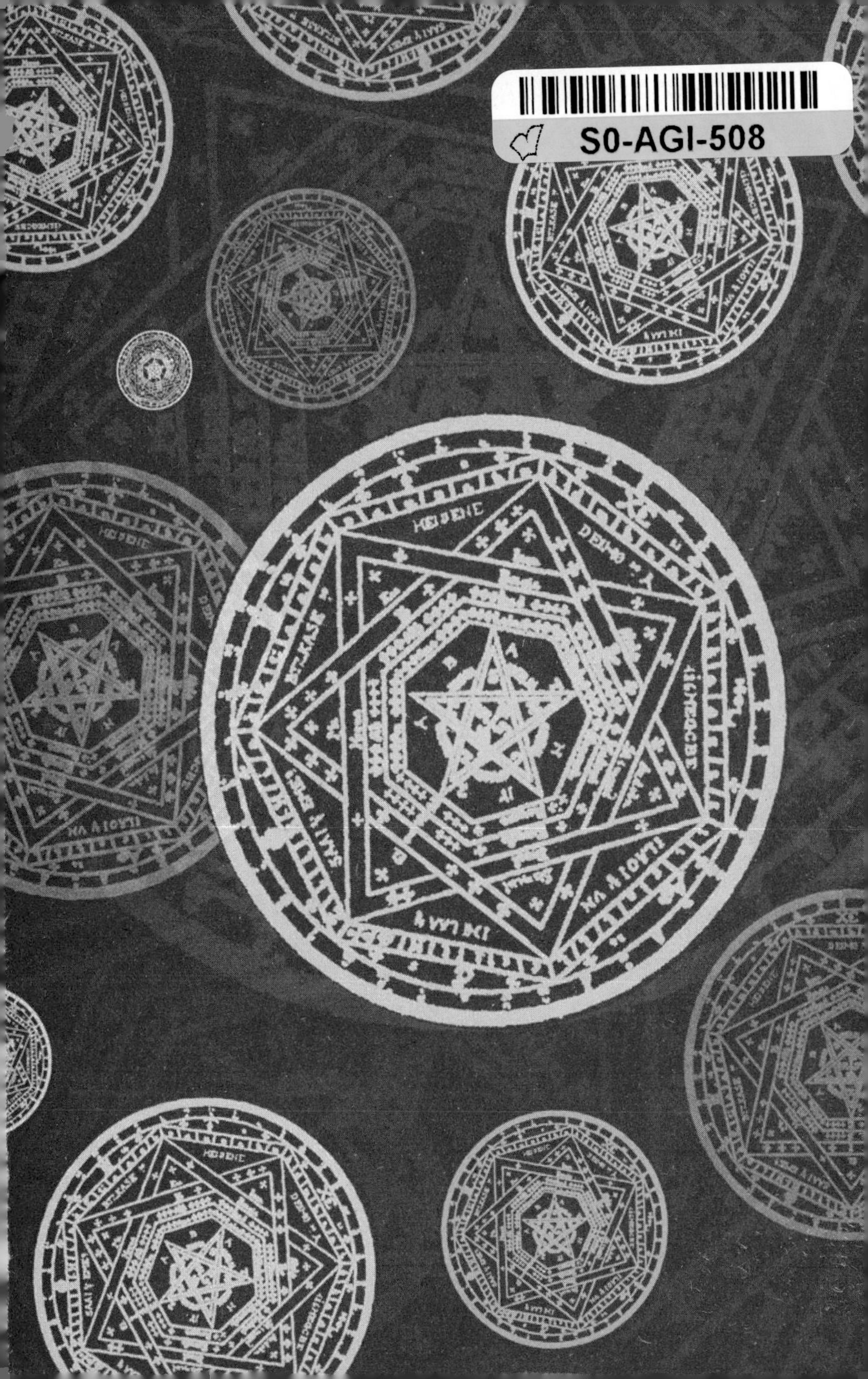

ALSO AVAILABLE FROM 🐸TOKYOPOP®

MANGA

ANGELIC LAYER*
BABY BIRTH* (September 2003)
BATTLE ROYALE*
BRAIN POWERED* (June 2003)
BRIGADOON* (August 2003)
CARDCAPTOR SAKURA
CARDCAPTOR SAKURA: MASTER OF THE CLOW*
CLAMP SCHOOL DETECTIVES*
CHOBITS*
CHRONICLES OF THE CURSED SWORD (July 2003)
CLOVER
CONFIDENTIAL CONFESSIONS* (July 2003)
CORRECTOR YUI
COWBOY BEBOP*
COWBOY BEBOP: SHOOTING STAR* (June 2003)
DEMON DIARY (May 2003)
DIGIMON
DRAGON HUNTER (June 2003)
DRAGON KNIGHTS*
DUKLYON: CLAMP SCHOOL DEFENDERS* (September 2003)
ERICA SAKURAZAWA* (May 2003)
ESCAFLOWNE* (July 2003)
FAKE* (May 2003)
FLCL* (September 2003)
FORBIDDEN DANCE* (August 2003)
GATE KEEPERS*
G-GUNDAM* (June 2003)
GRAVITATION* (June 2003)
GTO*
GUNDAM WING
GUNDAM WING: ENDLESS WALTZ*
GUNDAM: THE LAST OUTPOST*
HAPPY MANIA*
HARLEM BEAT
INITIAL D*
I.N.V.U.
ISLAND
JING: KING OF BANDITS* (June 2003)
JULINE
KARE KANO*
KINDAICHI CASE FILES* (June 2003)
KING OF HELL (June 2003)

KODOCHA*
LOVE HINA*
LUPIN III*
MAGIC KNIGHT RAYEARTH* (August 2003)
MAGIC KNIGHT RAYEARTH II* (COMING SOON)
MAN OF MANY FACES* (May 2003)
MARMALADE BOY*
MARS*
MIRACLE GIRLS
MIYUKI-CHAN IN WONDERLAND* (October 2003)
MONSTERS, INC.
NIEA_7* (August 2003)
PARADISE KISS*
PARASYTE
PEACH GIRL
PEACH GIRL: CHANGE OF HEART*
PET SHOP OF HORRORS* (June 2003)
PLANET LADDER
PLANETS* (October 2003)
PRIEST
RAGNAROK
RAVE MASTER*
REAL BOUT HIGH SCHOOL*
REALITY CHECK
REBIRTH
REBOUND*
SABER MARIONETTE J* (July 2003)
SAILOR MOON
SAINT TAIL
SAMURAI DEEPER KYO* (June 2003)
SCRYED*
SHAOLIN SISTERS*
SHIRAHIME-SYO* (December 2003)
THE SKULL MAN*
SORCERER HUNTERS
TOKYO MEW MEW*
UNDER THE GLASS MOON (June 2003)
VAMPIRE GAME* (June 2003)
WILD ACT* (July 2003)
WISH*
X-DAY* (August 2003)
ZODIAC P.I.* (July 2003)

CINE-MANGA™

AKIRA*
CARDCAPTORS
JIMMY NEUTRON (COMING SOON)
KIM POSSIBLE
LIZZIE McGUIRE
SPONGEBOB SQUAREPANTS (COMING SOON)
SPY KIDS 2

NOVELS

SAILOR MOON
KARMA CLUB (COMING SOON)

TOKYOPOP KIDS

STRAY SHEEP (September 2003)

ART BOOKS

CARDCAPTOR SAKURA*
MAGIC KNIGHT RAYEARTH*

ANIME GUIDES

GUNDAM TECHNICAL MANUALS
COWBOY BEBOP
SAILOR MOON SCOUT GUIDES

REBIRTH

VOLUME 2

STORY AND ART BY
WOO

HAMBURG • LONDON • LOS ANGELES • TOKYO

Translator - Lauren Na
English Adaption - Taliesin Jaffe
Associate Editor - Bryce P. Coleman
Retouch & Lettering - M. Caren McCaleb
Lettering - Anna Kernbaum
Cover Design - Patrick Hook

Editor - Luis Reyes
Digital Imaging Manager - Chris Buford
Pre-Press Manager - Antonio DePietro
Production Managers - Jennifer Miller and Mutsumi Miyazaki
Art Director - Matt Alford
Managing Editor - Jill Freshney
VP of Production - Ron Klamert
President and C.O.O. - John Parker
Publisher and C.E.O. - Stuart Levy

E-mail: info@TOKYOPOP.com
Come visit us online at www.TOKYOPOP.com

A  Manga

TOKYOPOP Inc.
5900 Wilshire Blvd. Suite 2000
Los Angeles, CA 90036

Rebirth Vol. 2

ISBN: 1-59182-217-3

First TOKYOPOP® printing: May 2003

10 9 8 7 6 5 4 3

Printed in the USA

REBIRTH

Vol ❷

Revenge
Three hundred years ago the Sorcerer Kalutika Maybus sealed the vampire Deshwitat in limbo after killing his fiancée, Lilith. For centuries, Deshwitat's mind calculated revenge while his body slumbered... until now. A band of spiritual investigators has inadvertently broken the seal that binds him and released Deshwitat to the world.

Redemption
A lot has changed since the 17th century. Carriages have bee replaced by cars, the Internet connects the world, and vampires have become the stuff of legends. But beneath the veneer of technology, magic and religion still reign supreme. Kalutika is the most powerful person in the world, although few actually know he exists. Prophecy foretold that Kalutika would destroy the Earth. Deshwitat's quest is now not just one of revenge, but of redemption... for himself, and the world.

Rebirth
Joined by an excommunicated exorcist and a spiritual investigator orphaned by his fangs, Deshwitat begins his bloodquest. The hunted is now the hunter.

CHAPTER 5: CO-EXISTING ENEMIES^2

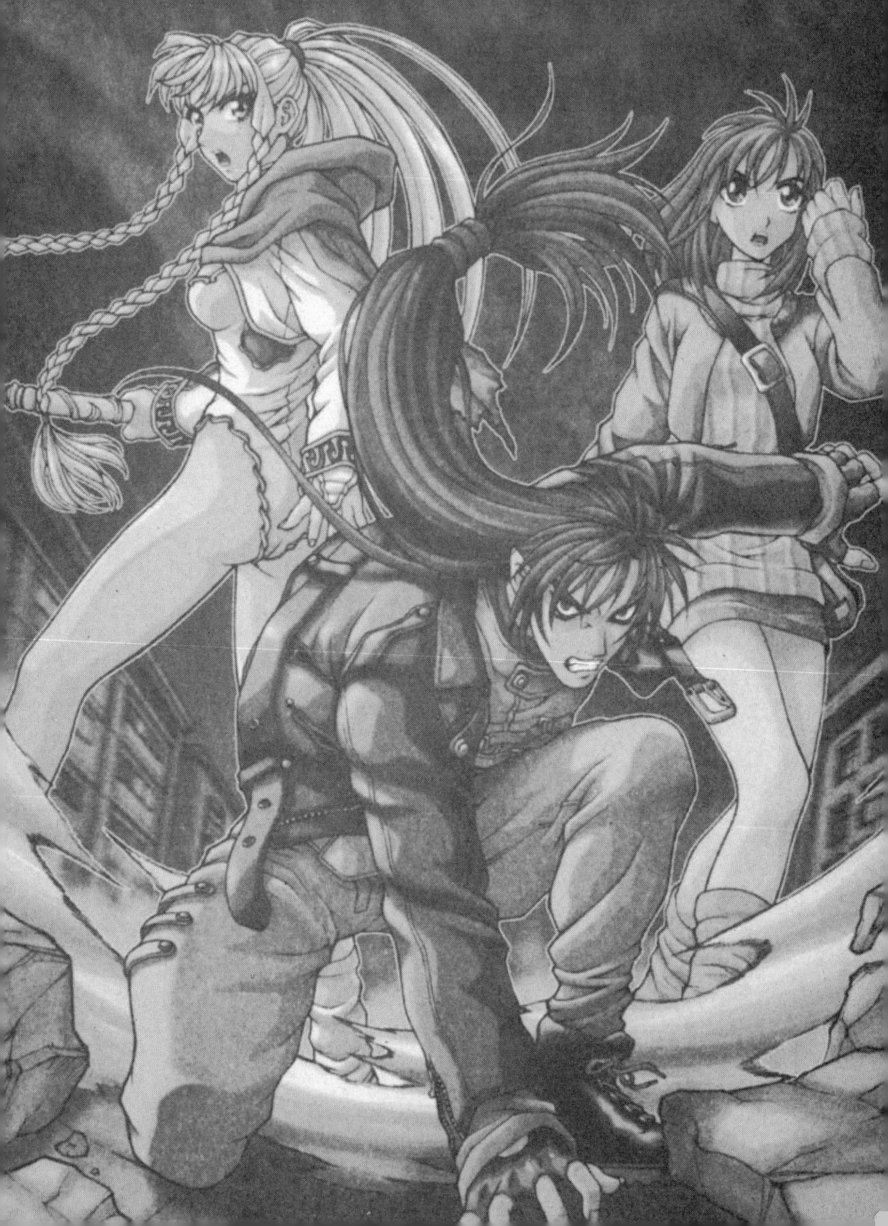

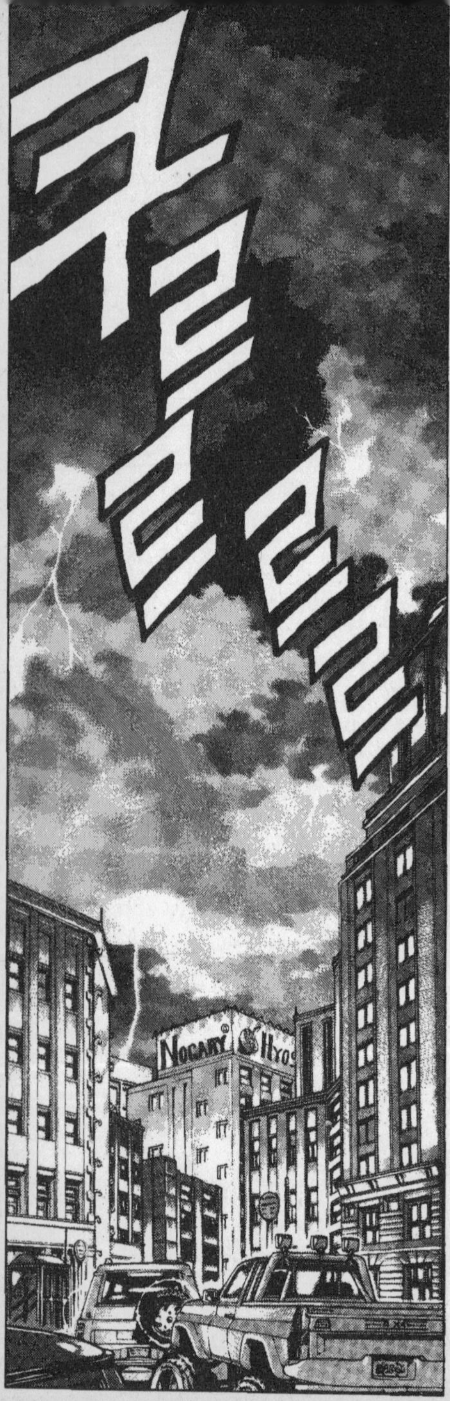
NOGARY

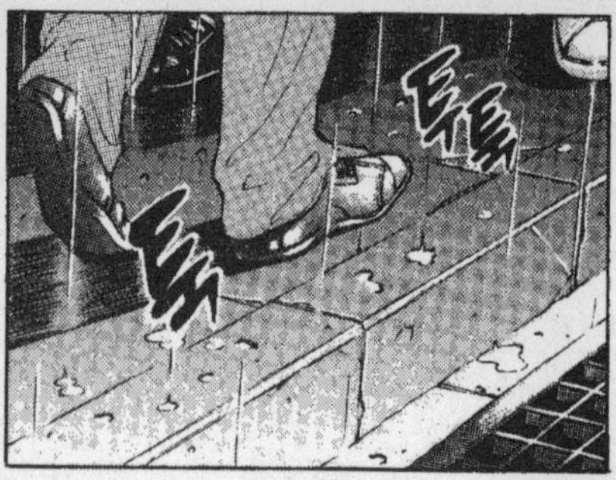

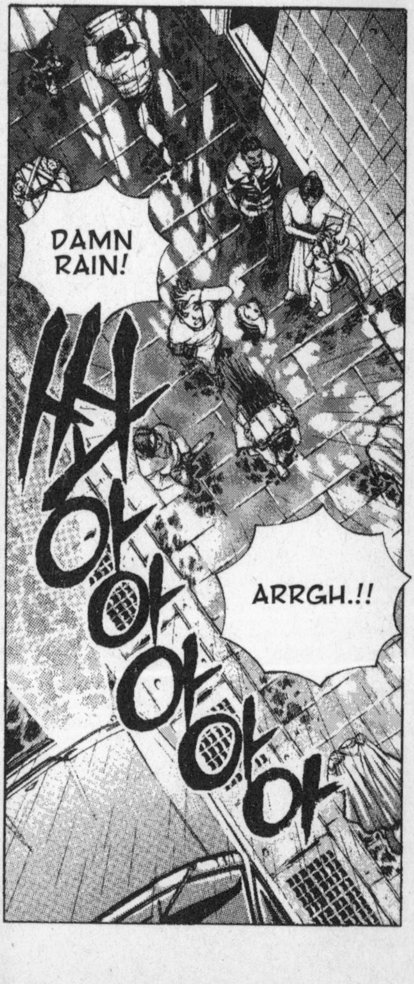
DAMN RAIN!
쏴아아아아아
ARRGH.!!

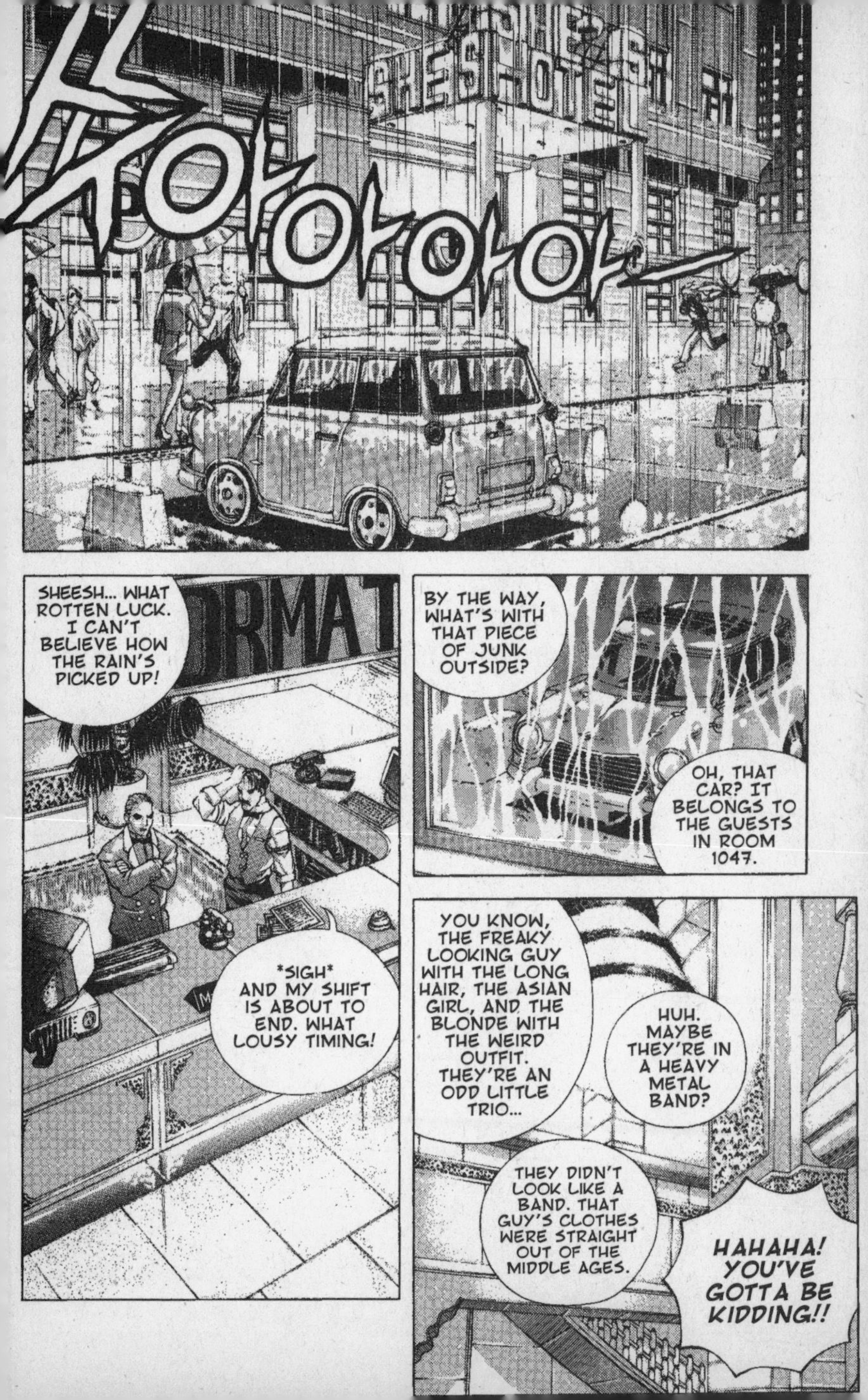
KOLOLOLOLOL
SHESHOTEL
SHEESH... WHAT ROTTEN LUCK. I CAN'T BELIEVE HOW THE RAIN'S PICKED UP!
SIGH AND MY SHIFT IS ABOUT TO END. WHAT LOUSY TIMING!
BY THE WAY, WHAT'S WITH THAT PIECE OF JUNK OUTSIDE?
OH, THAT CAR? IT BELONGS TO THE GUESTS IN ROOM 1047.
YOU KNOW, THE FREAKY LOOKING GUY WITH THE LONG HAIR, THE ASIAN GIRL, AND THE BLONDE WITH THE WEIRD OUTFIT. THEY'RE AN ODD LITTLE TRIO...
HUH. MAYBE THEY'RE IN A HEAVY METAL BAND?
THEY DIDN'T LOOK LIKE A BAND. THAT GUY'S CLOTHES WERE STRAIGHT OUT OF THE MIDDLE AGES.
HAHAHA! YOU'VE GOTTA BE KIDDING!!

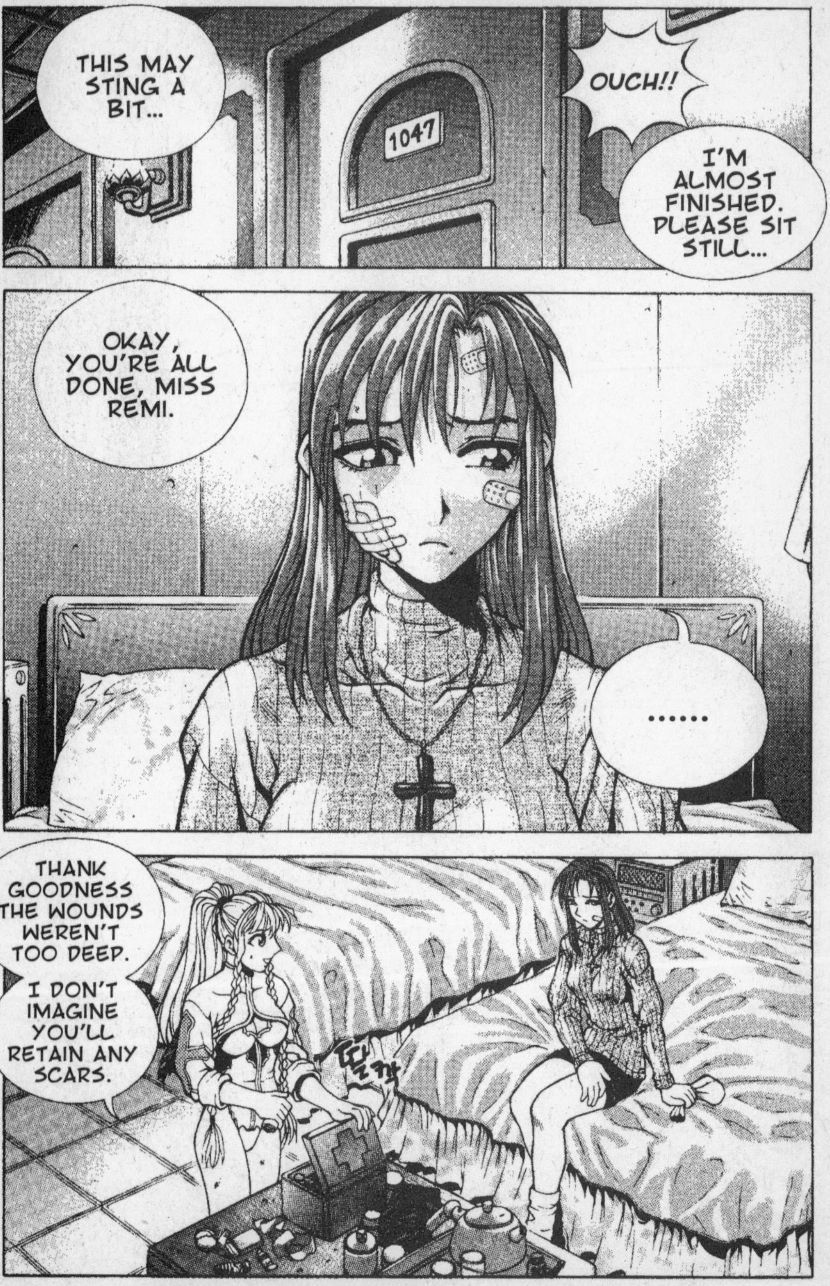
THIS MAY STING A BIT...
OUCH!!
I'M ALMOST FINISHED. PLEASE SIT STILL...
OKAY, YOU'RE ALL DONE, MISS REMI.
......
THANK GOODNESS THE WOUNDS WEREN'T TOO DEEP.
I DON'T IMAGINE YOU'LL RETAIN ANY SCARS.

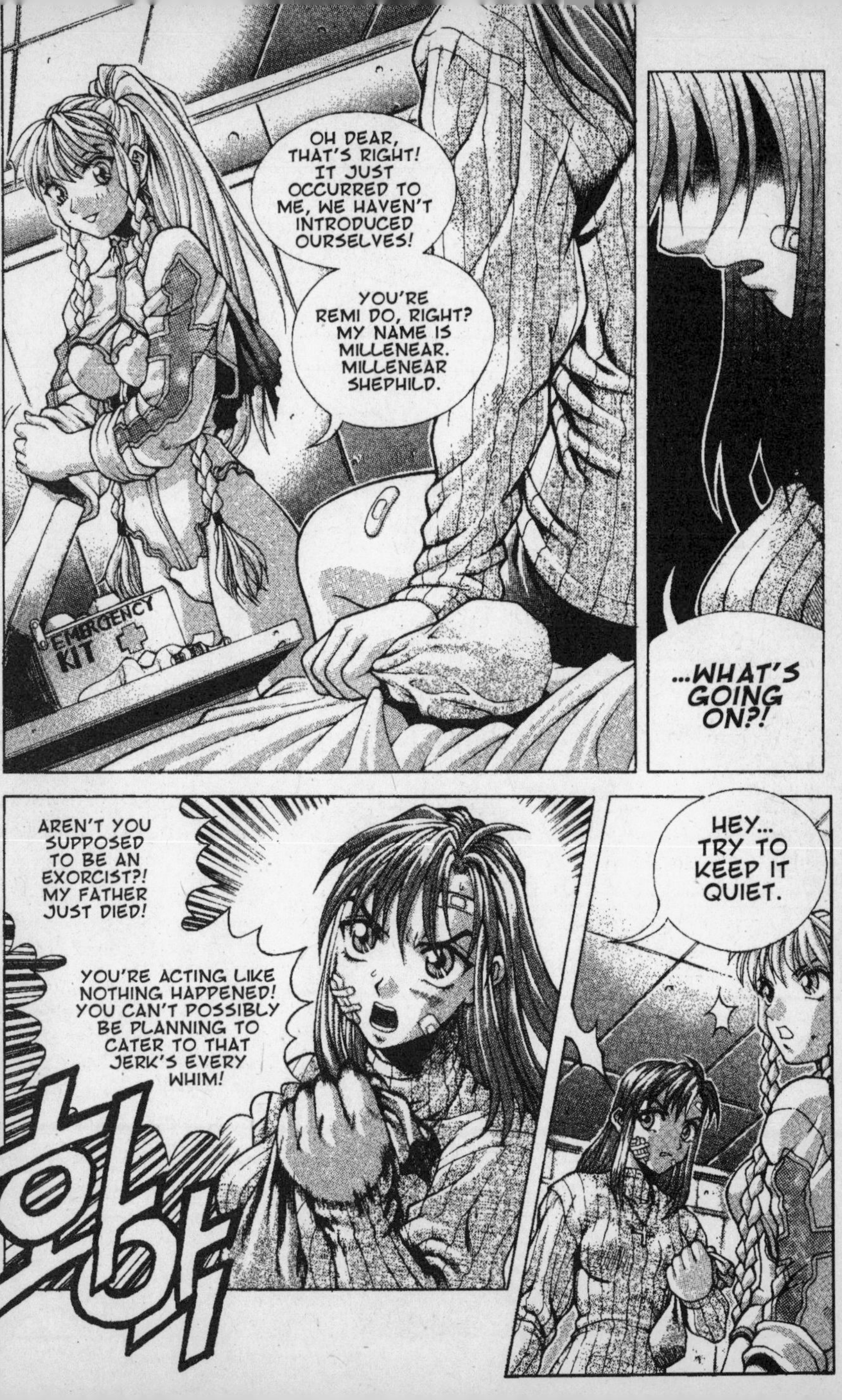
OH DEAR, THAT'S RIGHT! IT JUST OCCURRED TO ME, WE HAVEN'T INTRODUCED OURSELVES!
YOU'RE REMI DO, RIGHT? MY NAME IS MILLENEAR. MILLENEAR SHEPHILD.
EMERGENCY KIT
...WHAT'S GOING ON?!
AREN'T YOU SUPPOSED TO BE AN EXORCIST?! MY FATHER JUST DIED!
YOU'RE ACTING LIKE NOTHING HAPPENED! YOU CAN'T POSSIBLY BE PLANNING TO CATER TO THAT JERK'S EVERY WHIM!
HEY... TRY TO KEEP IT QUIET.

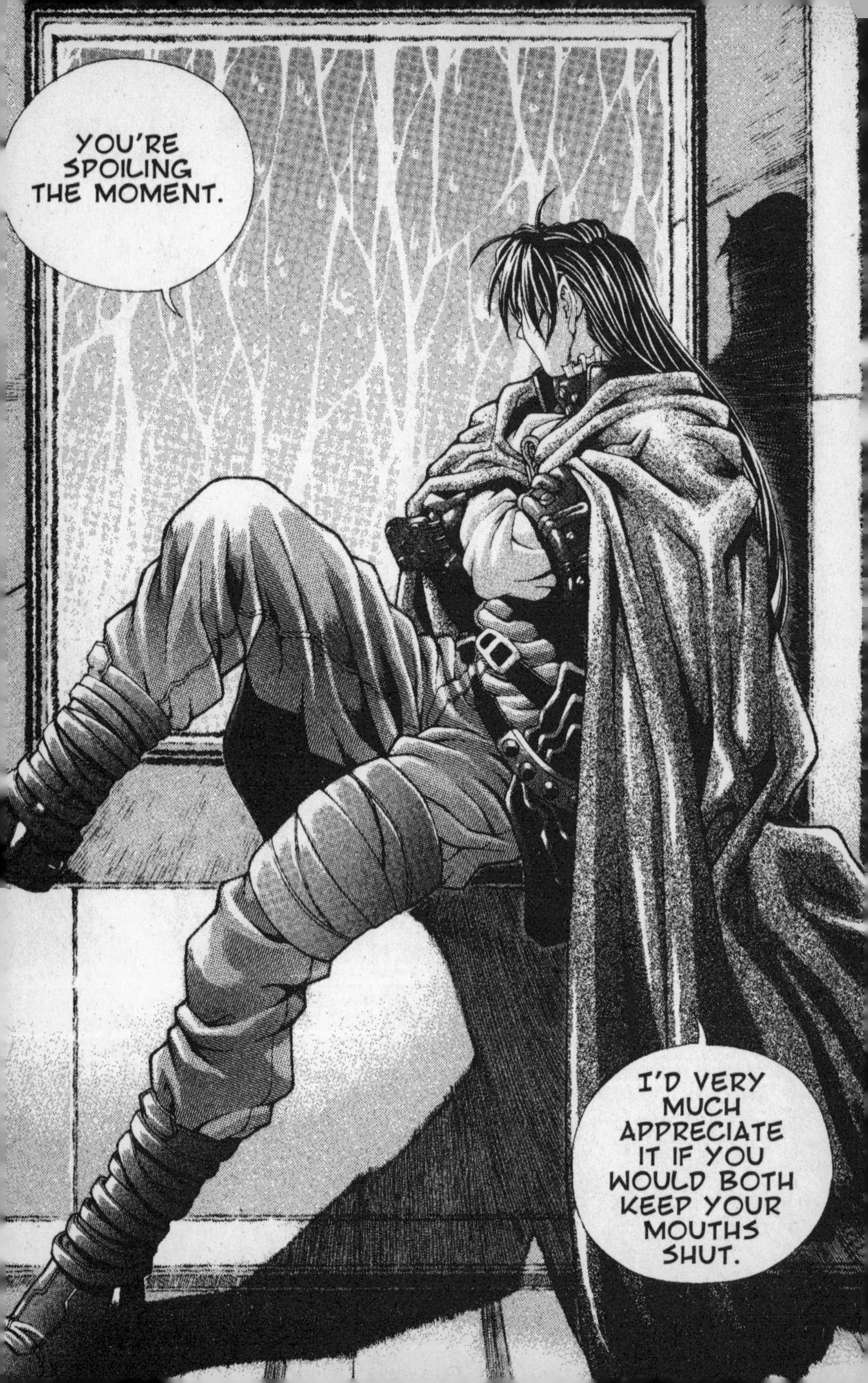
YOU'RE SPOILING THE MOMENT.
I'D VERY MUCH APPRECIATE IT IF YOU WOULD BOTH KEEP YOUR MOUTHS SHUT.

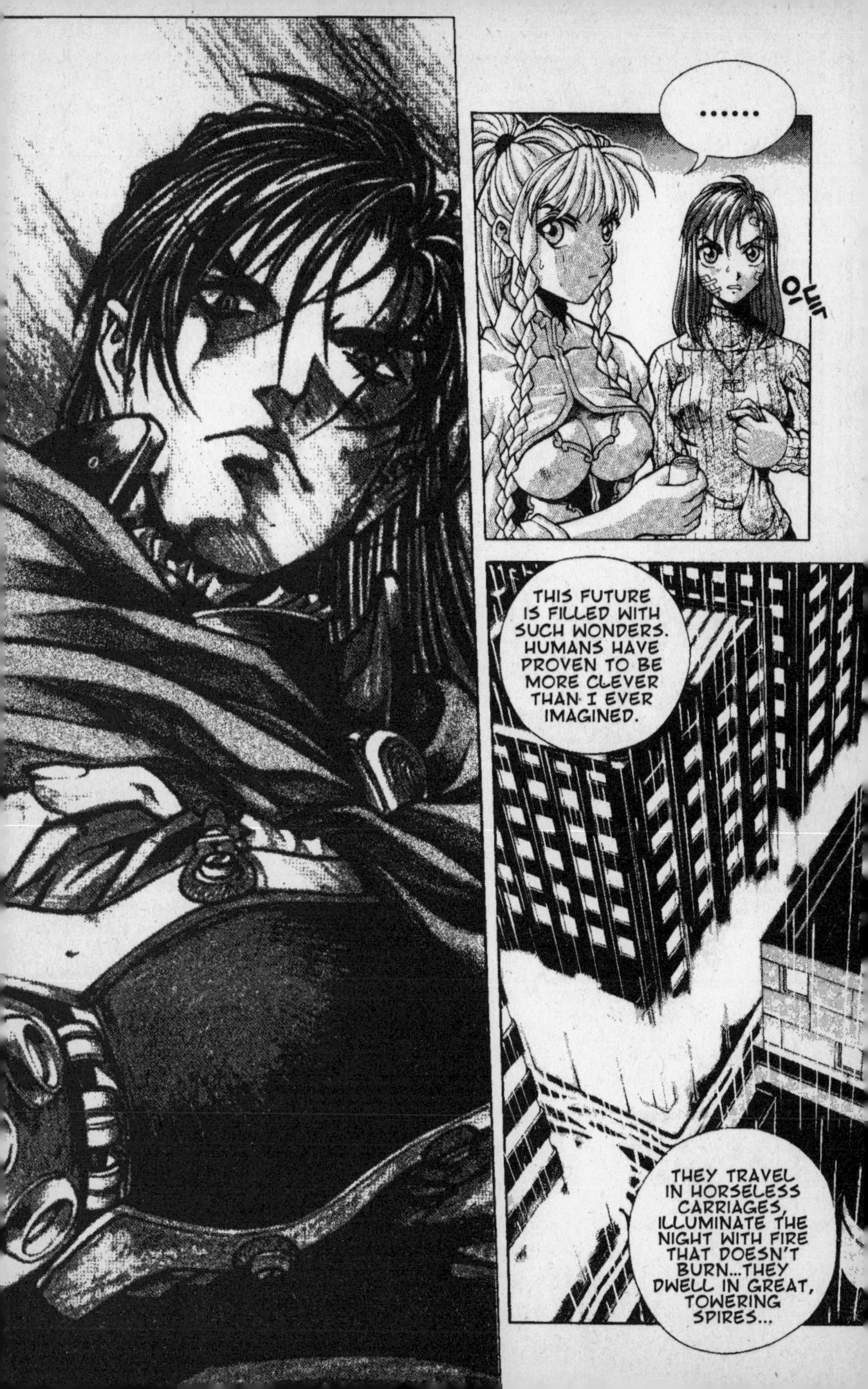

......
으쓱
THIS FUTURE IS FILLED WITH SUCH WONDERS. HUMANS HAVE PROVEN TO BE MORE CLEVER THAN I EVER IMAGINED.
THEY TRAVEL IN HORSELESS CARRIAGES, ILLUMINATE THE NIGHT WITH FIRE THAT DOESN'T BURN...THEY DWELL IN GREAT, TOWERING SPIRES...

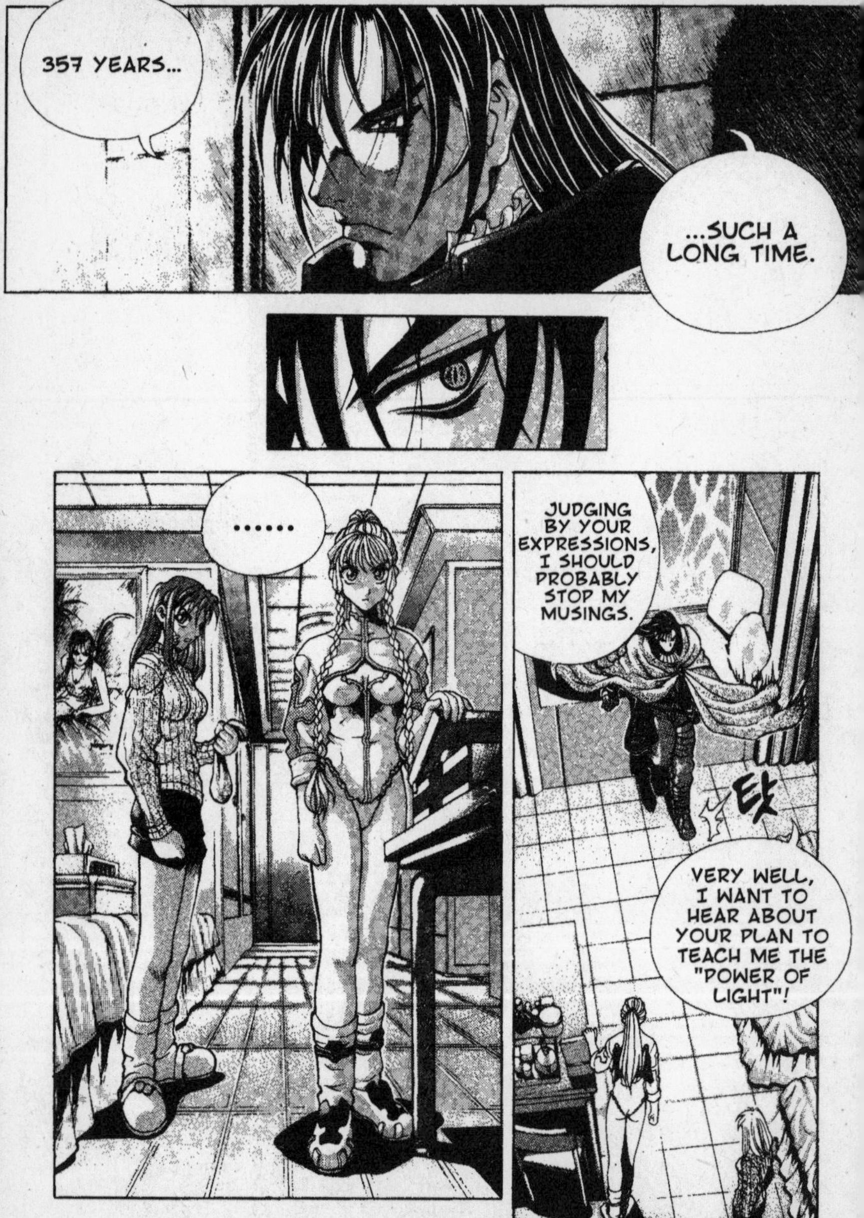
357 YEARS...
...SUCH A LONG TIME.
....
JUDGING BY YOUR EXPRESSIONS, I SHOULD PROBABLY STOP MY MUSINGS.
탁
VERY WELL, I WANT TO HEAR ABOUT YOUR PLAN TO TEACH ME THE "POWER OF LIGHT"!

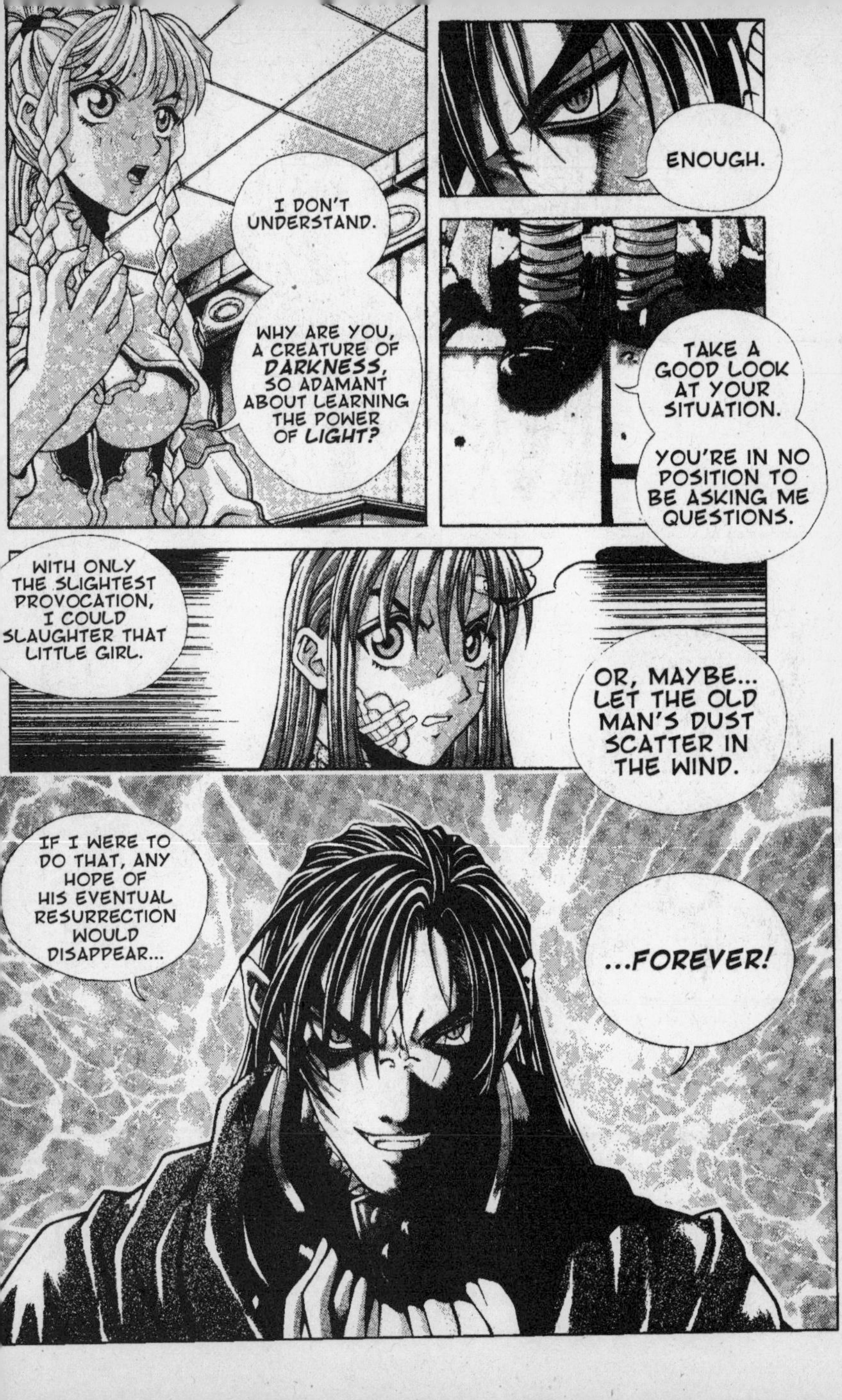
I DON'T UNDERSTAND.
WHY ARE YOU, A CREATURE OF DARKNESS, SO ADAMANT ABOUT LEARNING THE POWER OF LIGHT?
ENOUGH.
TAKE A GOOD LOOK AT YOUR SITUATION.
YOU'RE IN NO POSITION TO BE ASKING ME QUESTIONS.
WITH ONLY THE SLIGHTEST PROVOCATION, I COULD SLAUGHTER THAT LITTLE GIRL.
OR, MAYBE... LET THE OLD MAN'S DUST SCATTER IN THE WIND.
IF I WERE TO DO THAT, ANY HOPE OF HIS EVENTUAL RESURRECTION WOULD DISAPPEAR...
...FOREVER!

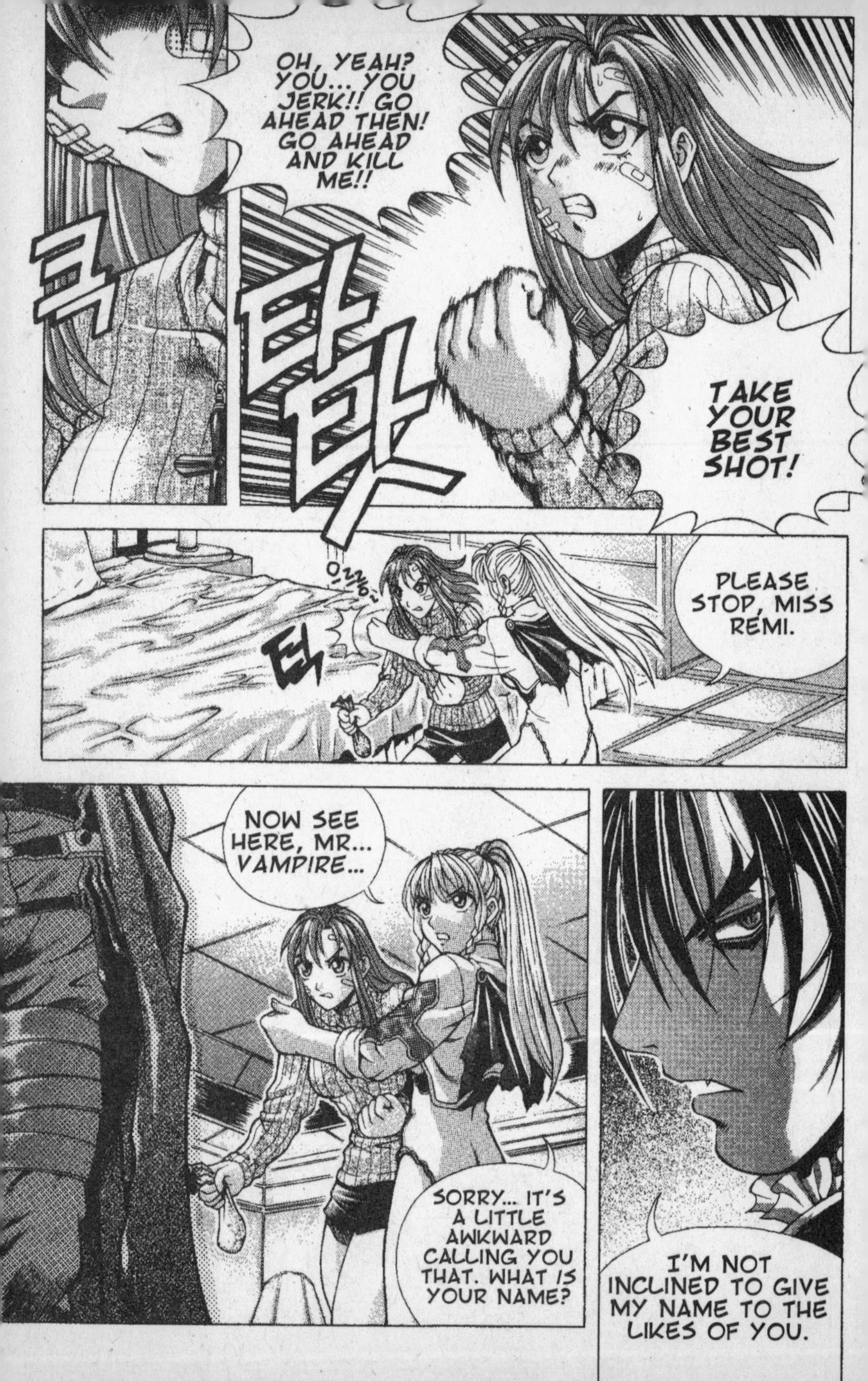
크
OH, YEAH? YOU... YOU JERK!! GO AHEAD THEN! GO AHEAD AND KILL ME!!
탁
탁
TAKE YOUR BEST SHOT!
턱
PLEASE STOP, MISS REMI.
NOW SEE HERE, MR... VAMPIRE...
SORRY... IT'S A LITTLE AWKWARD CALLING YOU THAT. WHAT *IS* YOUR NAME?
I'M NOT INCLINED TO GIVE MY NAME TO THE LIKES OF YOU.

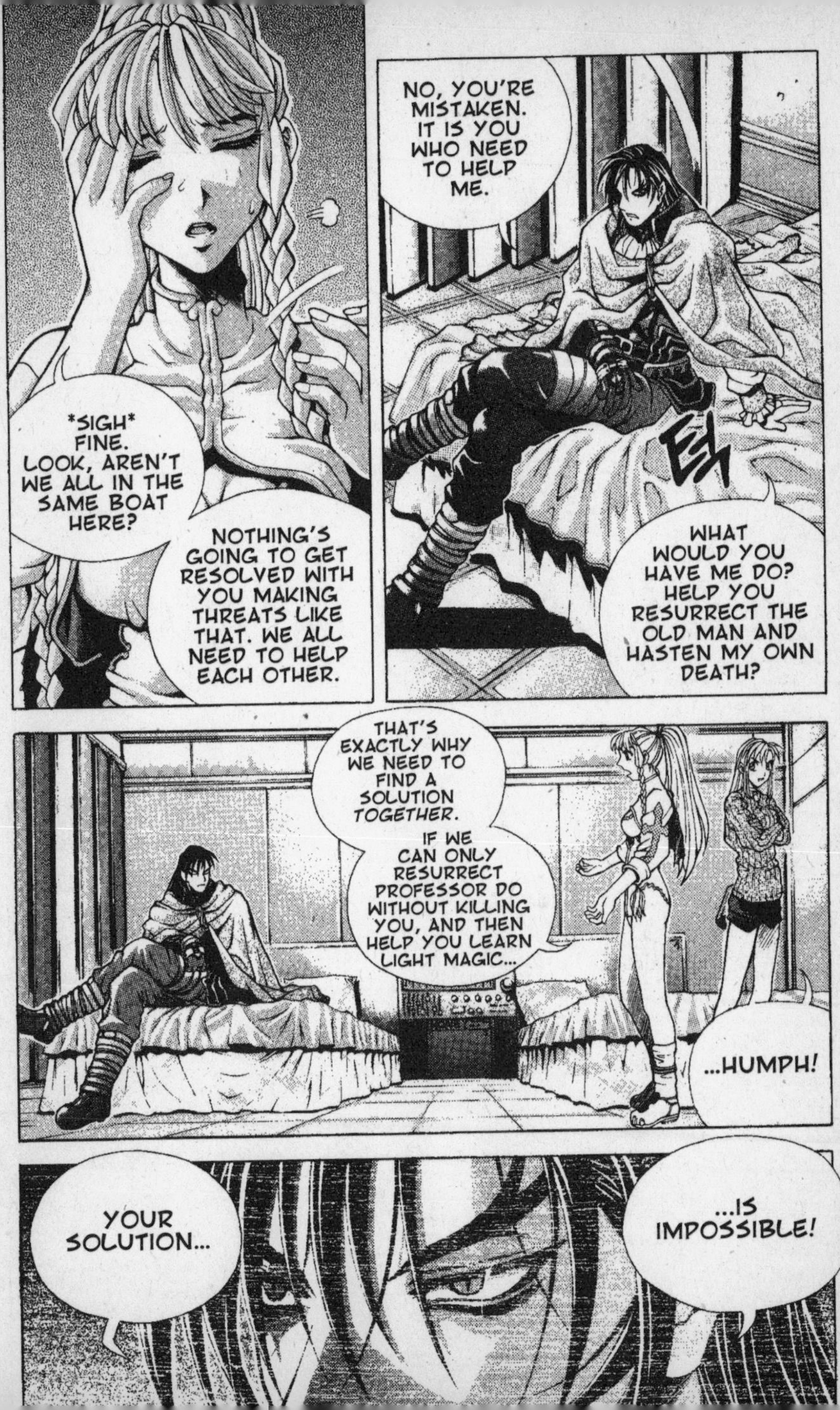
SIGH FINE. LOOK, AREN'T WE ALL IN THE SAME BOAT HERE?
NOTHING'S GOING TO GET RESOLVED WITH YOU MAKING THREATS LIKE THAT. WE ALL NEED TO HELP EACH OTHER.
NO, YOU'RE MISTAKEN. IT IS YOU WHO NEED TO HELP ME.
WHAT WOULD YOU HAVE ME DO? HELP YOU RESURRECT THE OLD MAN AND HASTEN MY OWN DEATH?
THAT'S EXACTLY WHY WE NEED TO FIND A SOLUTION *TOGETHER*.
IF WE CAN ONLY RESURRECT PROFESSOR DO WITHOUT KILLING YOU, AND THEN HELP YOU LEARN LIGHT MAGIC...
...HUMPH!
YOUR SOLUTION...
...IS IMPOSSIBLE!

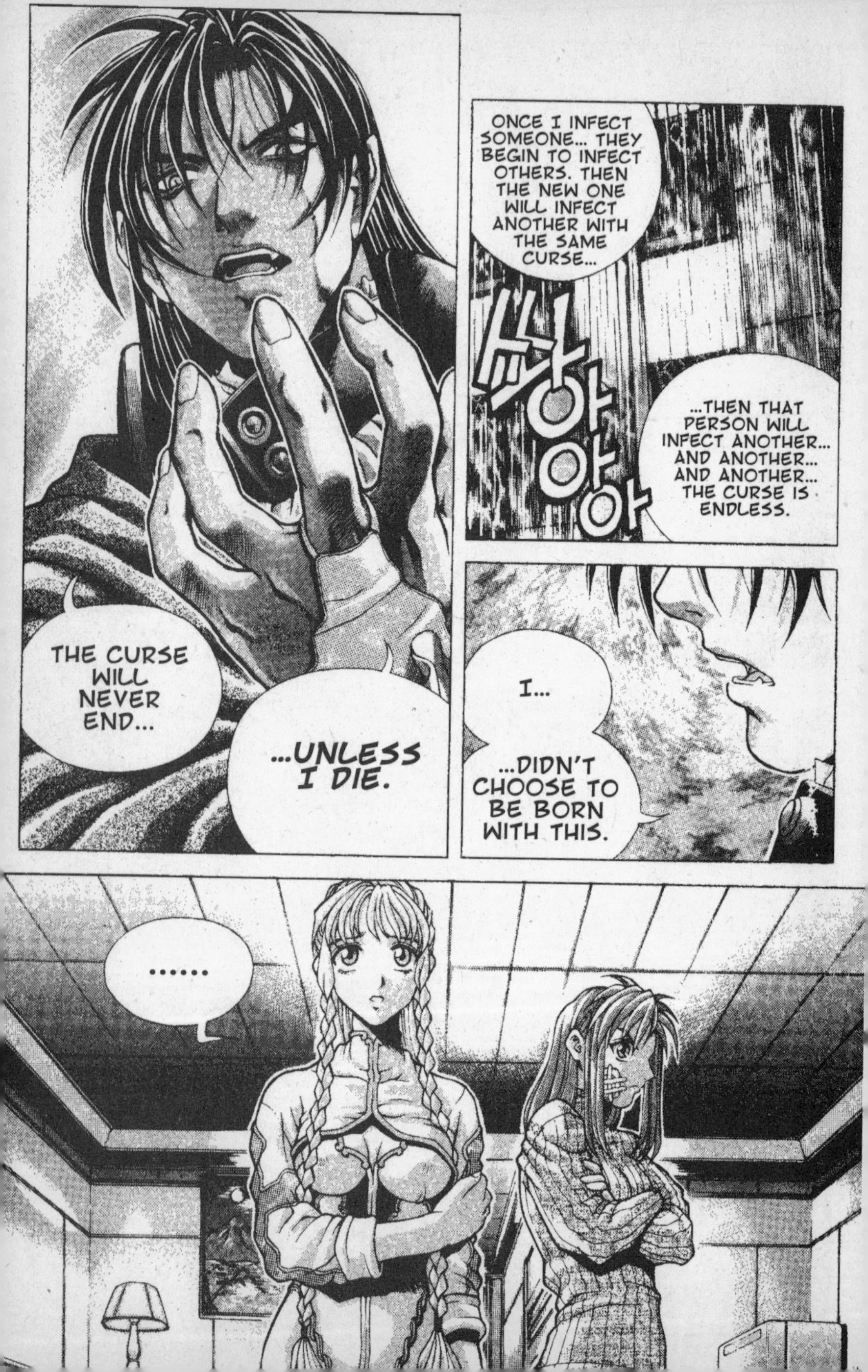
THE CURSE WILL NEVER END...
...UNLESS I DIE.
ONCE I INFECT SOMEONE... THEY BEGIN TO INFECT OTHERS. THEN THE NEW ONE WILL INFECT ANOTHER WITH THE SAME CURSE...
쑤아아아
...THEN THAT PERSON WILL INFECT ANOTHER... AND ANOTHER... AND ANOTHER... THE CURSE IS ENDLESS.
I...
...DIDN'T CHOOSE TO BE BORN WITH THIS.
......

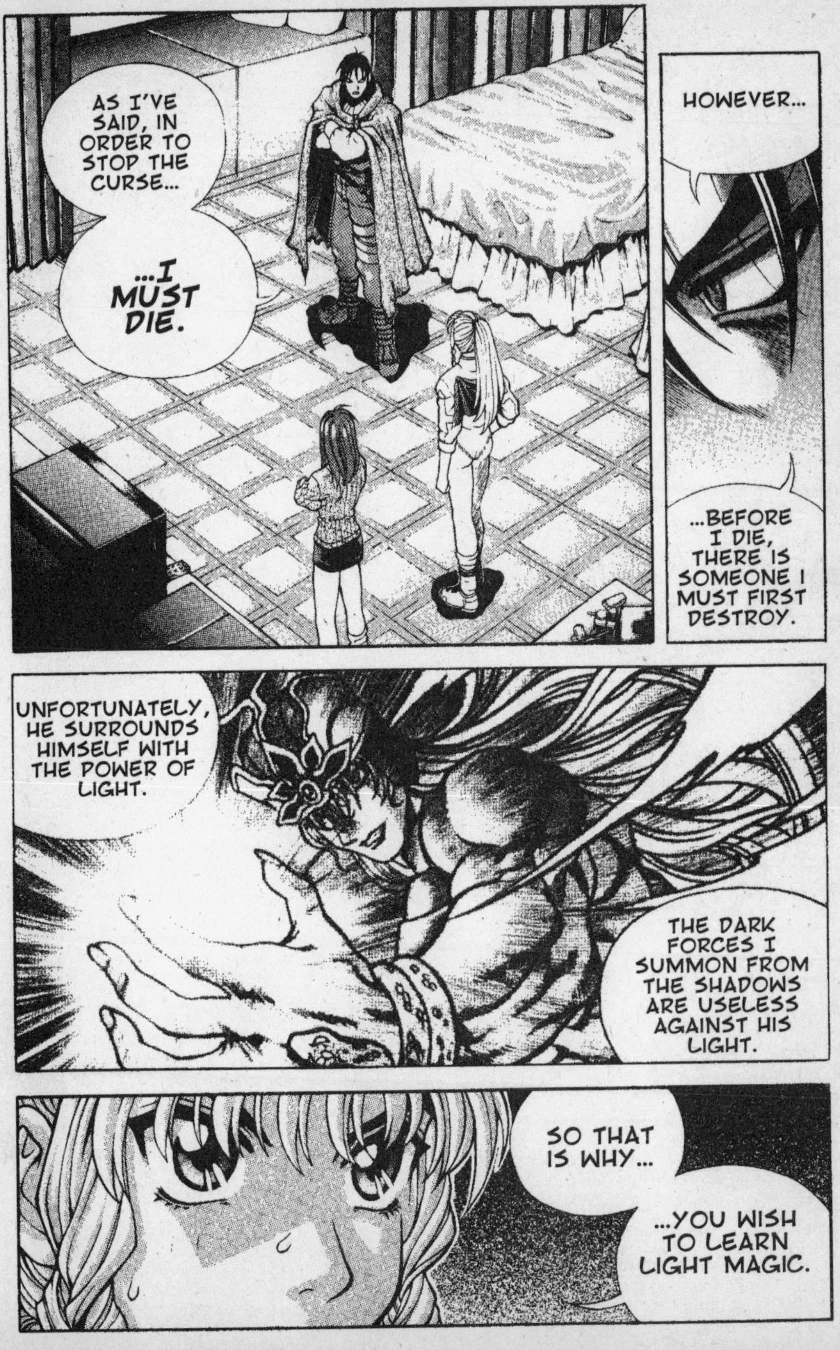

AS I'VE SAID, IN ORDER TO STOP THE CURSE...
...I MUST DIE.
HOWEVER...
...BEFORE I DIE, THERE IS SOMEONE I MUST FIRST DESTROY.
UNFORTUNATELY, HE SURROUNDS HIMSELF WITH THE POWER OF LIGHT.
THE DARK FORCES I SUMMON FROM THE SHADOWS ARE USELESS AGAINST HIS LIGHT.
SO THAT IS WHY...
...YOU WISH TO LEARN LIGHT MAGIC.

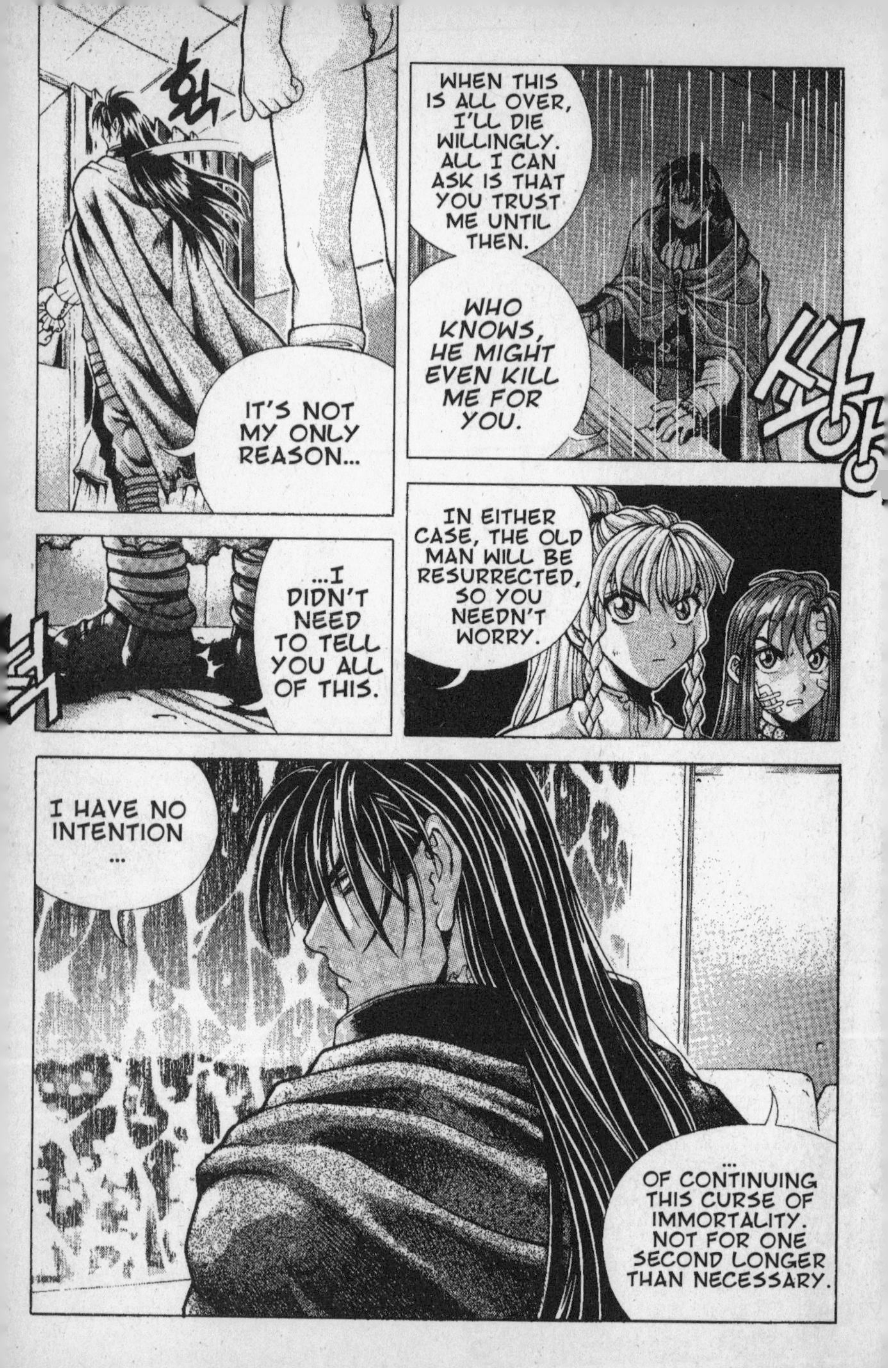
IT'S NOT MY ONLY REASON...
WHEN THIS IS ALL OVER, I'LL DIE WILLINGLY. ALL I CAN ASK IS THAT YOU TRUST ME UNTIL THEN.
WHO KNOWS, HE MIGHT EVEN KILL ME FOR YOU.
...I DIDN'T NEED TO TELL YOU ALL OF THIS.
IN EITHER CASE, THE OLD MAN WILL BE RESURRECTED, SO YOU NEEDN'T WORRY.
I HAVE NO INTENTION ...
... OF CONTINUING THIS CURSE OF IMMORTALITY. NOT FOR ONE SECOND LONGER THAN NECESSARY.

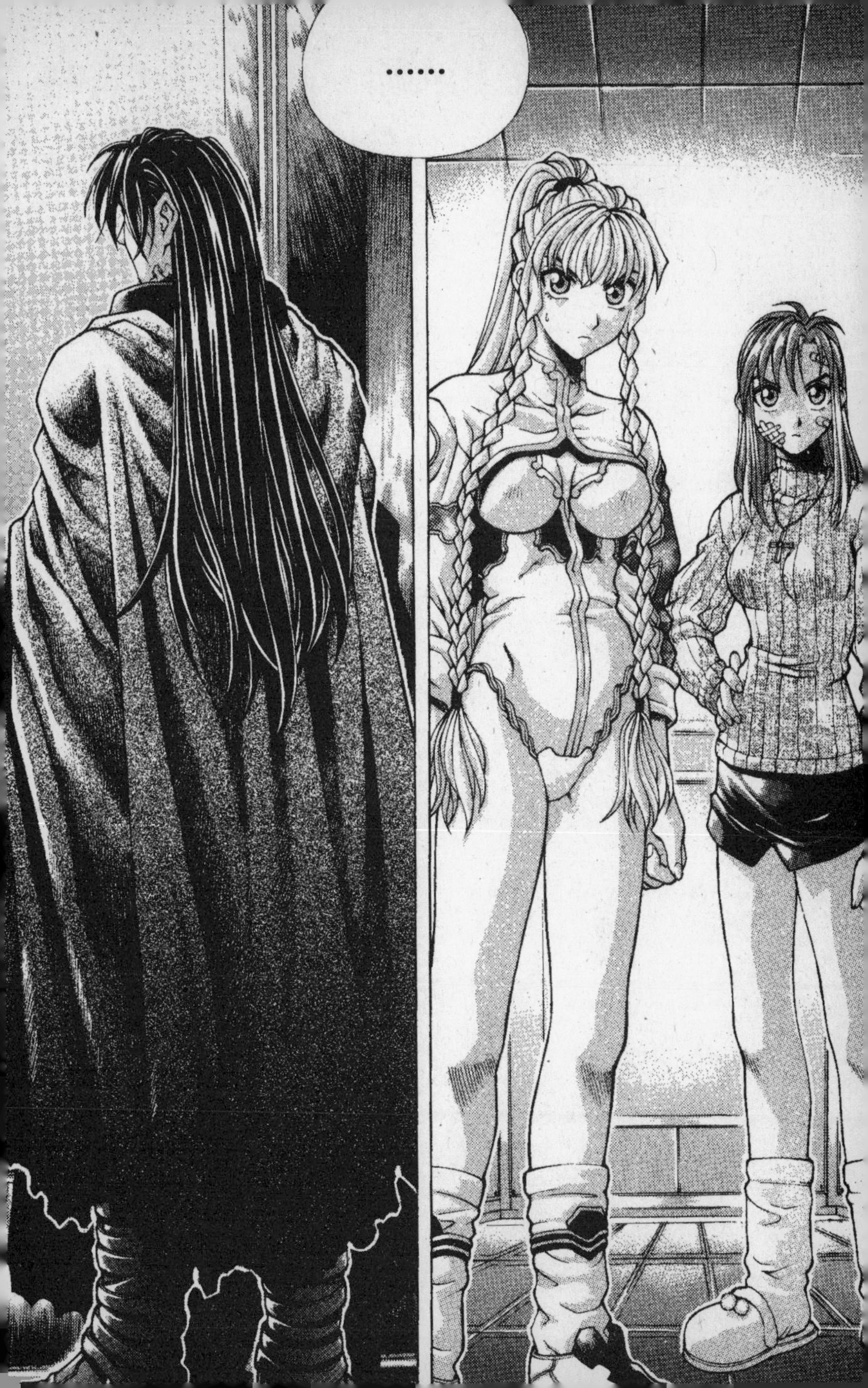
......

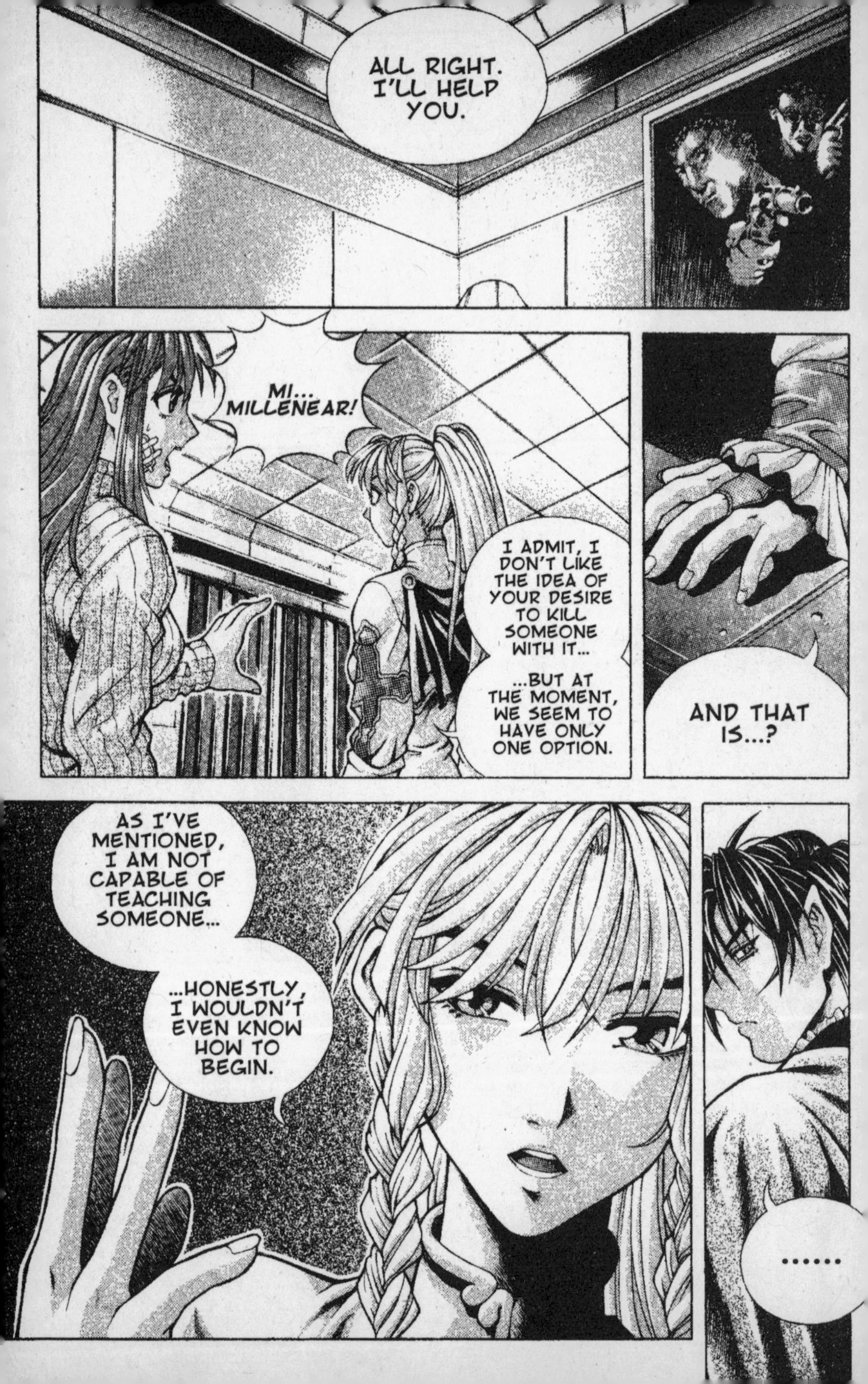
ALL RIGHT. I'LL HELP YOU.
MI... MILLENEAR!
I ADMIT, I DON'T LIKE THE IDEA OF YOUR DESIRE TO KILL SOMEONE WITH IT...
...BUT AT THE MOMENT, WE SEEM TO HAVE ONLY ONE OPTION.
AND THAT IS...?
AS I'VE MENTIONED, I AM NOT CAPABLE OF TEACHING SOMEONE...
...HONESTLY, I WOULDN'T EVEN KNOW HOW TO BEGIN.
......

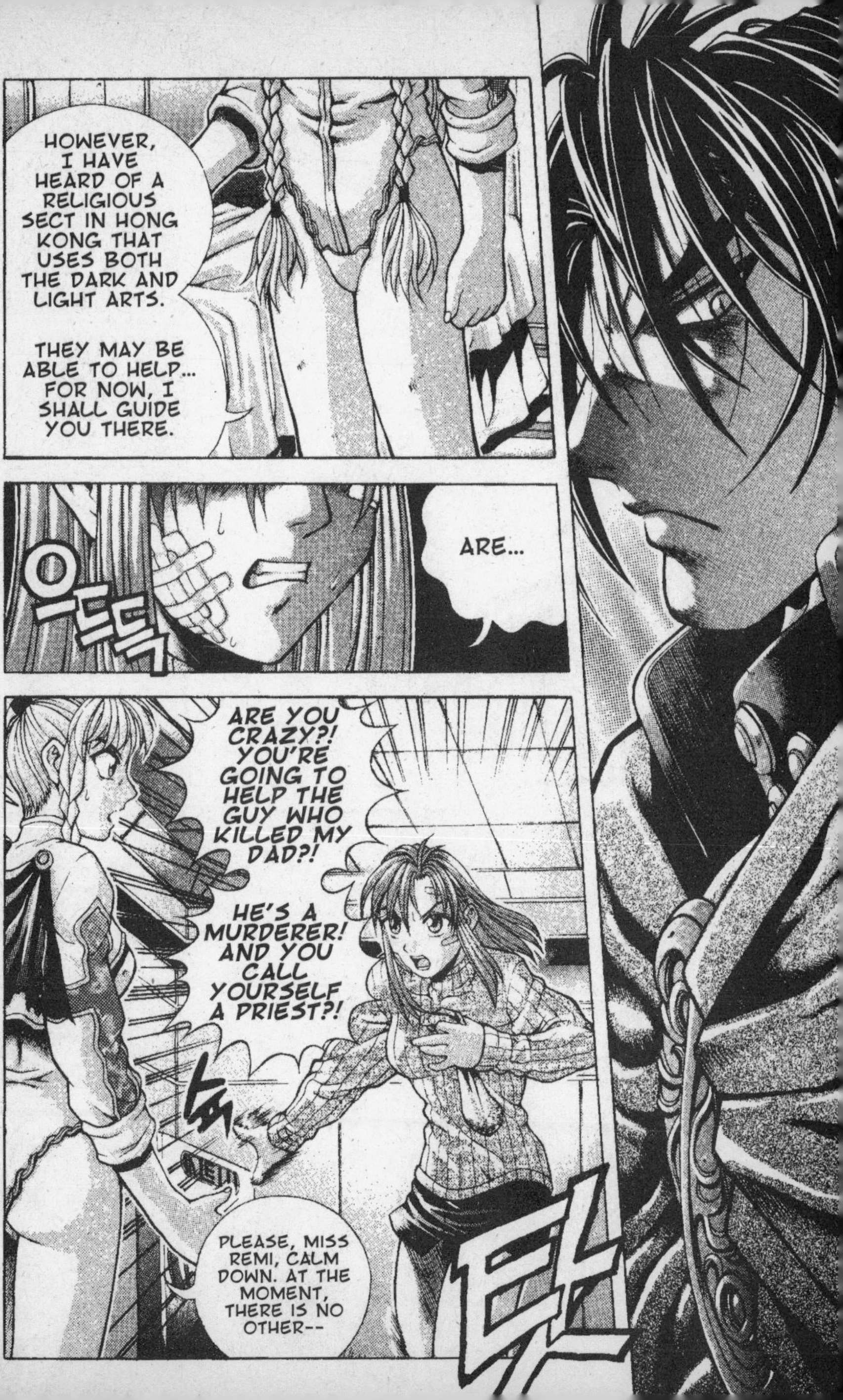
HOWEVER, I HAVE HEARD OF A RELIGIOUS SECT IN HONG KONG THAT USES BOTH THE DARK AND LIGHT ARTS.
THEY MAY BE ABLE TO HELP... FOR NOW, I SHALL GUIDE YOU THERE.
ARE...
ARE YOU CRAZY?! YOU'RE GOING TO HELP THE GUY WHO KILLED MY DAD?!
HE'S A MURDERER! AND YOU CALL YOURSELF A PRIEST?!
PLEASE, MISS REMI, CALM DOWN. AT THE MOMENT, THERE IS NO OTHER--

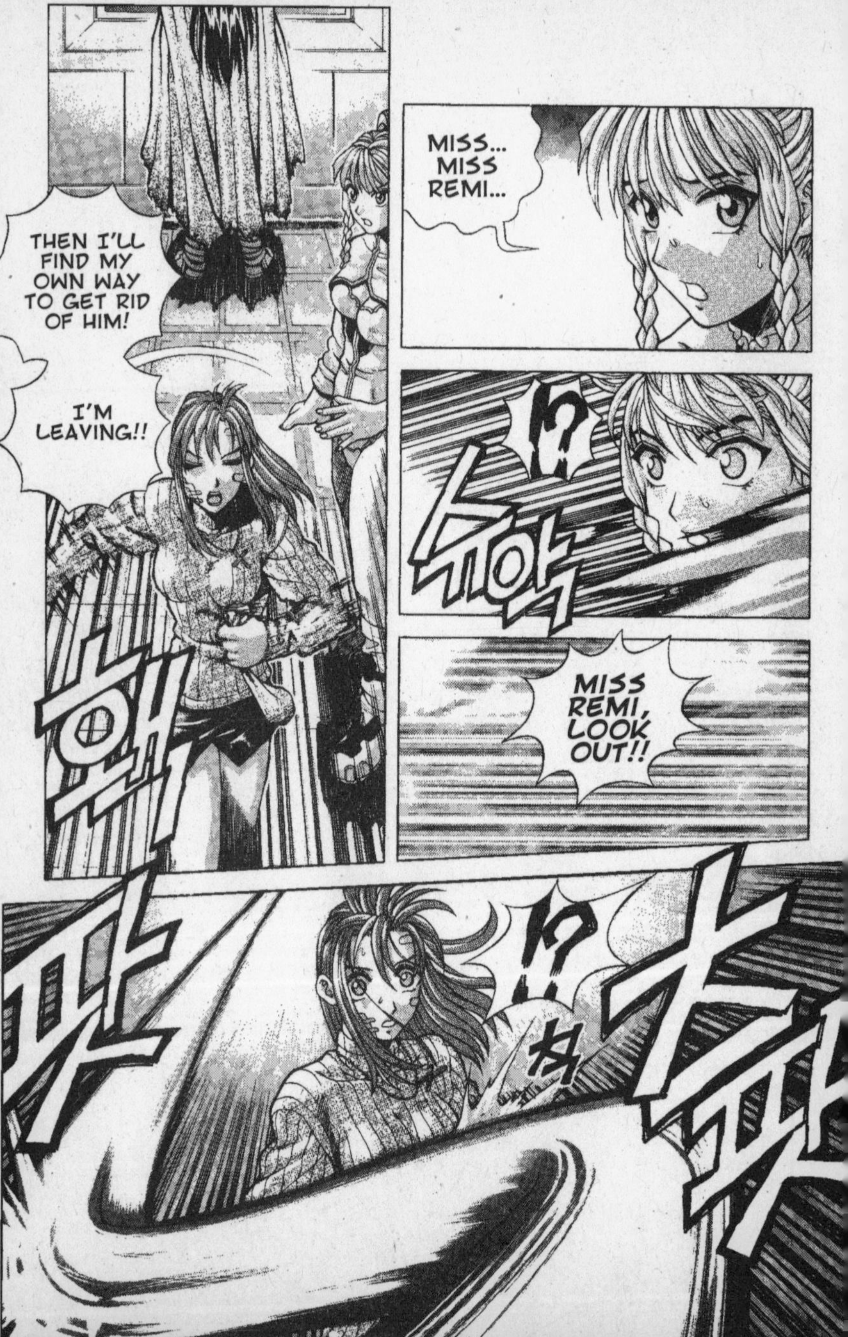
THEN I'LL FIND MY OWN WAY TO GET RID OF HIM!
I'M LEAVING!!
MISS... MISS REMI...
!?
MISS REMI, LOOK OUT!!
!?

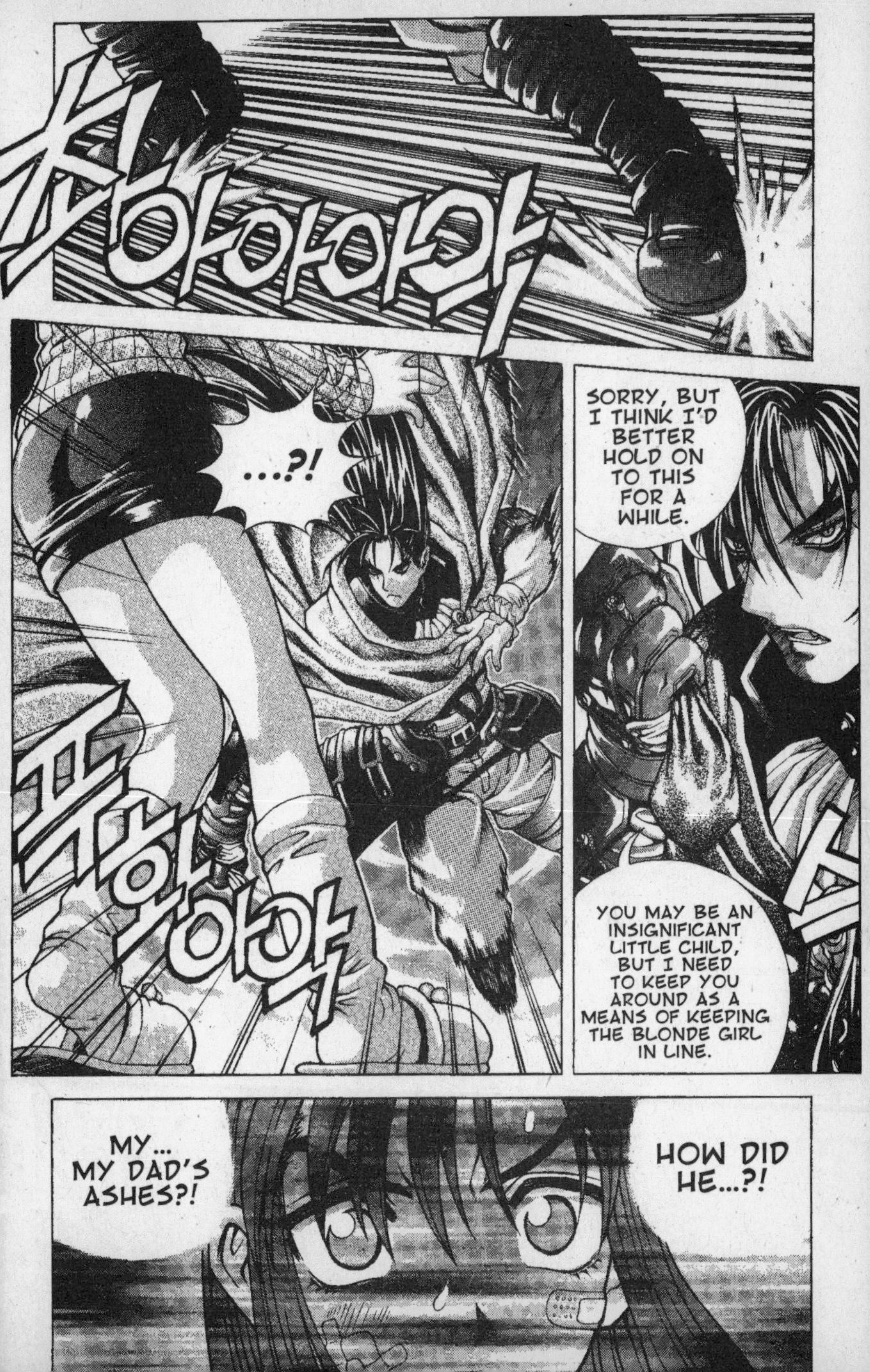
...?!
SORRY, BUT I THINK I'D BETTER HOLD ON TO THIS FOR A WHILE.
YOU MAY BE AN INSIGNIFICANT LITTLE CHILD, BUT I NEED TO KEEP YOU AROUND AS A MEANS OF KEEPING THE BLONDE GIRL IN LINE.
MY... MY DAD'S ASHES?!
HOW DID HE...?!

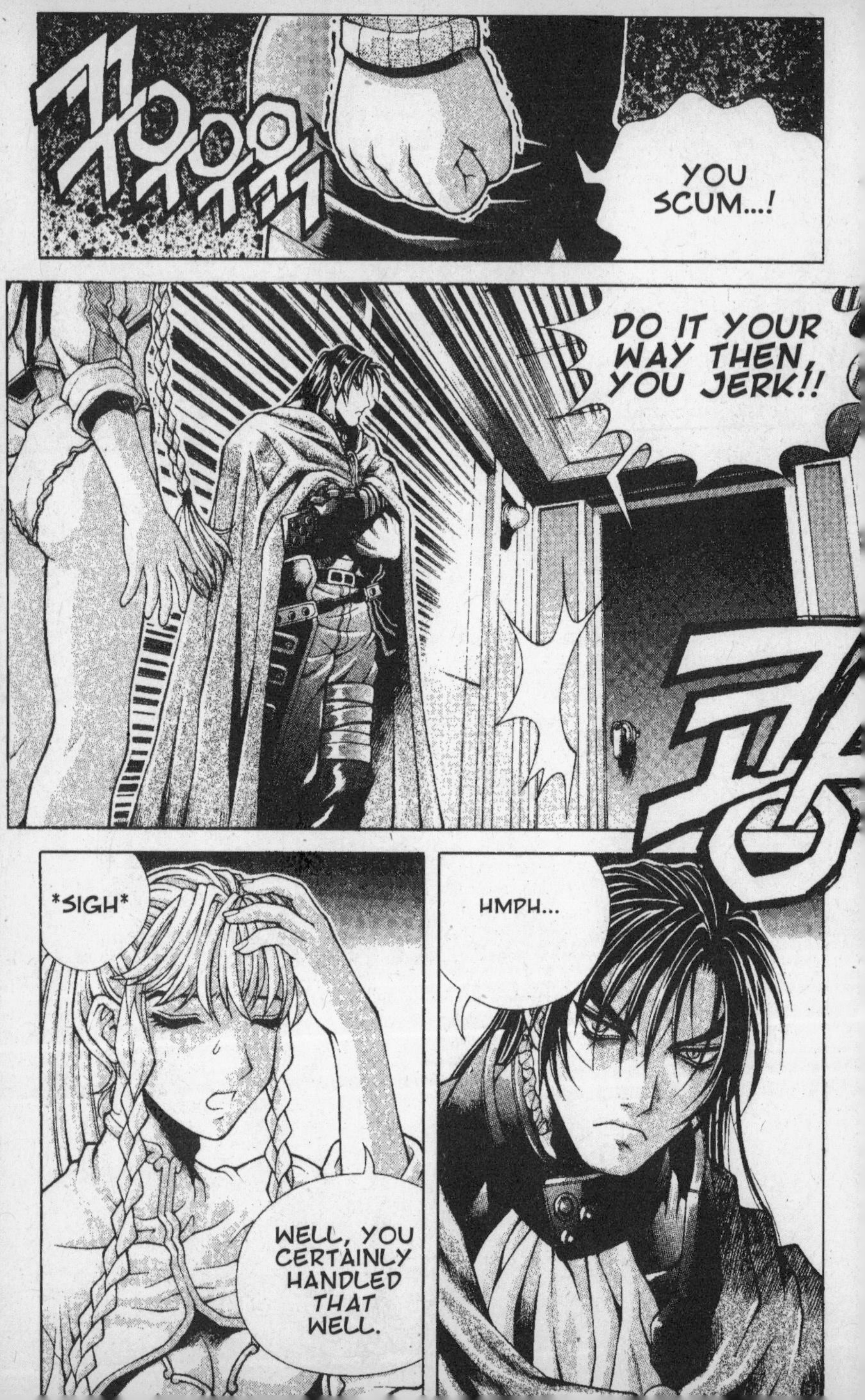
YOU SCUM...!
DO IT YOUR WAY THEN, YOU JERK!!
SIGH
WELL, YOU CERTAINLY HANDLED THAT WELL.
HMPH...

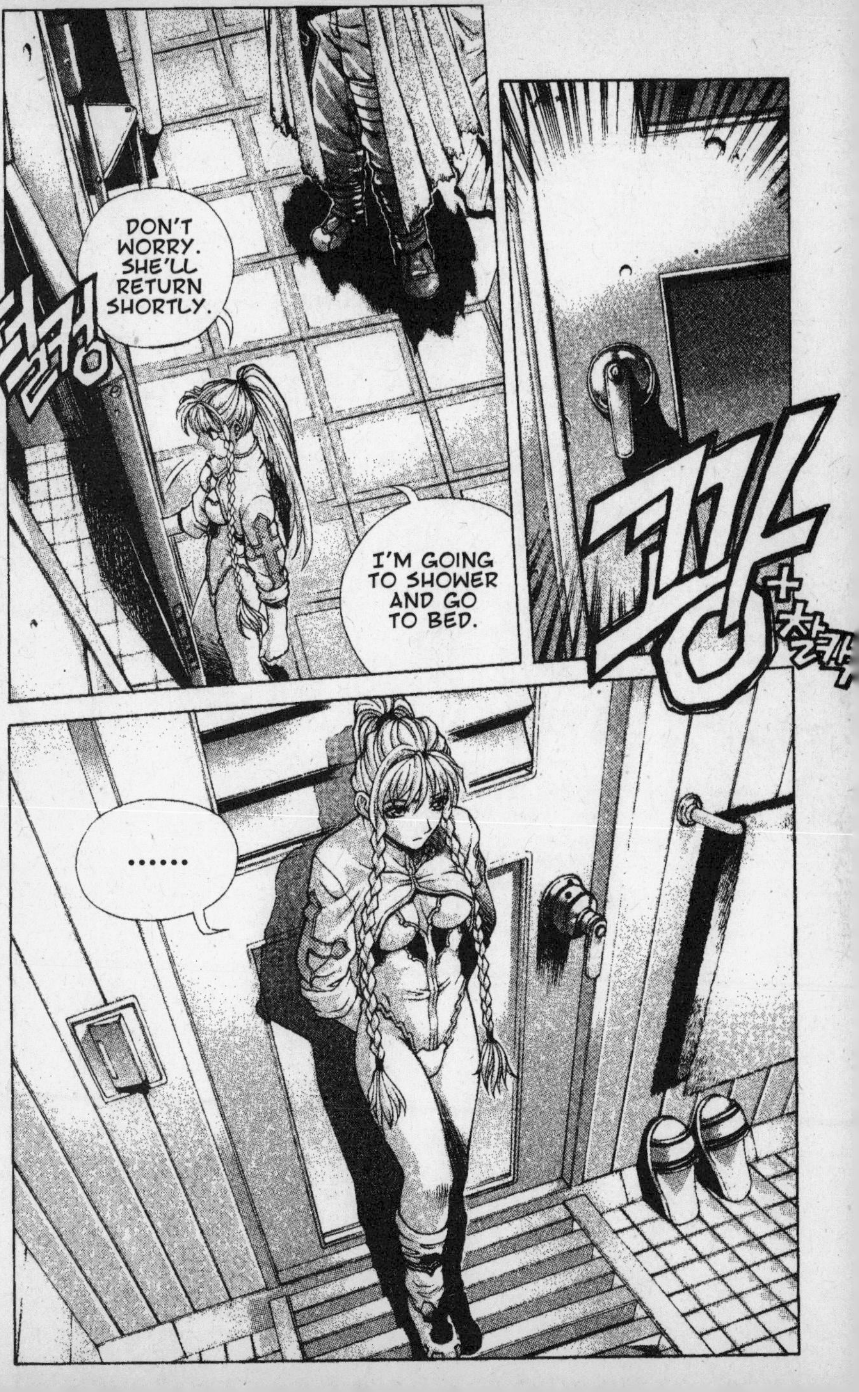
DON'T WORRY. SHE'LL RETURN SHORTLY.
덜컹
I'M GOING TO SHOWER AND GO TO BED.
......

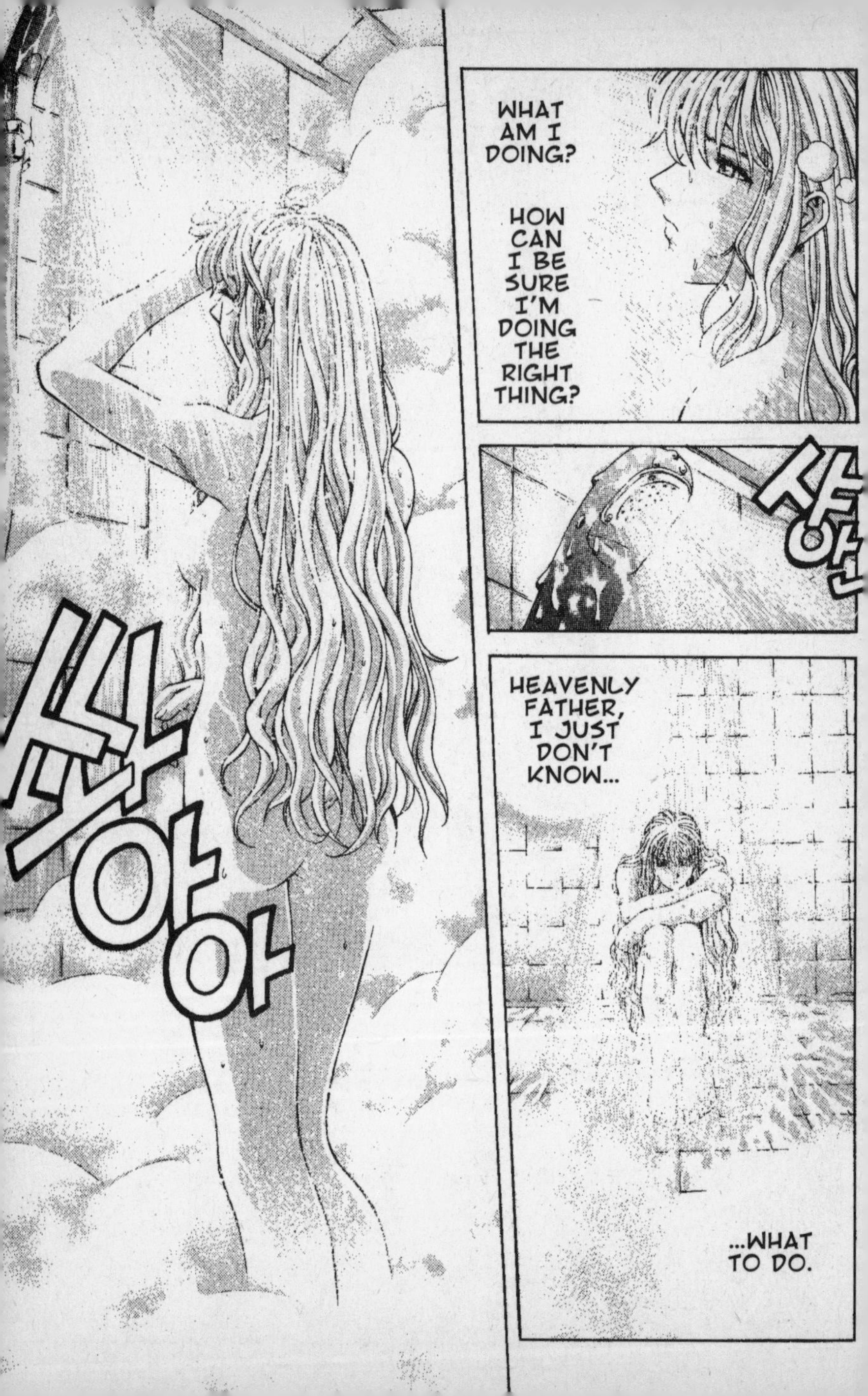
WHAT AM I DOING?
HOW CAN I BE SURE I'M DOING THE RIGHT THING?
HEAVENLY FATHER, I JUST DON'T KNOW...
...WHAT TO DO.

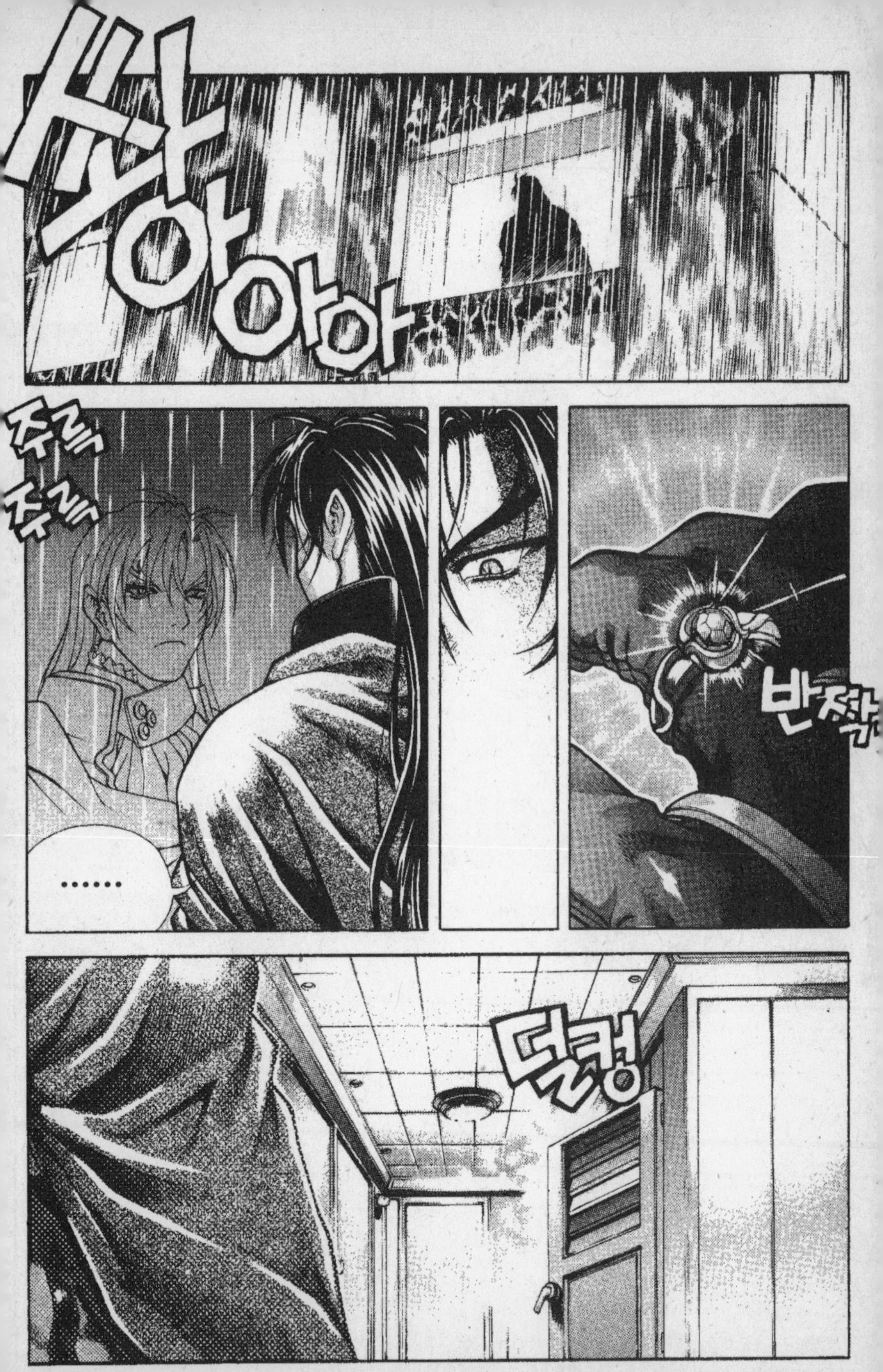
쏴아아아
주륵 주륵
……
반짝
덜컹

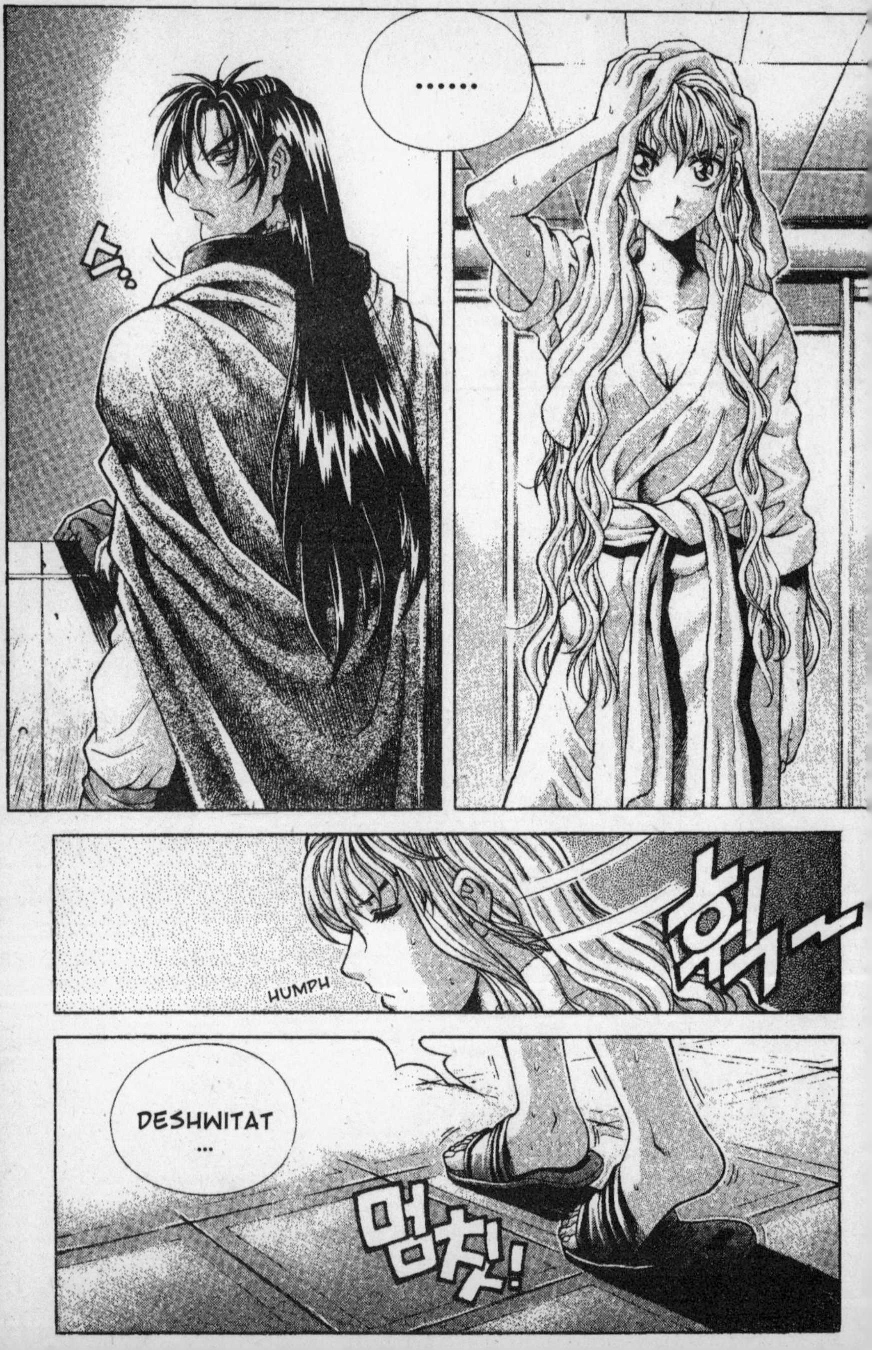
......
휙~
HUMPH
DESHWITAT ...
멈칫!

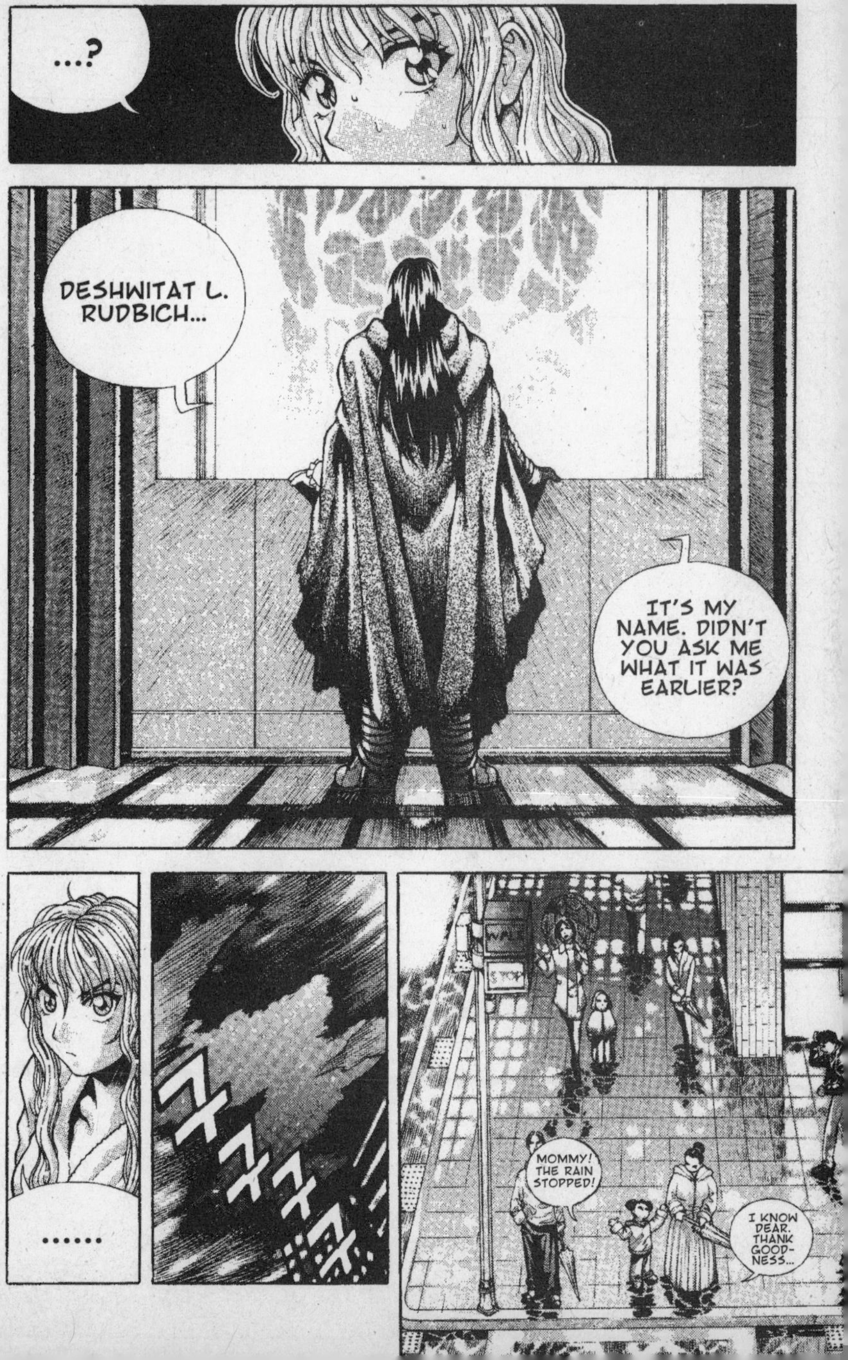
...?
DESHWITAT L. RUDBICH...
IT'S MY NAME. DIDN'T YOU ASK ME WHAT IT WAS EARLIER?
......
MOMMY! THE RAIN STOPPED!
I KNOW DEAR. THANK GOODNESS...

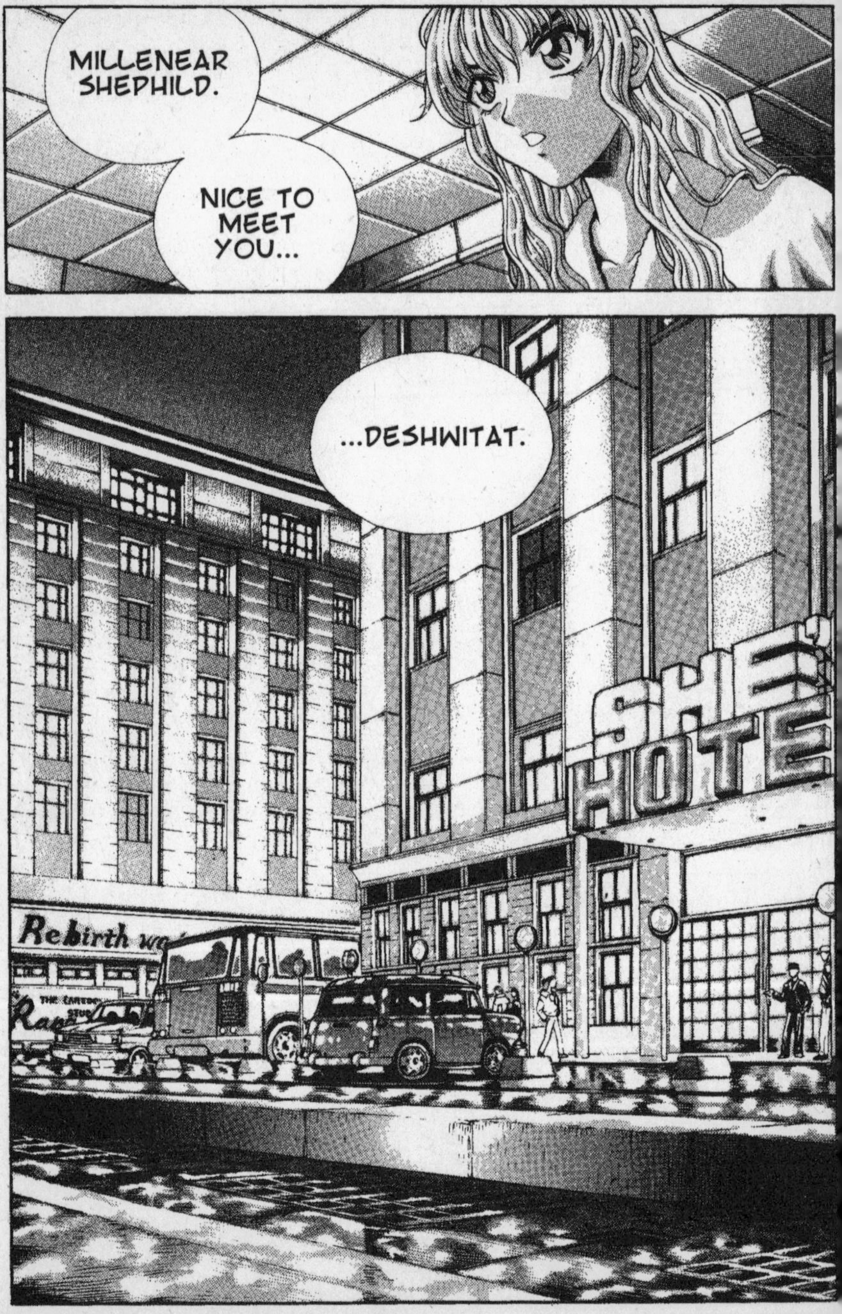
MILLENEAR SHEPHILD.
NICE TO MEET YOU...
...DESHWITAT.
Rebirth

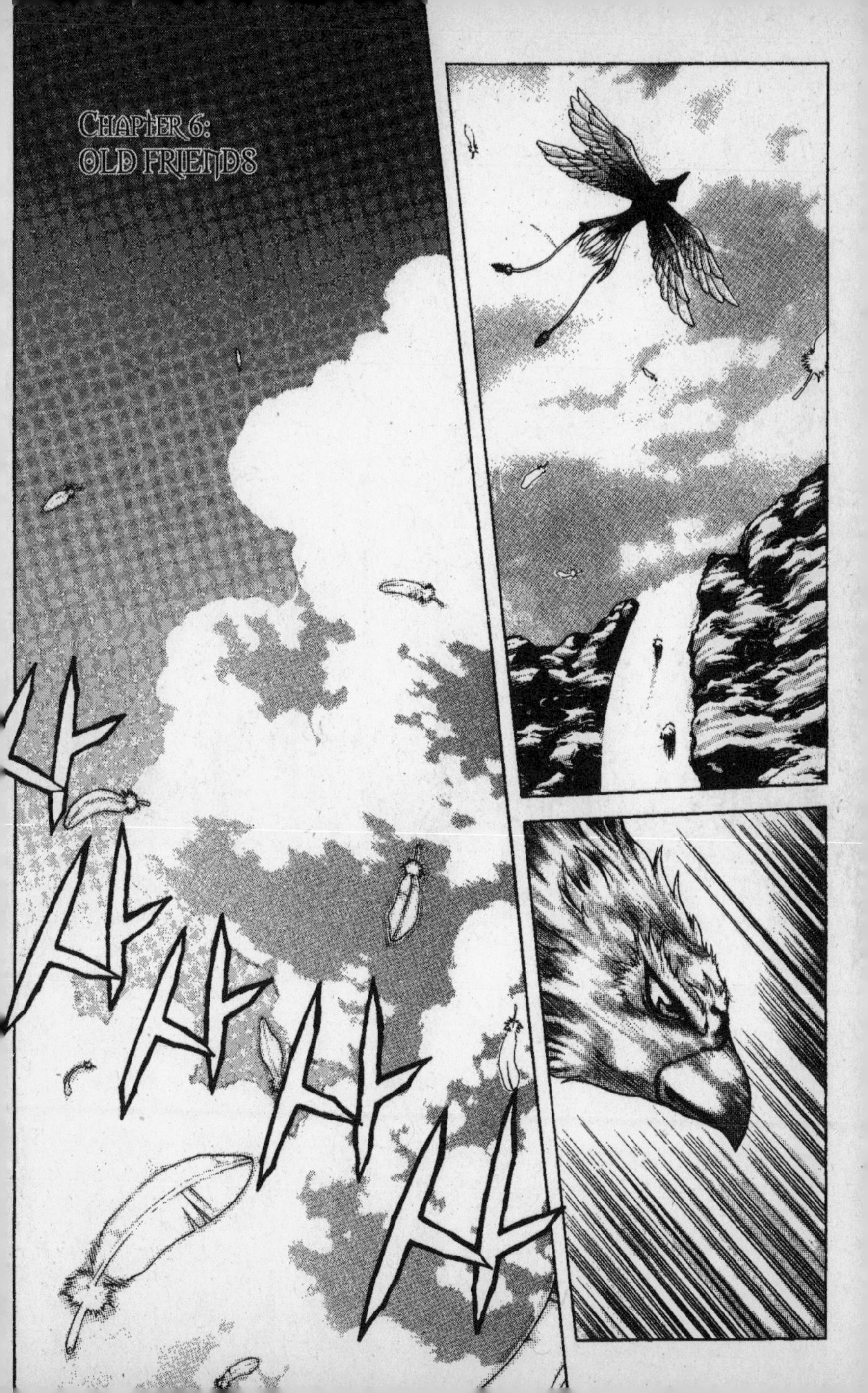
Chapter 6:
Old Friends

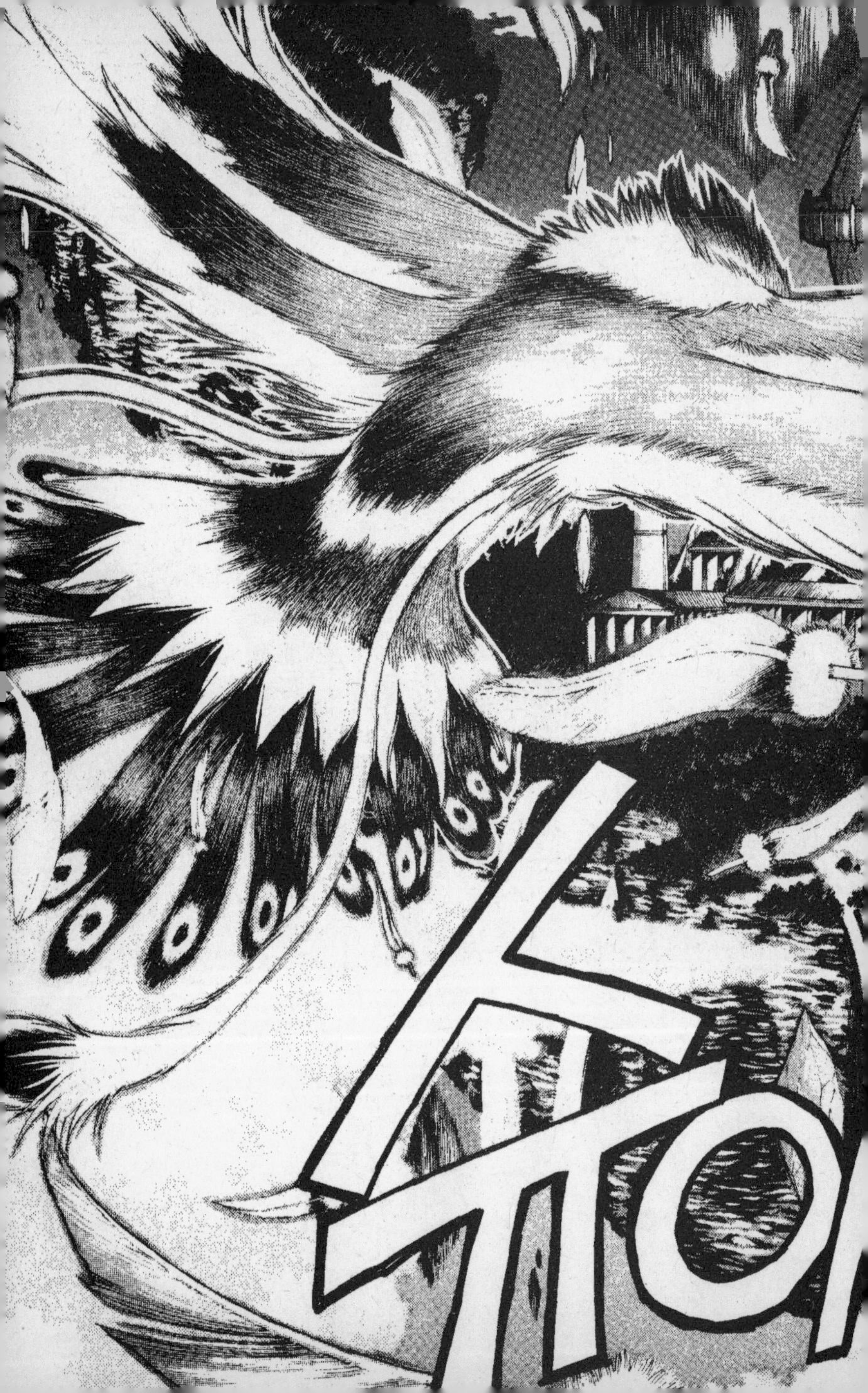

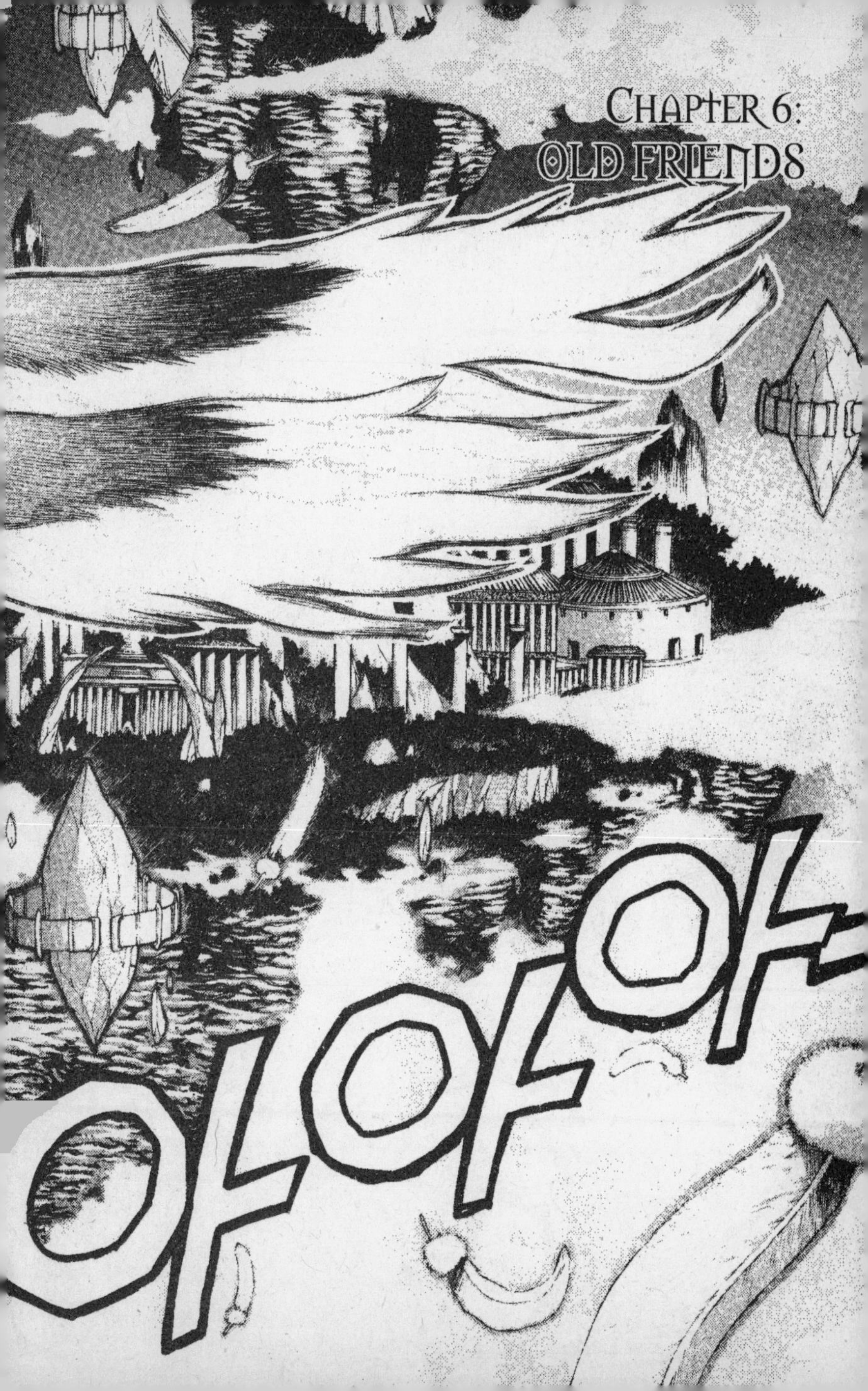
Chapter 6:
OLD FRIENDS

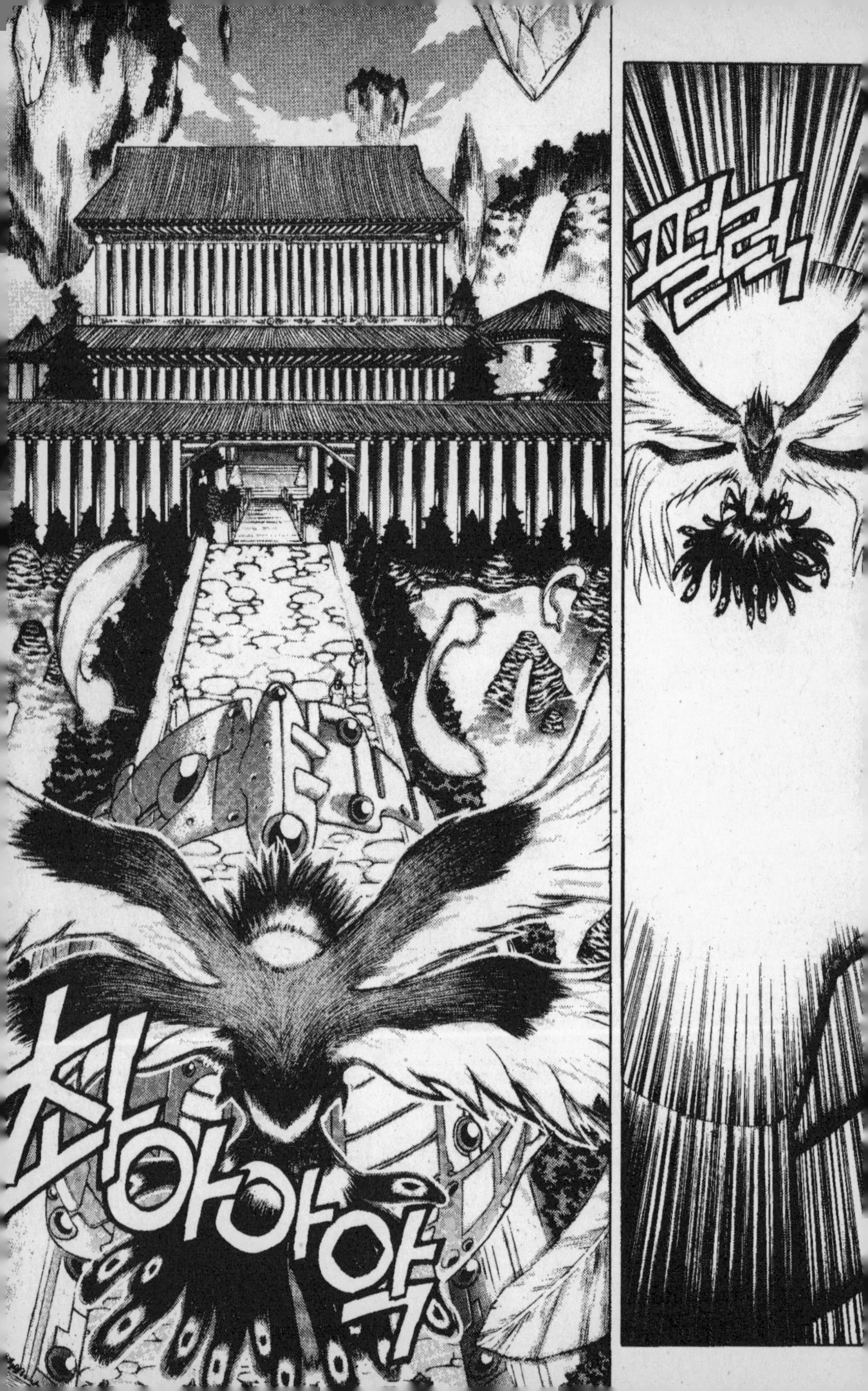
차아아아악
펄럭

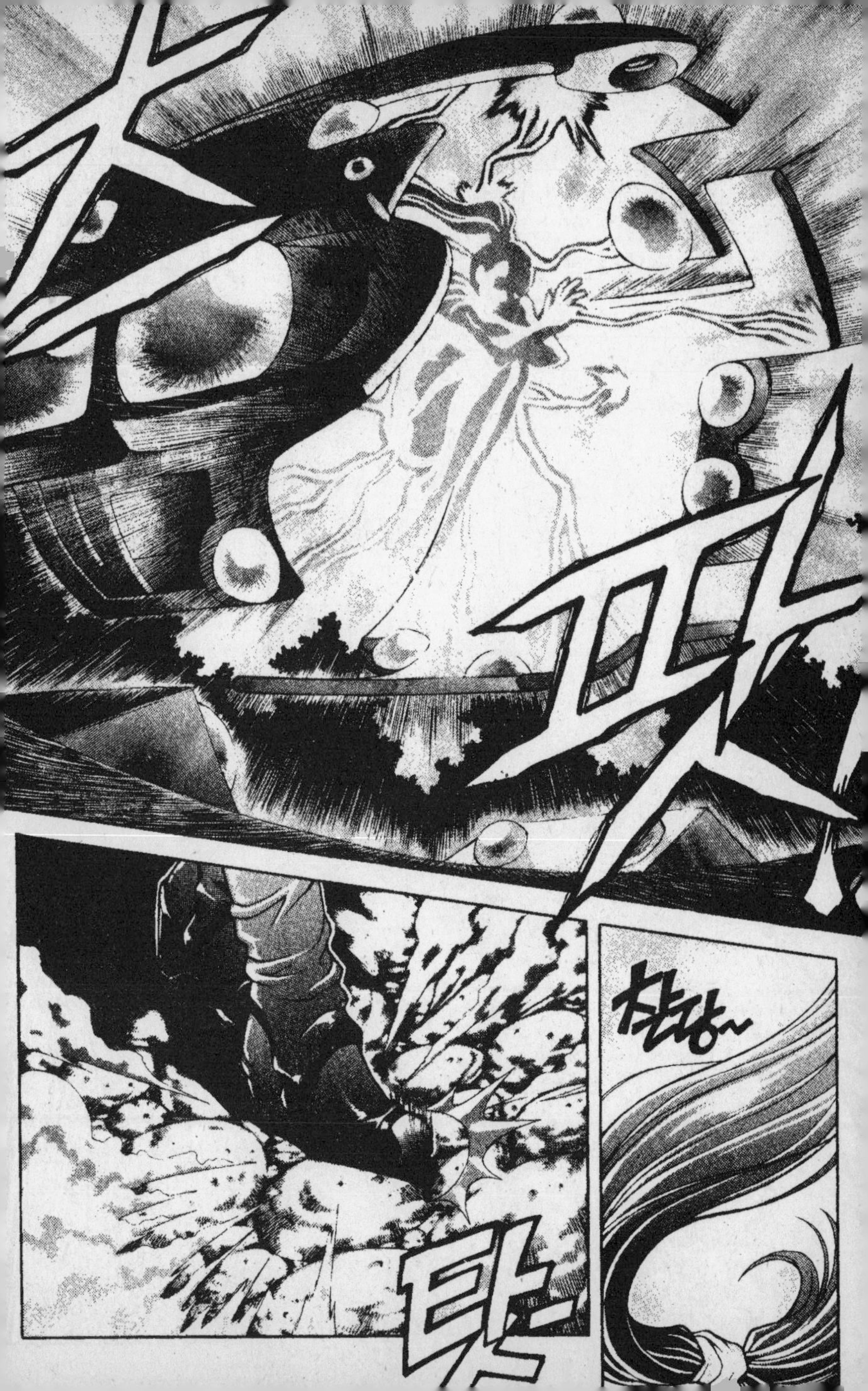
팟
탁
차랑~

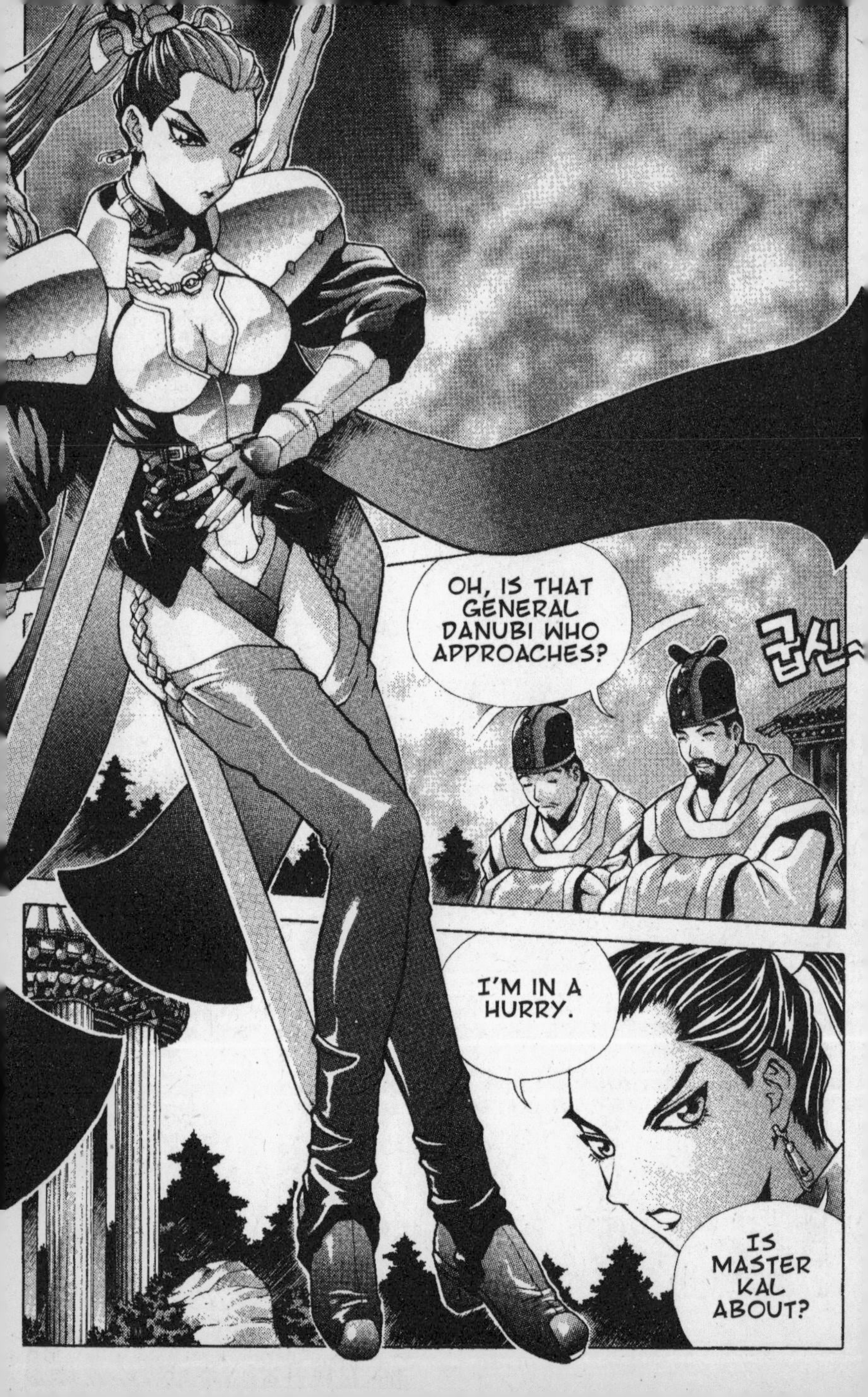
OH, IS THAT GENERAL DANUBI WHO APPROACHES?
굽신~
I'M IN A HURRY.
IS MASTER KAL ABOUT?

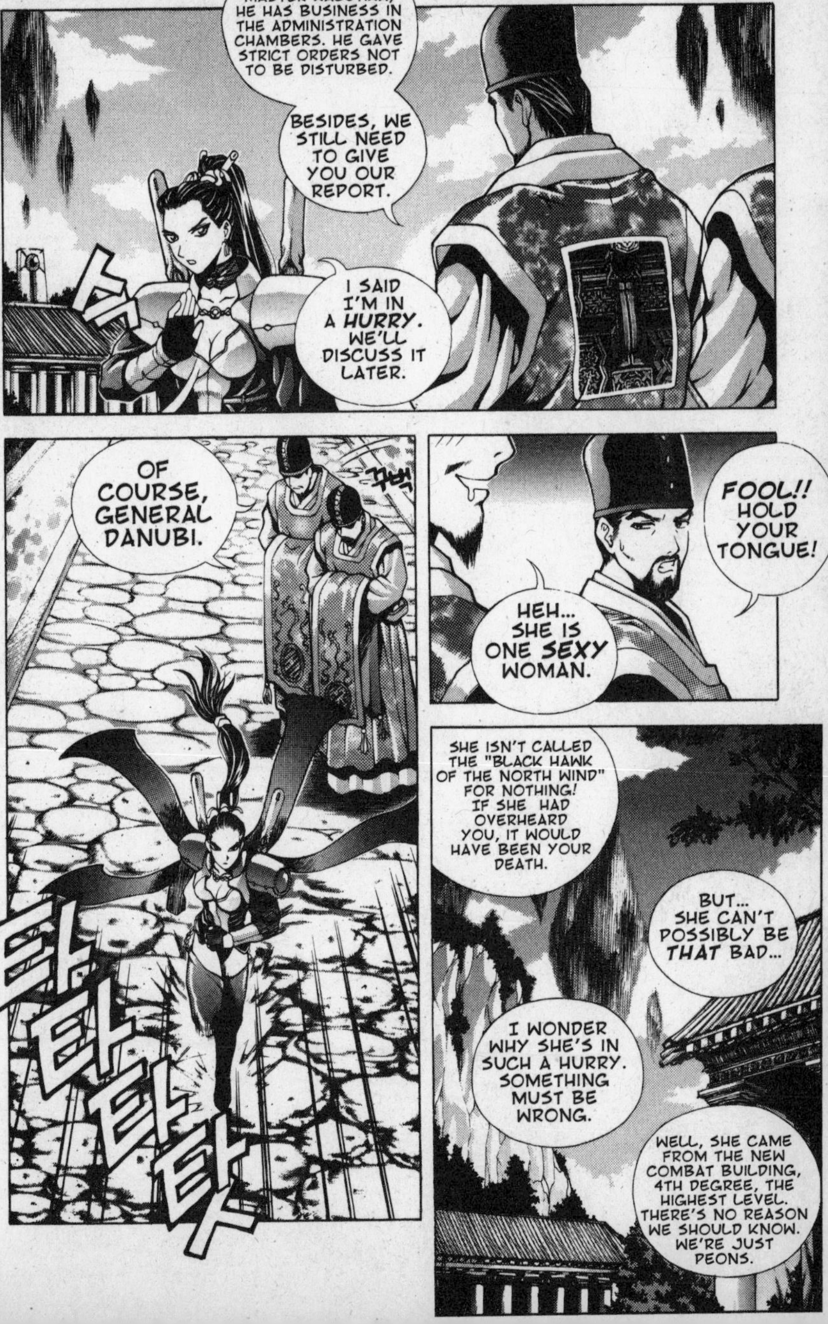
IF YOU ARE REFERRING TO MASTER KALUTIKA, HE HAS BUSINESS IN THE ADMINISTRATION CHAMBERS. HE GAVE STRICT ORDERS NOT TO BE DISTURBED.
BESIDES, WE STILL NEED TO GIVE YOU OUR REPORT.
I SAID I'M IN A *HURRY*. WE'LL DISCUSS IT LATER.
OF COURSE, GENERAL DANUBI.
타 타 타 탁
HEH... SHE IS ONE *SEXY* WOMAN.
FOOL!! HOLD YOUR TONGUE!
SHE ISN'T CALLED THE "BLACK HAWK OF THE NORTH WIND" FOR NOTHING! IF SHE HAD OVERHEARD YOU, IT WOULD HAVE BEEN YOUR DEATH.
BUT... SHE CAN'T POSSIBLY BE *THAT* BAD...
I WONDER WHY SHE'S IN SUCH A HURRY. SOMETHING MUST BE WRONG.
WELL, SHE CAME FROM THE NEW COMBAT BUILDING, 4TH DEGREE, THE HIGHEST LEVEL. THERE'S NO REASON WE SHOULD KNOW. WE'RE JUST PEONS.

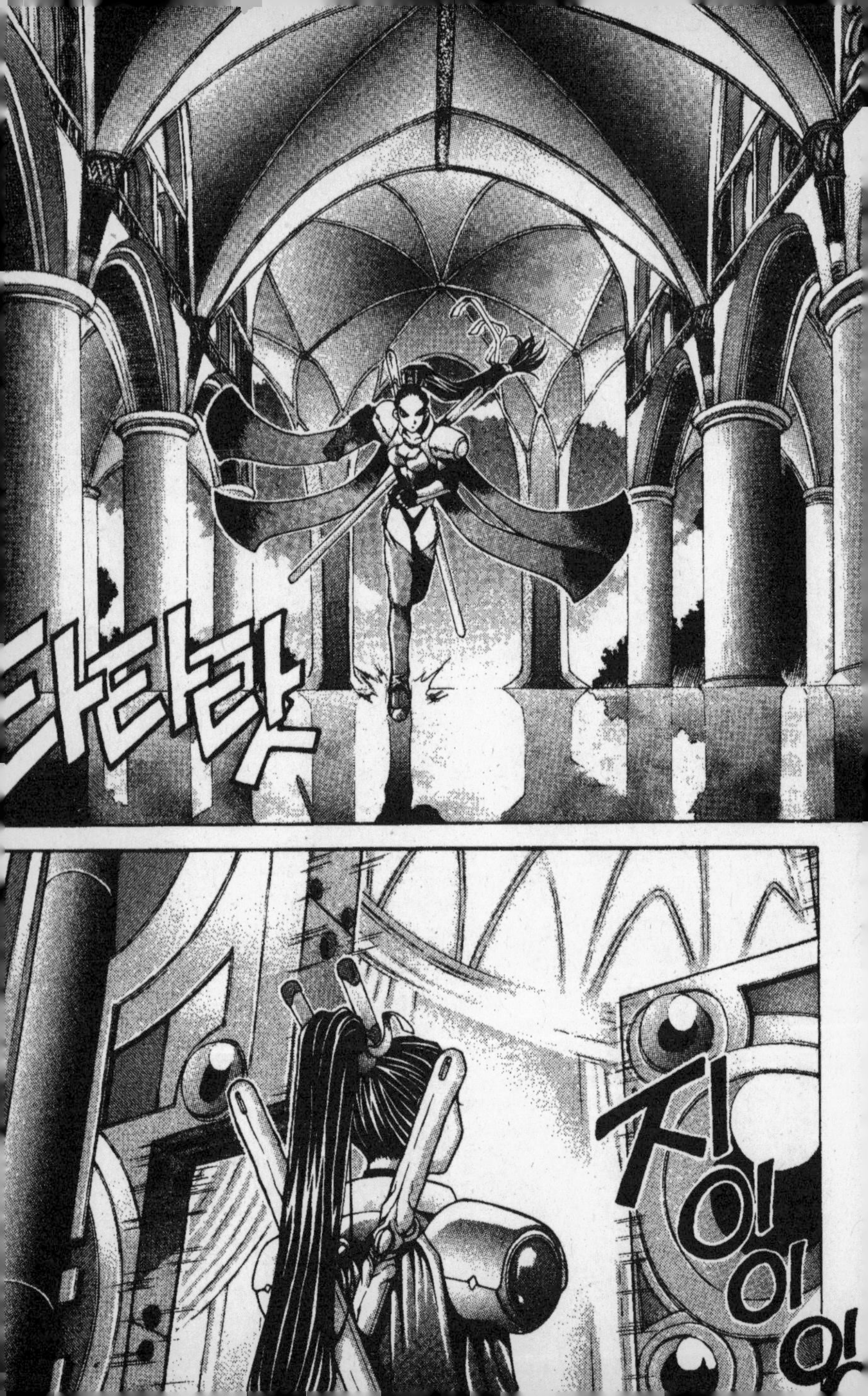
타타탓
지이이이이!

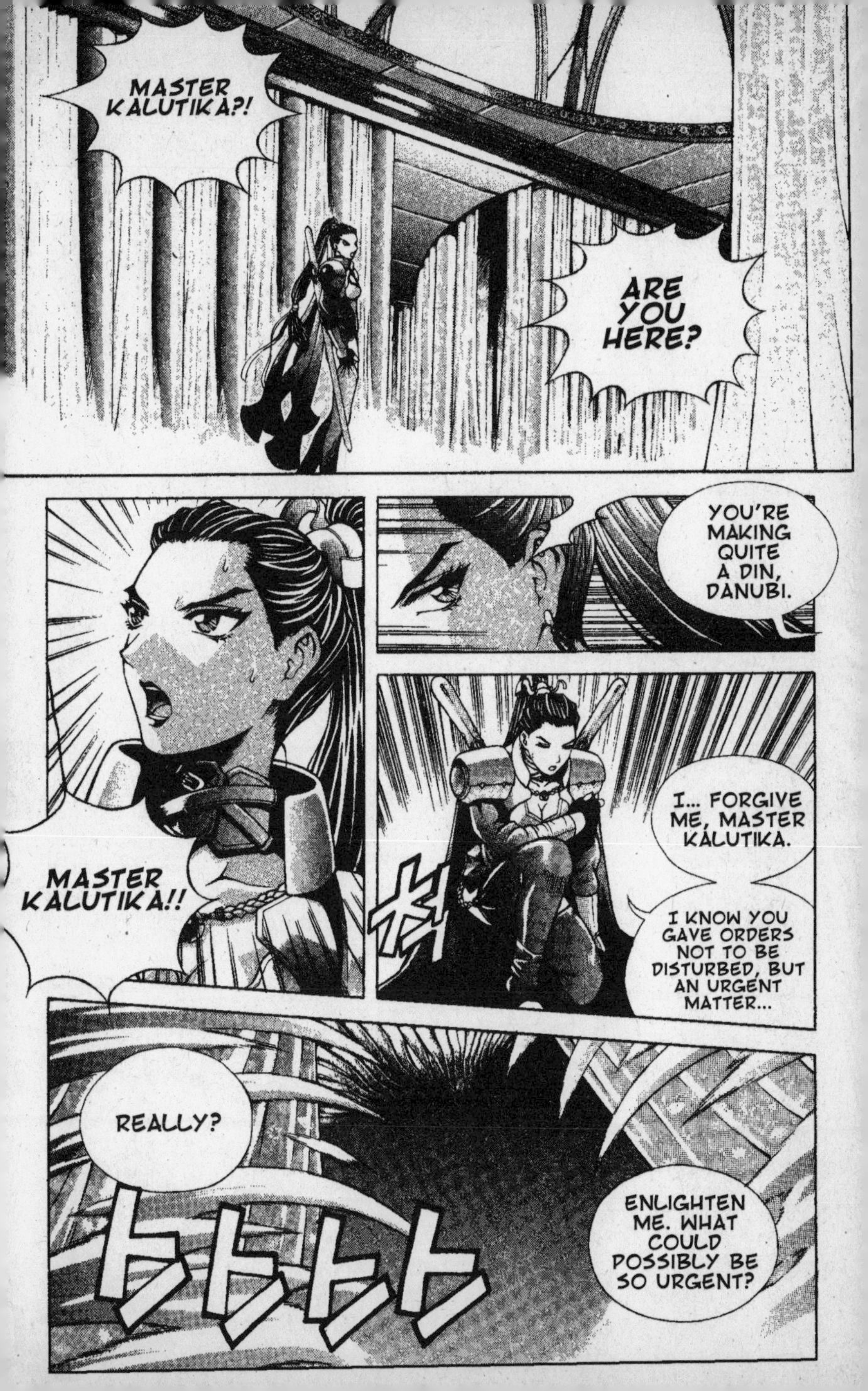
MASTER KALUTIKA?!
ARE YOU HERE?
MASTER KALUTIKA!!
YOU'RE MAKING QUITE A DIN, DANUBI.
I... FORGIVE ME, MASTER KALUTIKA.
I KNOW YOU GAVE ORDERS NOT TO BE DISTURBED, BUT AN URGENT MATTER...
REALLY?
ENLIGHTEN ME. WHAT COULD POSSIBLY BE SO URGENT?

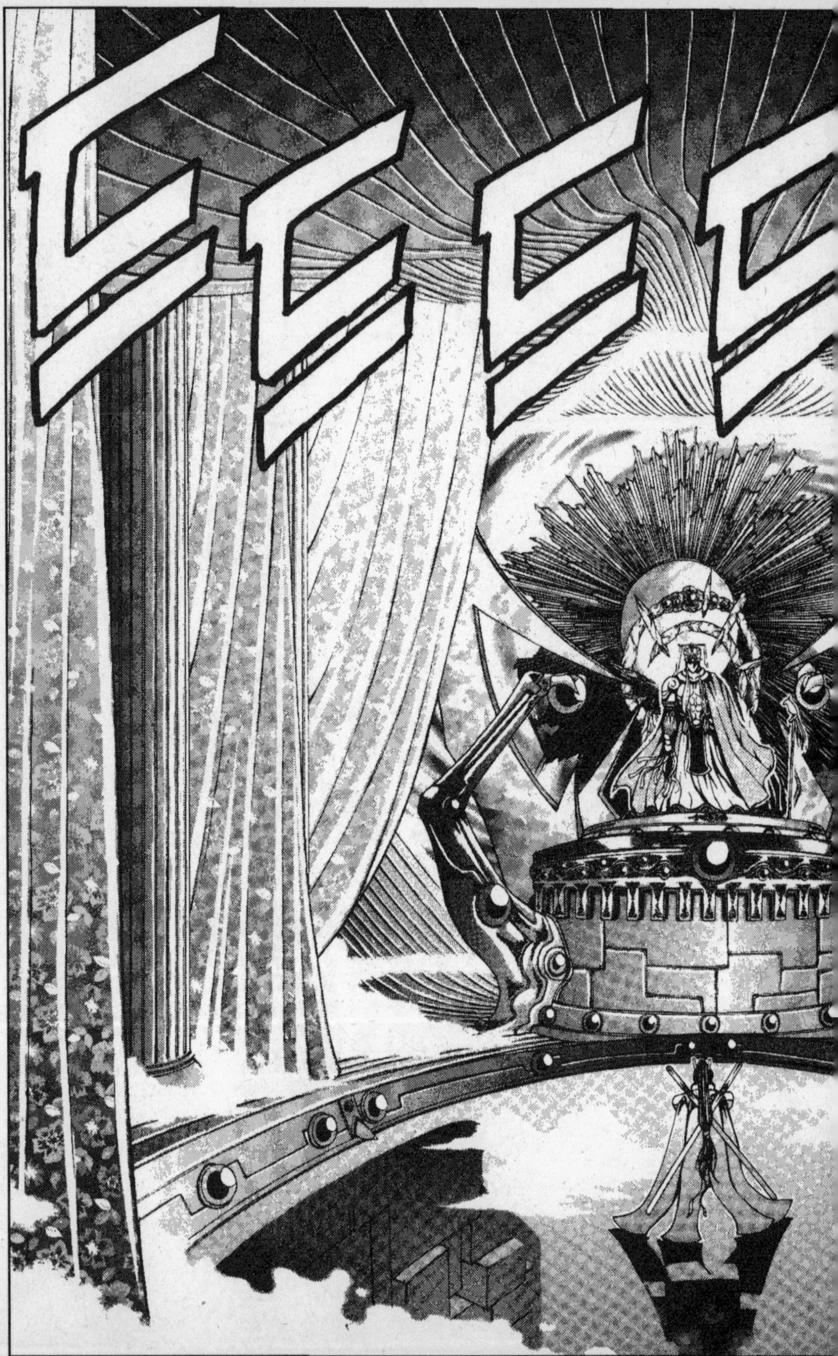

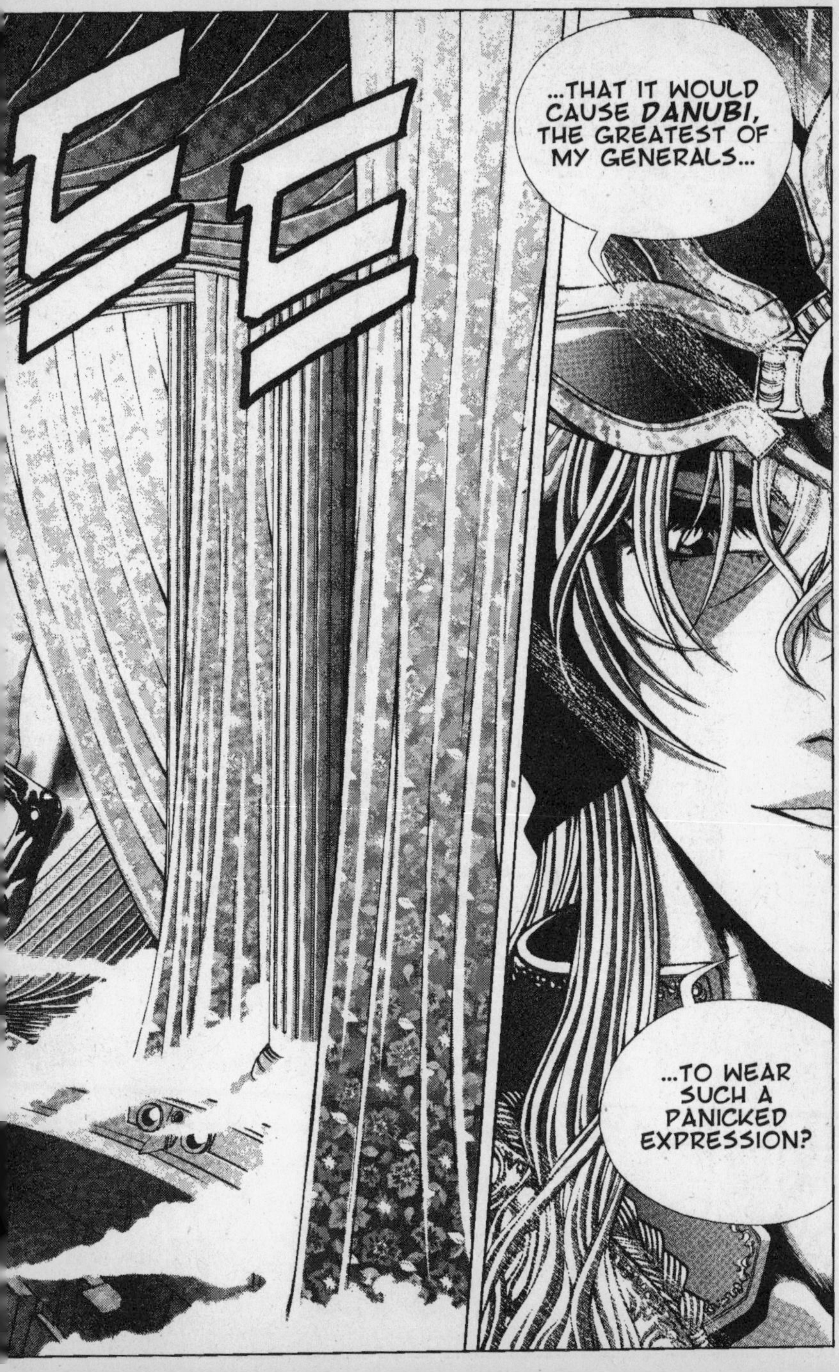

...THAT IT WOULD CAUSE DANUBI, THE GREATEST OF MY GENERALS...
...TO WEAR SUCH A PANICKED EXPRESSION?

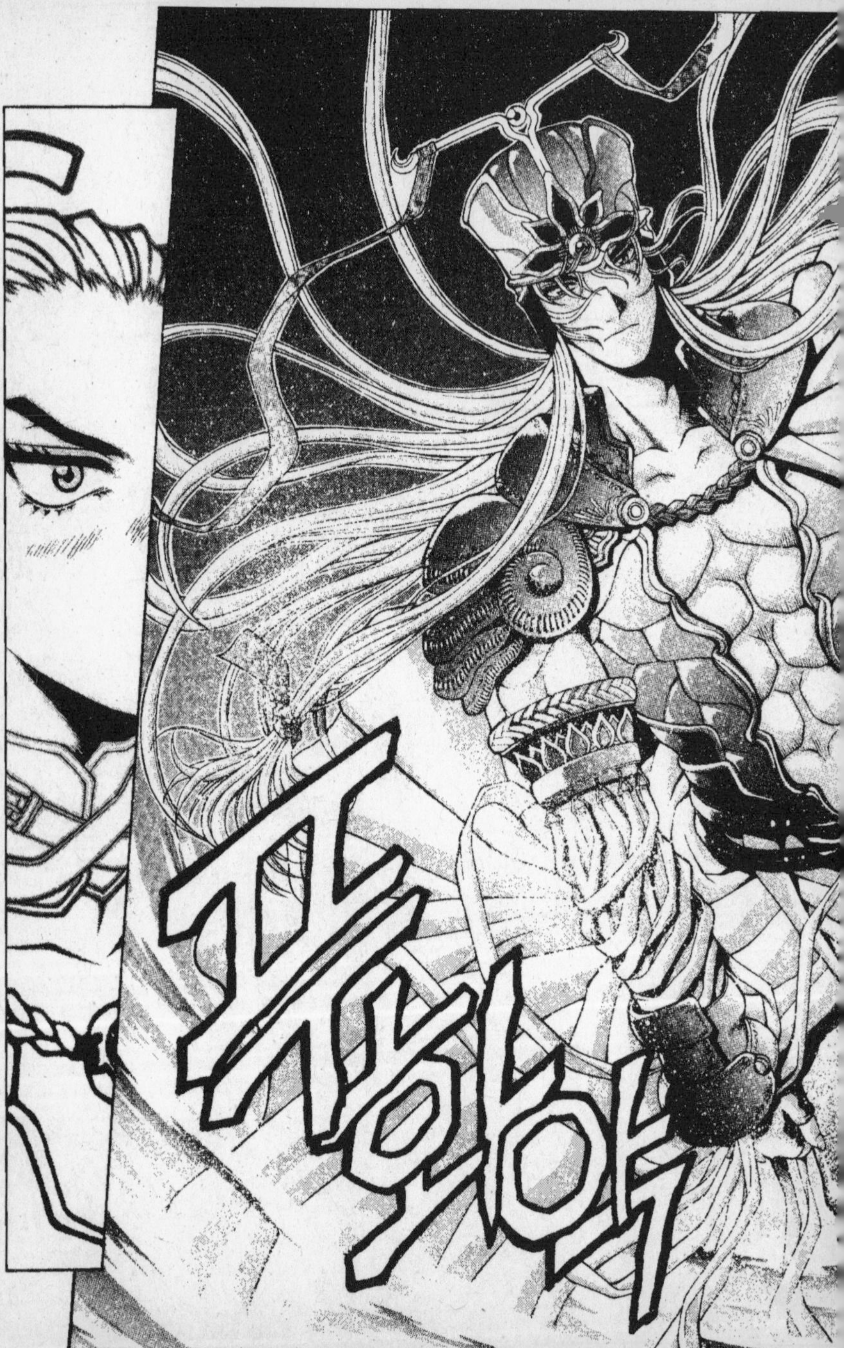

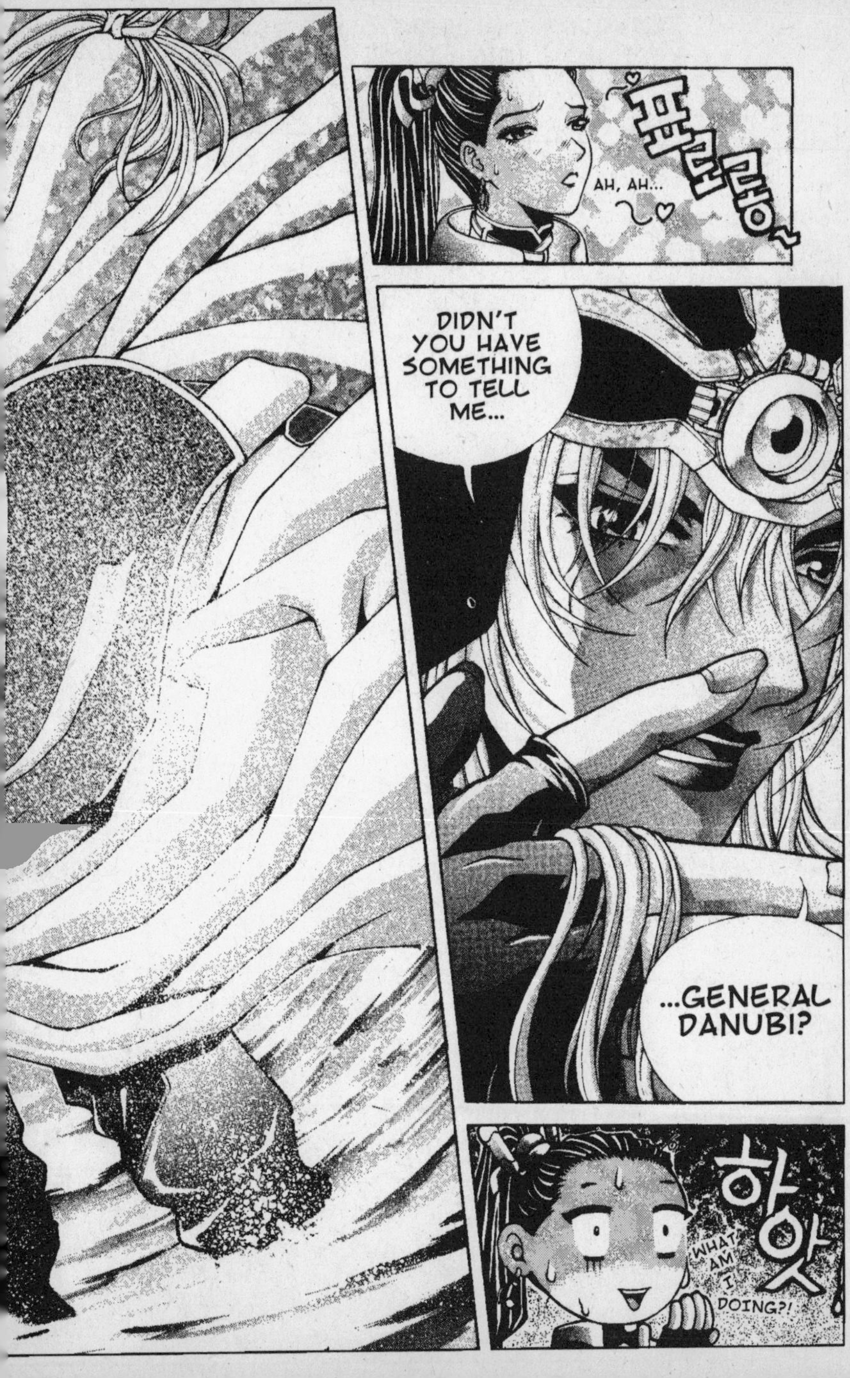
표르릉~
AH, AH...
DIDN'T YOU HAVE SOMETHING TO TELL ME...
...GENERAL DANUBI?
하앗
WHAT AM I DOING?!

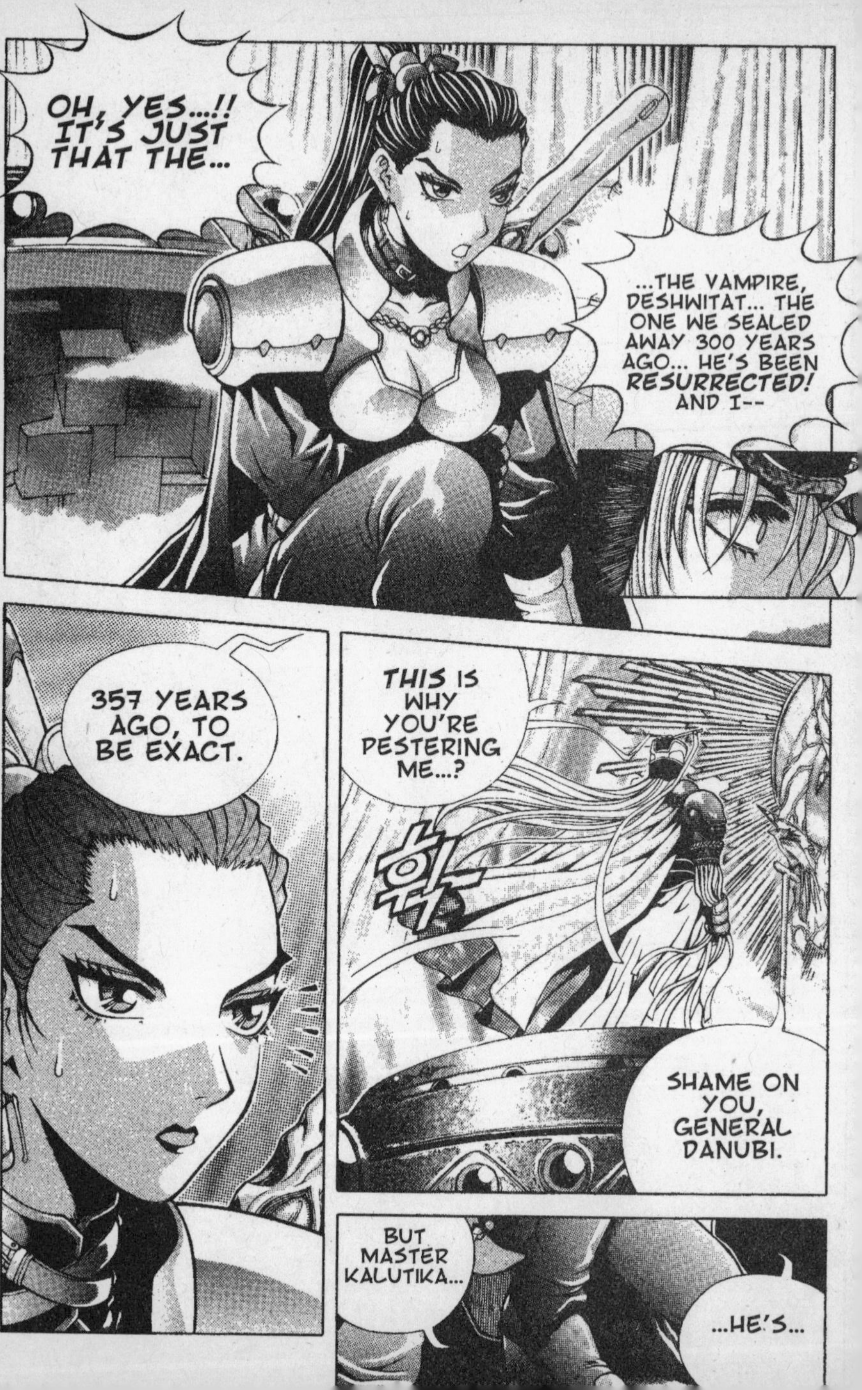
OH, YES...!! IT'S JUST THAT THE...
...THE VAMPIRE, DESHWITAT... THE ONE WE SEALED AWAY 300 YEARS AGO... HE'S BEEN RESURRECTED! AND I--
357 YEARS AGO, TO BE EXACT.
THIS IS WHY YOU'RE PESTERING ME...?
SHAME ON YOU, GENERAL DANUBI.
BUT MASTER KALUTIKA...
...HE'S...

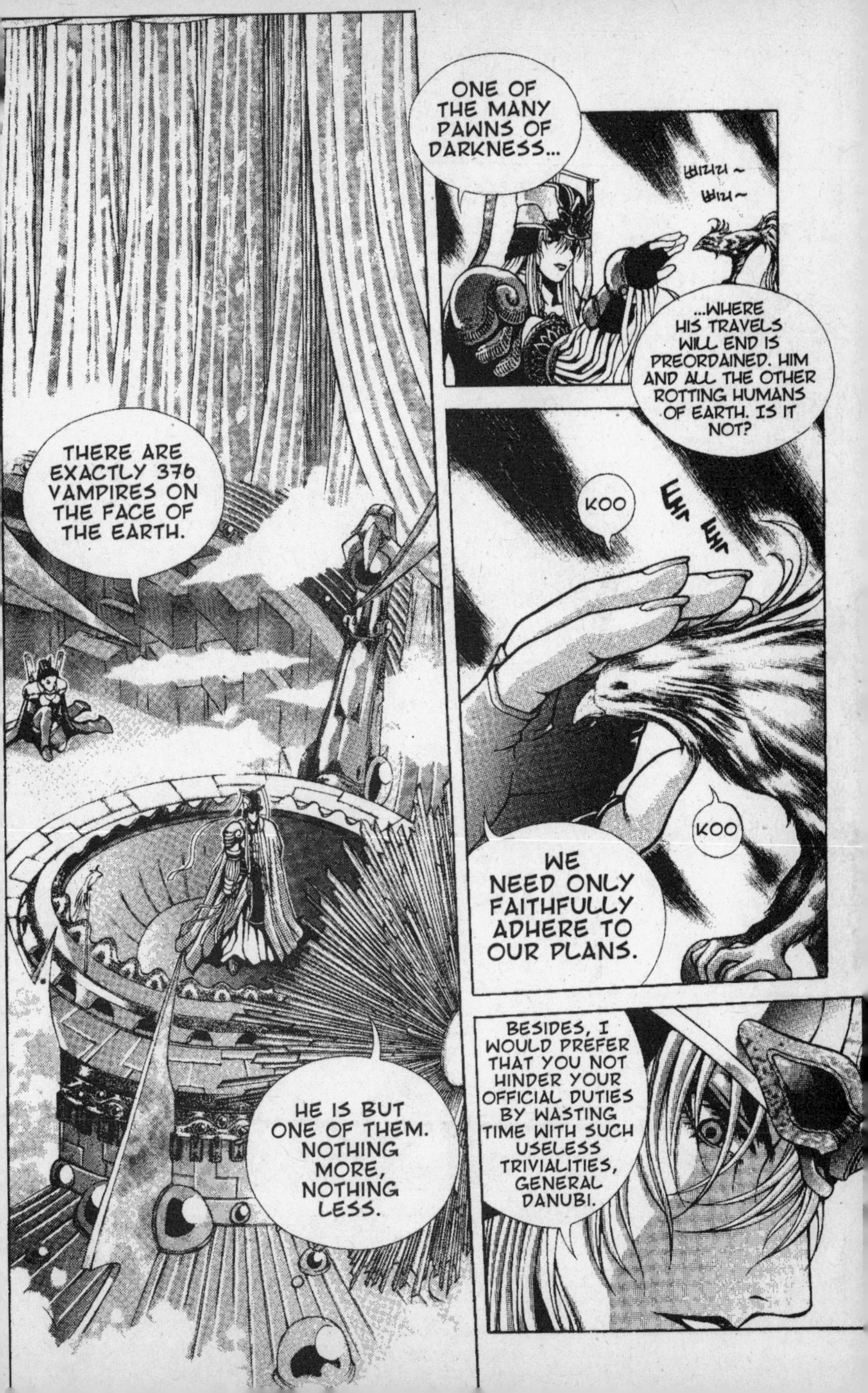
THERE ARE EXACTLY 376 VAMPIRES ON THE FACE OF THE EARTH.
HE IS BUT ONE OF THEM. NOTHING MORE, NOTHING LESS.
ONE OF THE MANY PAWNS OF DARKNESS...
삐리리~
삐리~
...WHERE HIS TRAVELS WILL END IS PREORDAINED. HIM AND ALL THE OTHER ROTTING HUMANS OF EARTH. IS IT NOT?
KOO
KOO
WE NEED ONLY FAITHFULLY ADHERE TO OUR PLANS.
BESIDES, I WOULD PREFER THAT YOU NOT HINDER YOUR OFFICIAL DUTIES BY WASTING TIME WITH SUCH USELESS TRIVIALITIES, GENERAL DANUBI.

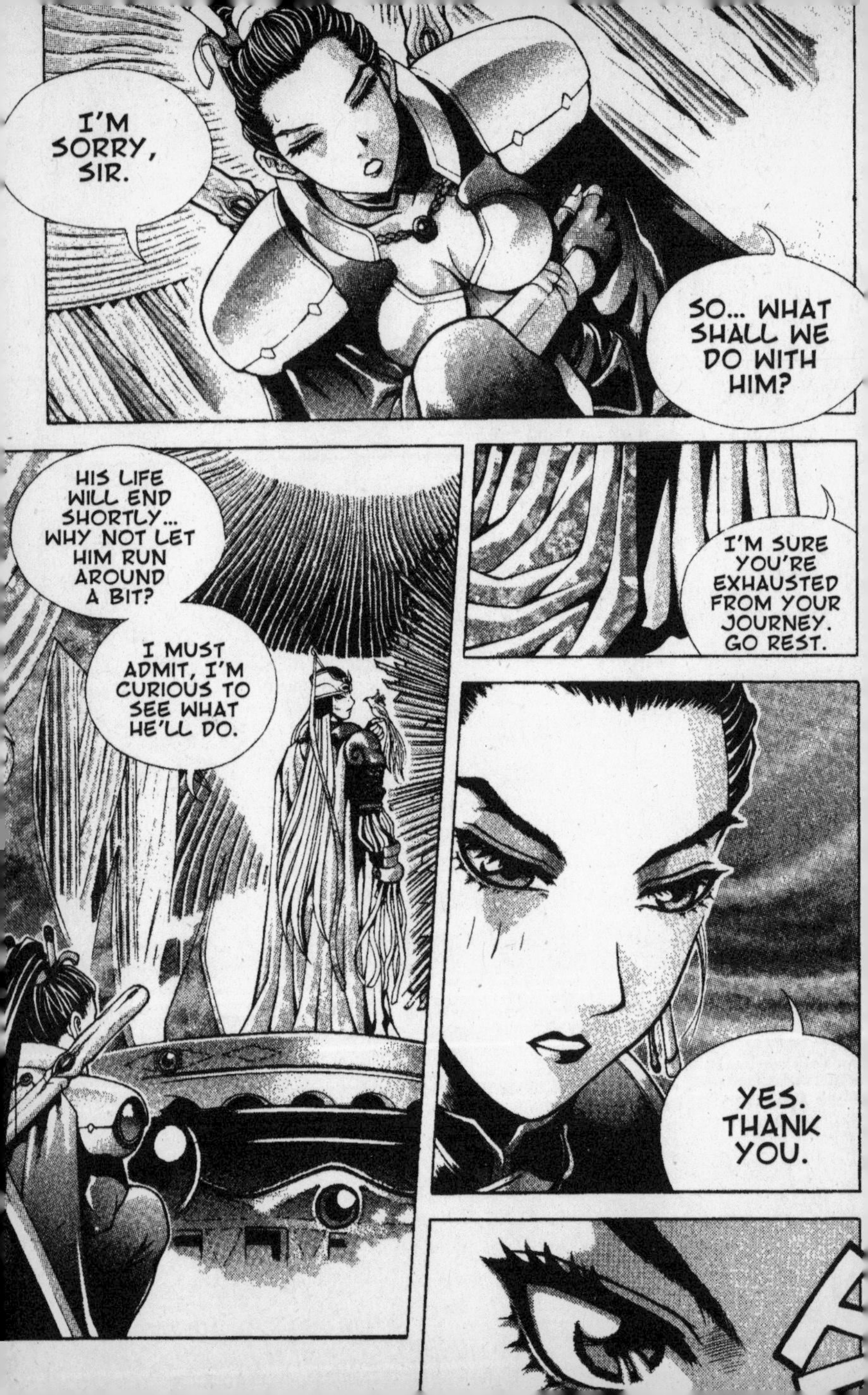
I'M SORRY, SIR.
SO... WHAT SHALL WE DO WITH HIM?
HIS LIFE WILL END SHORTLY... WHY NOT LET HIM RUN AROUND A BIT?
I MUST ADMIT, I'M CURIOUS TO SEE WHAT HE'LL DO.
I'M SURE YOU'RE EXHAUSTED FROM YOUR JOURNEY. GO REST.
YES. THANK YOU.

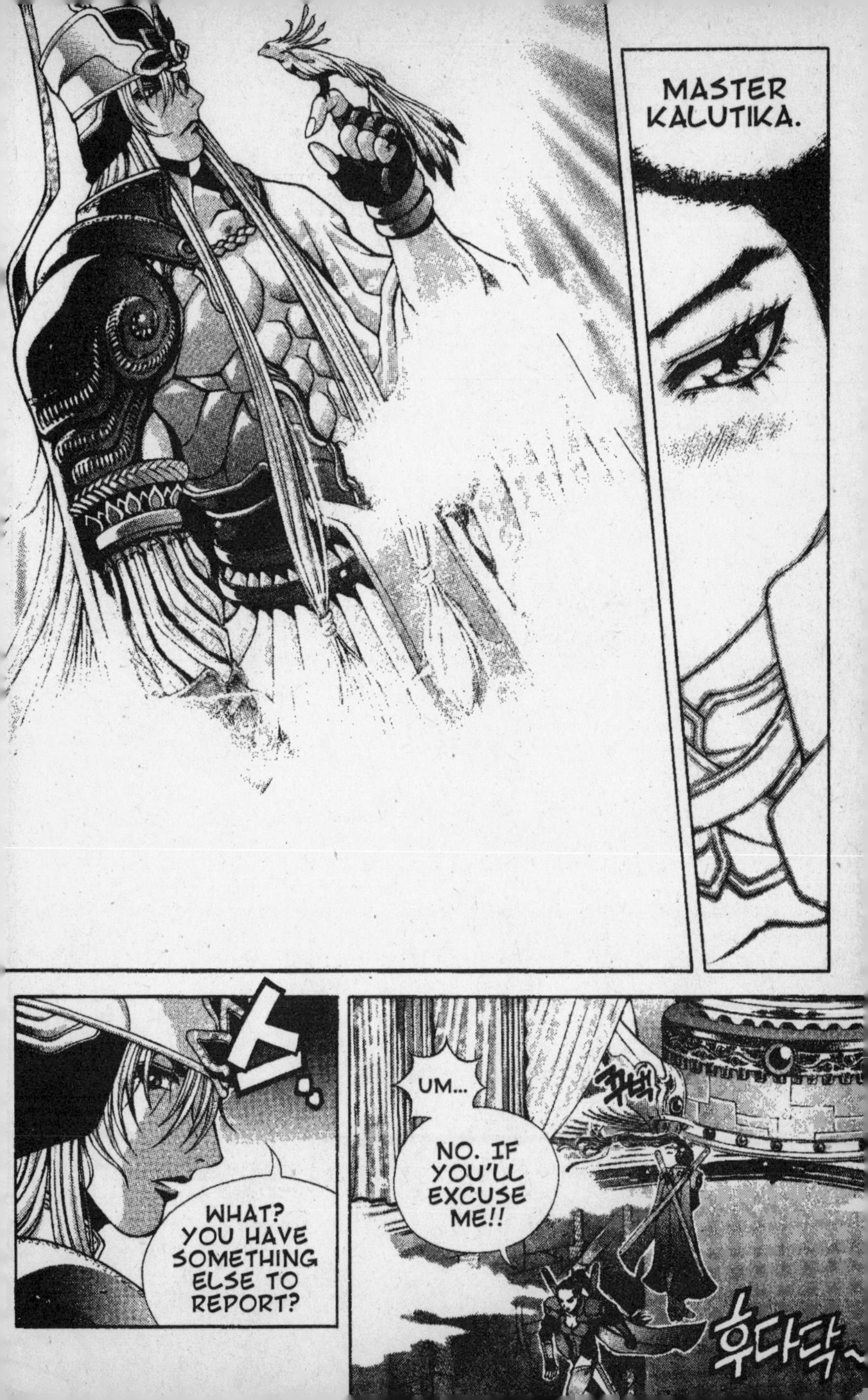
MASTER KALUTIKA.
WHAT? YOU HAVE SOMETHING ELSE TO REPORT?
UM...
NO. IF YOU'LL EXCUSE ME!!
후다닥~

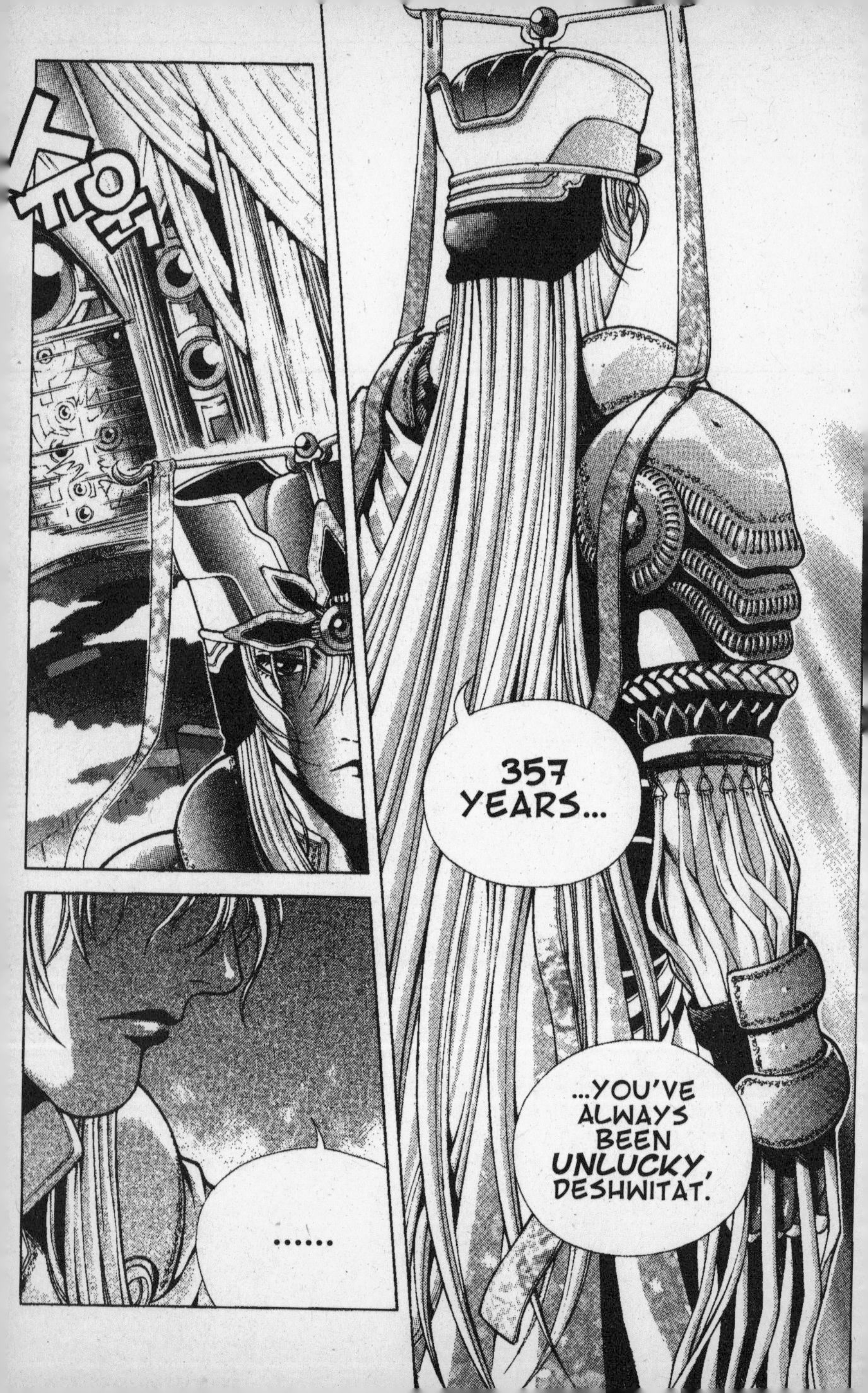
......
357 YEARS...
...YOU'VE ALWAYS BEEN UNLUCKY, DESHWITAT.

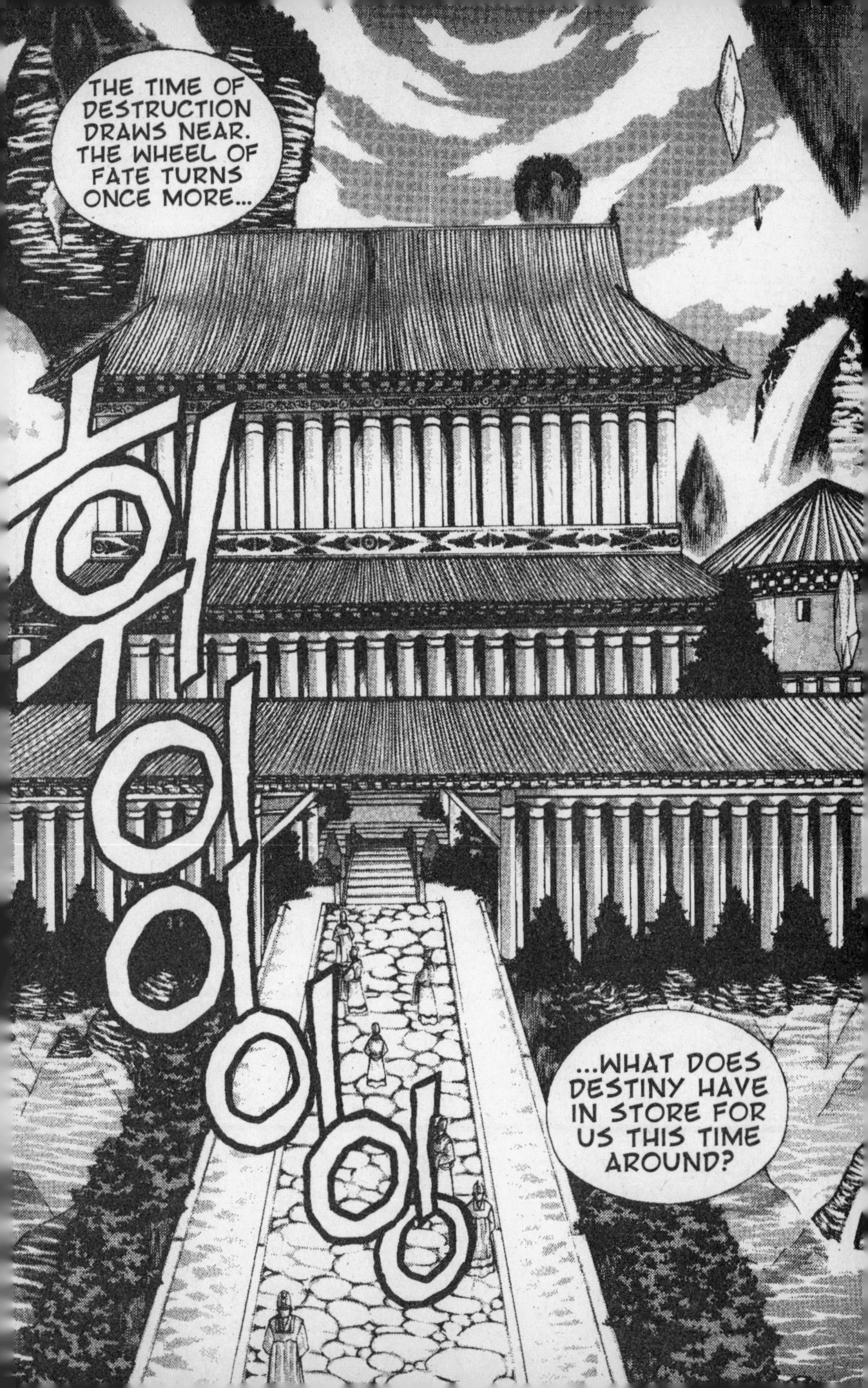
THE TIME OF DESTRUCTION DRAWS NEAR. THE WHEEL OF FATE TURNS ONCE MORE...
...WHAT DOES DESTINY HAVE IN STORE FOR US THIS TIME AROUND?

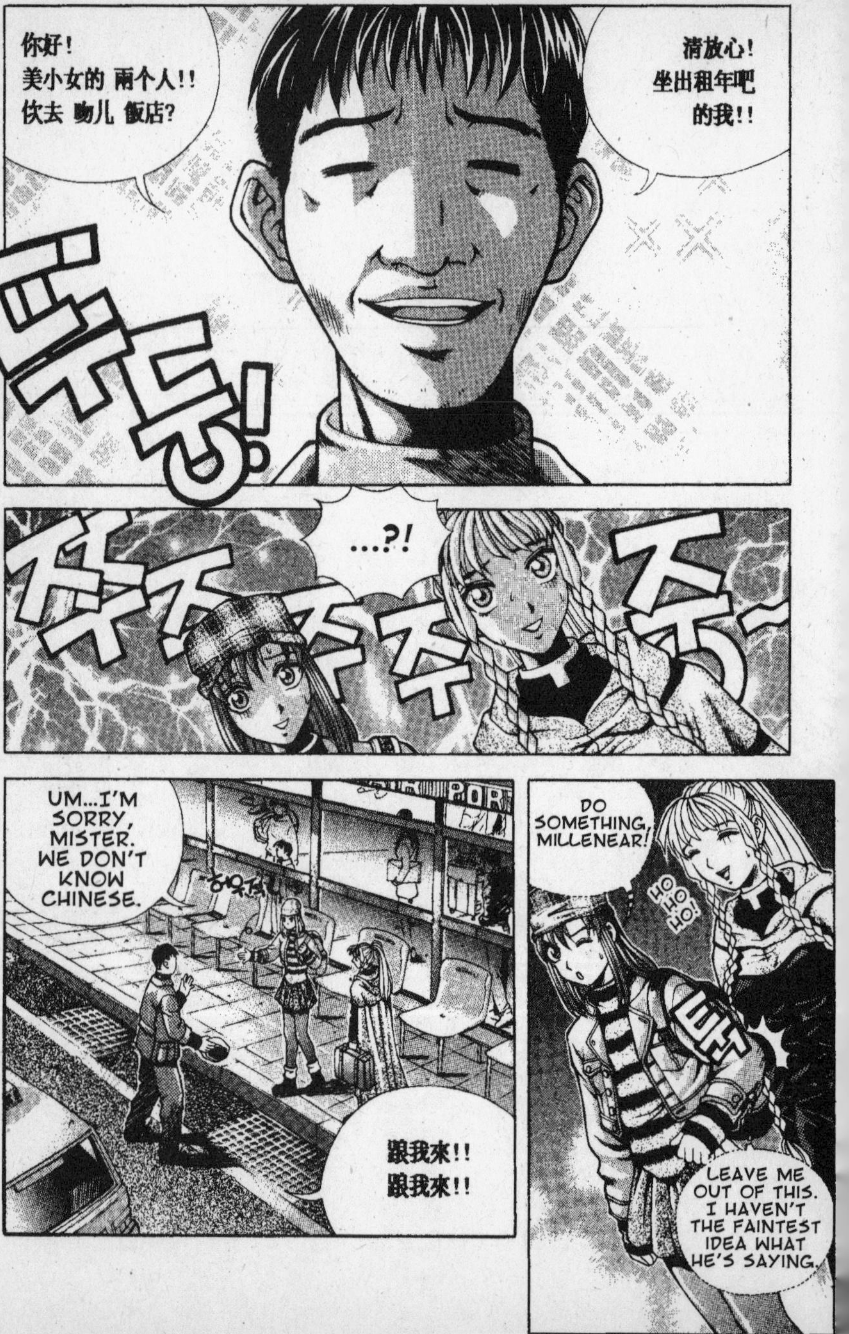

你好！
美小女的 兩个人!!
伙去 哪儿 飯店?
清放心！
坐出租年吧
的我!!
...?!
UM...I'M SORRY, MISTER. WE DON'T KNOW CHINESE.
跟我來!!
跟我來!!
DO SOMETHING, MILLENEAR!
HO HO HO!
LEAVE ME OUT OF THIS. I HAVEN'T THE FAINTEST IDEA WHAT HE'S SAYING.

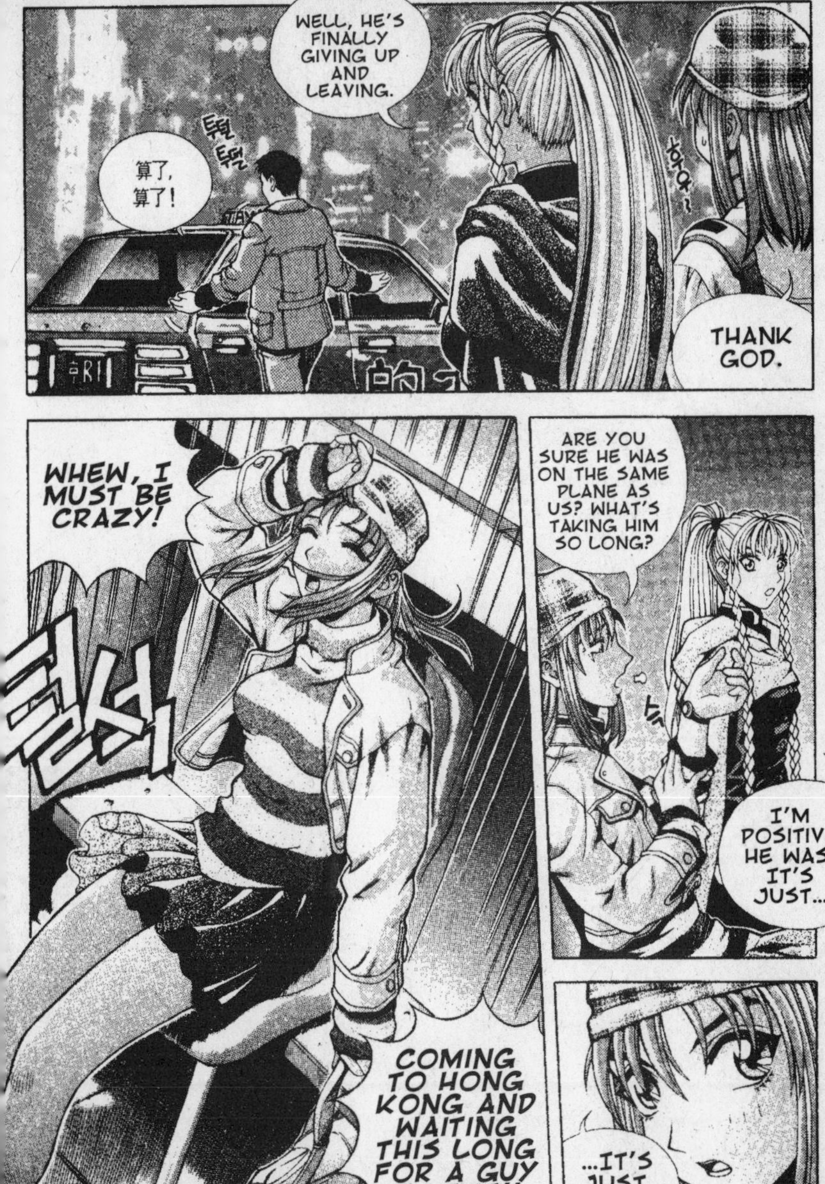

WELL, HE'S FINALLY GIVING UP AND LEAVING.
算了，算了！
THANK GOD.
WHEW, I MUST BE CRAZY!
COMING TO HONG KONG AND WAITING THIS LONG FOR A GUY I HATE!!
ARE YOU SURE HE WAS ON THE SAME PLANE AS US? WHAT'S TAKING HIM SO LONG?
I'M POSITIVE HE WAS. IT'S JUST...
...IT'S JUST, WHAT?

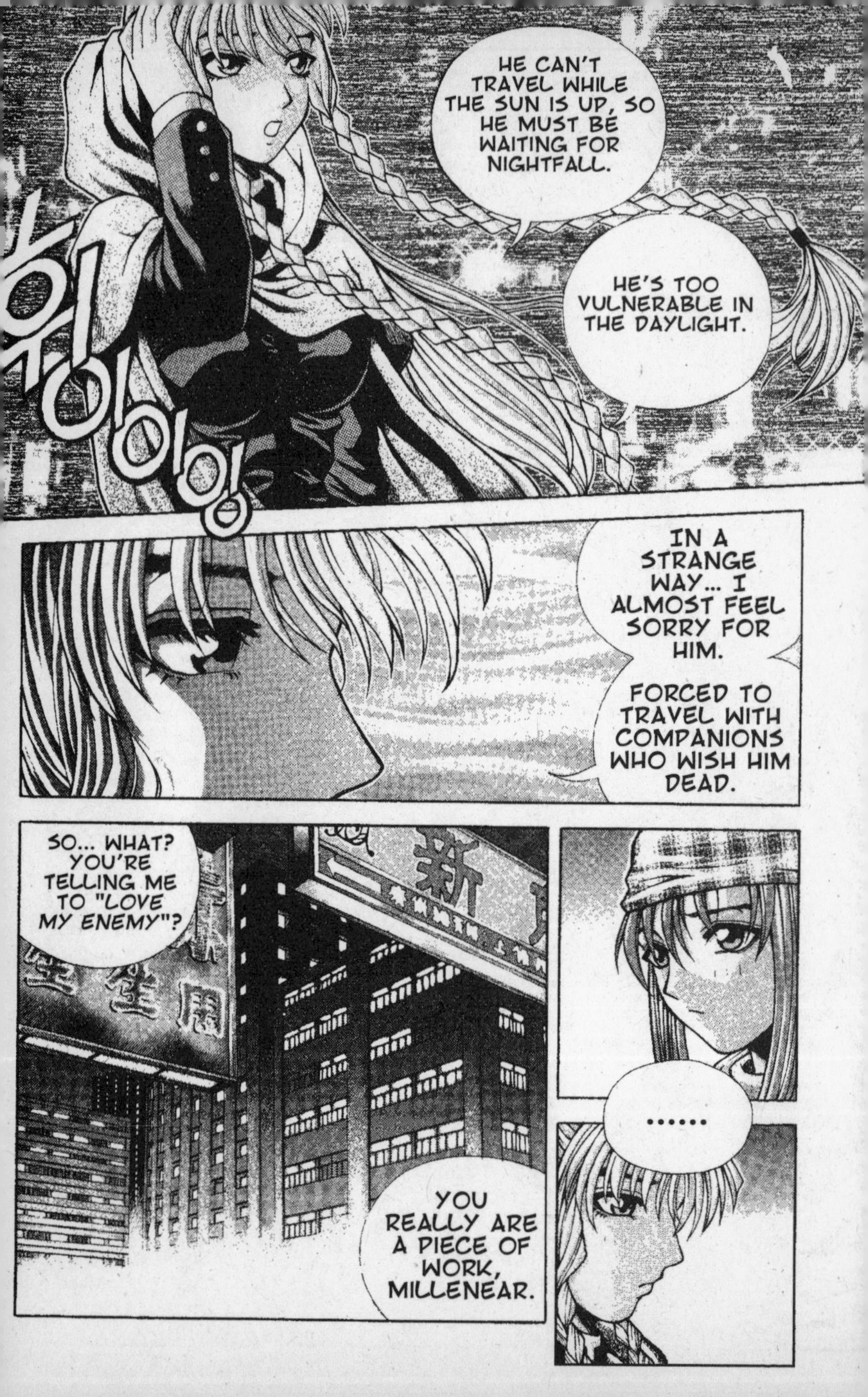
HE CAN'T TRAVEL WHILE THE SUN IS UP, SO HE MUST BE WAITING FOR NIGHTFALL.
HE'S TOO VULNERABLE IN THE DAYLIGHT.
IN A STRANGE WAY... I ALMOST FEEL SORRY FOR HIM.
FORCED TO TRAVEL WITH COMPANIONS WHO WISH HIM DEAD.
SO... WHAT? YOU'RE TELLING ME TO "LOVE MY ENEMY"?
......
YOU REALLY ARE A PIECE OF WORK, MILLENEAR.

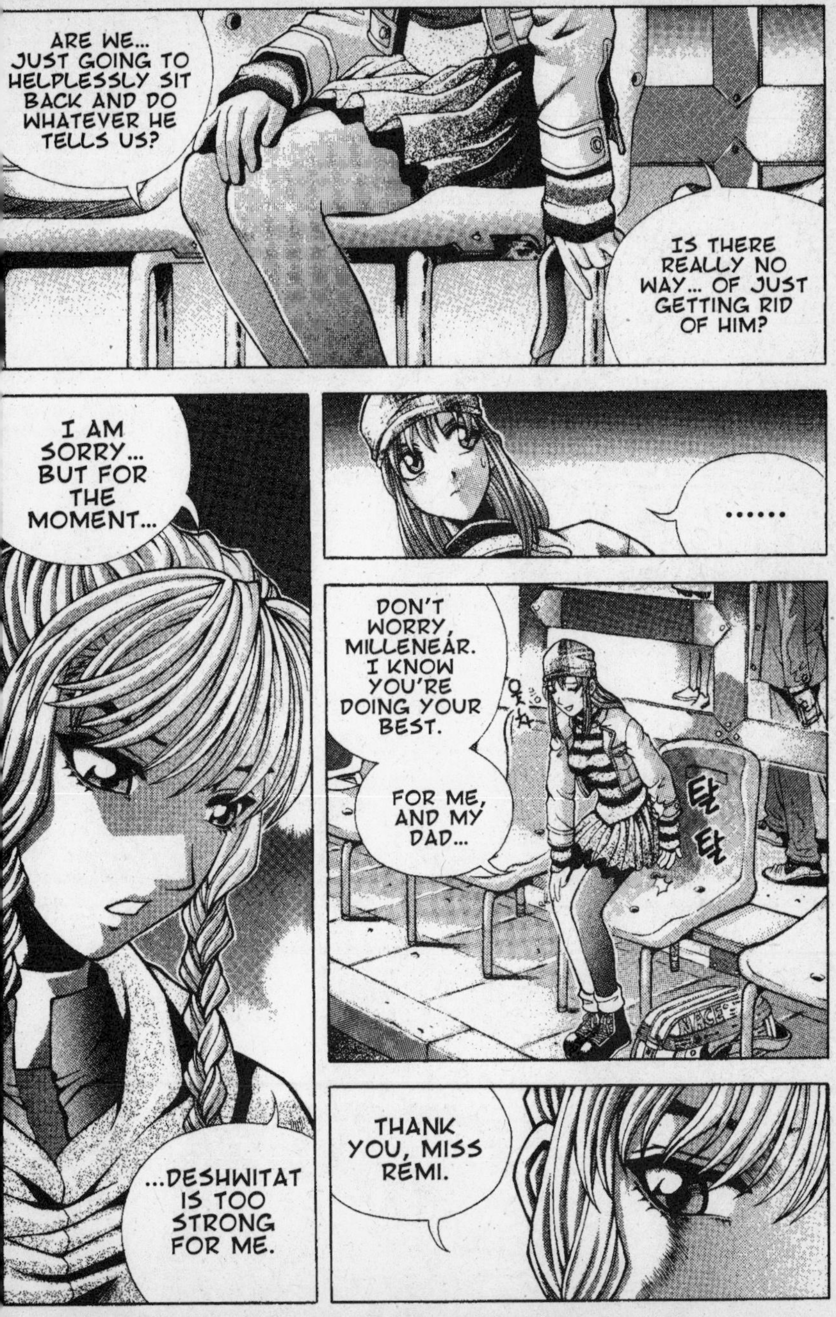
ARE WE... JUST GOING TO HELPLESSLY SIT BACK AND DO WHATEVER HE TELLS US?
IS THERE REALLY NO WAY... OF JUST GETTING RID OF HIM?
I AM SORRY... BUT FOR THE MOMENT...
...DESHWITAT IS TOO STRONG FOR ME.
......
DON'T WORRY, MILLENEAR. I KNOW YOU'RE DOING YOUR BEST.
FOR ME, AND MY DAD...
탁 탁
THANK YOU, MISS REMI.

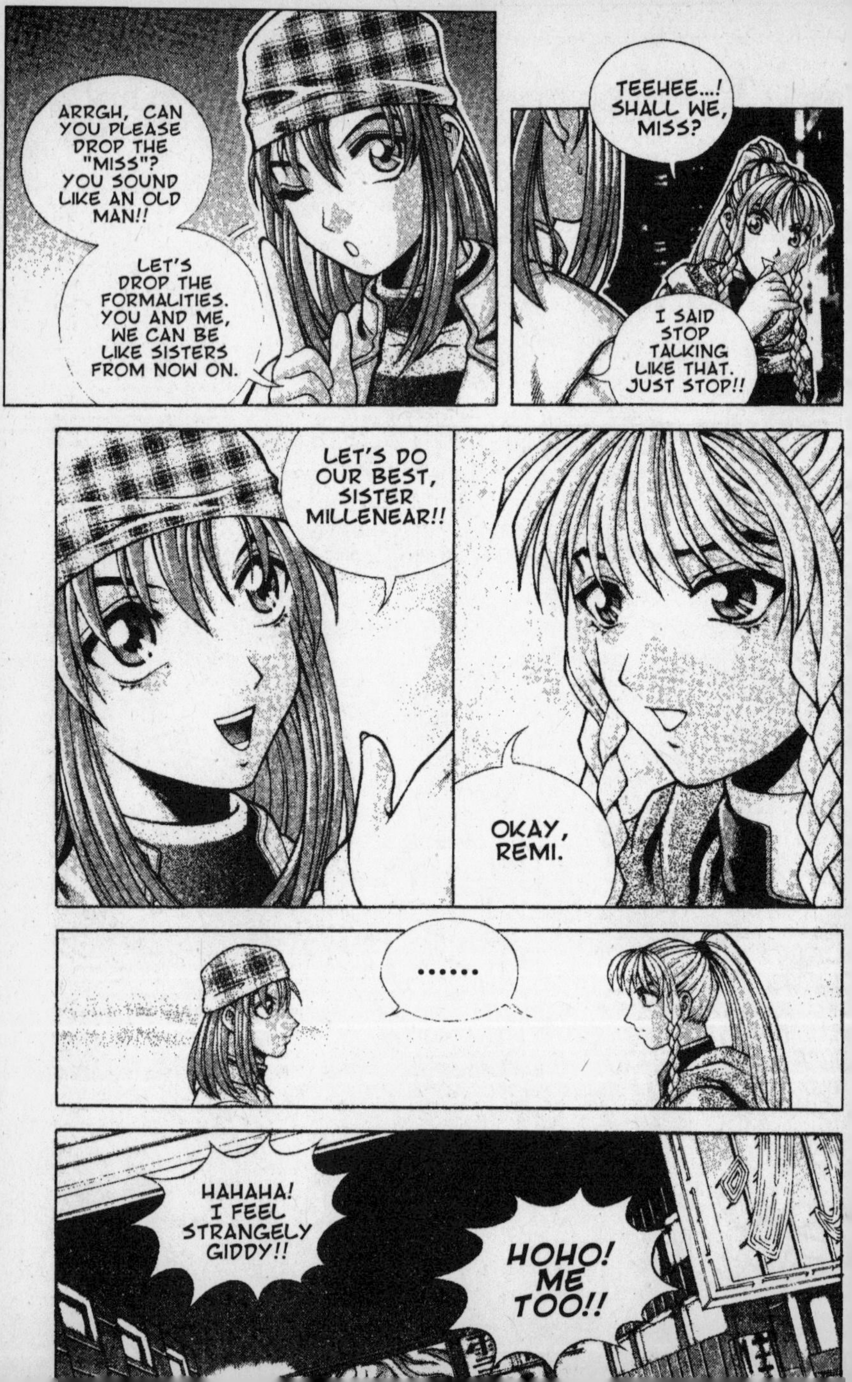
ARRGH, CAN YOU PLEASE DROP THE "MISS"? YOU SOUND LIKE AN OLD MAN!!
LET'S DROP THE FORMALITIES. YOU AND ME, WE CAN BE LIKE SISTERS FROM NOW ON.
TEEHEE...! SHALL WE, MISS?
I SAID STOP TALKING LIKE THAT. JUST STOP!!
LET'S DO OUR BEST, SISTER MILLENEAR!!
OKAY, REMI.
......
HAHAHA! I FEEL STRANGELY GIDDY!!
HOHO! ME TOO!!

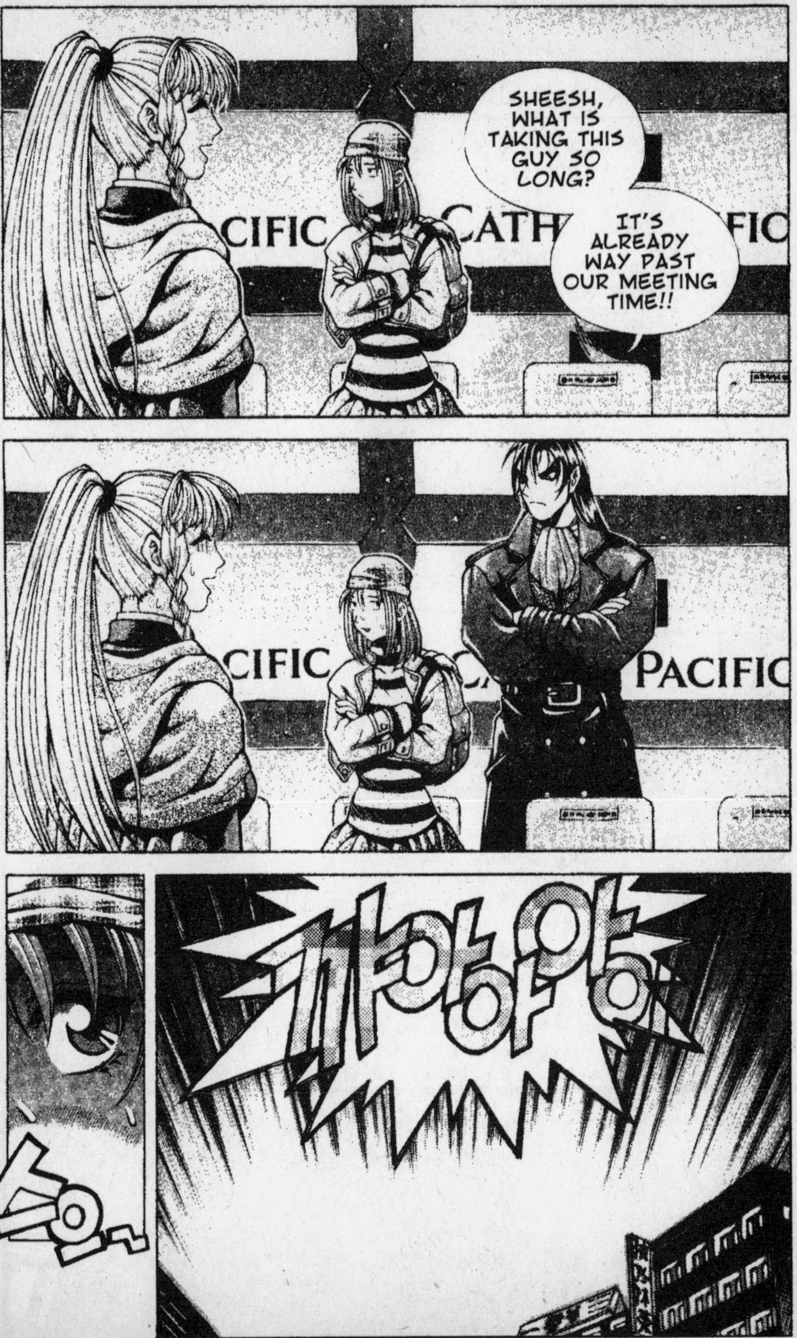
SHEESH, WHAT IS TAKING THIS GUY SO LONG?
IT'S ALREADY WAY PAST OUR MEETING TIME!!

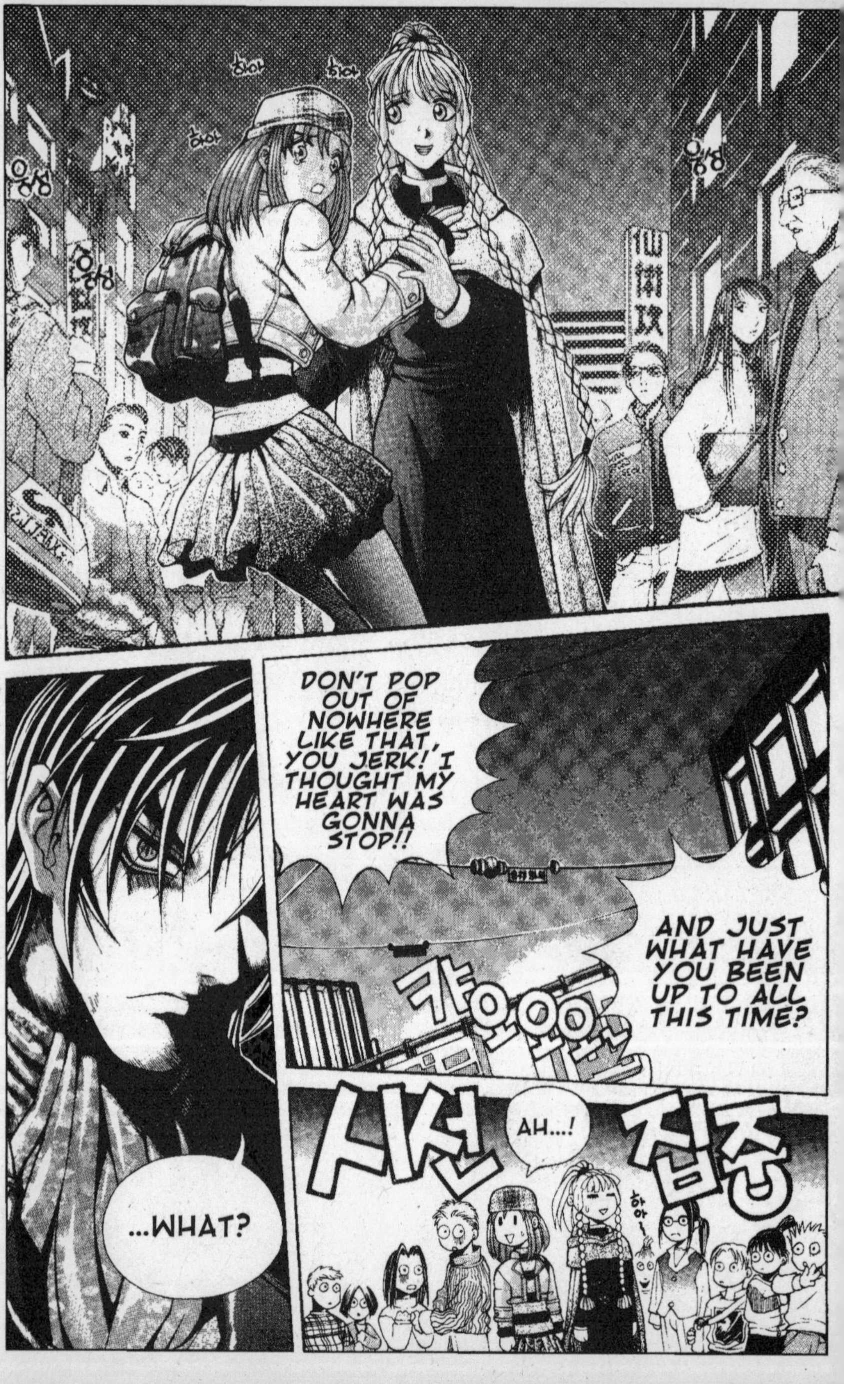
하아
하아
하아
웅성
웅성
웅성
...WHAT?
DON'T POP OUT OF NOWHERE LIKE THAT, YOU JERK! I THOUGHT MY HEART WAS GONNA STOP!!
AND JUST WHAT HAVE YOU BEEN UP TO ALL THIS TIME?
갸오오오
시선
AH...!
집중
하아~

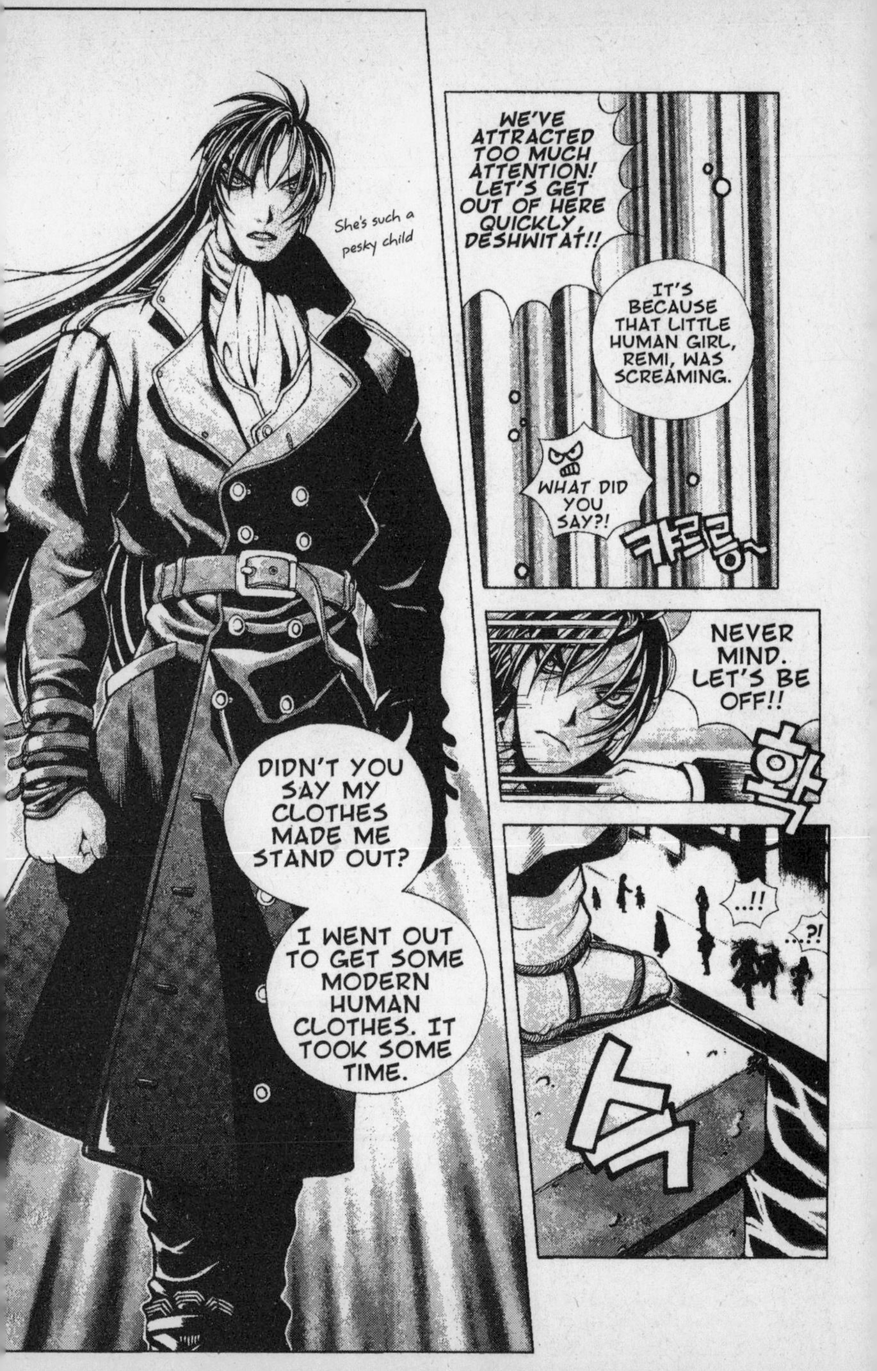
She's such a pesky child
DIDN'T YOU SAY MY CLOTHES MADE ME STAND OUT?
I WENT OUT TO GET SOME MODERN HUMAN CLOTHES. IT TOOK SOME TIME.
WE'VE ATTRACTED TOO MUCH ATTENTION! LET'S GET OUT OF HERE QUICKLY, DESHWITAT!!
IT'S BECAUSE THAT LITTLE HUMAN GIRL, REMI, WAS SCREAMING.
WHAT DID YOU SAY?!
NEVER MIND. LET'S BE OFF!!
확
...!!
...?!

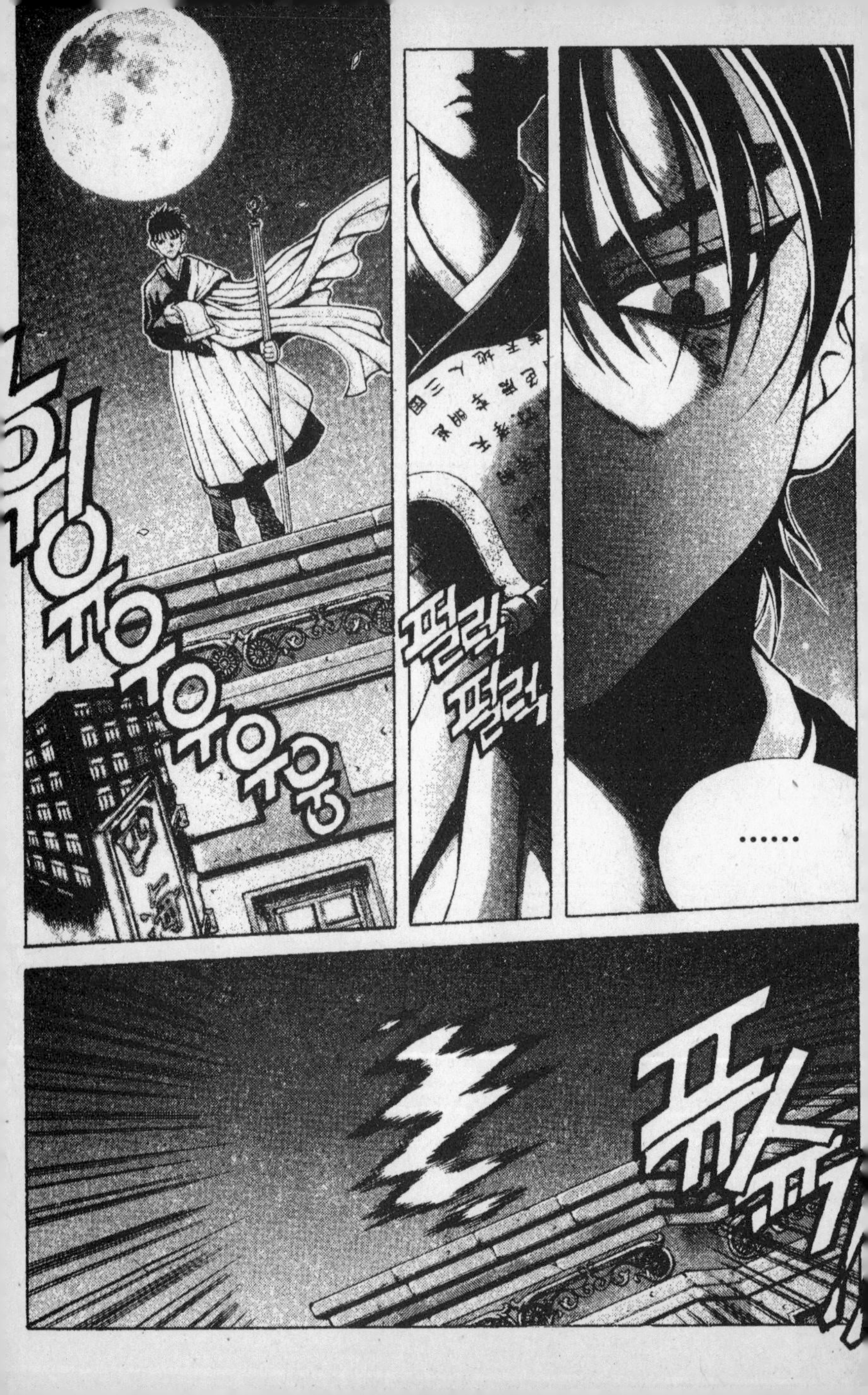
펄럭
펄럭
......

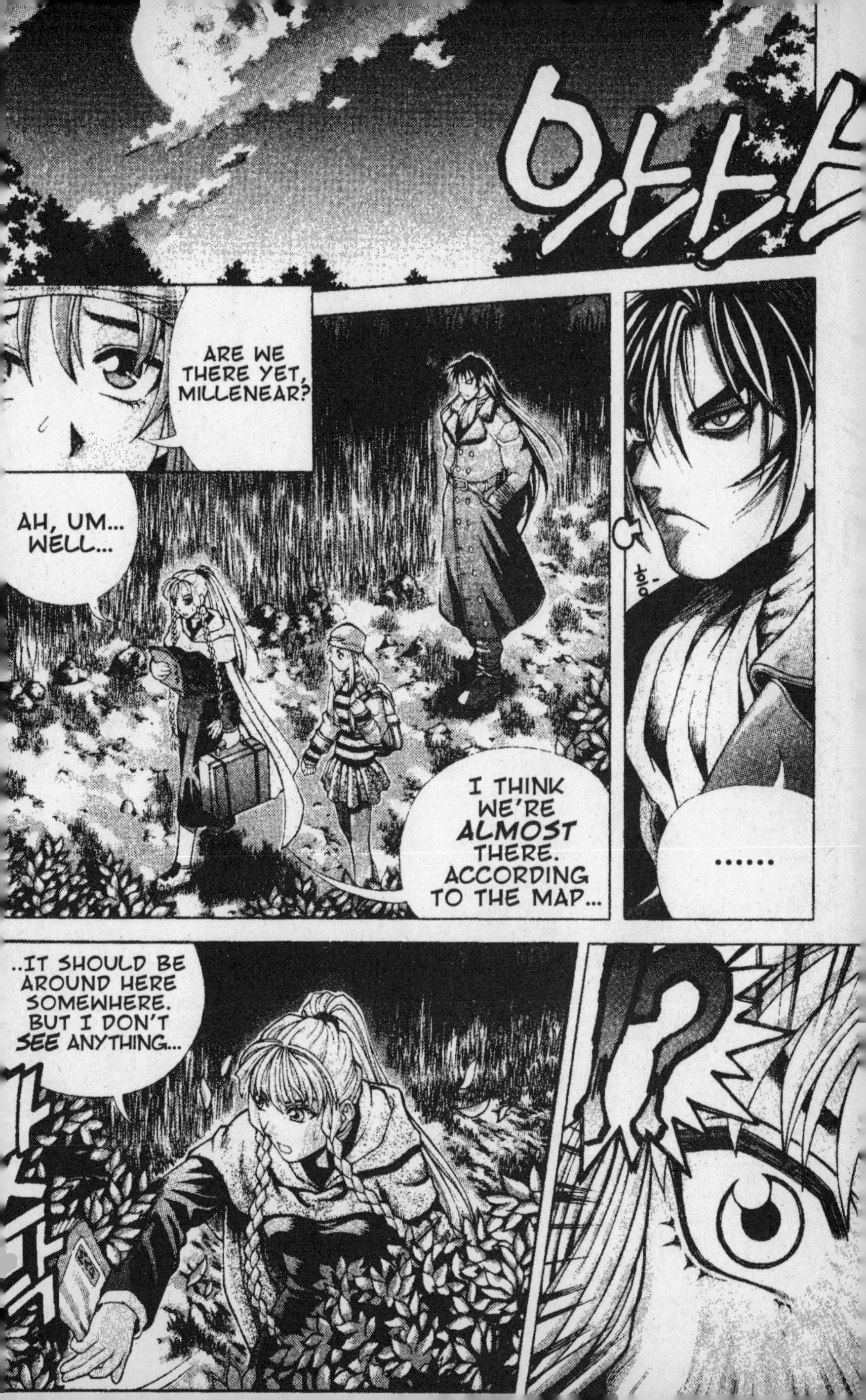
ARE WE THERE YET, MILLENEAR?
AH, UM... WELL...
I THINK WE'RE ALMOST THERE. ACCORDING TO THE MAP...
......
..IT SHOULD BE AROUND HERE SOMEWHERE. BUT I DON'T SEE ANYTHING...

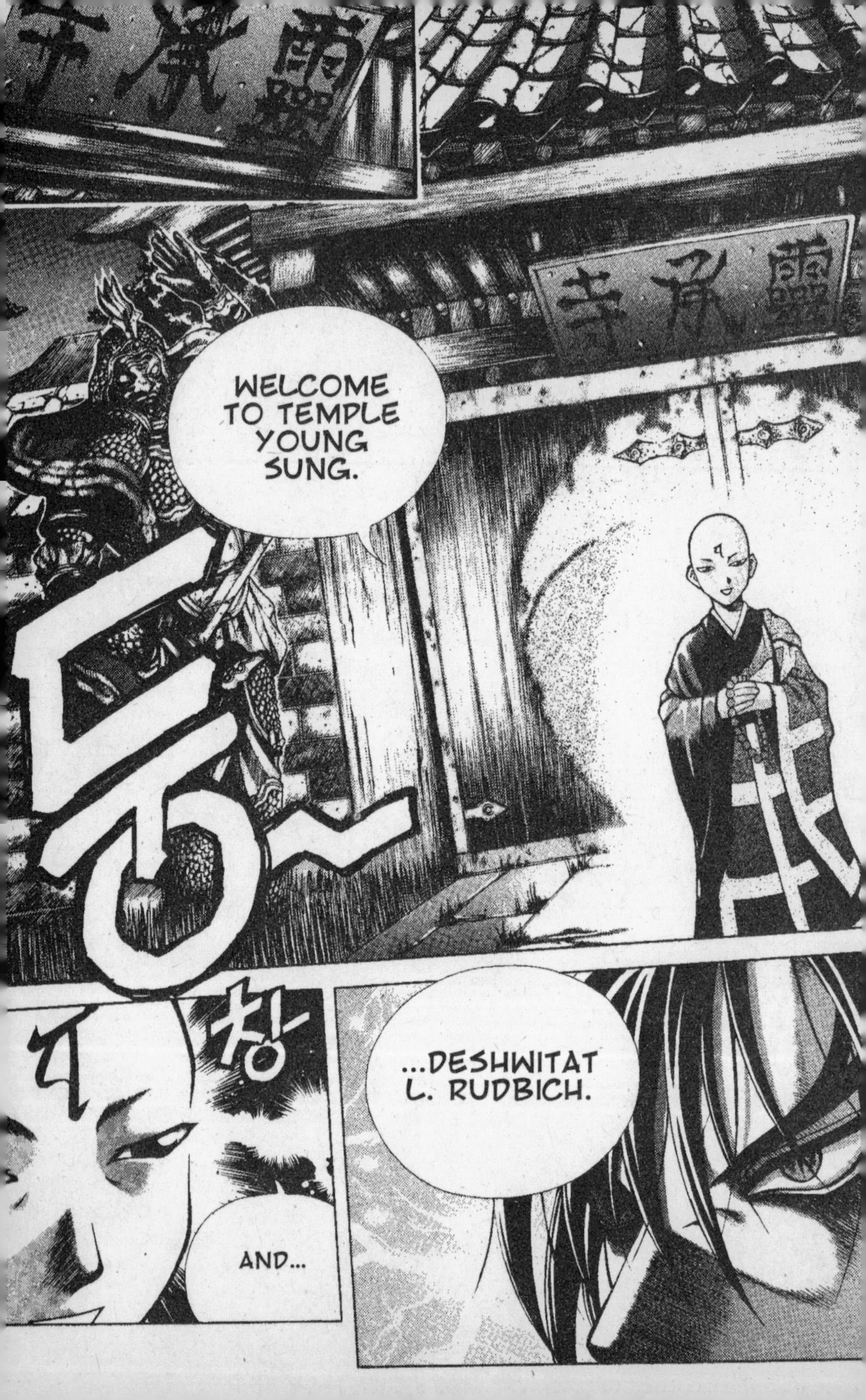
WELCOME TO TEMPLE YOUNG SUNG.
AND...
...DESHWITAT L. RUDBICH.

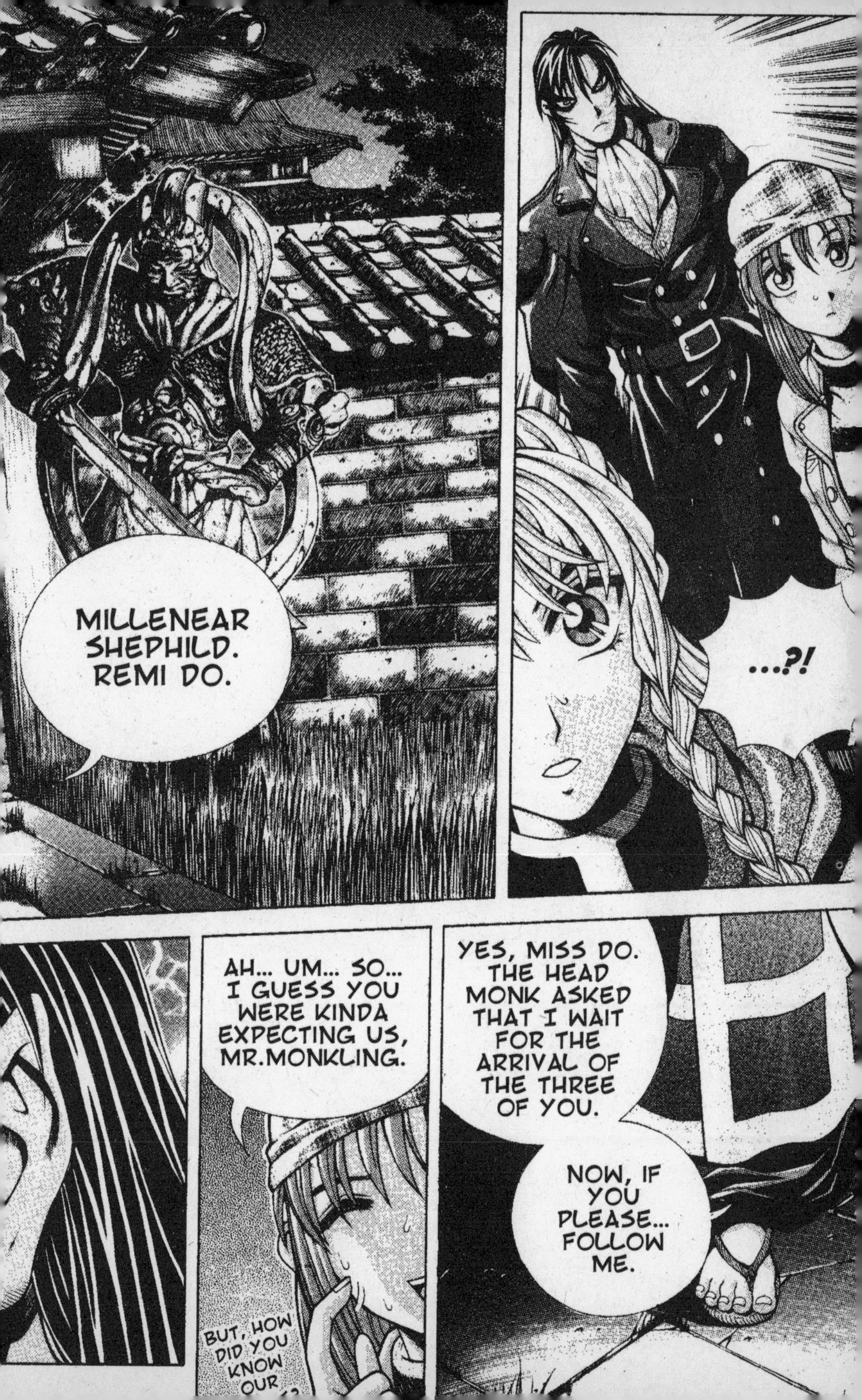
MILLENEAR SHEPHILD. REMI DO.
...?!
AH... UM... SO... I GUESS YOU WERE KINDA EXPECTING US, MR.MONKLING.
BUT, HOW DID YOU KNOW OUR
YES, MISS DO. THE HEAD MONK ASKED THAT I WAIT FOR THE ARRIVAL OF THE THREE OF YOU.
NOW, IF YOU PLEASE... FOLLOW ME.

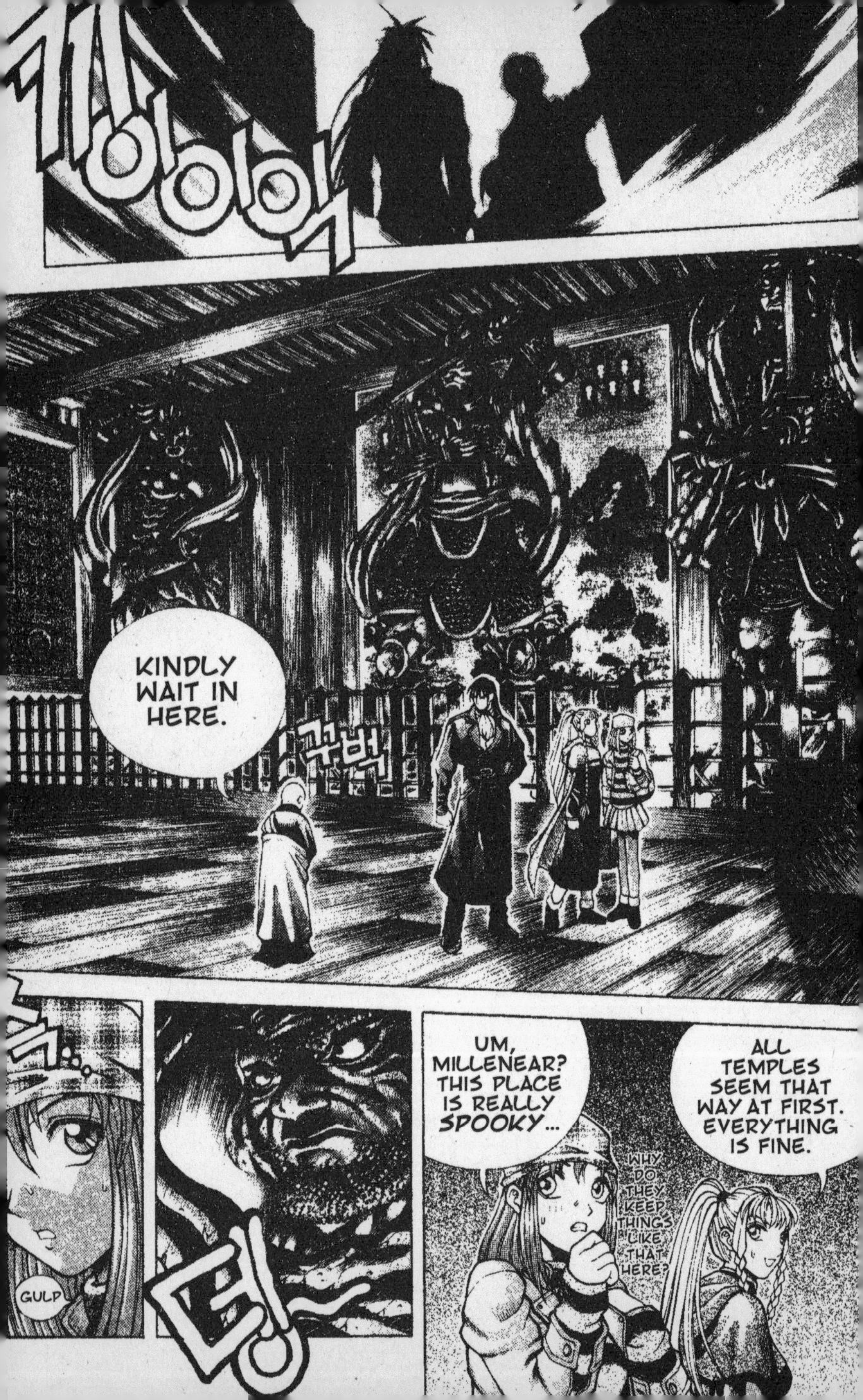
KINDLY WAIT IN HERE.
꾸벅
GULP
UM, MILLENEAR? THIS PLACE IS REALLY SPOOKY...
ALL TEMPLES SEEM THAT WAY AT FIRST. EVERYTHING IS FINE.
WHY DO THEY KEEP THINGS LIKE THAT HERE?

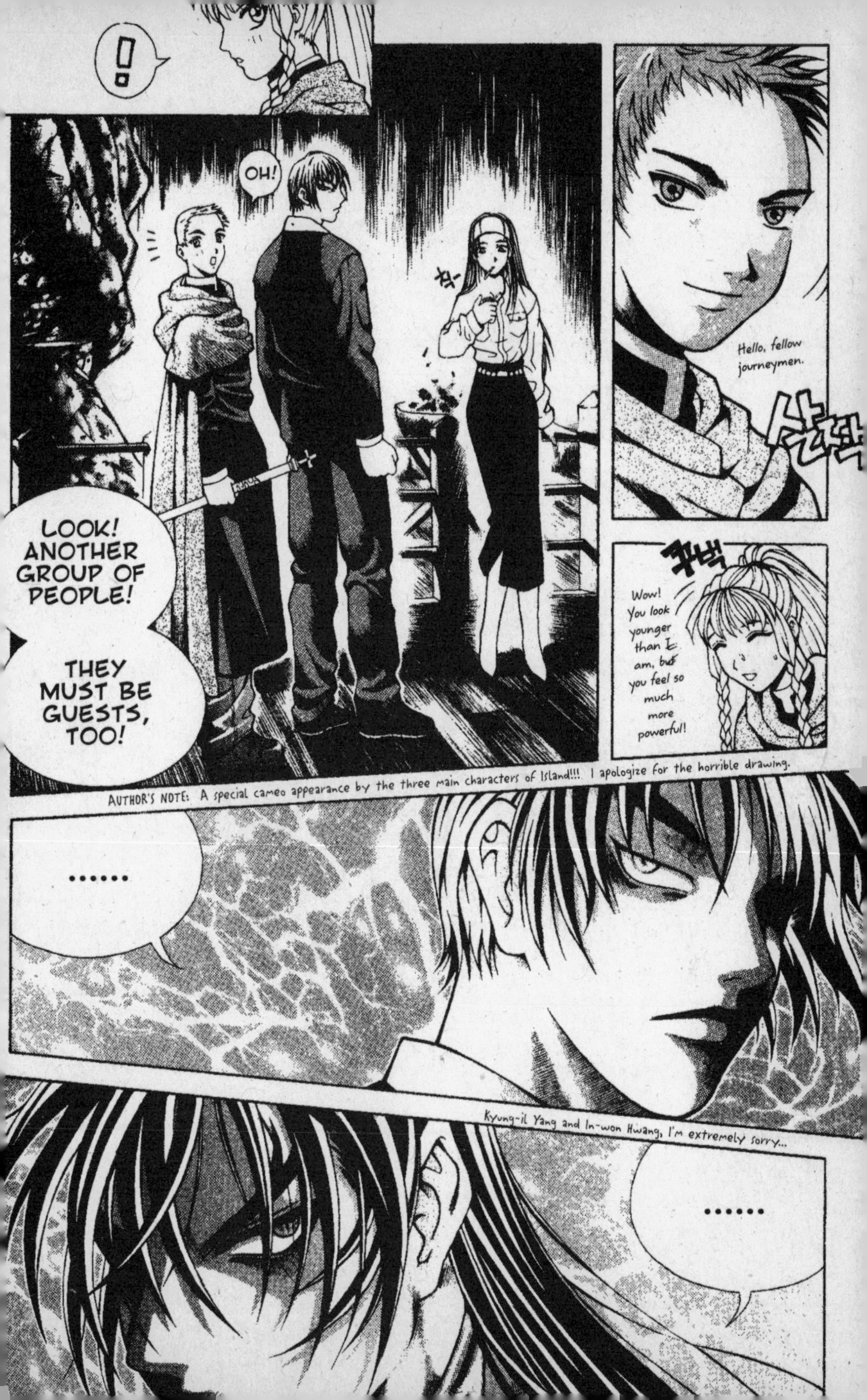
!
OH!
LOOK! ANOTHER GROUP OF PEOPLE!
THEY MUST BE GUESTS, TOO!
Hello, fellow journeymen.
Wow! You look younger than I am, but you feel so much more powerful!
AUTHOR'S NOTE: A special cameo appearance by the three main characters of Island!!! I apologize for the horrible drawing.
......
Kyung-il Yang and In-won Hwang, I'm extremely sorry...
......

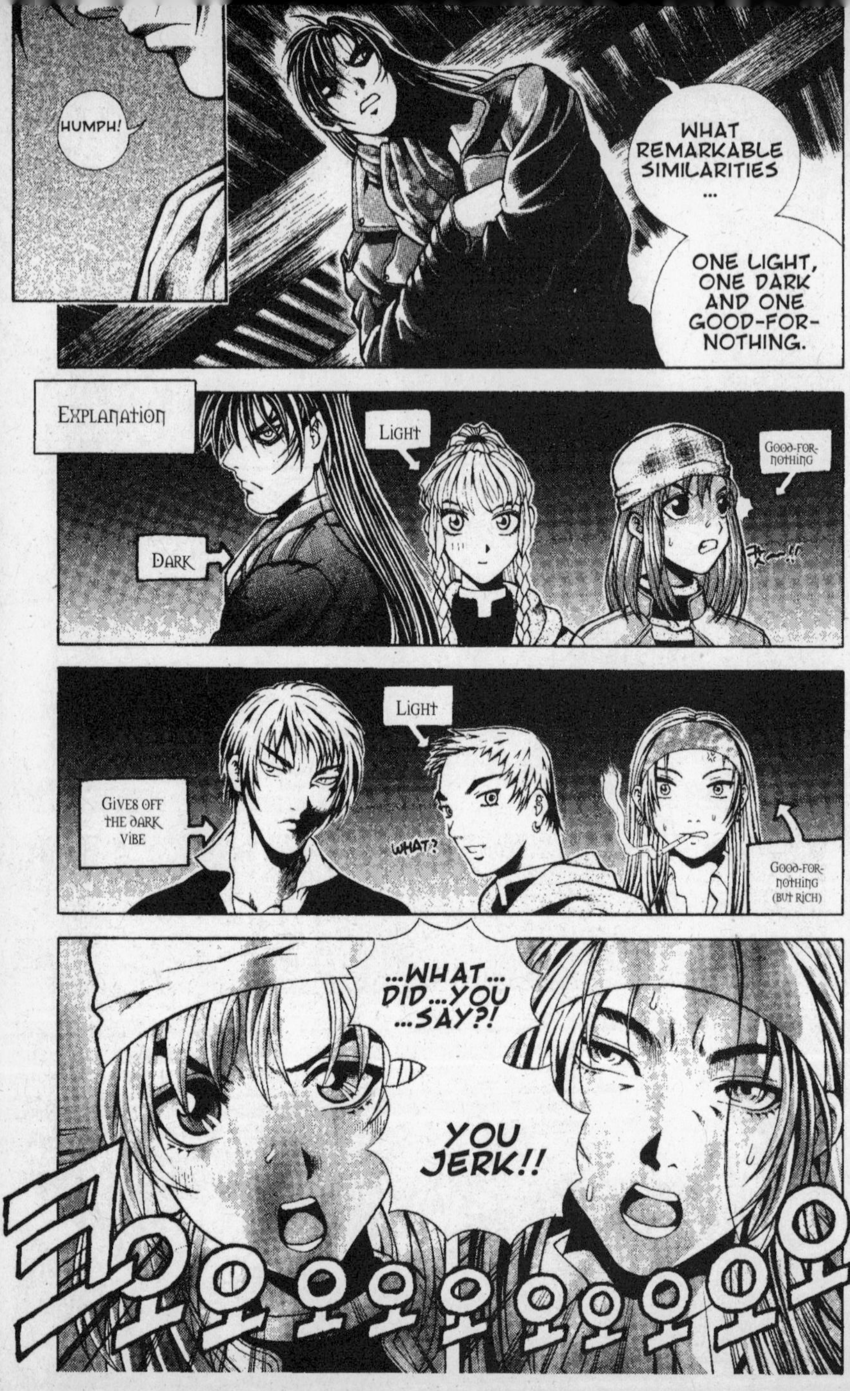
HUMPH!
WHAT REMARKABLE SIMILARITIES ...
ONE LIGHT, ONE DARK AND ONE GOOD-FOR-NOTHING.
EXPLANATION
DARK
LIGHT
GOOD-FOR-NOTHING
GIVES OFF THE DARK VIBE
LIGHT
WHAT?
GOOD-FOR-NOTHING (BUT RICH)
...WHAT... DID...YOU ...SAY?!
YOU JERK!!

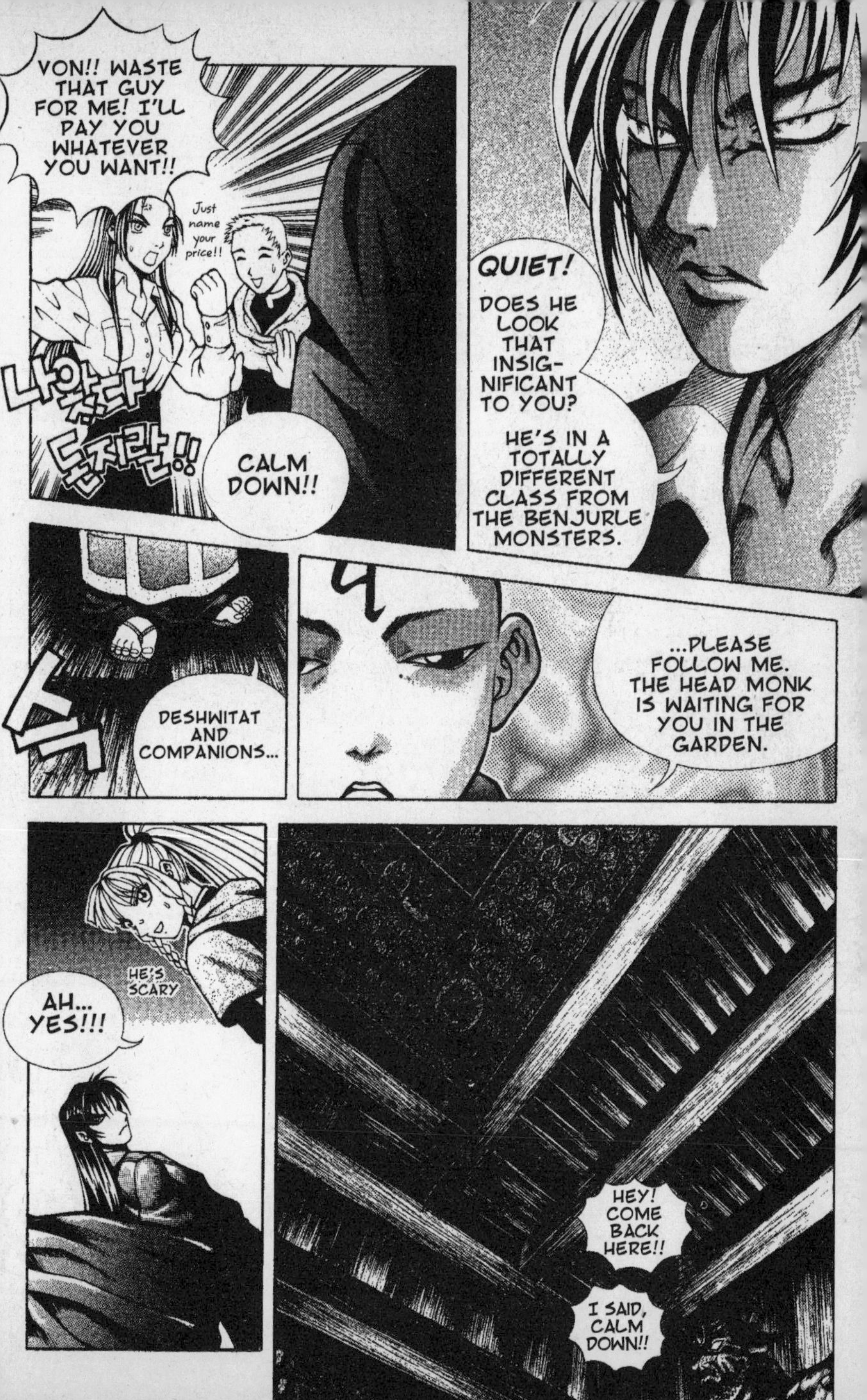
VON!! WASTE THAT GUY FOR ME! I'LL PAY YOU WHATEVER YOU WANT!!
Just name your price!!
나왔다 돈지랄!!
CALM DOWN!!
QUIET!
DOES HE LOOK THAT INSIGNIFICANT TO YOU?
HE'S IN A TOTALLY DIFFERENT CLASS FROM THE BENJURLE MONSTERS.
DESHWITAT AND COMPANIONS...
...PLEASE FOLLOW ME. THE HEAD MONK IS WAITING FOR YOU IN THE GARDEN.
HE'S SCARY
AH... YES!!!
HEY! COME BACK HERE!!
I SAID, CALM DOWN!!

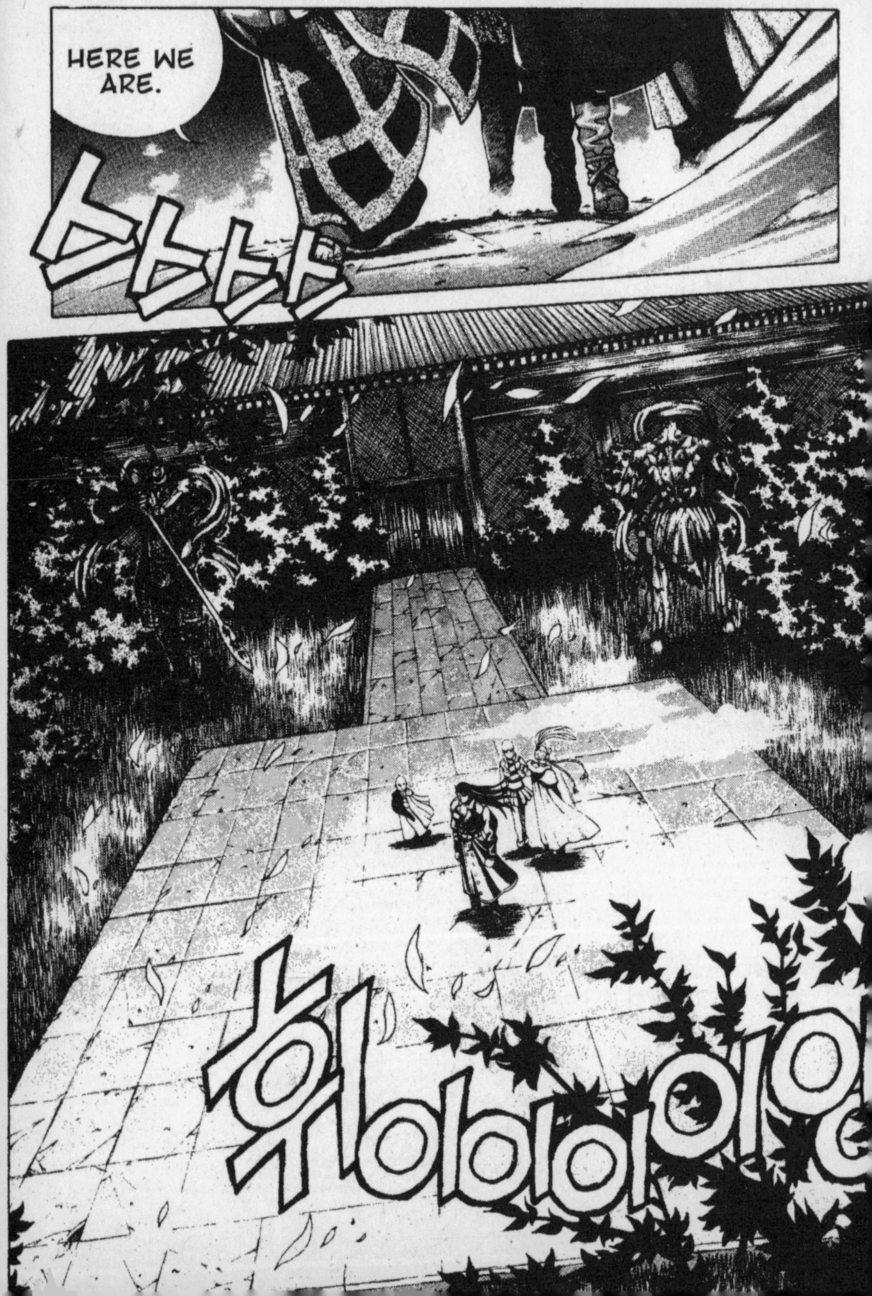
HERE WE ARE.

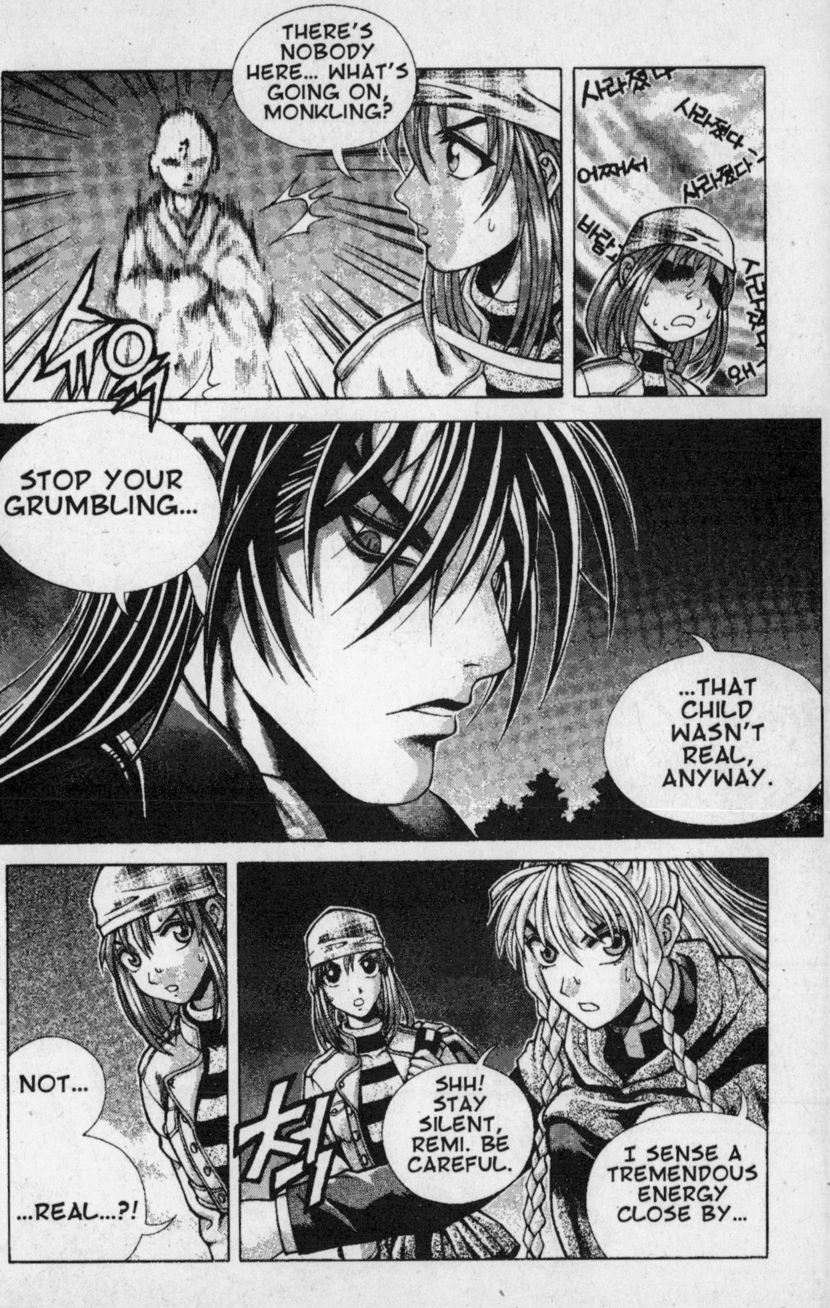
THERE'S NOBODY HERE... WHAT'S GOING ON, MONKLING?
사라졌다
사라졌다
어째서
사라졌다!
바람?
사라졌다 왜~
STOP YOUR GRUMBLING...
...THAT CHILD WASN'T REAL, ANYWAY.
NOT...
...REAL...?!
SHH! STAY SILENT, REMI. BE CAREFUL.
I SENSE A TREMENDOUS ENERGY CLOSE BY...

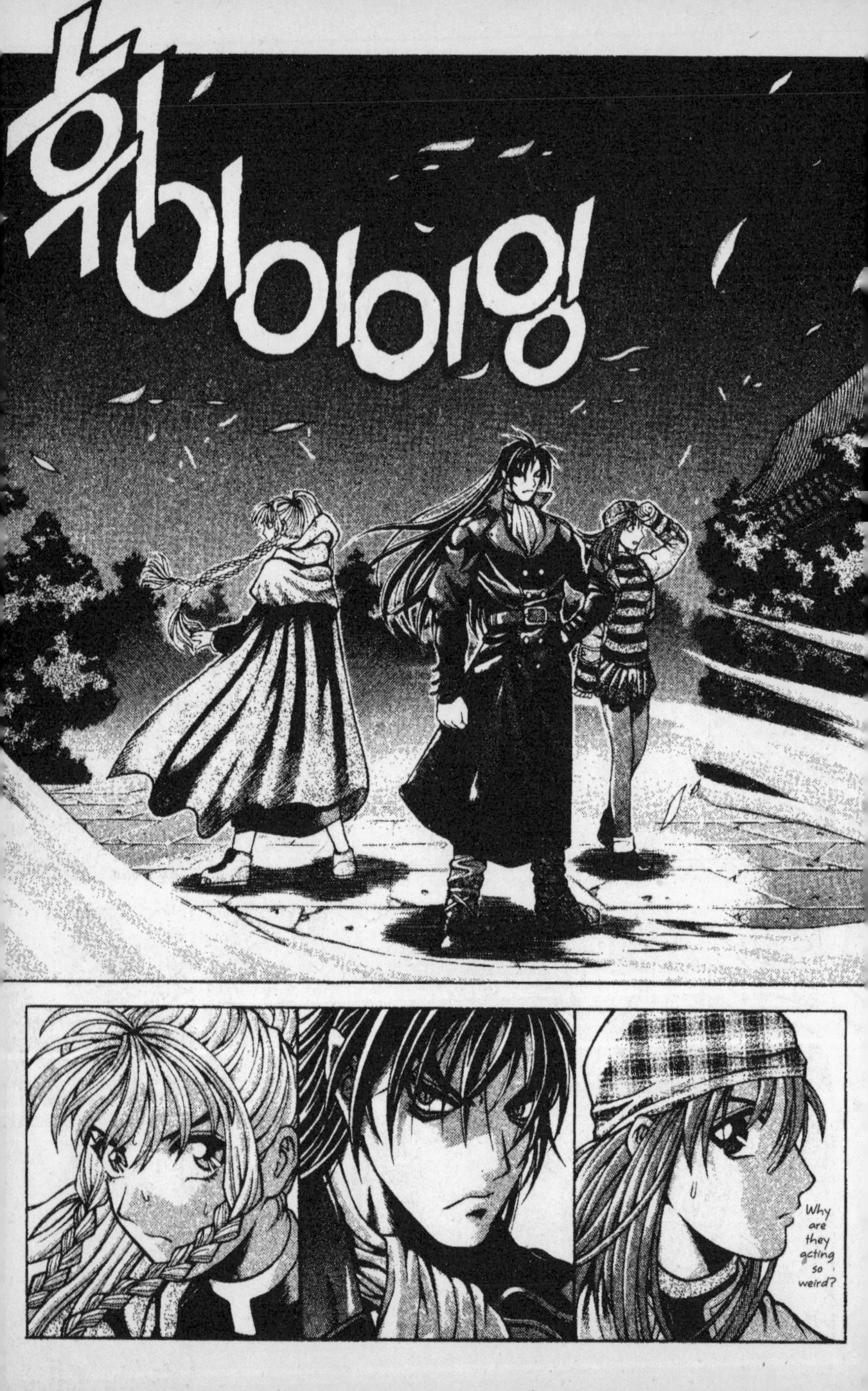
휘이이이잉!
Why are they acting so weird?

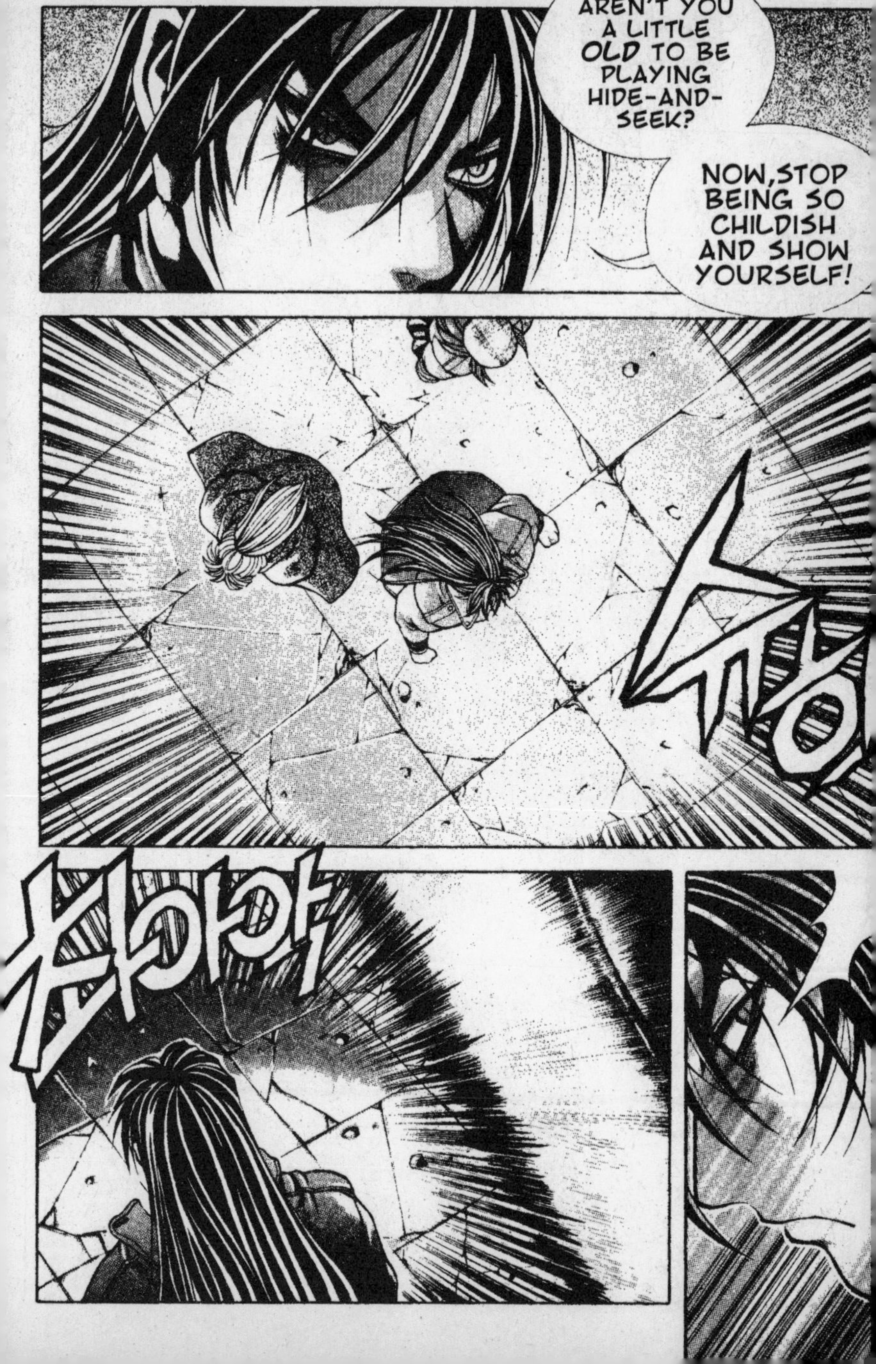
ARE'NT YOU A LITTLE OLD TO BE PLAYING HIDE-AND-SEEK?
NOW, STOP BEING SO CHILDISH AND SHOW YOURSELF!

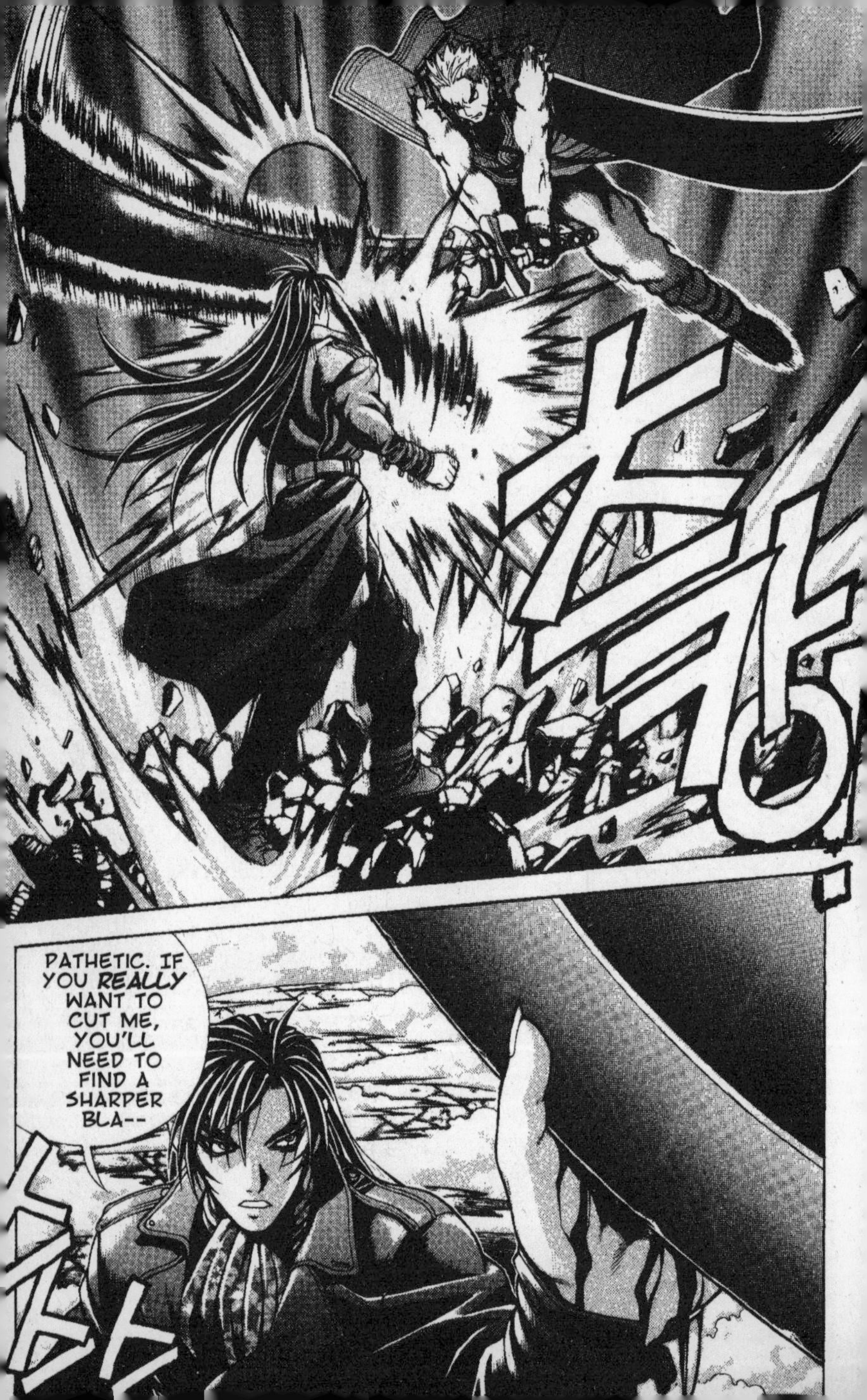
PATHETIC. IF YOU *REALLY* WANT TO CUT ME, YOU'LL NEED TO FIND A SHARPER BLA--

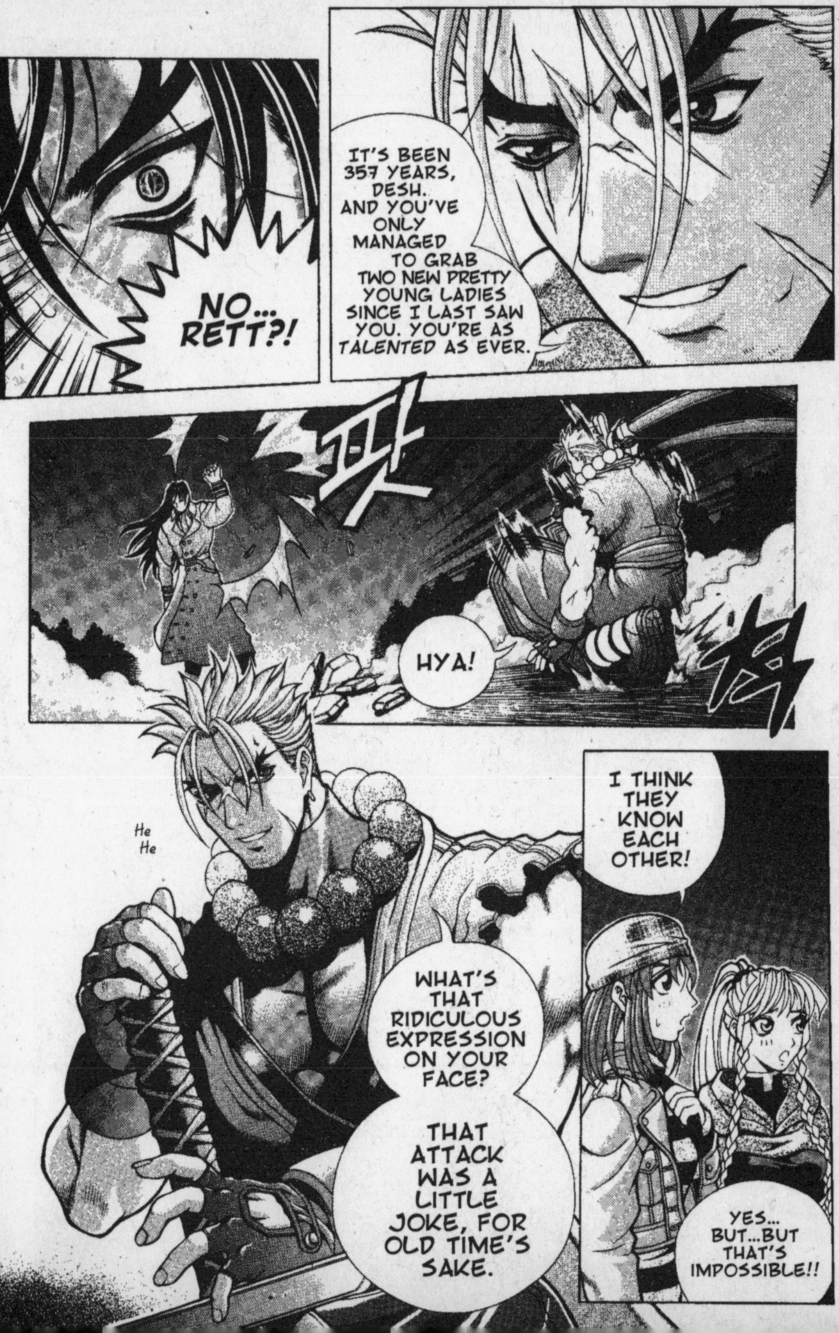
NO... RETT?!
IT'S BEEN 357 YEARS, DESH. AND YOU'VE ONLY MANAGED TO GRAB TWO NEW PRETTY YOUNG LADIES SINCE I LAST SAW YOU. YOU'RE AS TALENTED AS EVER.
HYA!
He He
WHAT'S THAT RIDICULOUS EXPRESSION ON YOUR FACE?
THAT ATTACK WAS A LITTLE JOKE, FOR OLD TIME'S SAKE.
I THINK THEY KNOW EACH OTHER!
YES... BUT...BUT THAT'S IMPOSSIBLE!!

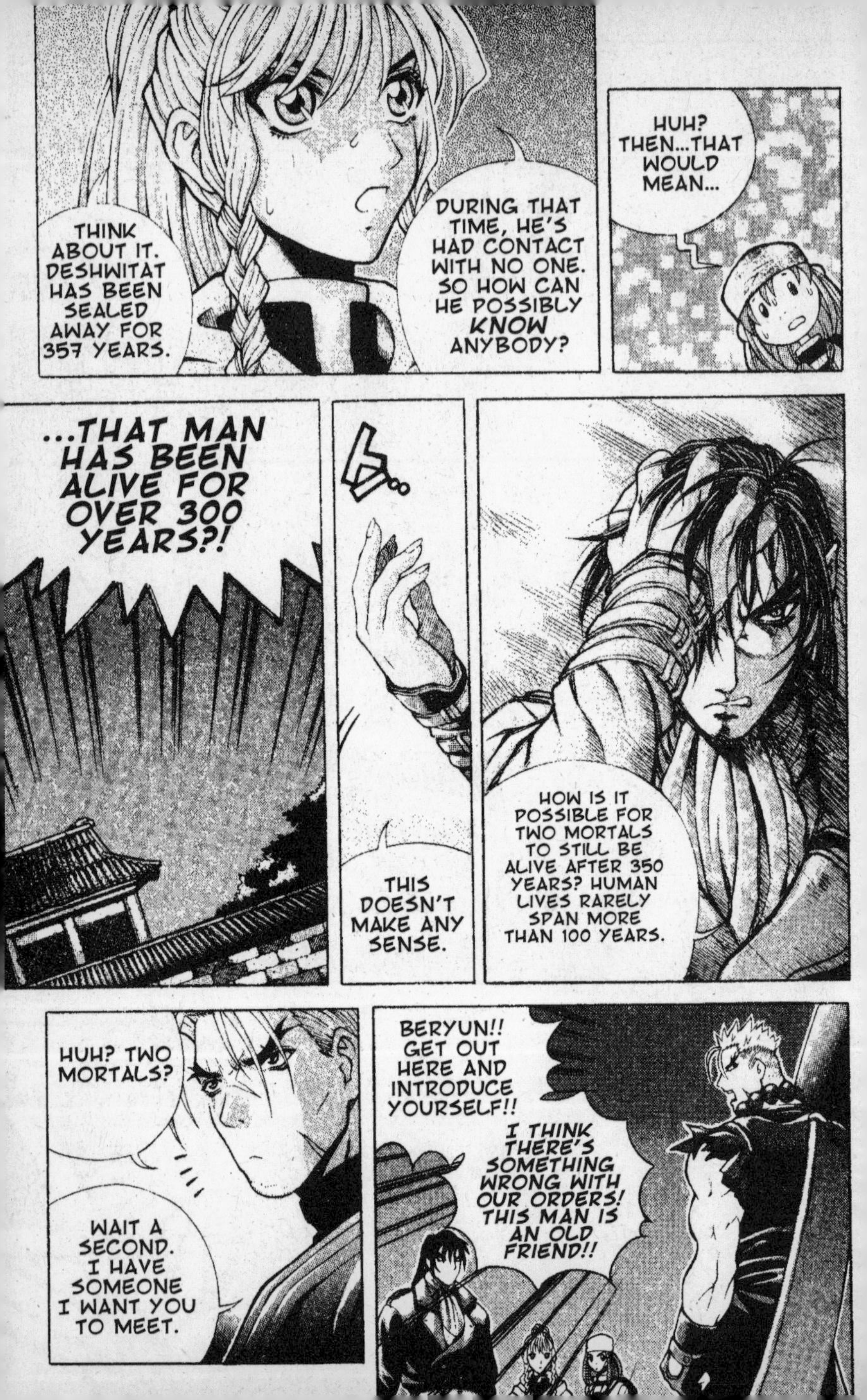
THINK ABOUT IT. DESHWITAT HAS BEEN SEALED AWAY FOR 357 YEARS.
DURING THAT TIME, HE'S HAD CONTACT WITH NO ONE. SO HOW CAN HE POSSIBLY *KNOW* ANYBODY?
HUH? THEN...THAT WOULD MEAN...
...THAT MAN HAS BEEN ALIVE FOR OVER 300 YEARS?!
THIS DOESN'T MAKE ANY SENSE.
HOW IS IT POSSIBLE FOR TWO MORTALS TO STILL BE ALIVE AFTER 350 YEARS? HUMAN LIVES RARELY SPAN MORE THAN 100 YEARS.
HUH? TWO MORTALS?
WAIT A SECOND. I HAVE SOMEONE I WANT YOU TO MEET.
BERYUN!! GET OUT HERE AND INTRODUCE YOURSELF!!
I THINK THERE'S SOMETHING WRONG WITH OUR ORDERS! THIS MAN IS AN OLD FRIEND!!

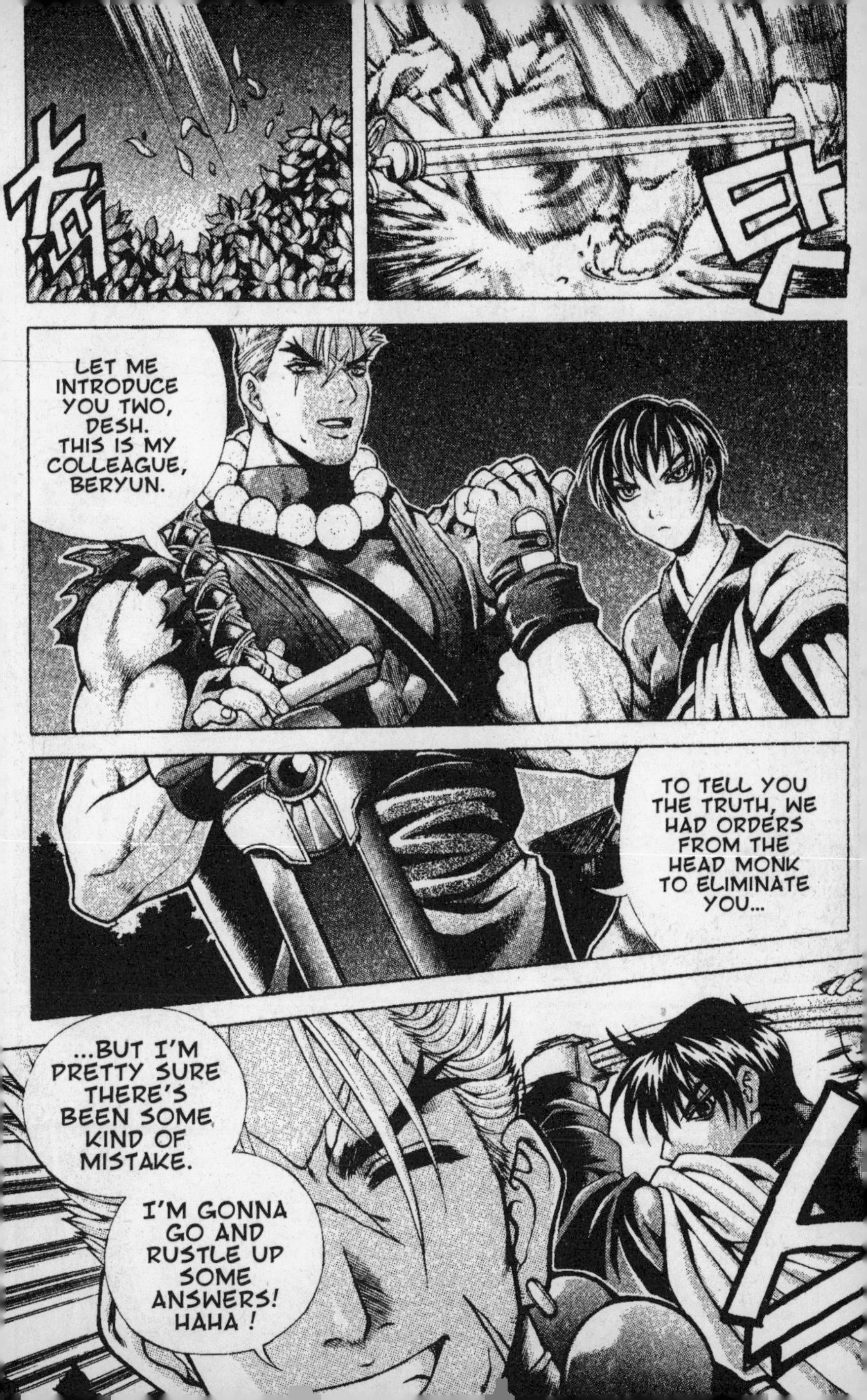
LET ME INTRODUCE YOU TWO, DESH. THIS IS MY COLLEAGUE, BERYUN.
TO TELL YOU THE TRUTH, WE HAD ORDERS FROM THE HEAD MONK TO ELIMINATE YOU...
...BUT I'M PRETTY SURE THERE'S BEEN SOME KIND OF MISTAKE.
I'M GONNA GO AND RUSTLE UP SOME ANSWERS! HAHA !

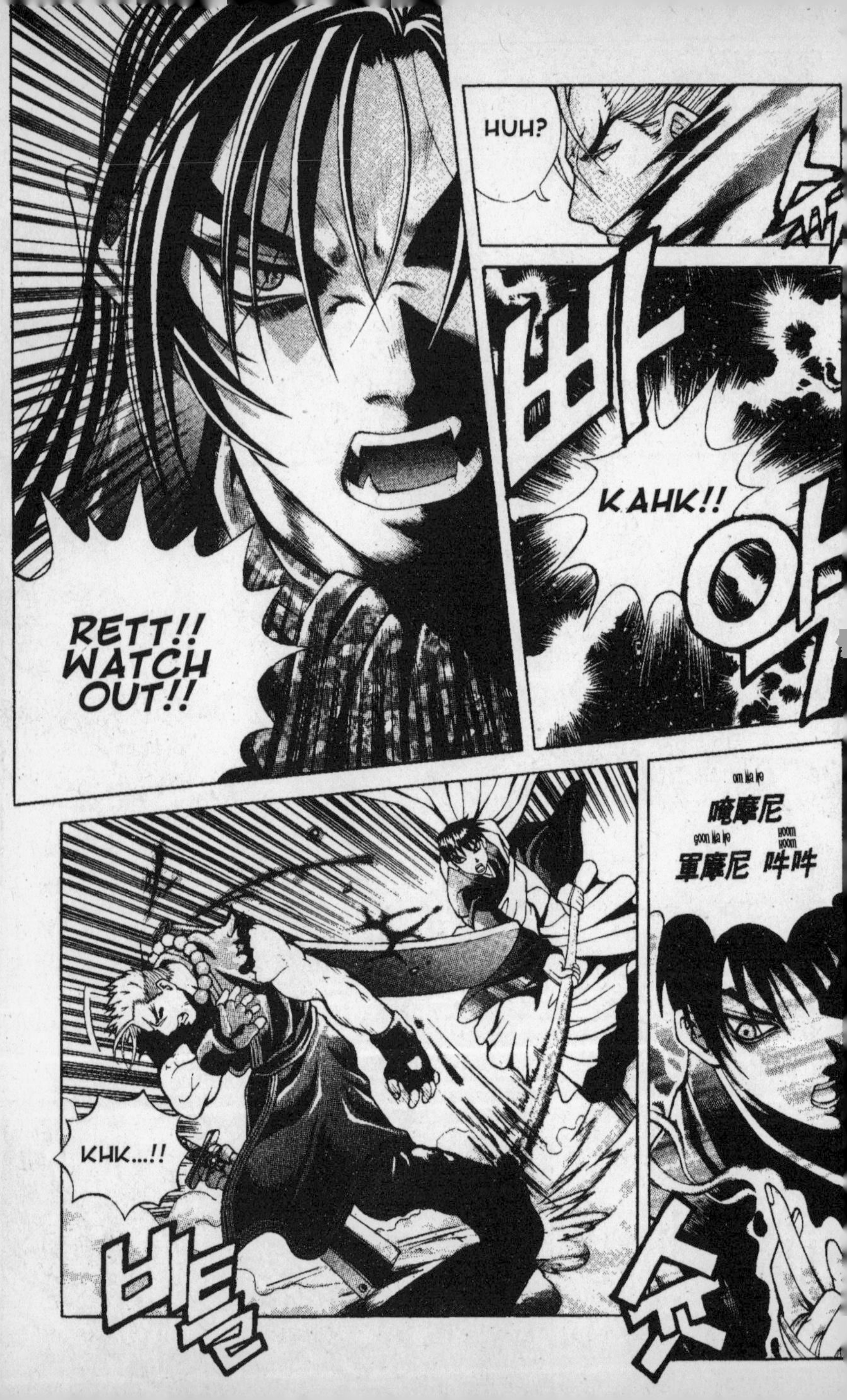
RETT!! WATCH OUT!!
HUH?
빠
KAHK!!
아
KHK...!!
비틀
om Ma ne
唵摩尼
goon Ma ne
軍摩尼
HOOM HOOM
吽吽

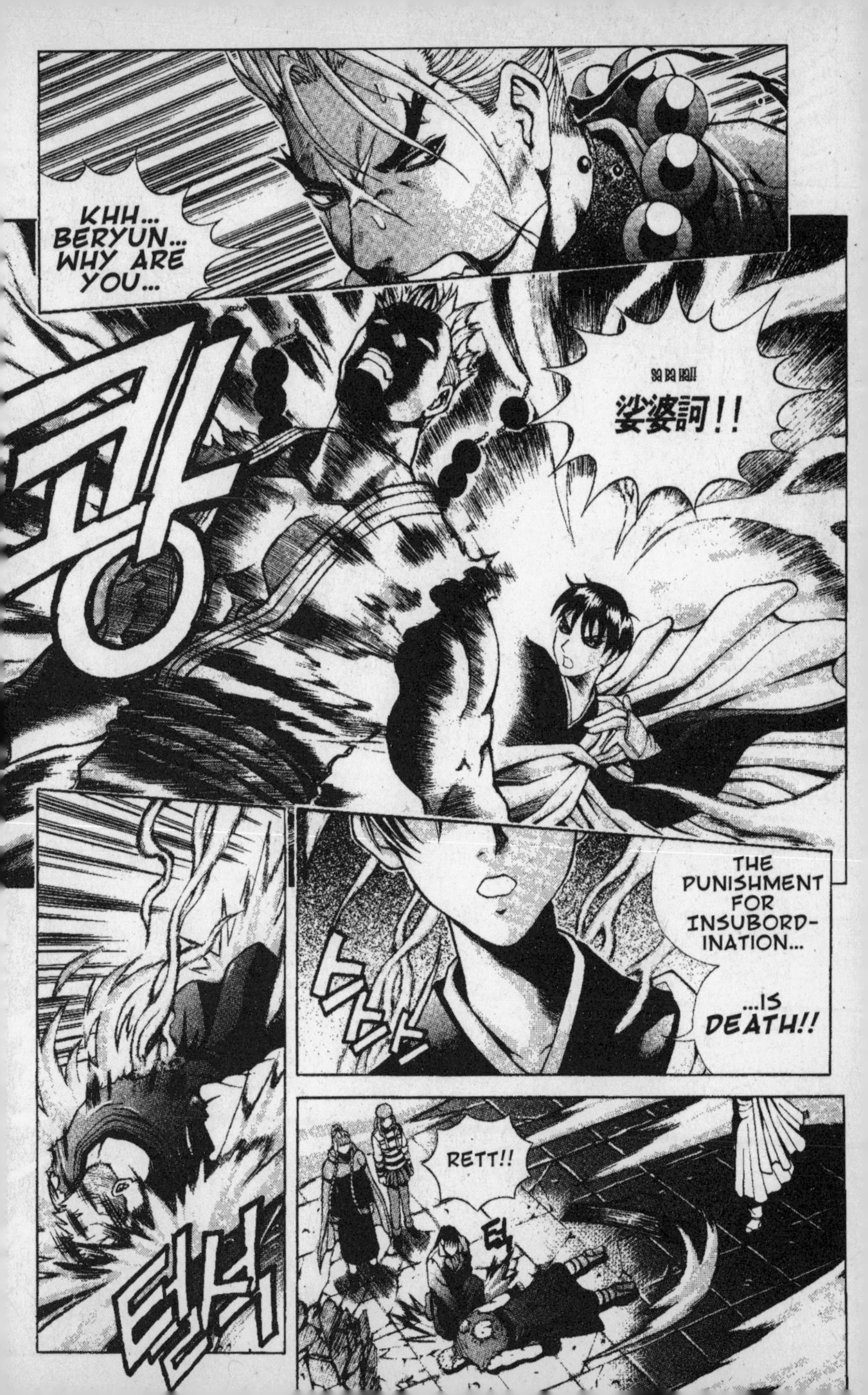
KHH... BERYUN... WHY ARE YOU...
SA BA HA!!
娑婆訶!!
THE PUNISHMENT FOR INSUBORD-INATION...
...IS DEATH!!
RETT!!

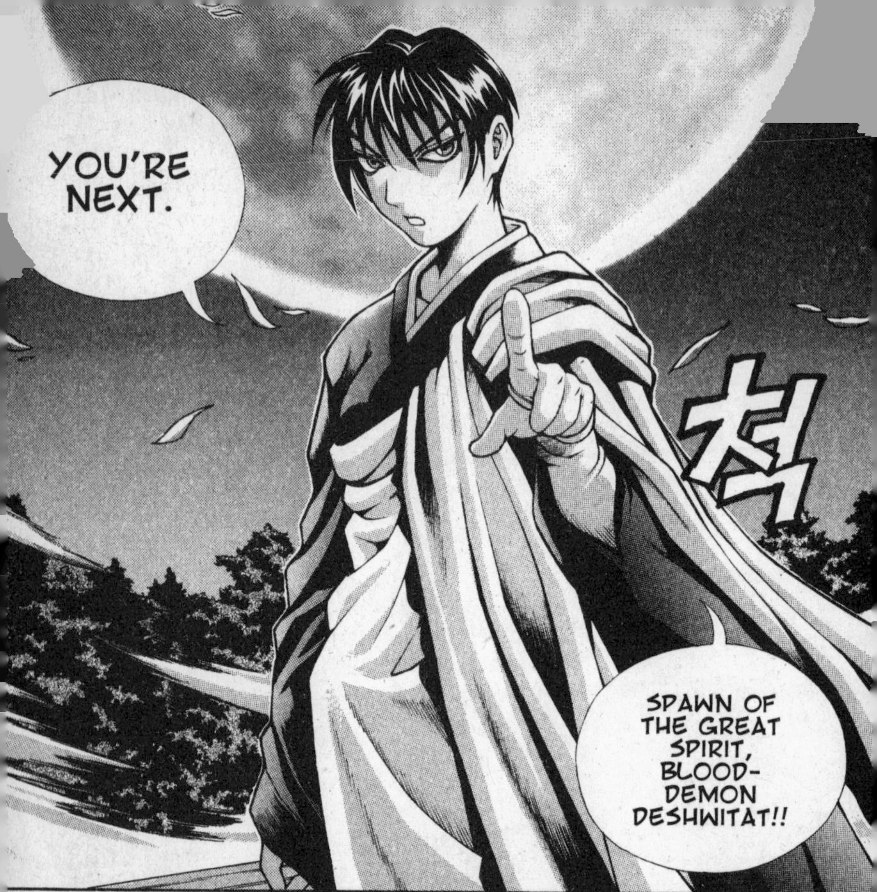
YOU'RE NEXT.
척
SPAWN OF THE GREAT SPIRIT, BLOOD-DEMON DESHWITAT!!

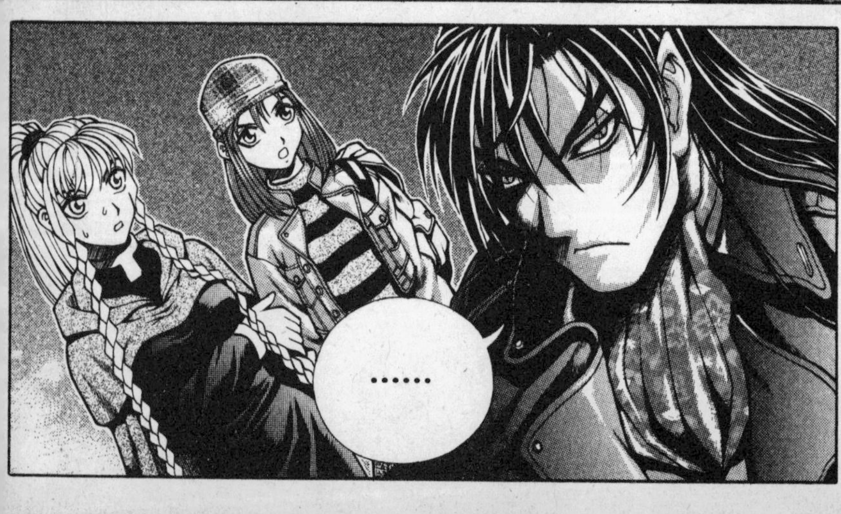
......

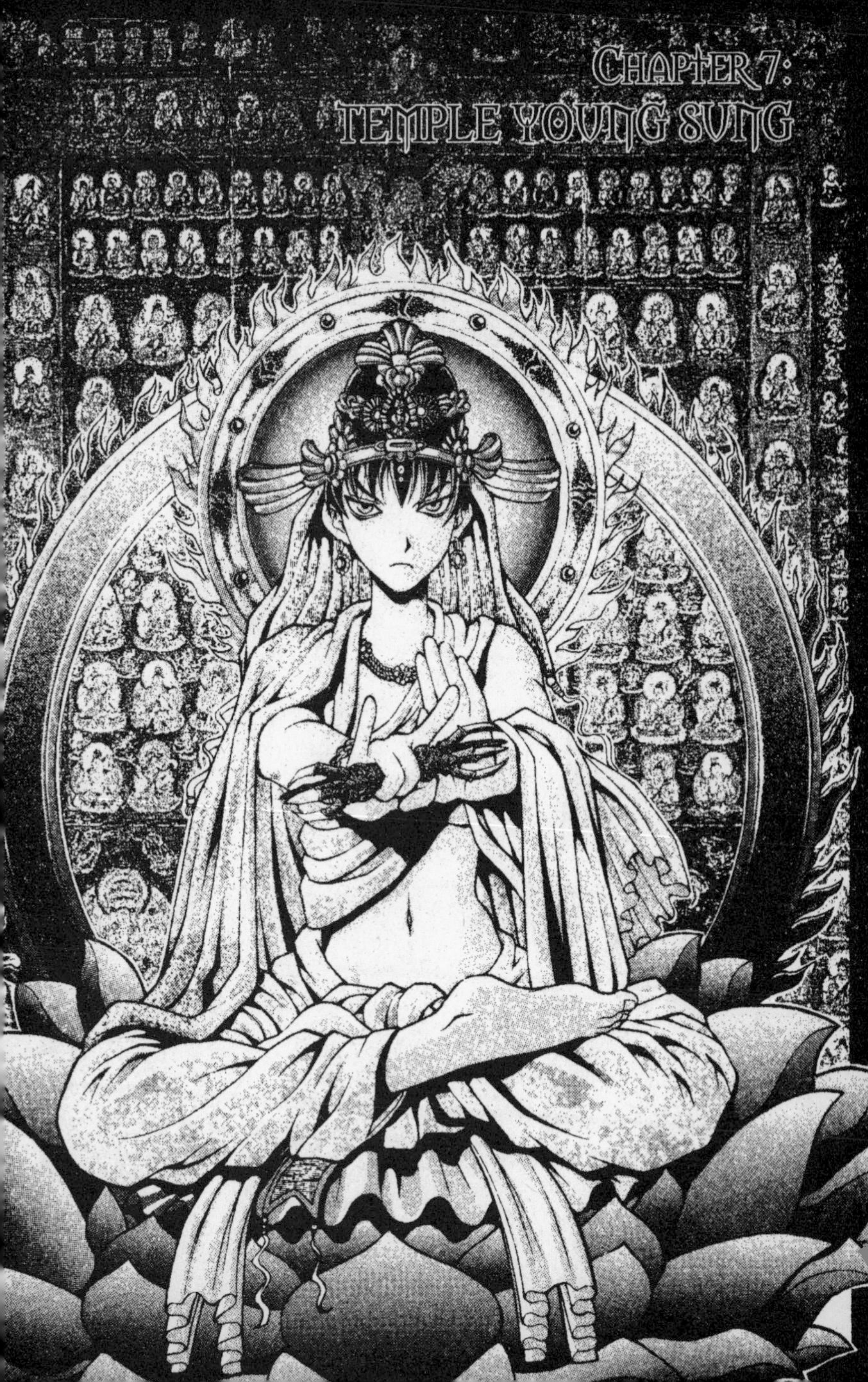
Chapter 7:
Temple Young Sung

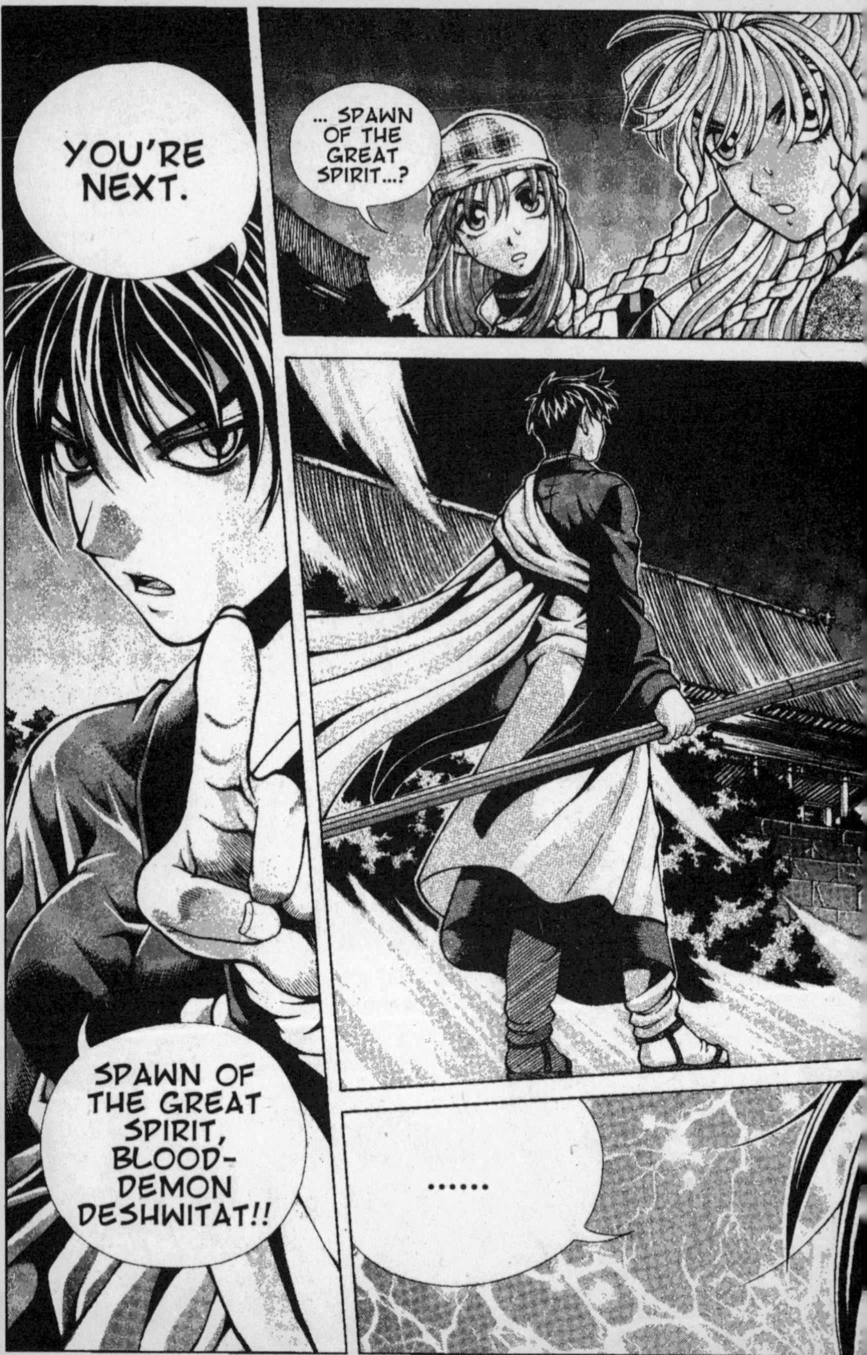
YOU'RE NEXT.
SPAWN OF THE GREAT SPIRIT, BLOOD-DEMON DESHWITAT!!
... SPAWN OF THE GREAT SPIRIT...?
......

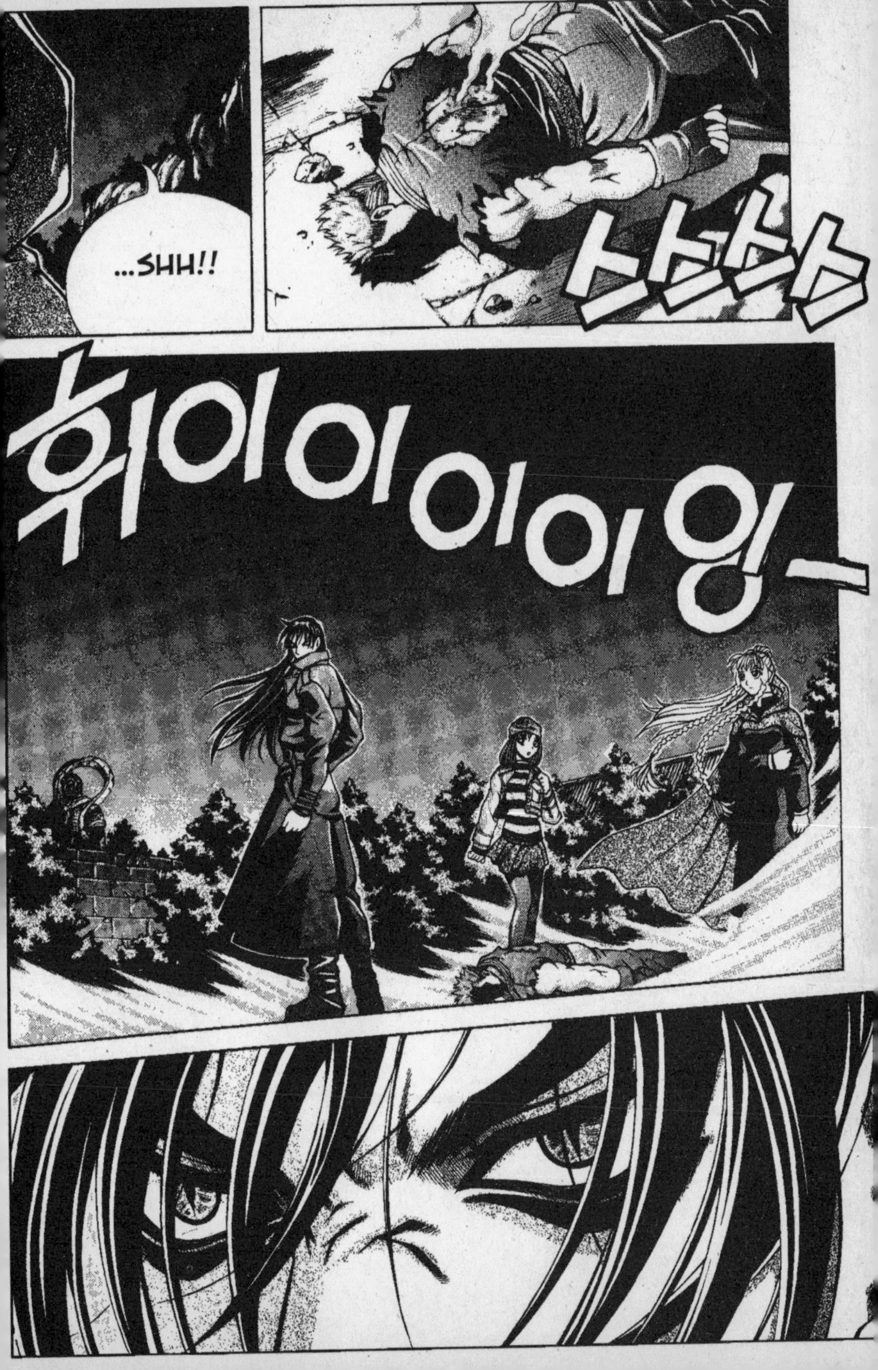
...SHH!!
휘이이이이잉–

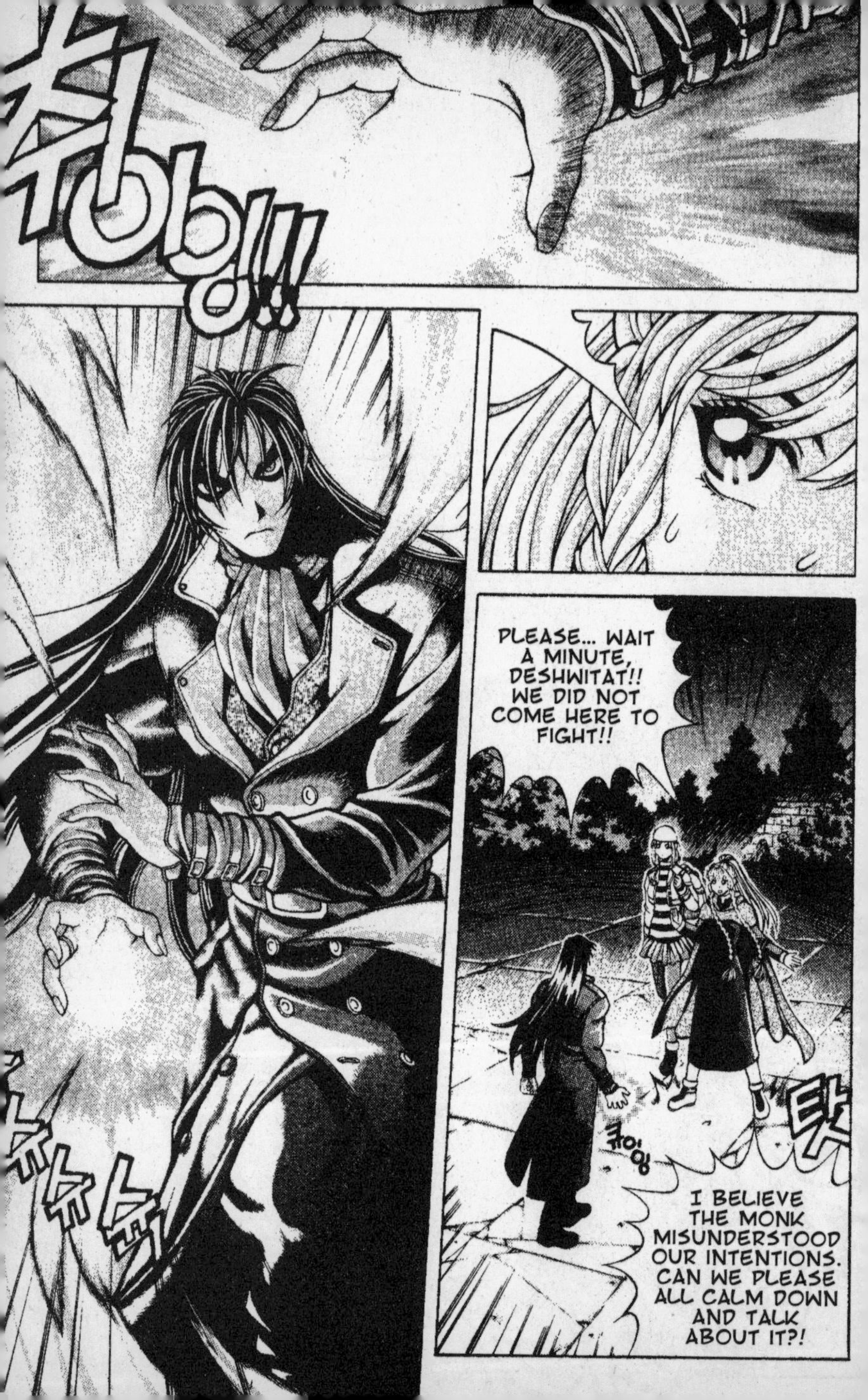
PLEASE... WAIT A MINUTE, DESHWITAT!! WE DID NOT COME HERE TO FIGHT!!
I BELIEVE THE MONK MISUNDERSTOOD OUR INTENTIONS. CAN WE PLEASE ALL CALM DOWN AND TALK ABOUT IT?!

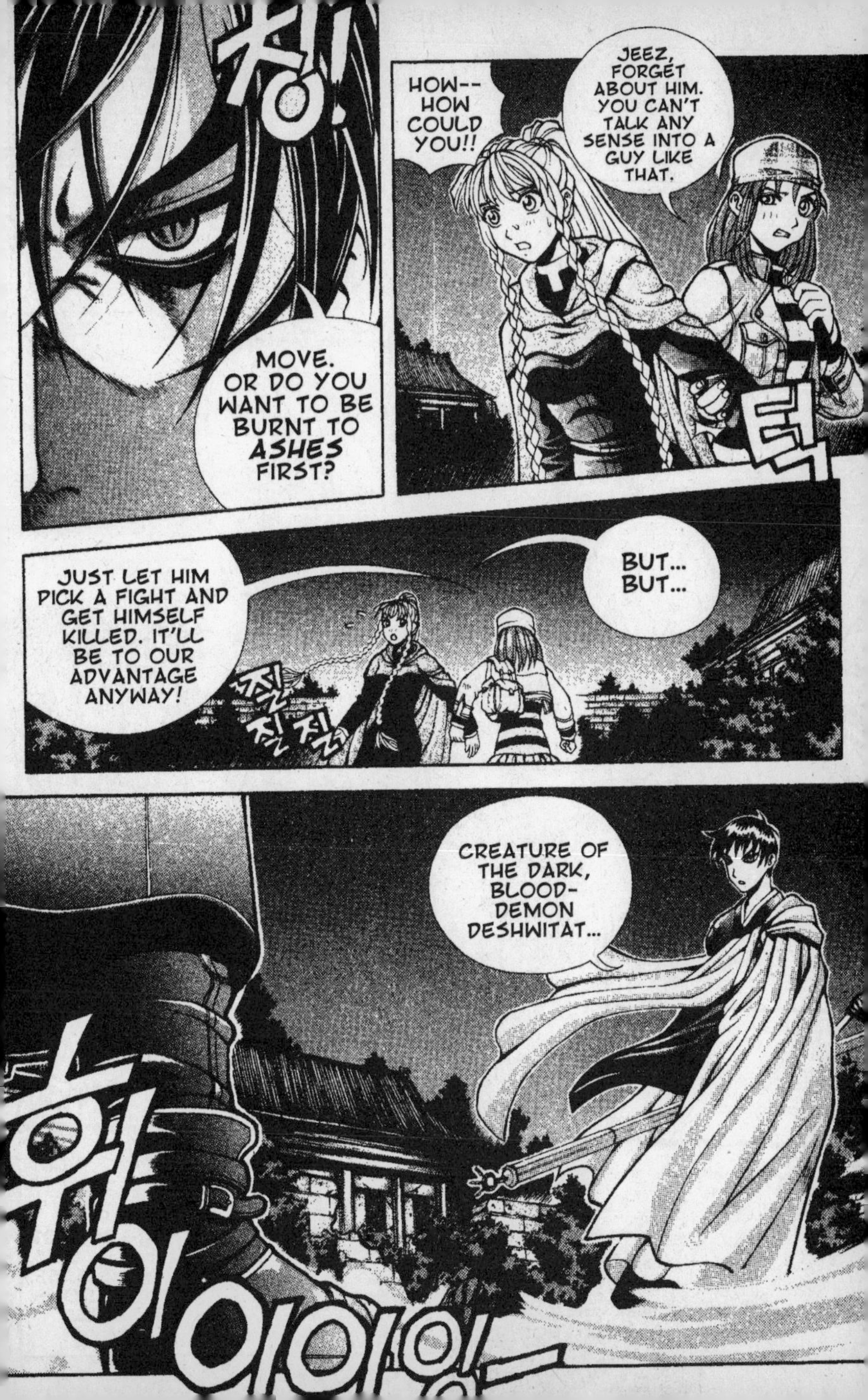
MOVE. OR DO YOU WANT TO BE BURNT TO ASHES FIRST?
HOW-- HOW COULD YOU!!
JEEZ, FORGET ABOUT HIM. YOU CAN'T TALK ANY SENSE INTO A GUY LIKE THAT.
JUST LET HIM PICK A FIGHT AND GET HIMSELF KILLED. IT'LL BE TO OUR ADVANTAGE ANYWAY!
BUT... BUT...
CREATURE OF THE DARK, BLOOD-DEMON DESHWITAT...

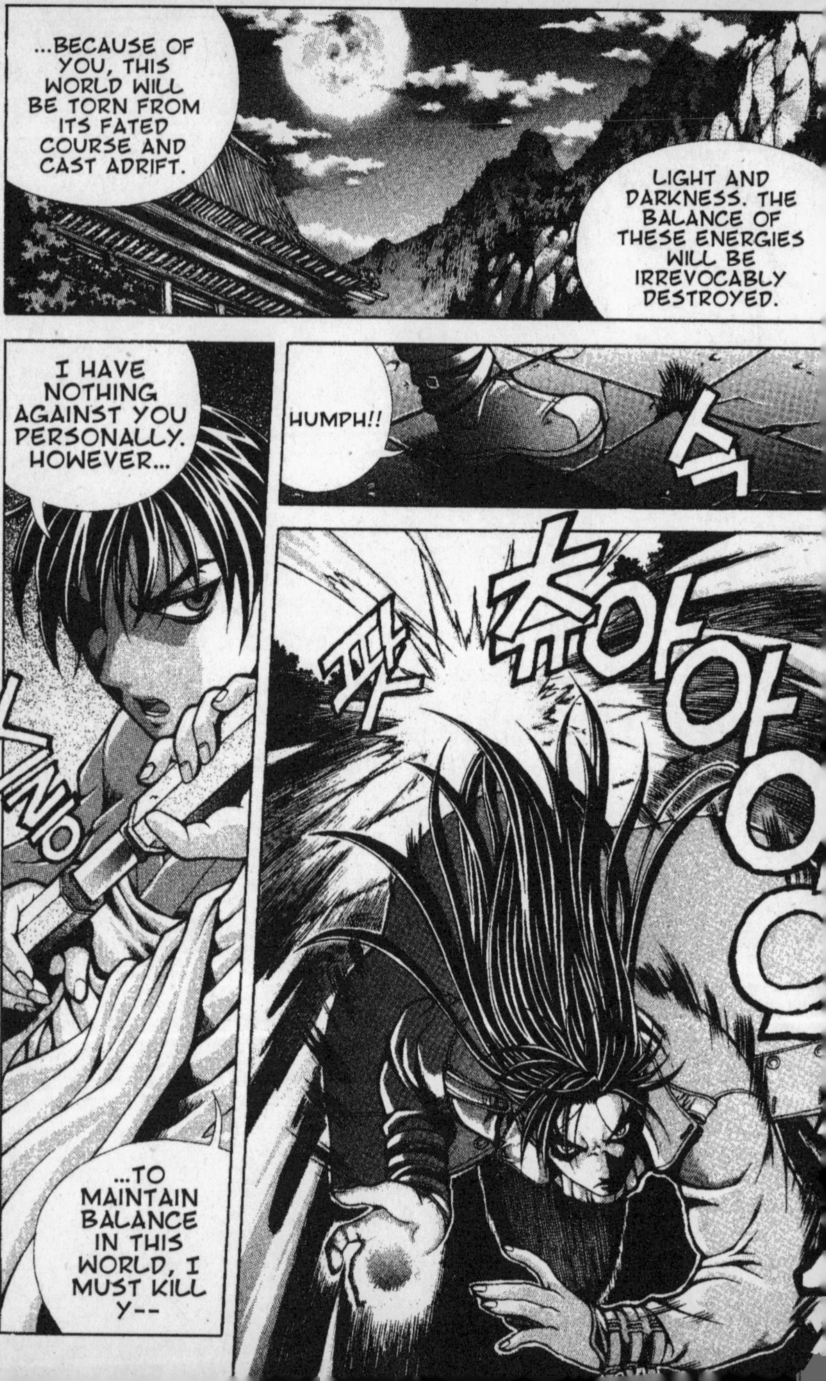
...BECAUSE OF YOU, THIS WORLD WILL BE TORN FROM ITS FATED COURSE AND CAST ADRIFT.
LIGHT AND DARKNESS. THE BALANCE OF THESE ENERGIES WILL BE IRREVOCABLY DESTROYED.
I HAVE NOTHING AGAINST YOU PERSONALLY. HOWEVER...
...TO MAINTAIN BALANCE IN THIS WORLD, I MUST KILL Y--
HUMPH!!

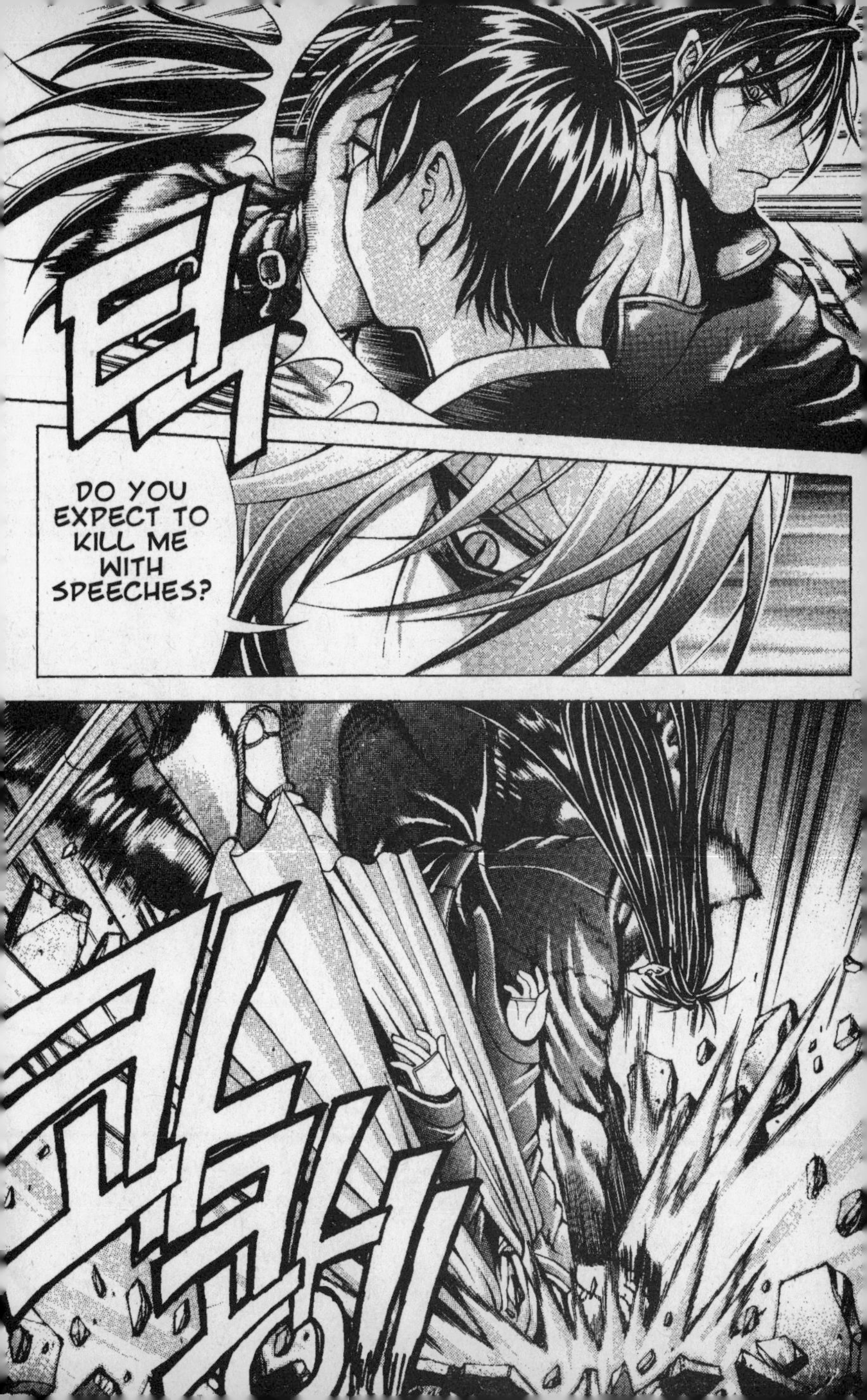
DO YOU EXPECT TO KILL ME WITH SPEECHES?

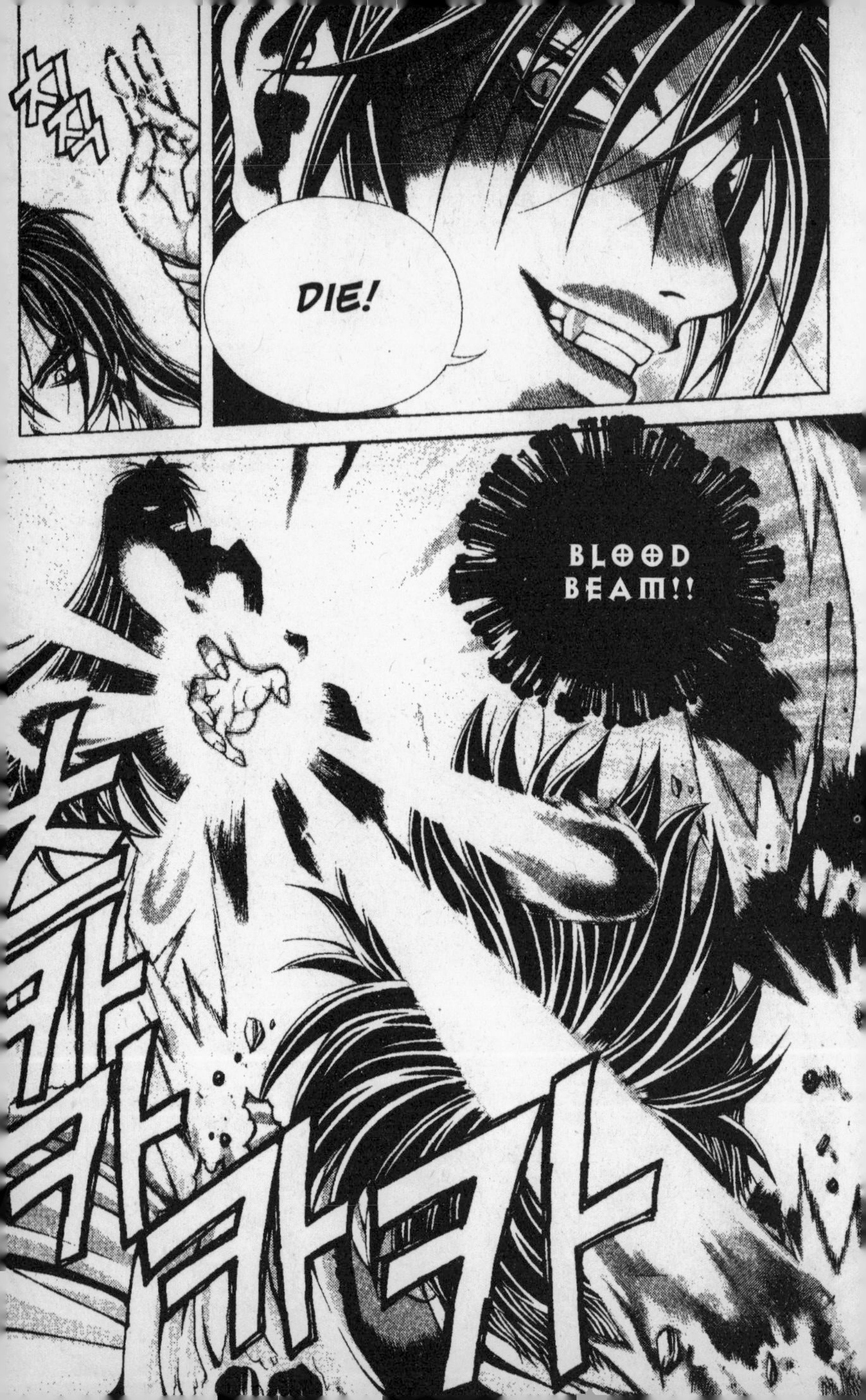
DIE!
BLOOD BEAM!!

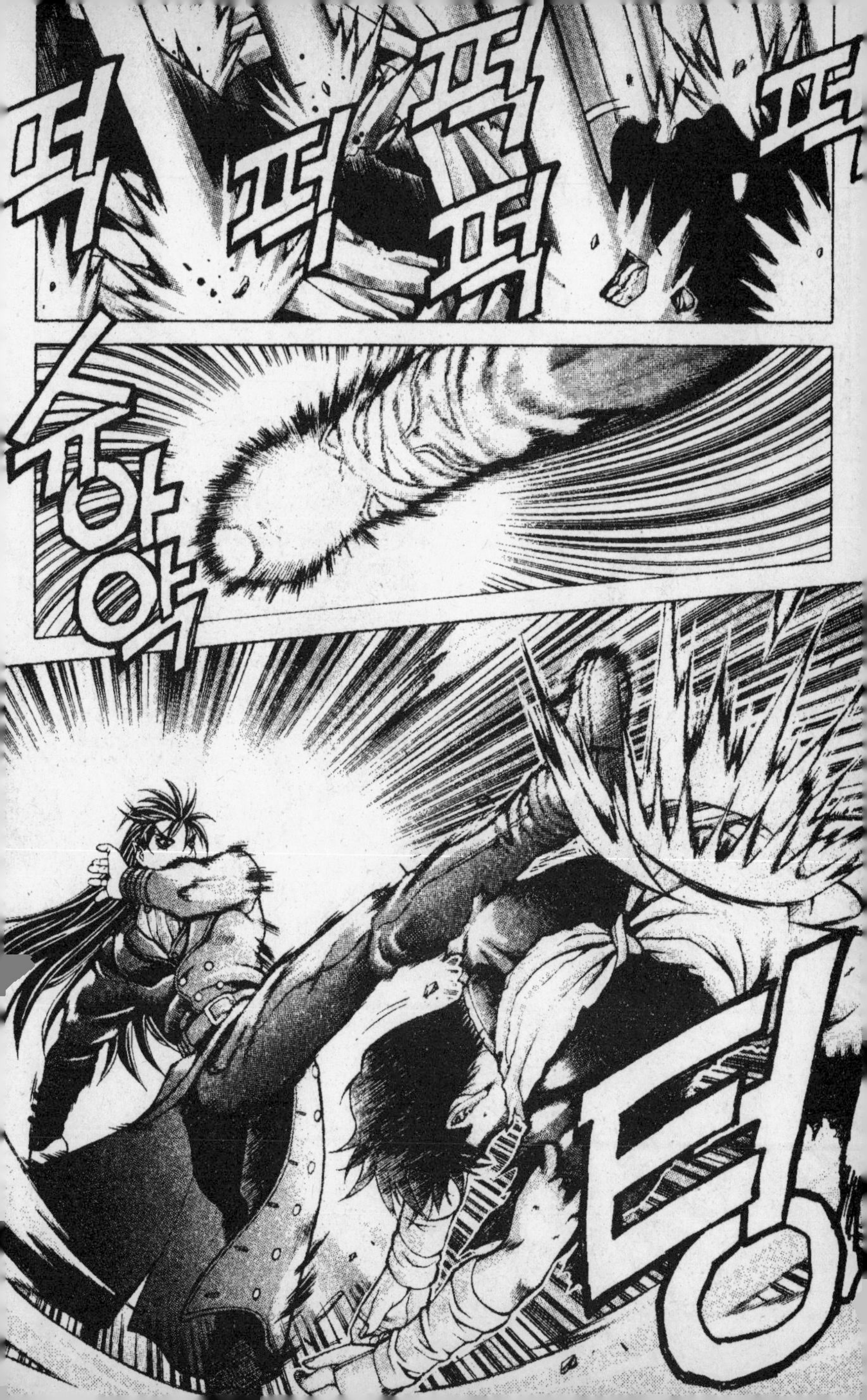
퍽
퍽
퍽
퍽
슈아악
덩

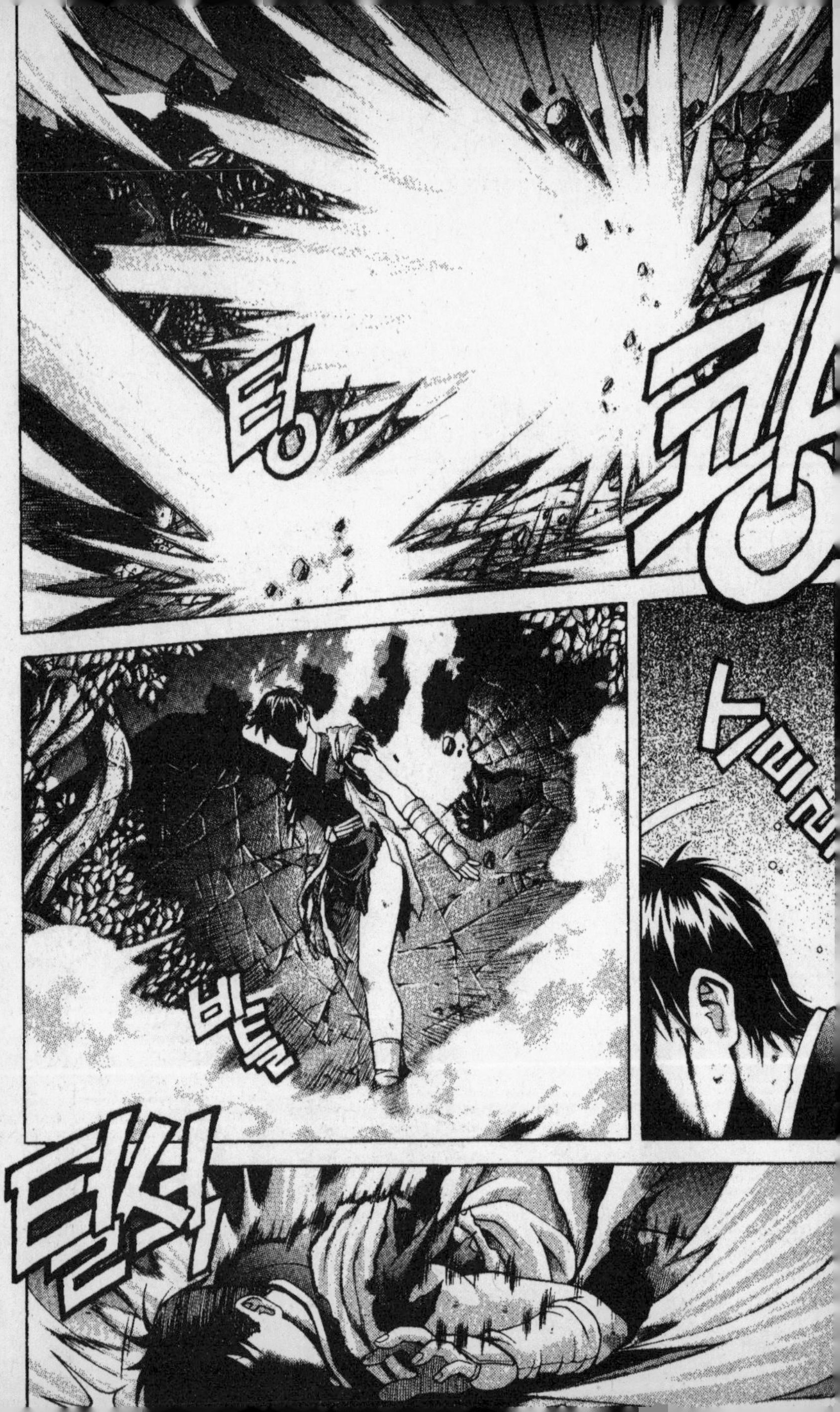
텅
쾅
비틀
니리리
털석

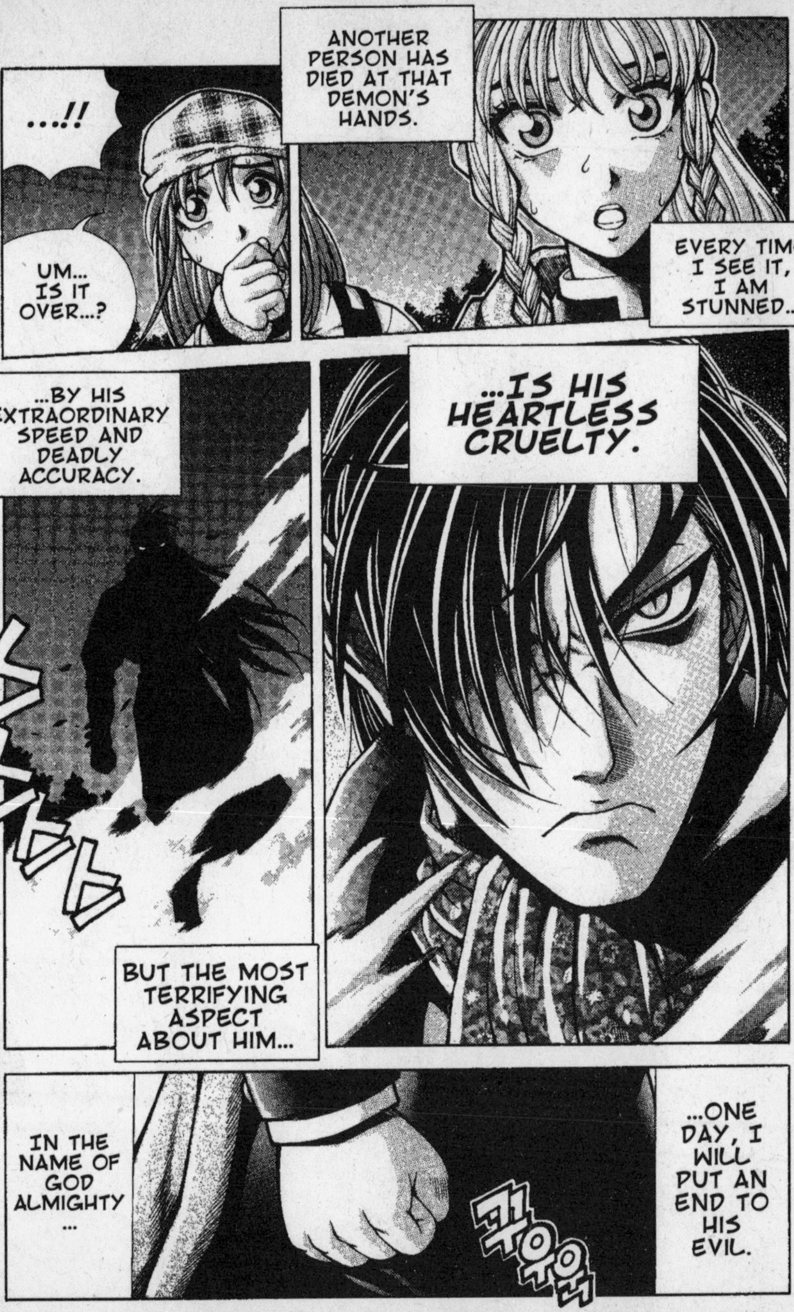

...!!
UM... IS IT OVER...?
ANOTHER PERSON HAS DIED AT THAT DEMON'S HANDS.
EVERY TIME I SEE IT, I AM STUNNED...
...BY HIS EXTRAORDINARY SPEED AND DEADLY ACCURACY.
BUT THE MOST TERRIFYING ASPECT ABOUT HIM...
...IS HIS HEARTLESS CRUELTY.
IN THE NAME OF GOD ALMIGHTY ...
...ONE DAY, I WILL PUT AN END TO HIS EVIL.

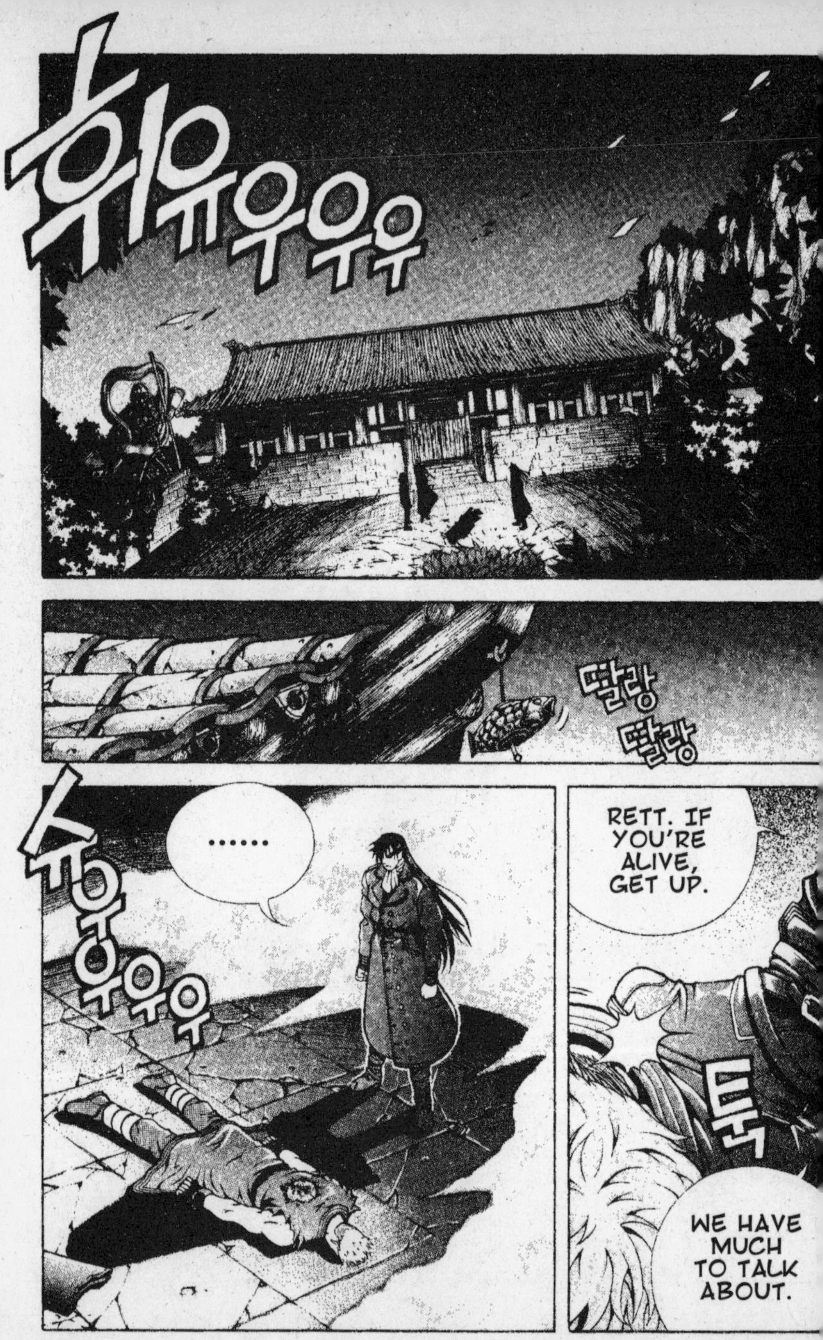

휘유우우
딸랑
딸랑
슈우우우
......
RETT. IF YOU'RE ALIVE, GET UP.
툭
WE HAVE MUCH TO TALK ABOUT.

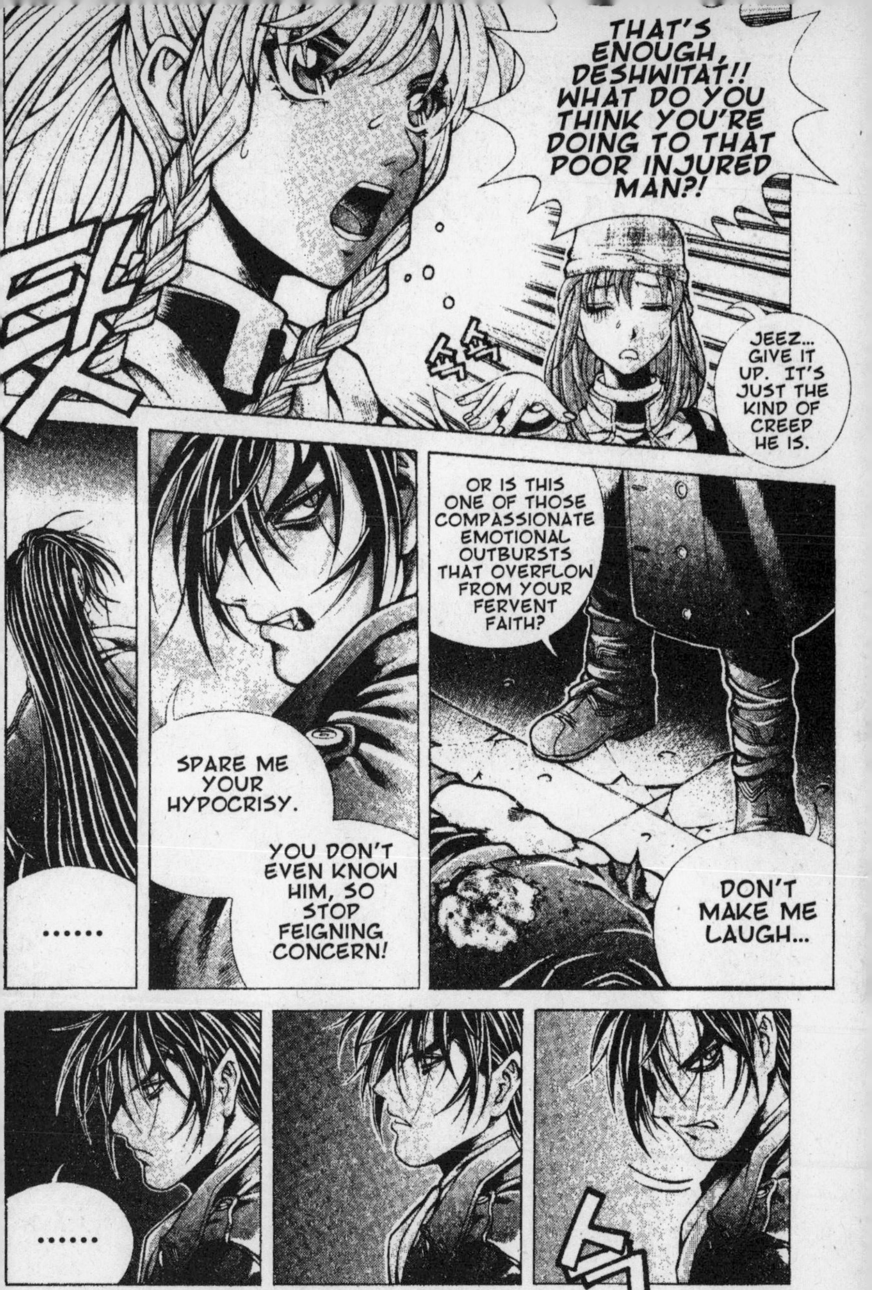
THAT'S ENOUGH, DESHWITAT!! WHAT DO YOU THINK YOU'RE DOING TO THAT POOR INJURED MAN?!
JEEZ... GIVE IT UP. IT'S JUST THE KIND OF CREEP HE IS.
......
SPARE ME YOUR HYPOCRISY.
YOU DON'T EVEN KNOW HIM, SO STOP FEIGNING CONCERN!
OR IS THIS ONE OF THOSE COMPASSIONATE EMOTIONAL OUTBURSTS THAT OVERFLOW FROM YOUR FERVENT FAITH?
DON'T MAKE ME LAUGH...
......

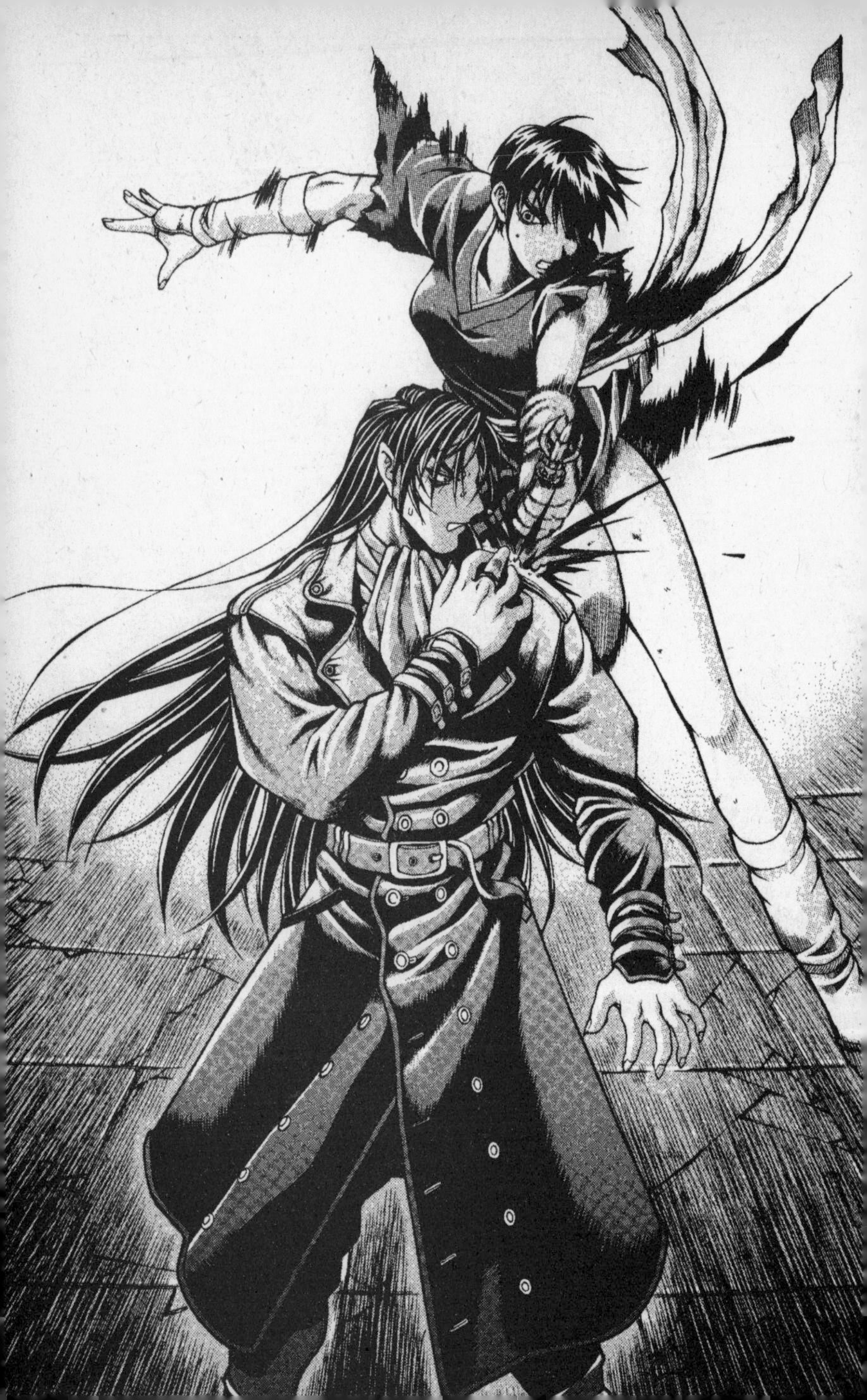

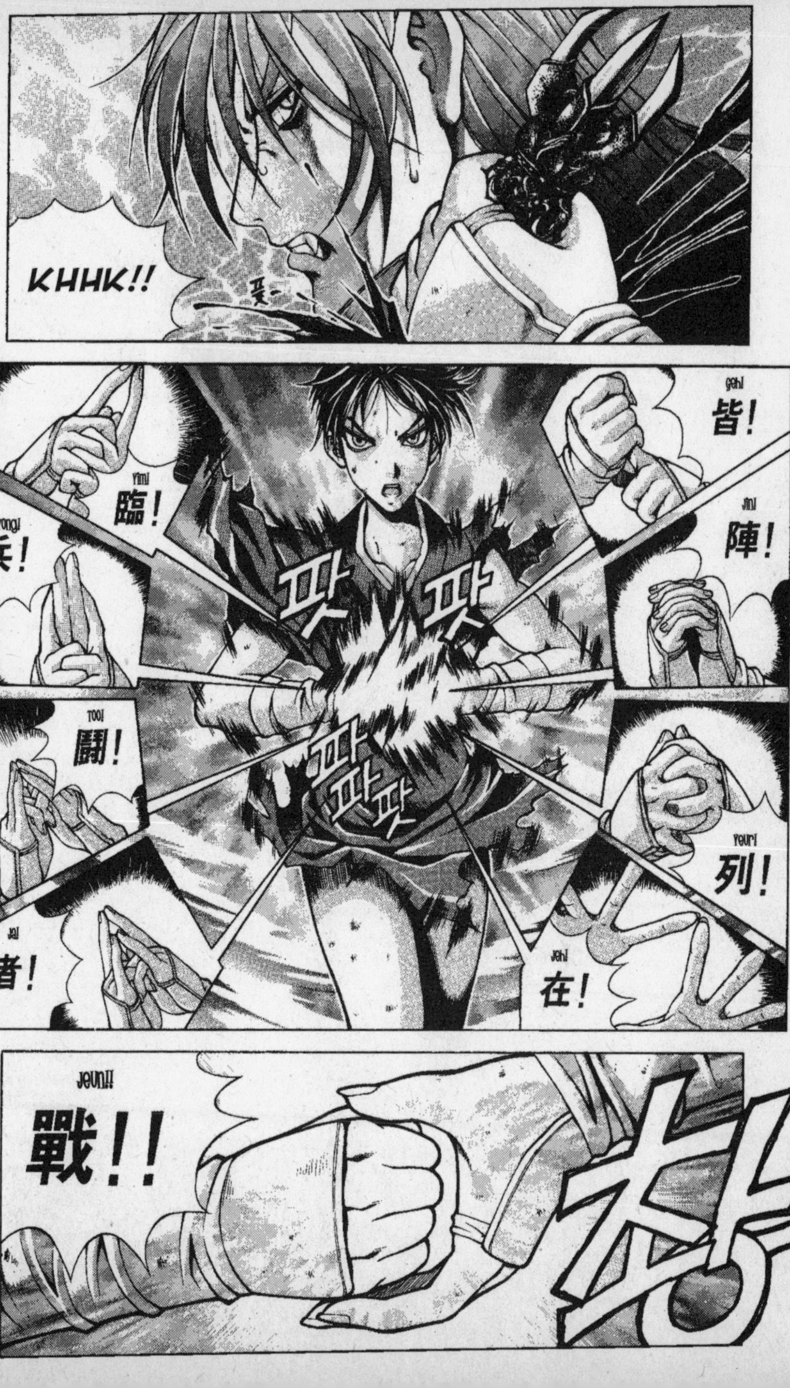
KHHK!!
푹
Yim!
臨!
Byong!
兵!
Geh!
皆!
Jin!
陣!
팟 팟
파 파 팟
Too!
鬪!
Yeul!
列!
Jah!
者!
Jeh!
在!
Jeun!!
戰!!

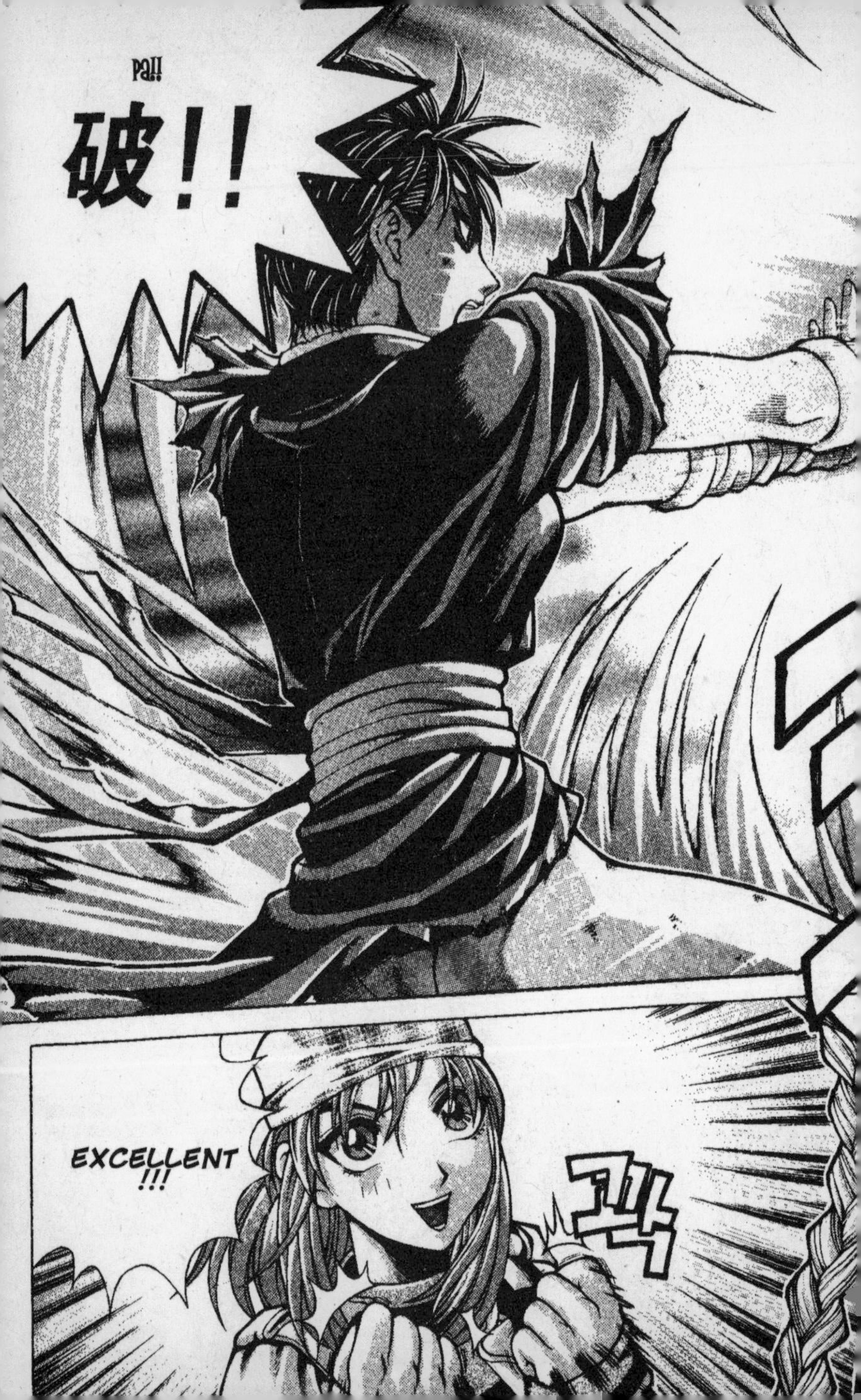
Pa!!
破!!
EXCELLENT !!!

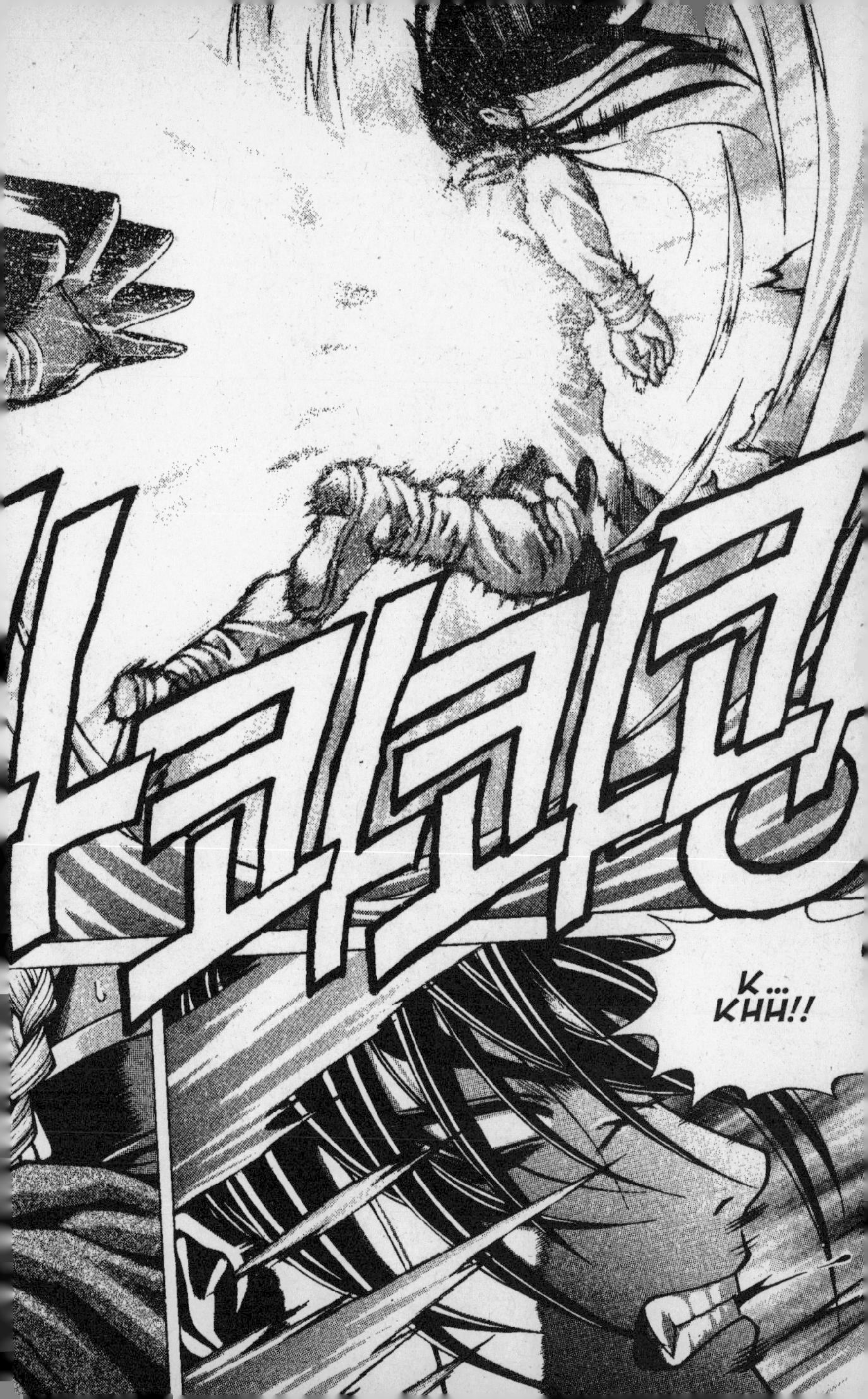
K... KHH!!

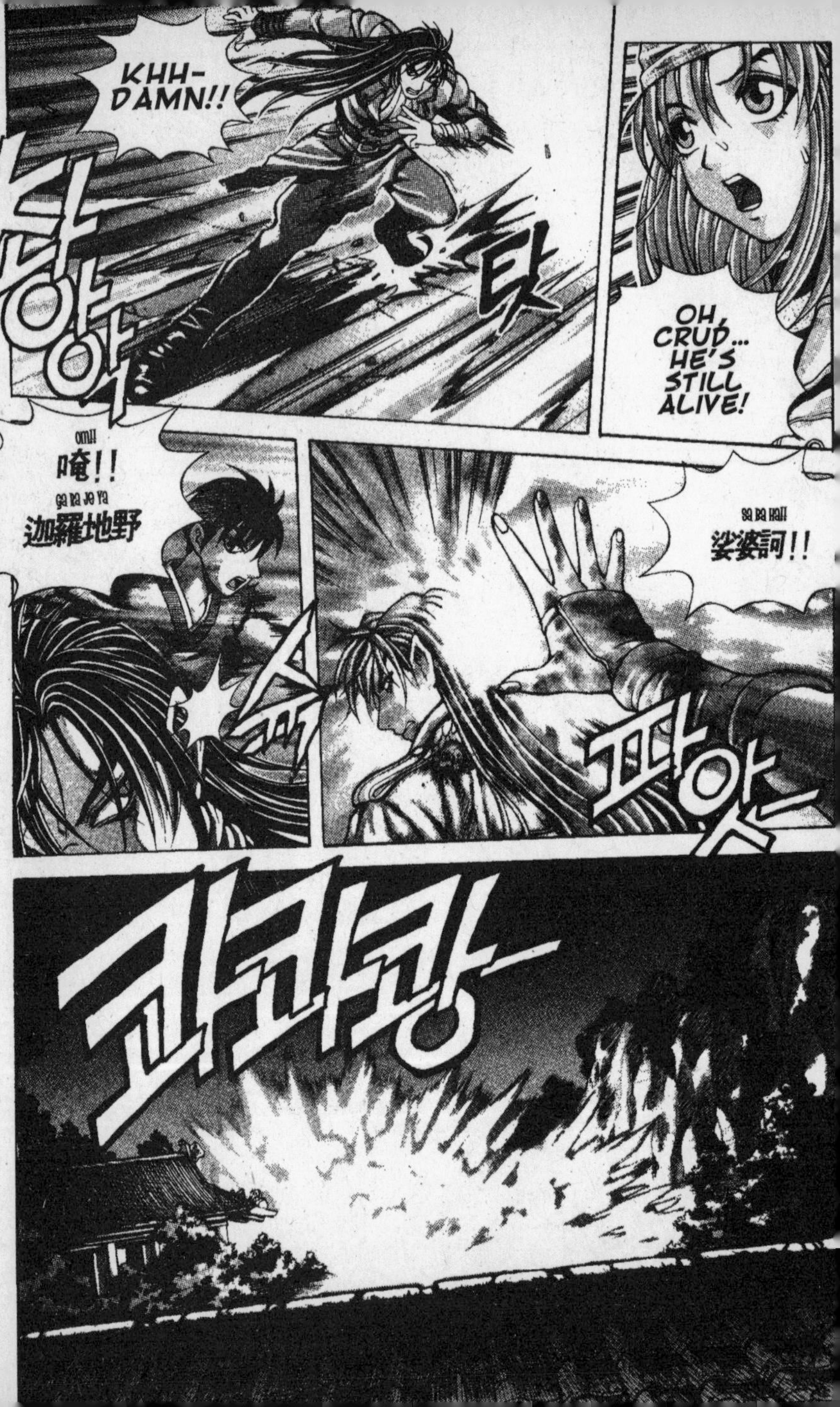
KHH-
DAMN!!
탓
OH, CRUD... HE'S STILL ALIVE!
om!!
唵!!
ga ra je ya
迦羅地野
sa ba ha!!
娑婆訶!!

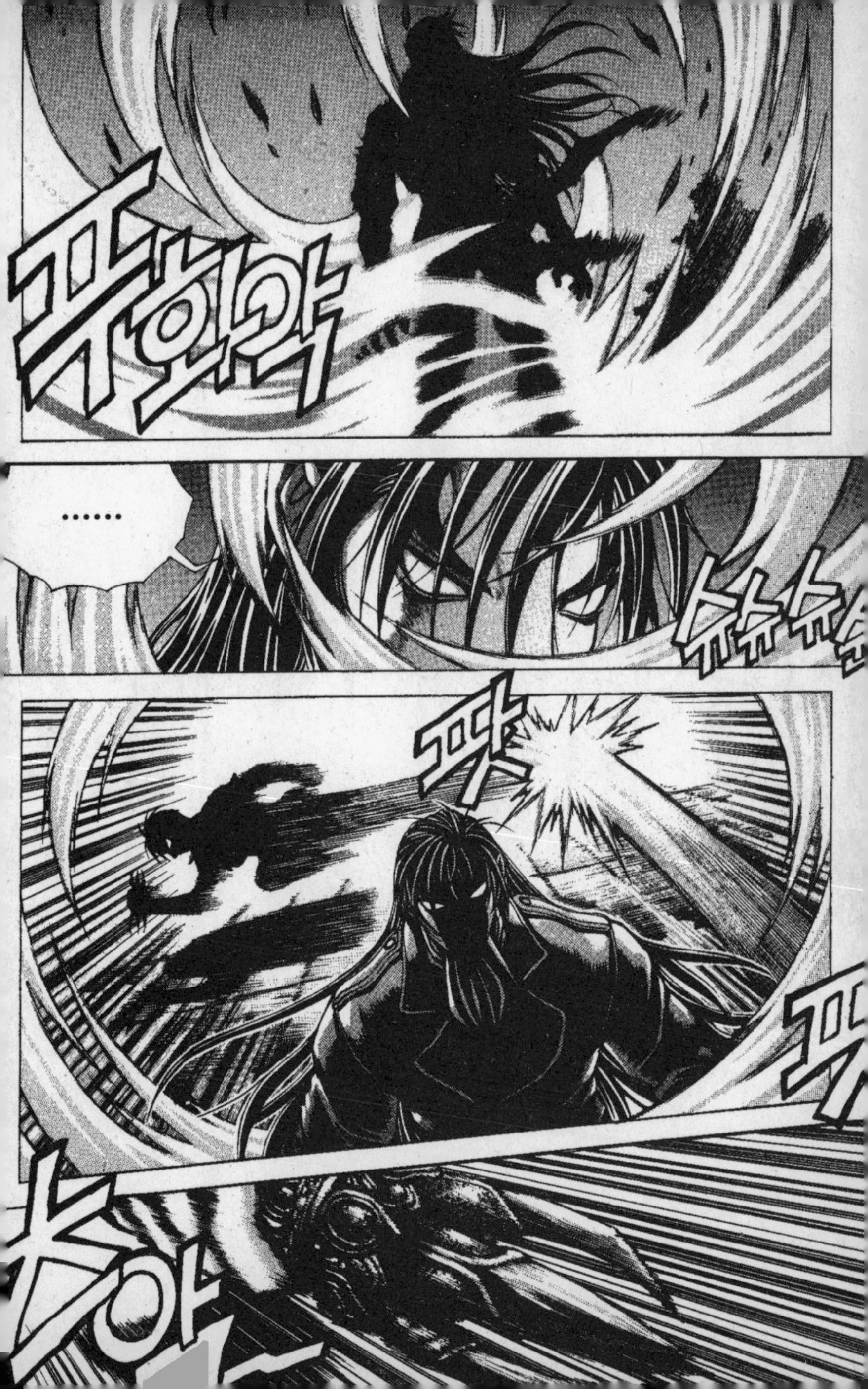
......
팍

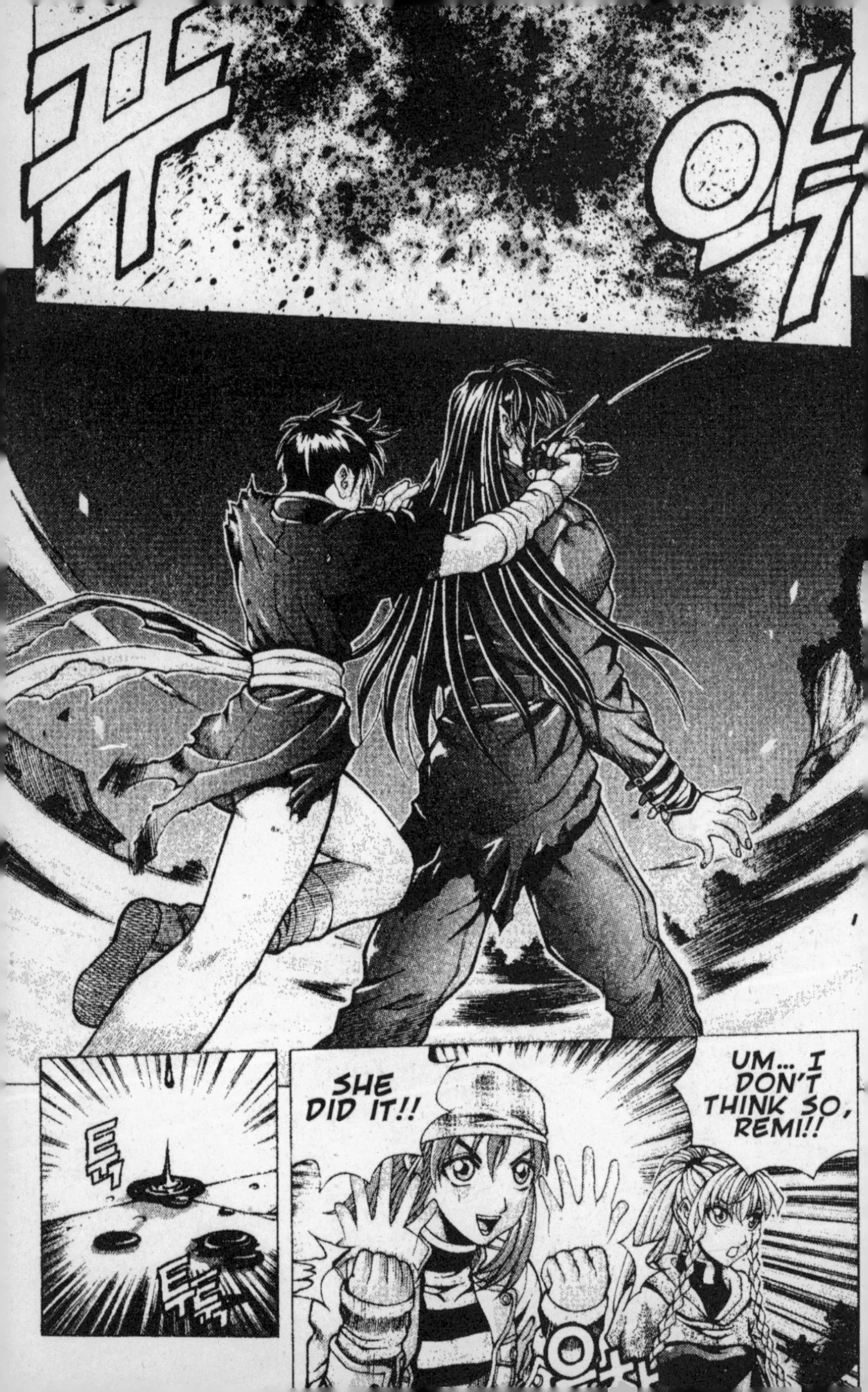
SHE DID IT!!
UM... I DON'T THINK SO, REMI!!

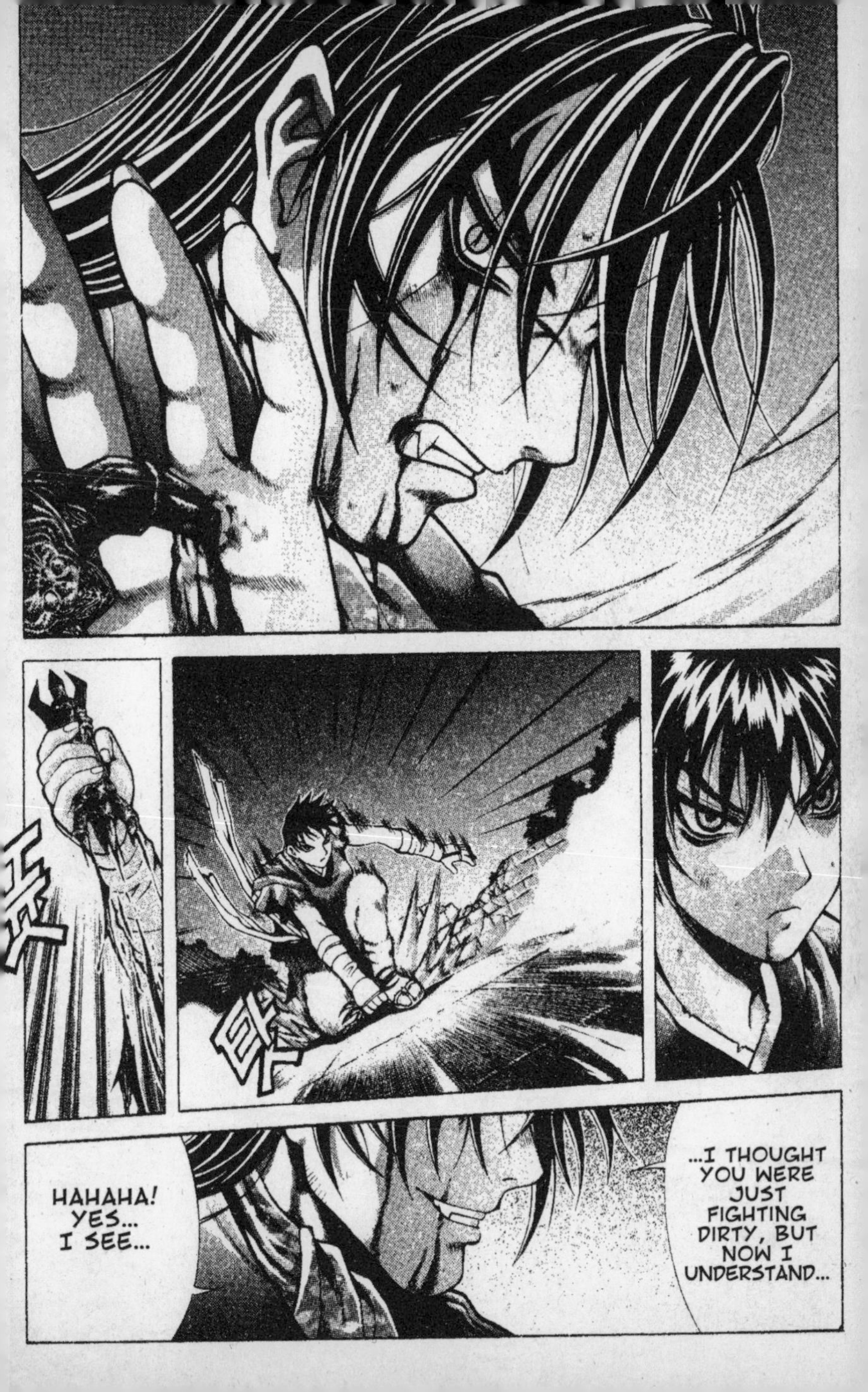
HAHAHA! YES... I SEE...
...I THOUGHT YOU WERE JUST FIGHTING DIRTY, BUT NOW I UNDERSTAND...

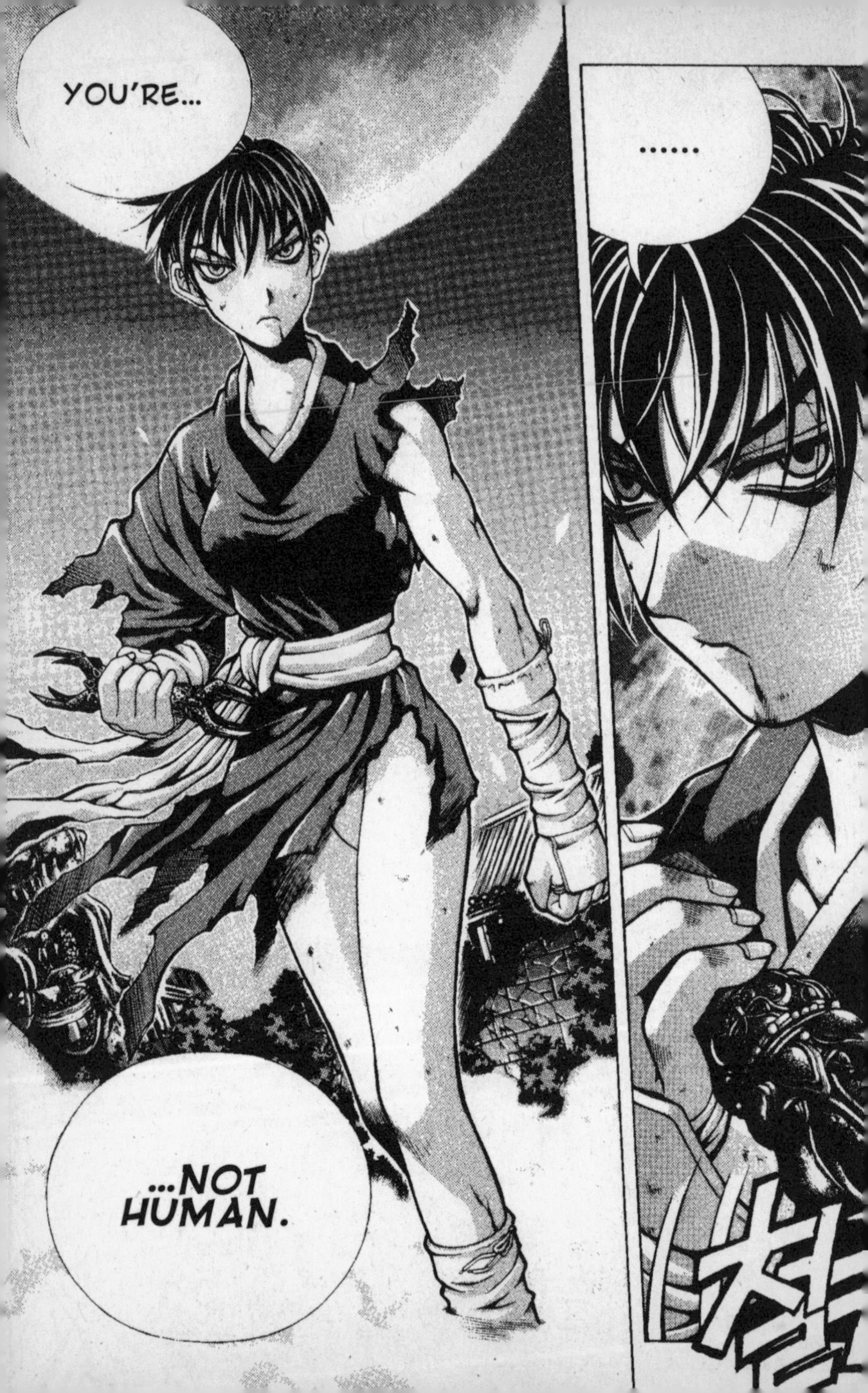
......
YOU'RE...
...NOT HUMAN.

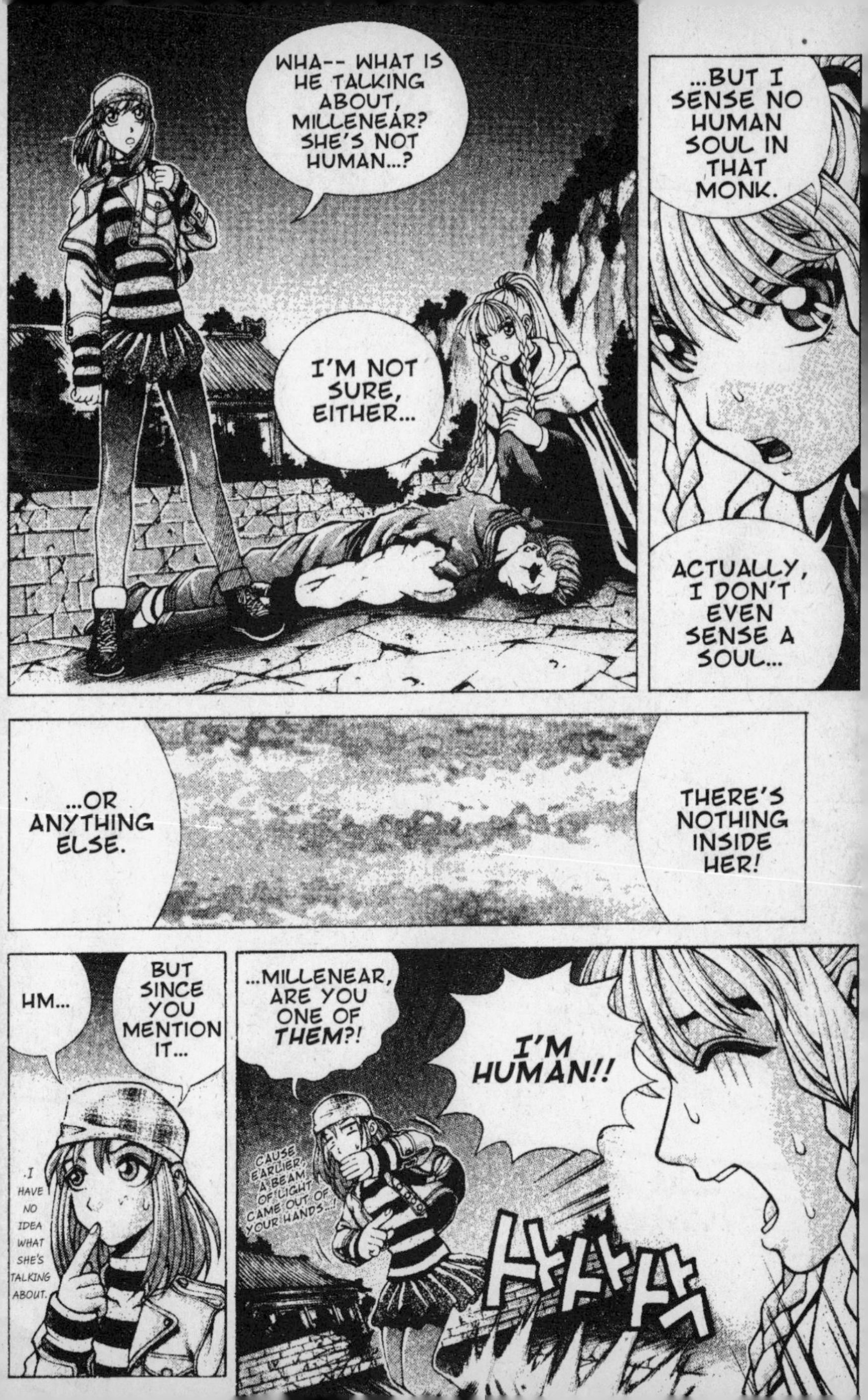
WHA-- WHAT IS HE TALKING ABOUT, MILLENEAR? SHE'S NOT HUMAN...?
I'M NOT SURE, EITHER...
...BUT I SENSE NO HUMAN SOUL IN THAT MONK.
ACTUALLY, I DON'T EVEN SENSE A SOUL...
...OR ANYTHING ELSE.
THERE'S NOTHING INSIDE HER!
HM...
BUT SINCE YOU MENTION IT...
I HAVE NO IDEA WHAT SHE'S TALKING ABOUT.
...MILLENEAR, ARE YOU ONE OF *THEM*?!
CAUSE EARLIER, A BEAM OF LIGHT CAME OUT OF YOUR HANDS...
I'M HUMAN!!

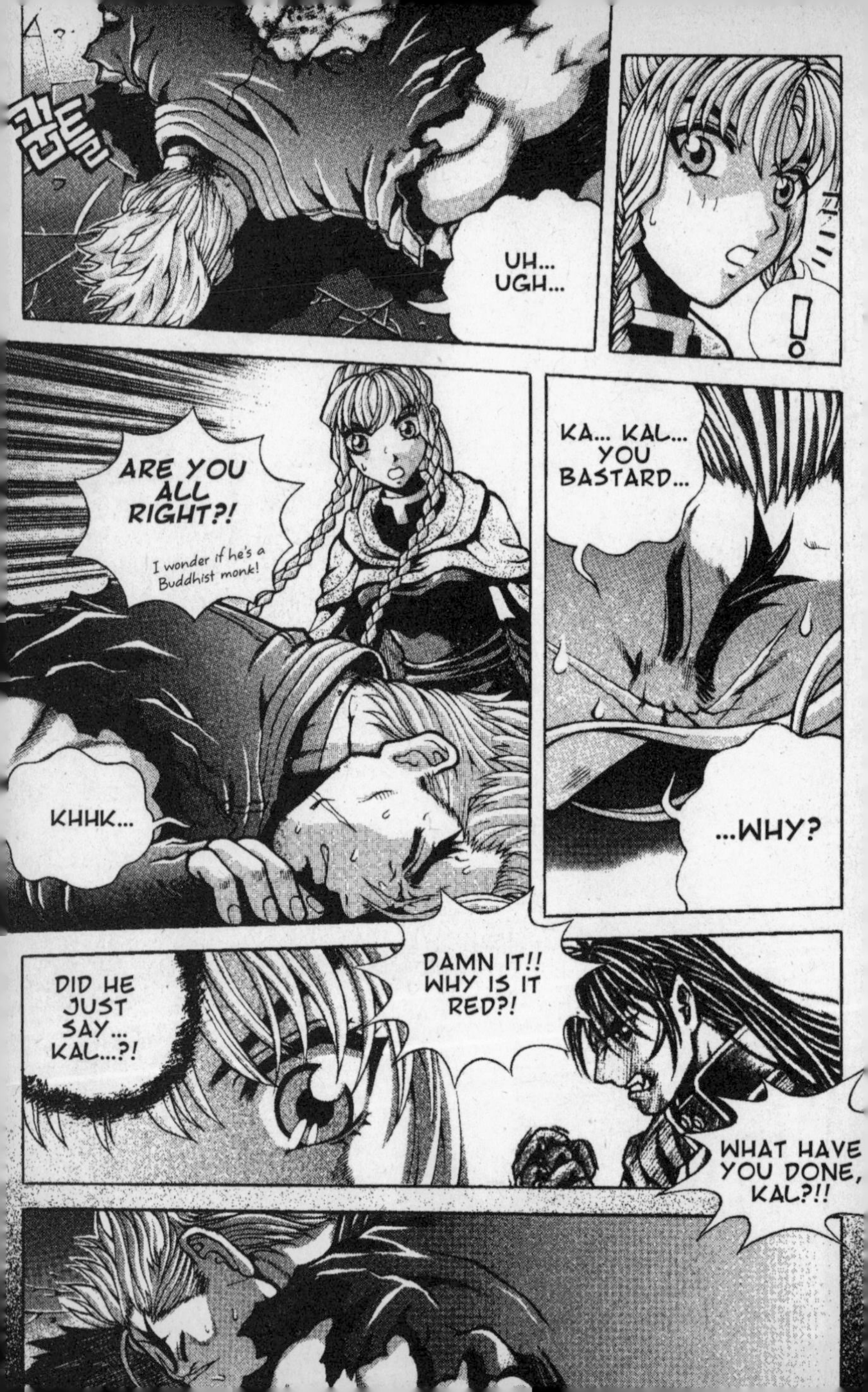
UH... UGH...
!
ARE YOU ALL RIGHT?!
I wonder if he's a Buddhist monk!
KHHK...
KA... KAL... YOU BASTARD...
...WHY?
DID HE JUST SAY... KAL...?!
DAMN IT!! WHY IS IT RED?!
WHAT HAVE YOU DONE, KAL?!!

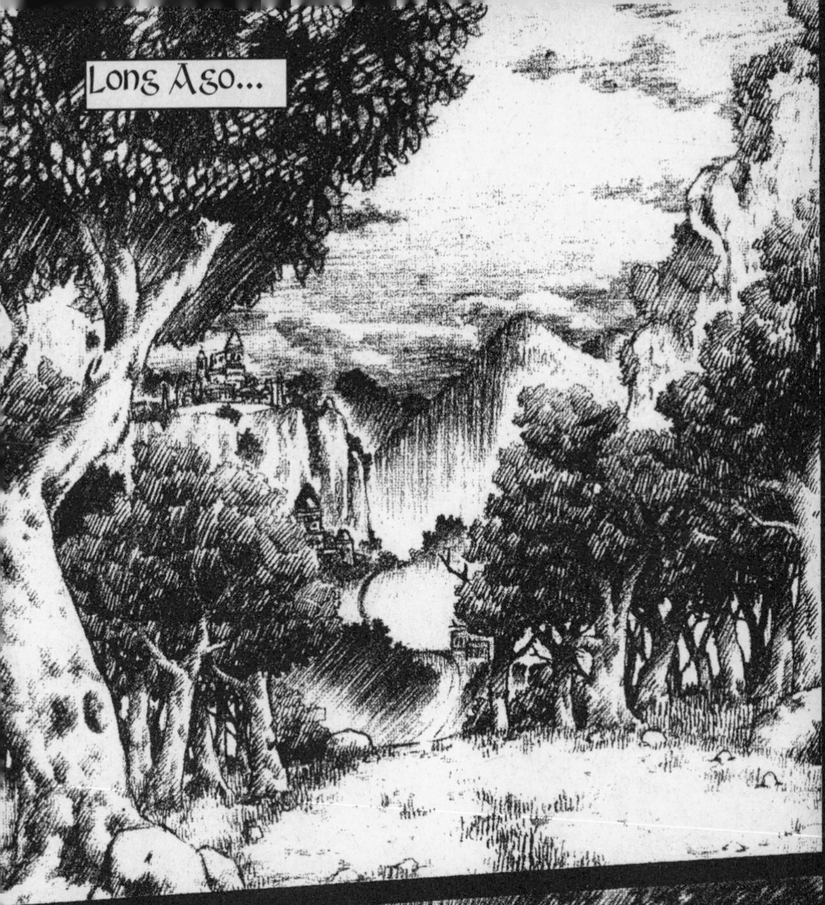
Long Ago...
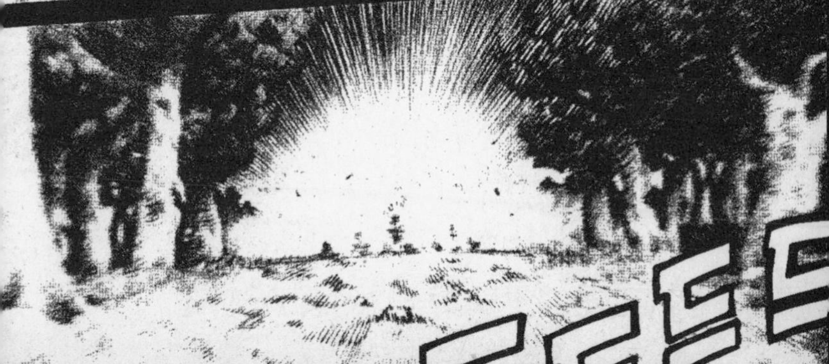

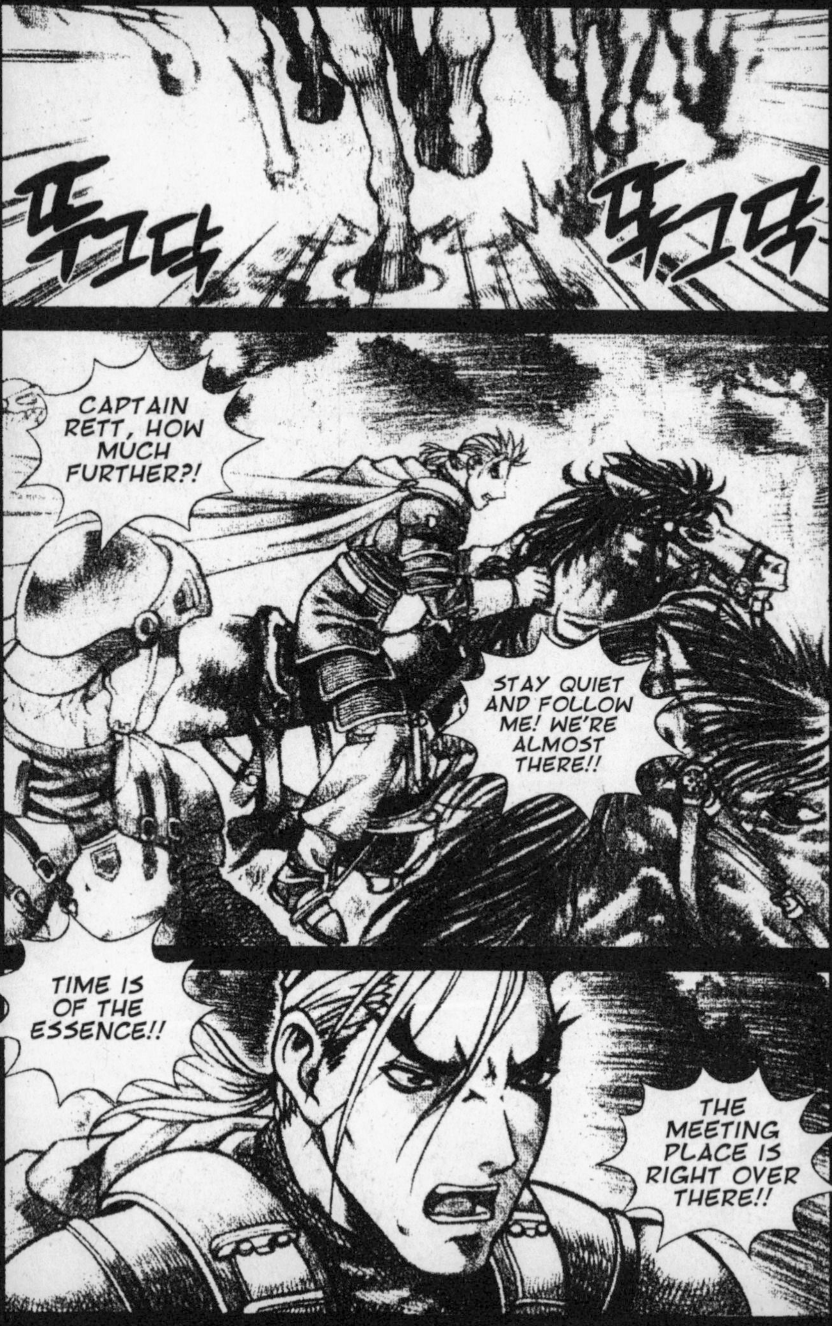
뚜그닥
뚜그닥
CAPTAIN RETT, HOW MUCH FURTHER?!
STAY QUIET AND FOLLOW ME! WE'RE ALMOST THERE!!
TIME IS OF THE ESSENCE!!
THE MEETING PLACE IS RIGHT OVER THERE!!

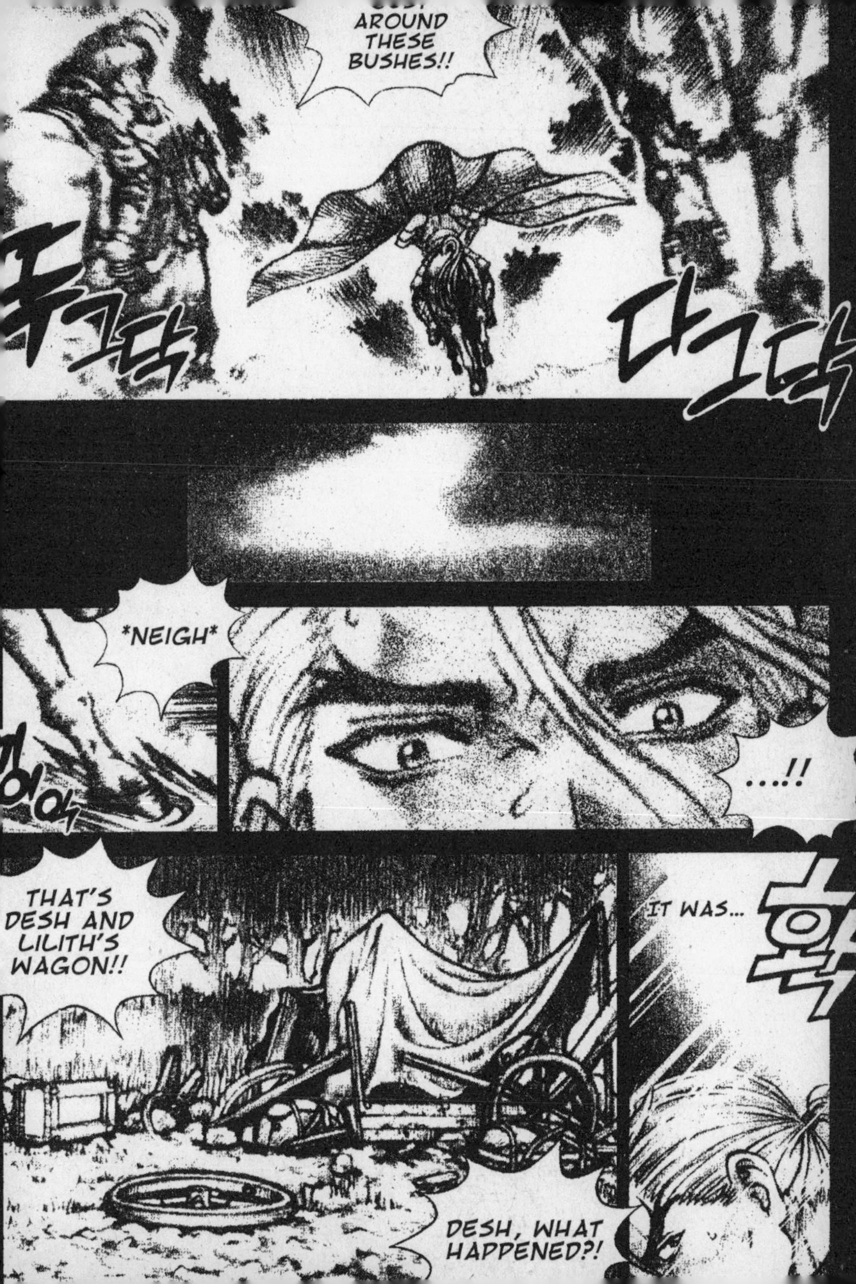
AROUND THESE BUSHES!!
두그닥
다그닥
NEIGH
...!!
THAT'S DESH AND LILITH'S WAGON!!
IT WAS...
DESH, WHAT HAPPENED?!

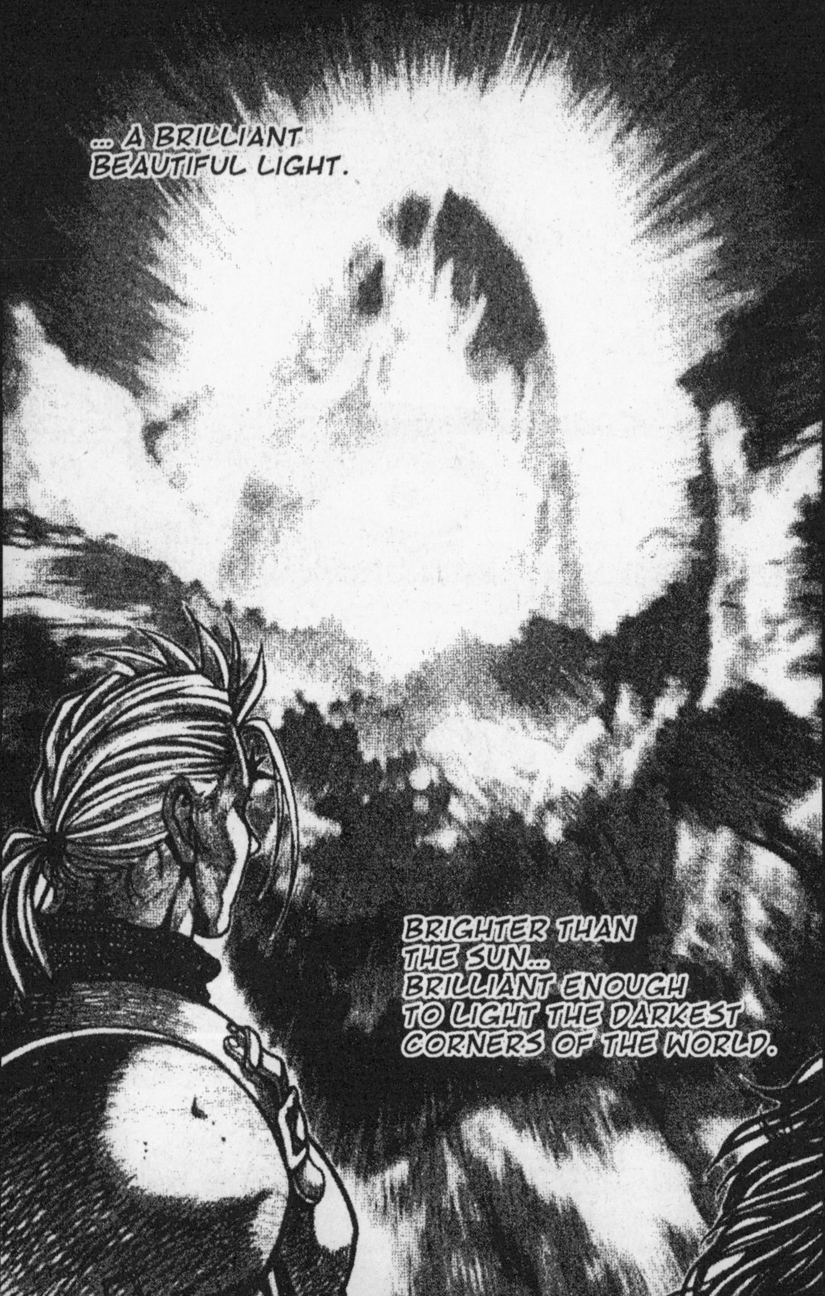

... A BRILLIANT BEAUTIFUL LIGHT.
BRIGHTER THAN THE SUN... BRILLIANT ENOUGH TO LIGHT THE DARKEST CORNERS OF THE WORLD.

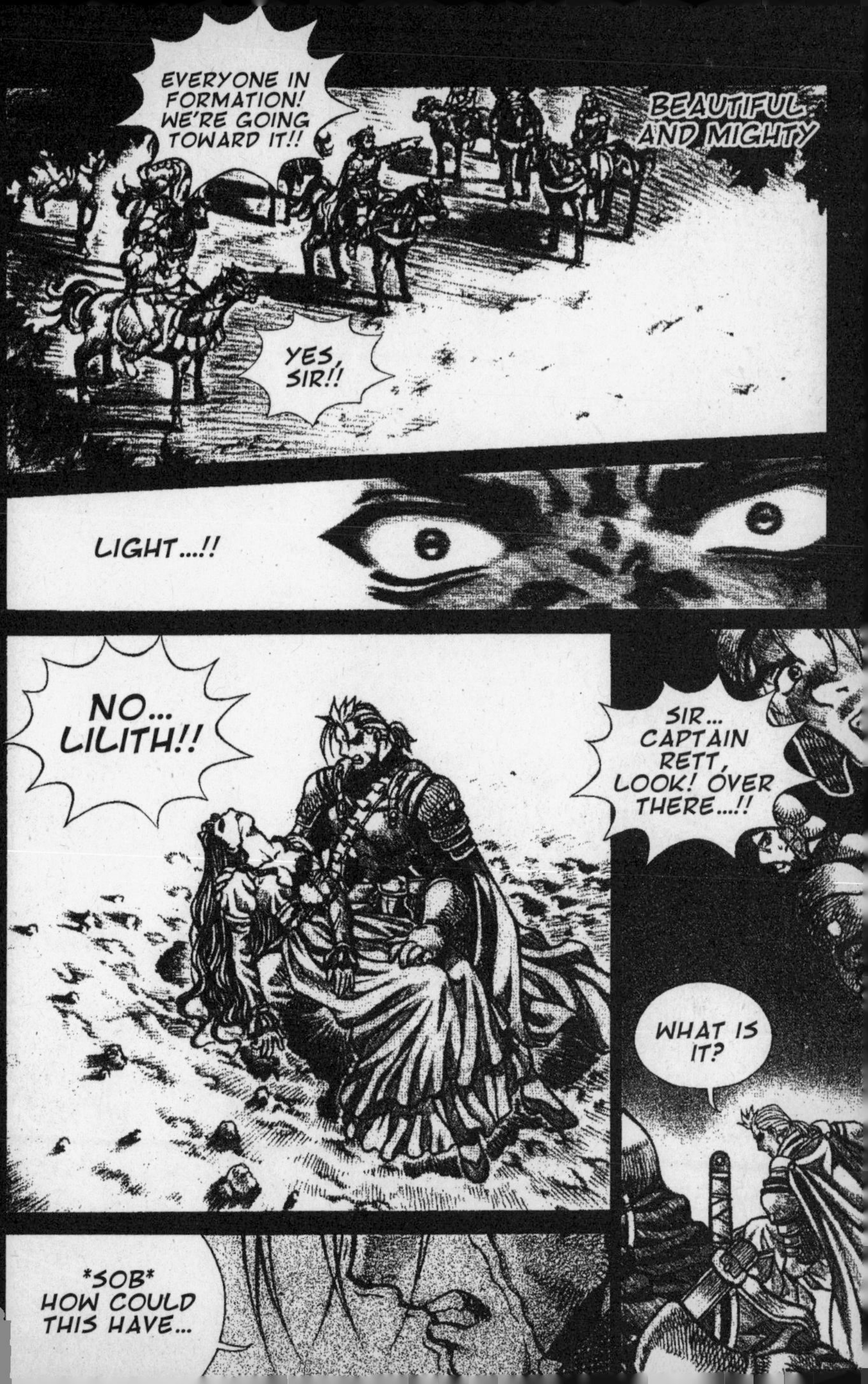
EVERYONE IN FORMATION! WE'RE GOING TOWARD IT!!
BEAUTIFUL AND MIGHTY
YES, SIR!!
LIGHT...!!
NO... LILITH!!
SOB HOW COULD THIS HAVE...
SIR... CAPTAIN RETT, LOOK! OVER THERE...!!
WHAT IS IT?

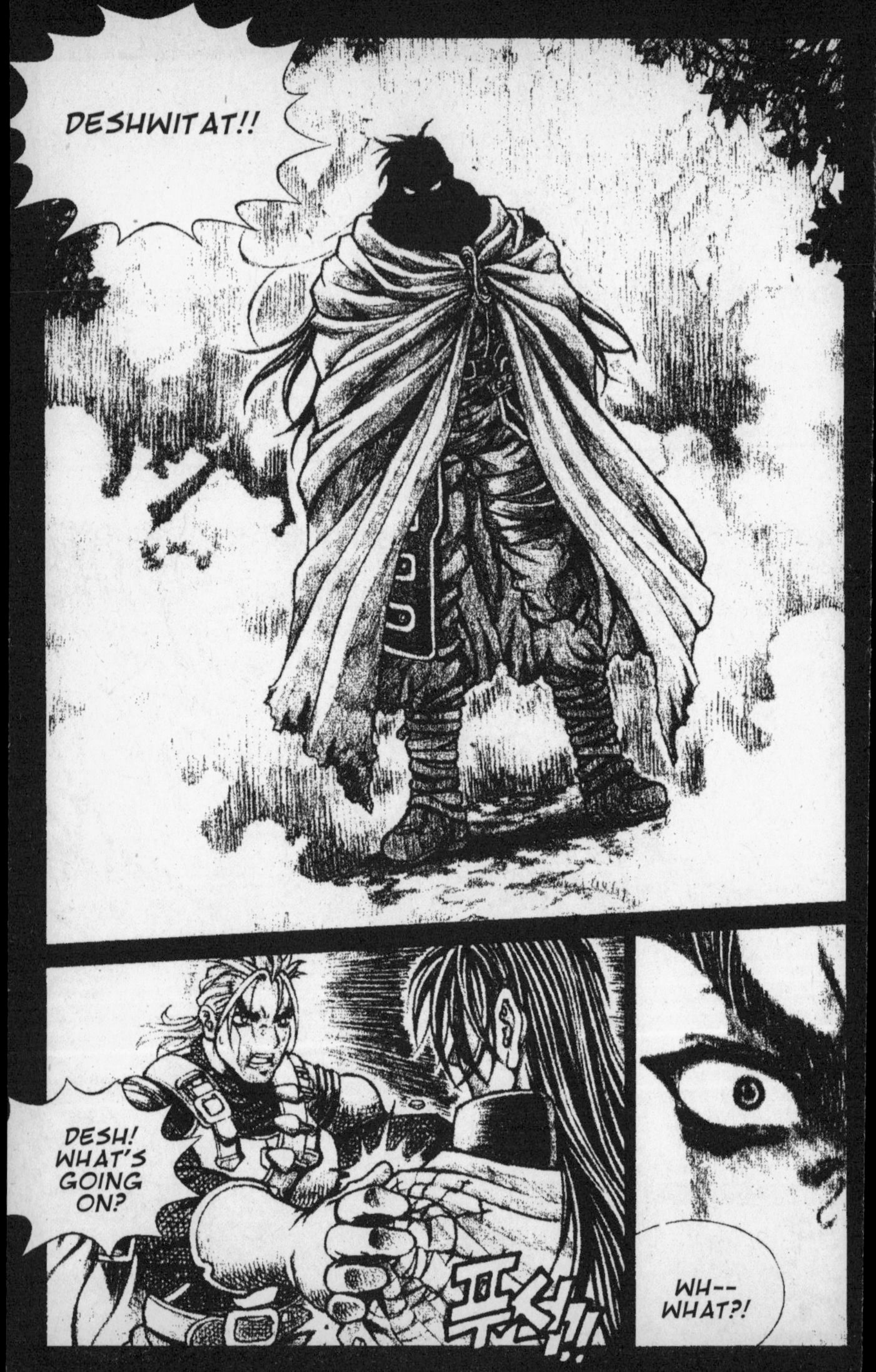
DESHWITAT!!
DESH! WHAT'S GOING ON?
WH-- WHAT?!

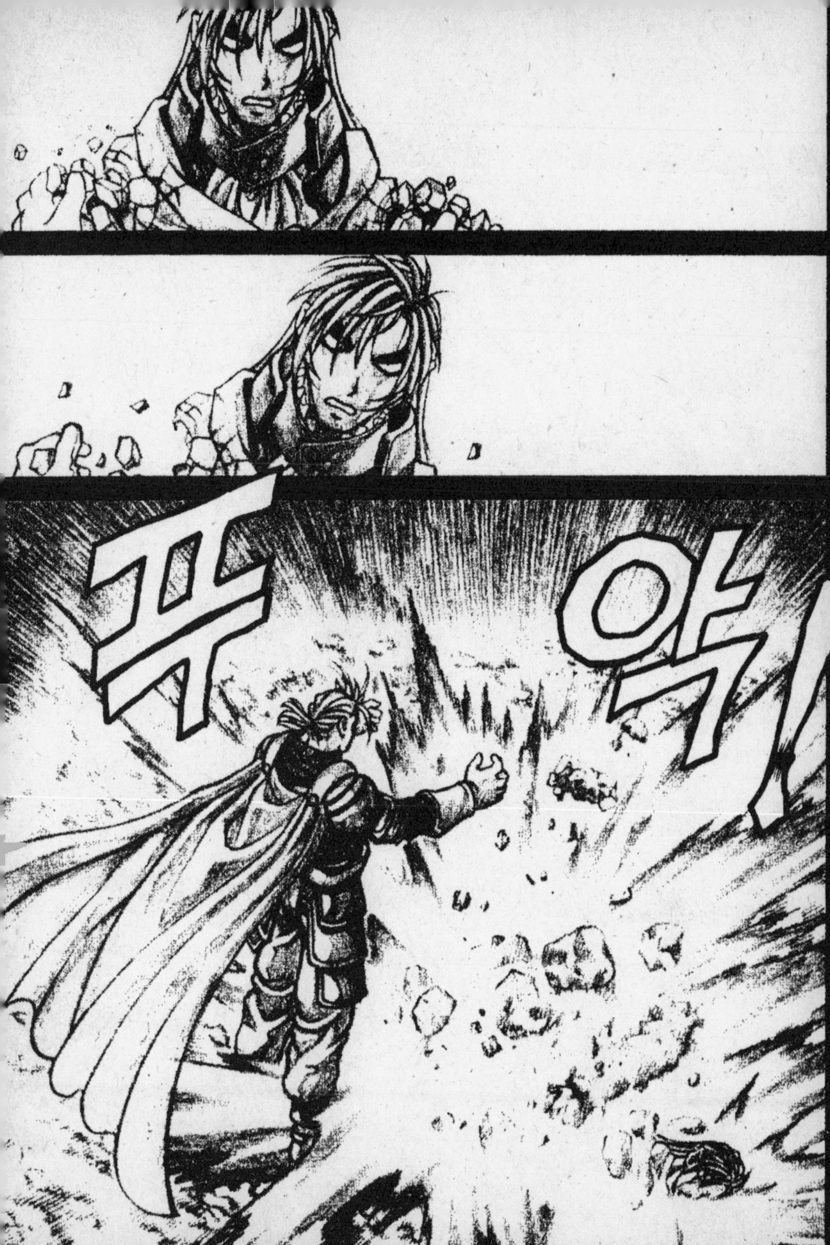
푸악!

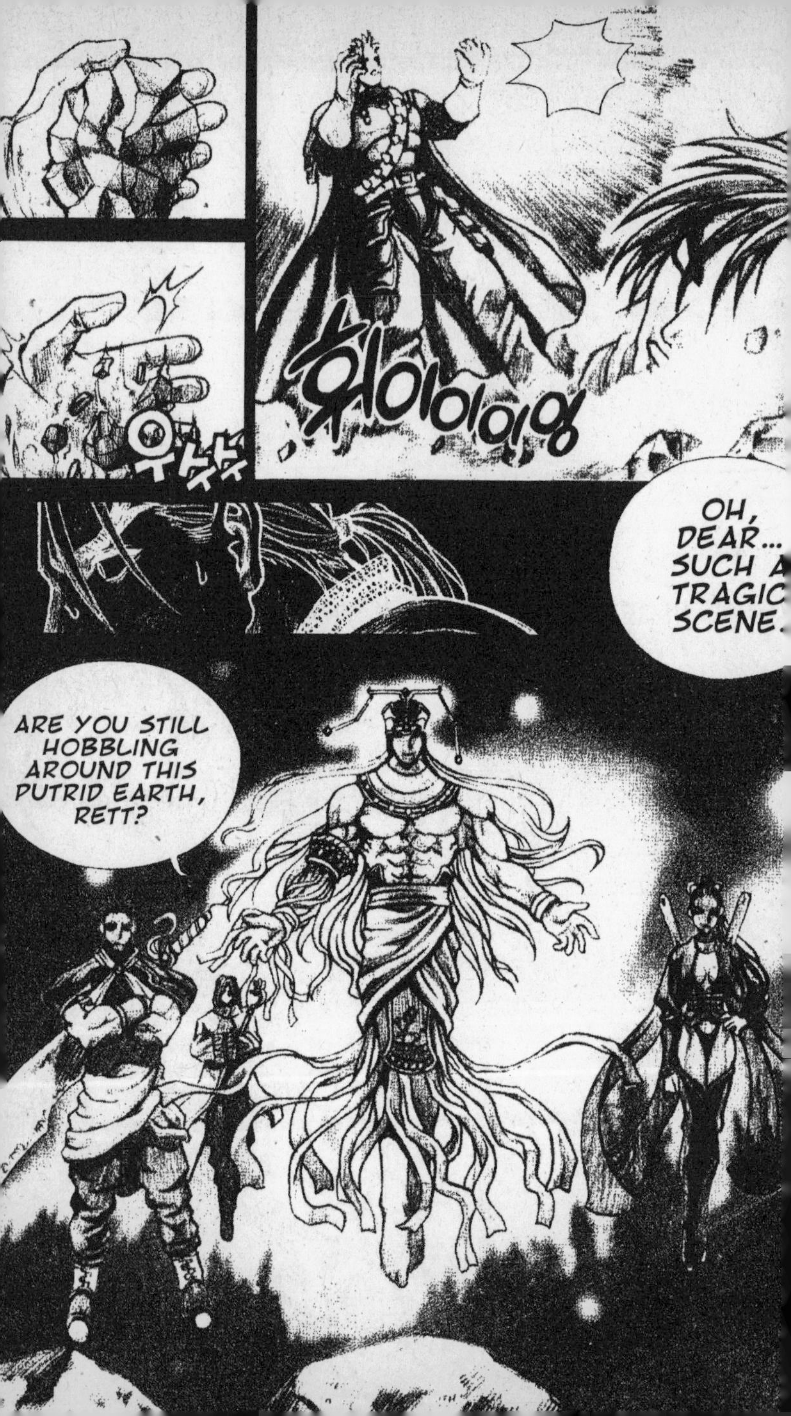
우수수
와이이이이잉
OH, DEAR... SUCH A TRAGIC SCENE.
ARE YOU STILL HOBBLING AROUND THIS PUTRID EARTH, RETT?

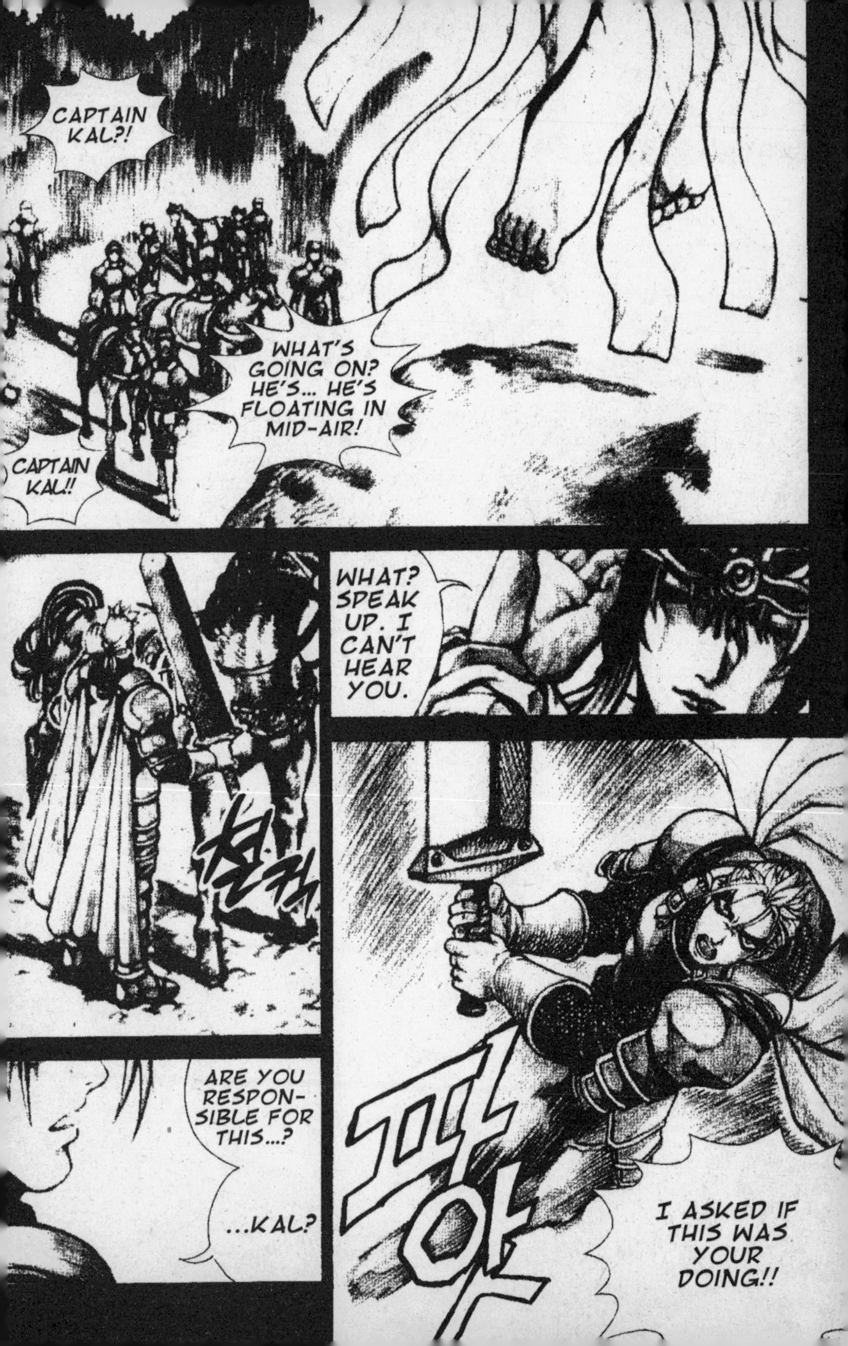
CAPTAIN KAL?!
WHAT'S GOING ON? HE'S... HE'S FLOATING IN MID-AIR!
CAPTAIN KAL!!
WHAT? SPEAK UP. I CAN'T HEAR YOU.
ARE YOU RESPONSIBLE FOR THIS...?
...KAL?
I ASKED IF THIS WAS YOUR DOING!!

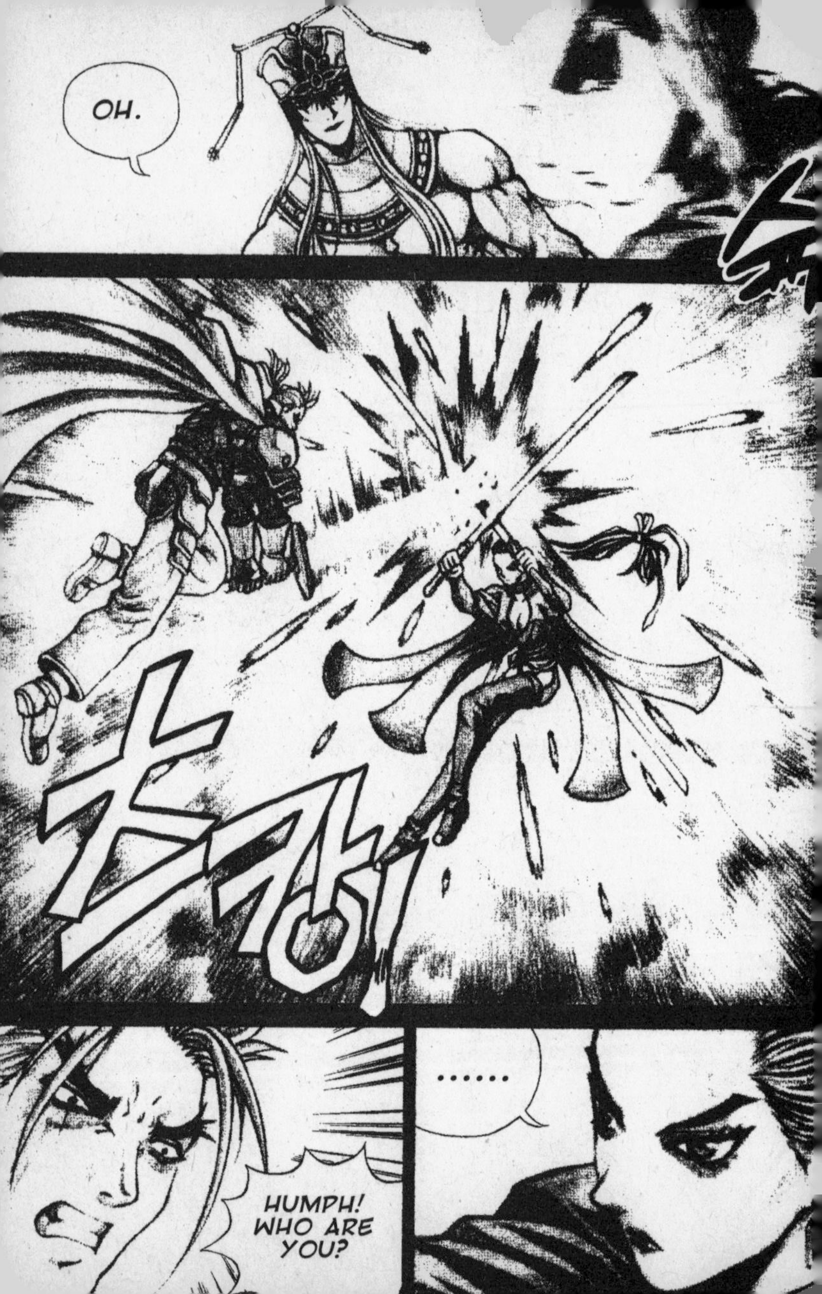
OH.
HUMPH! WHO ARE YOU?
......

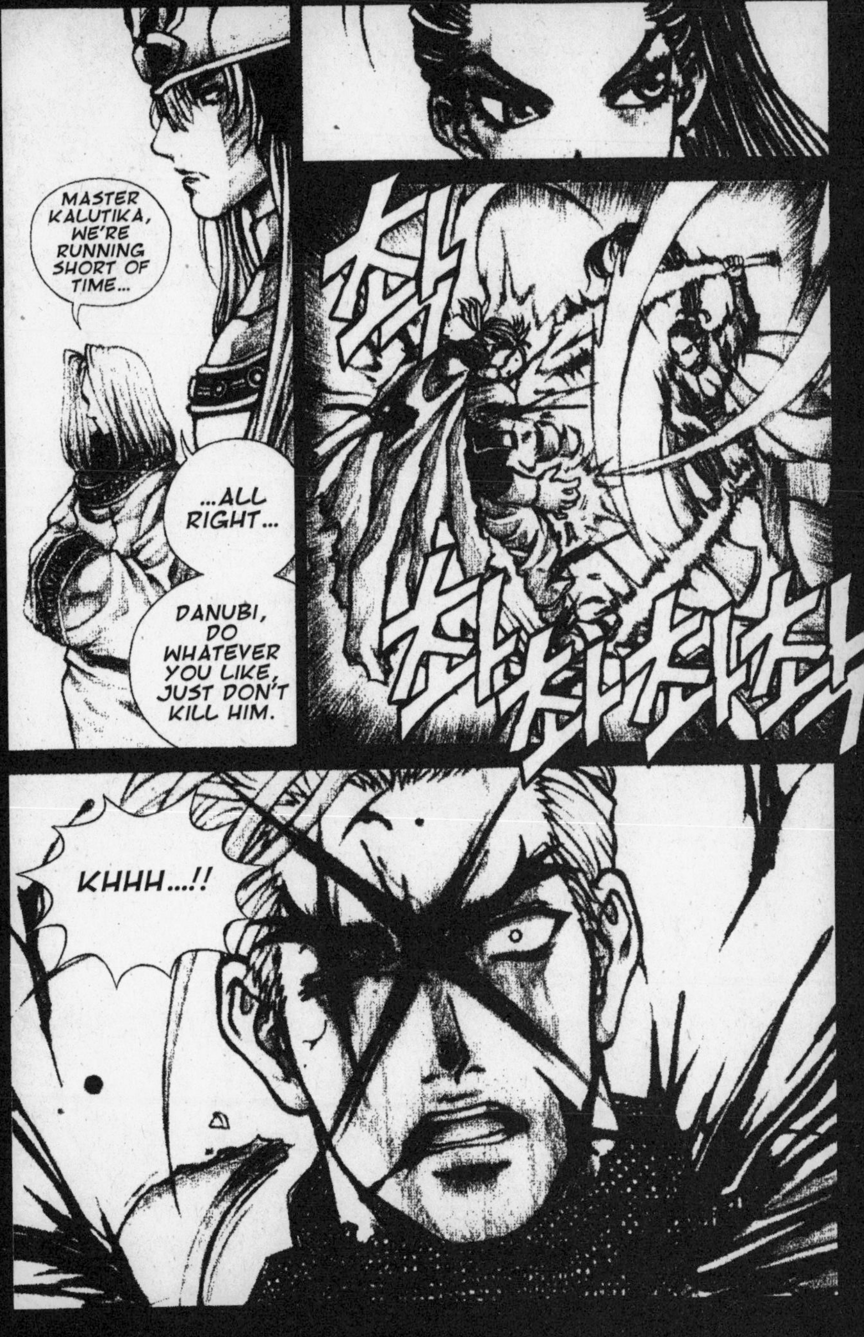
MASTER KALUTIKA, WE'RE RUNNING SHORT OF TIME...
...ALL RIGHT...
DANUBI, DO WHATEVER YOU LIKE, JUST DON'T KILL HIM.
KHHH...!!

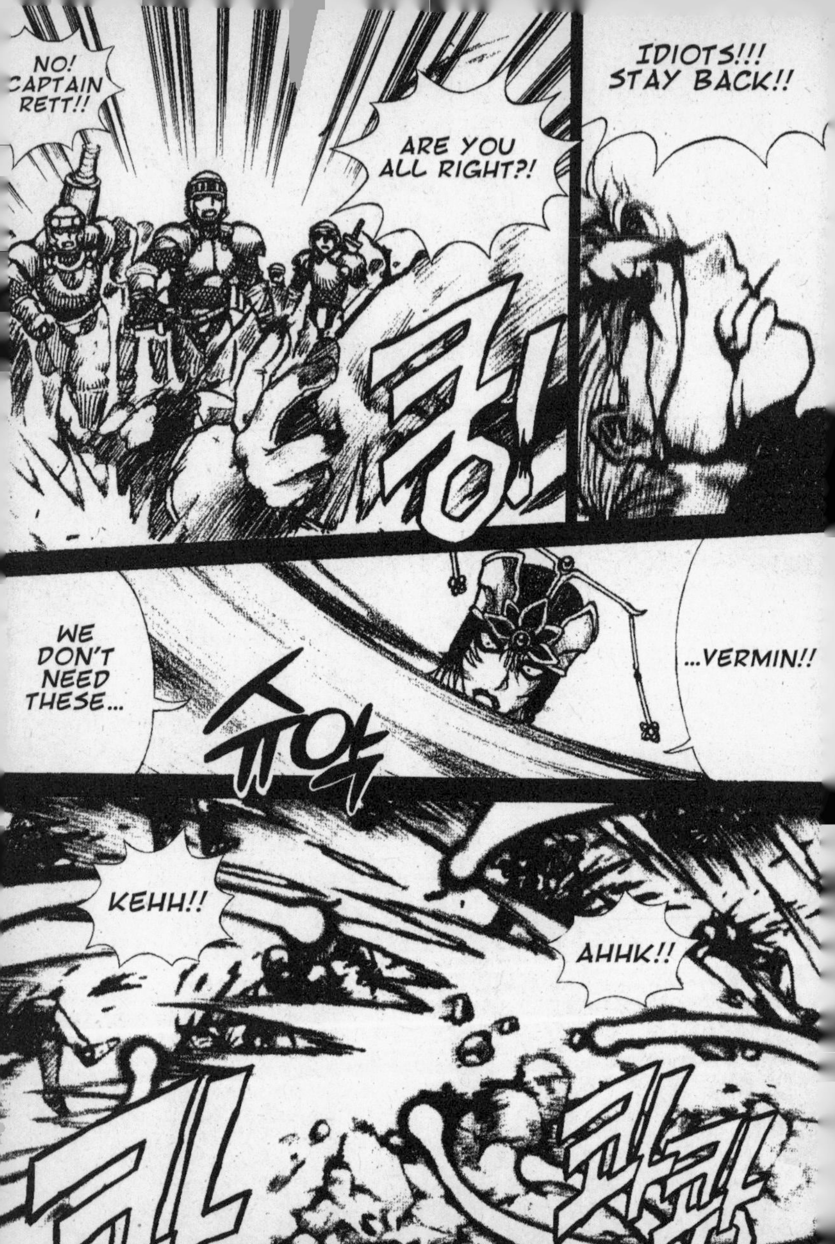
NO! CAPTAIN RETT!!
ARE YOU ALL RIGHT?!
IDIOTS!!! STAY BACK!!
WE DON'T NEED THESE...
...VERMIN!!
KEHH!!
AHHK!!

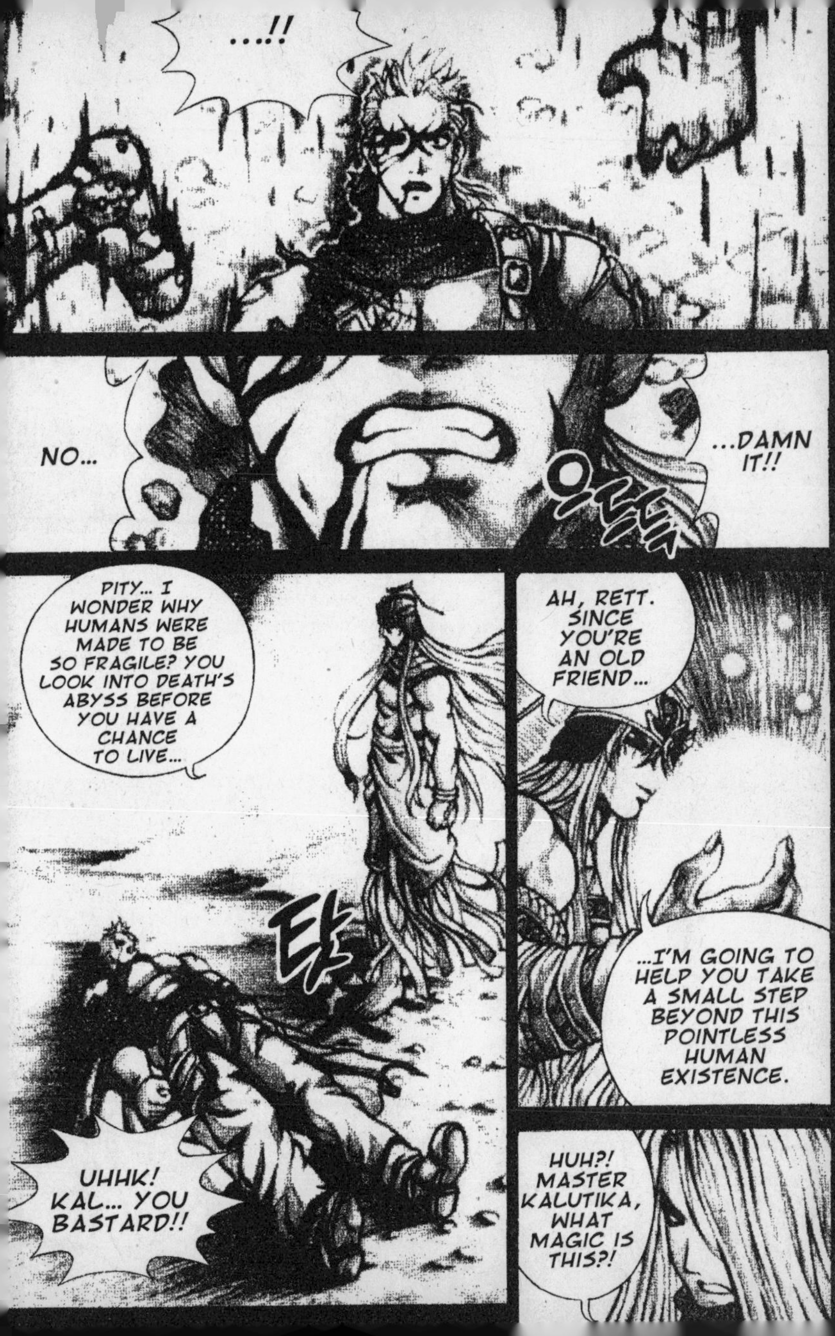
...!!
NO...
...DAMN IT!!
PITY... I WONDER WHY HUMANS WERE MADE TO BE SO FRAGILE? YOU LOOK INTO DEATH'S ABYSS BEFORE YOU HAVE A CHANCE TO LIVE...
탁
UHHK! KAL... YOU BASTARD!!
AH, RETT. SINCE YOU'RE AN OLD FRIEND...
...I'M GOING TO HELP YOU TAKE A SMALL STEP BEYOND THIS POINTLESS HUMAN EXISTENCE.
HUH?! MASTER KALUTIKA, WHAT MAGIC IS THIS?!

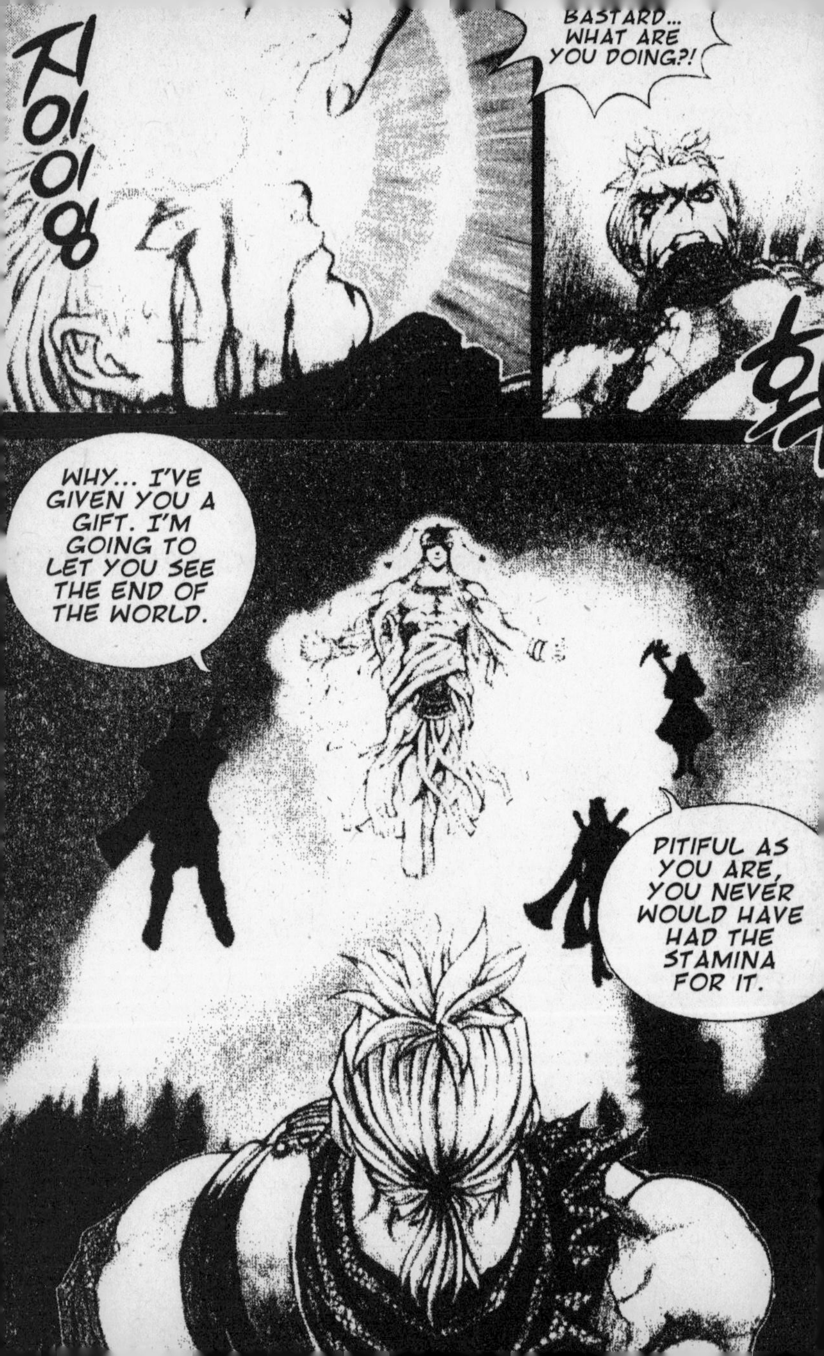

지이이잉
BASTARD... WHAT ARE YOU DOING?!
WHY... I'VE GIVEN YOU A GIFT. I'M GOING TO LET YOU SEE THE END OF THE WORLD.
PITIFUL AS YOU ARE, YOU NEVER WOULD HAVE HAD THE STAMINA FOR IT.

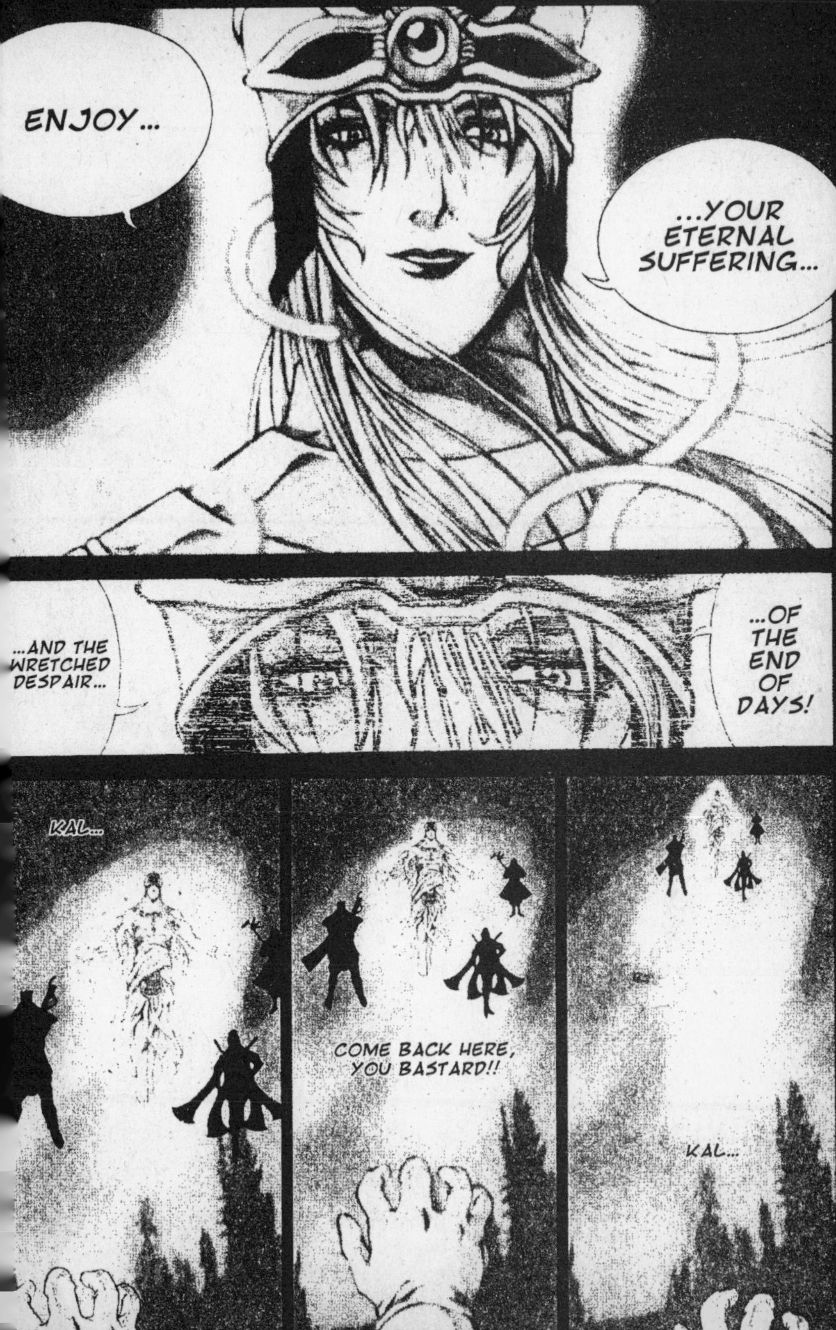
ENJOY...
...YOUR ETERNAL SUFFERING...
...AND THE WRETCHED DESPAIR...
...OF THE END OF DAYS!
KAL...
COME BACK HERE, YOU BASTARD!!
KAL...

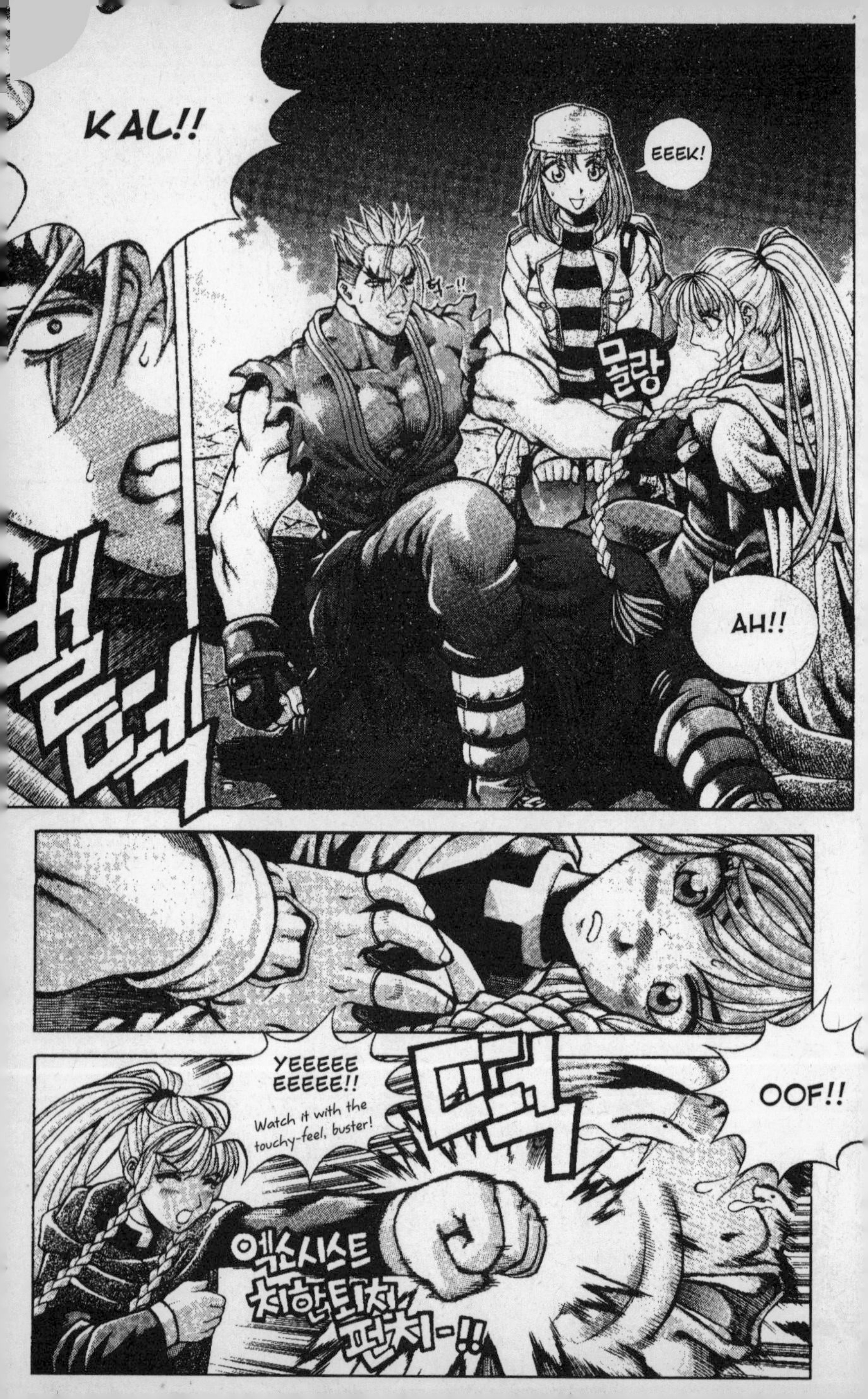

KAL!!
EEEK!
몰랑
AH!!
벌떡
YEEEEE EEEEE!!
Watch it with the touchy-feel, buster!
떡
OOF!!
엑소시스트 치한퇴치 펀치-!!

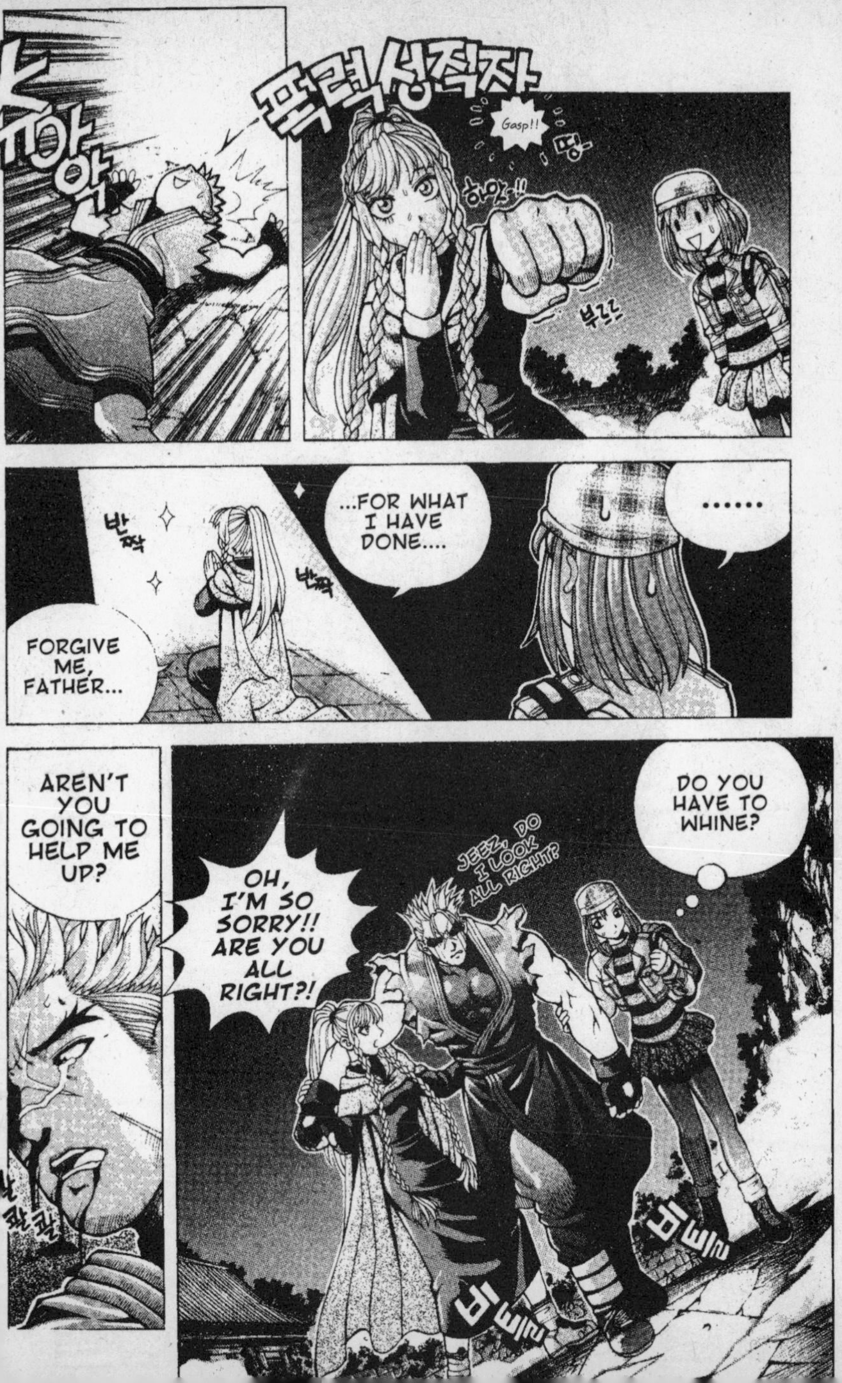

폭력성직자
Gasp!!
하앗!!
부르르
반짝
FORGIVE ME, FATHER...
반짝
...FOR WHAT I HAVE DONE....
......
AREN'T YOU GOING TO HELP ME UP?
OH, I'M SO SORRY!! ARE YOU ALL RIGHT?!
JEEZ, DO I LOOK ALL RIGHT?
DO YOU HAVE TO WHINE?

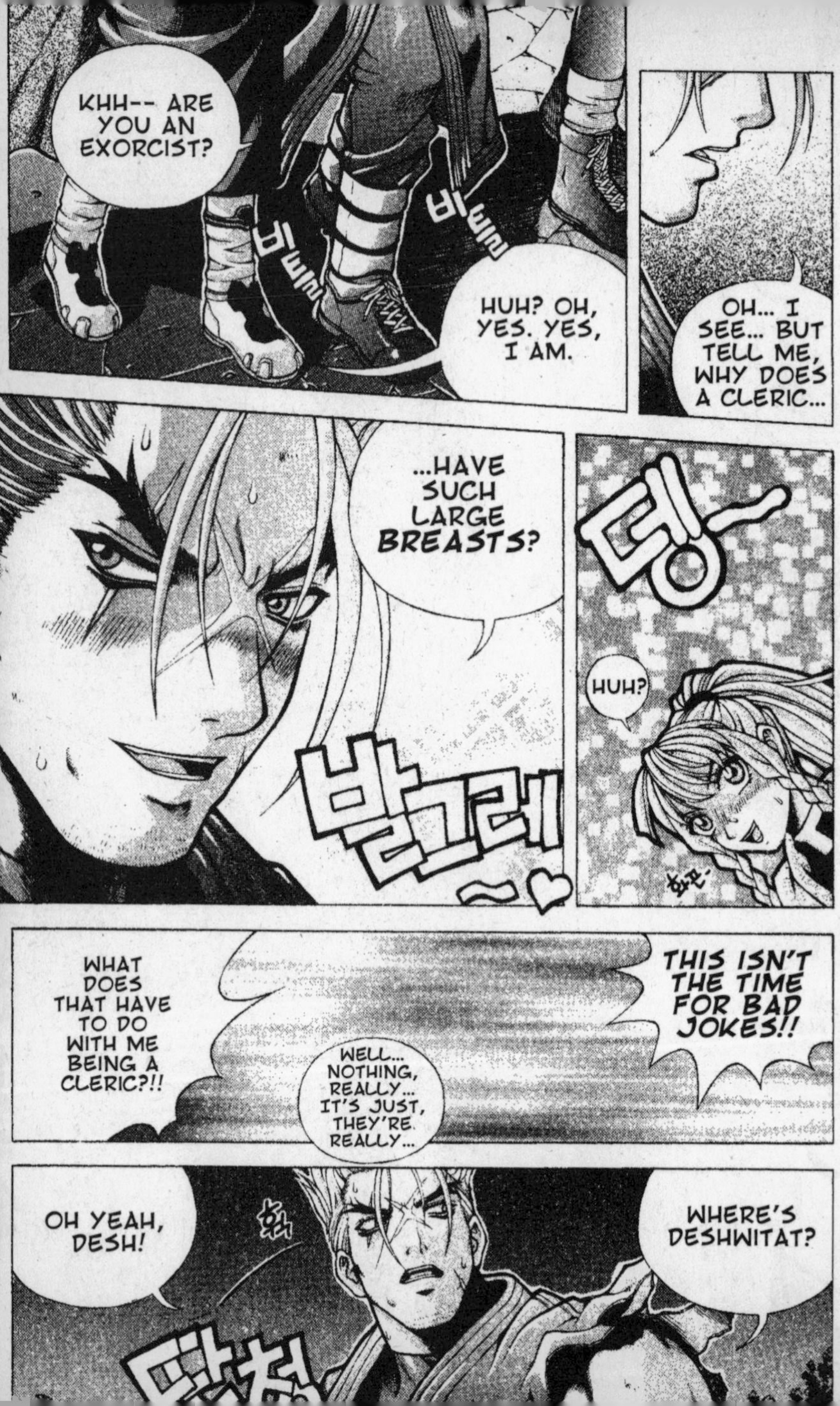
KHH-- ARE YOU AN EXORCIST?
비틀
비틀
HUH? OH, YES. YES, I AM.
OH... I SEE... BUT TELL ME, WHY DOES A CLERIC...
...HAVE SUCH LARGE BREASTS?
발그레~
덩~
HUH?
WHAT DOES THAT HAVE TO DO WITH ME BEING A CLERIC?!!
WELL... NOTHING, REALLY... IT'S JUST, THEY'RE REALLY...
THIS ISN'T THE TIME FOR BAD JOKES!!
OH YEAH, DESH!
WHERE'S DESHWITAT?

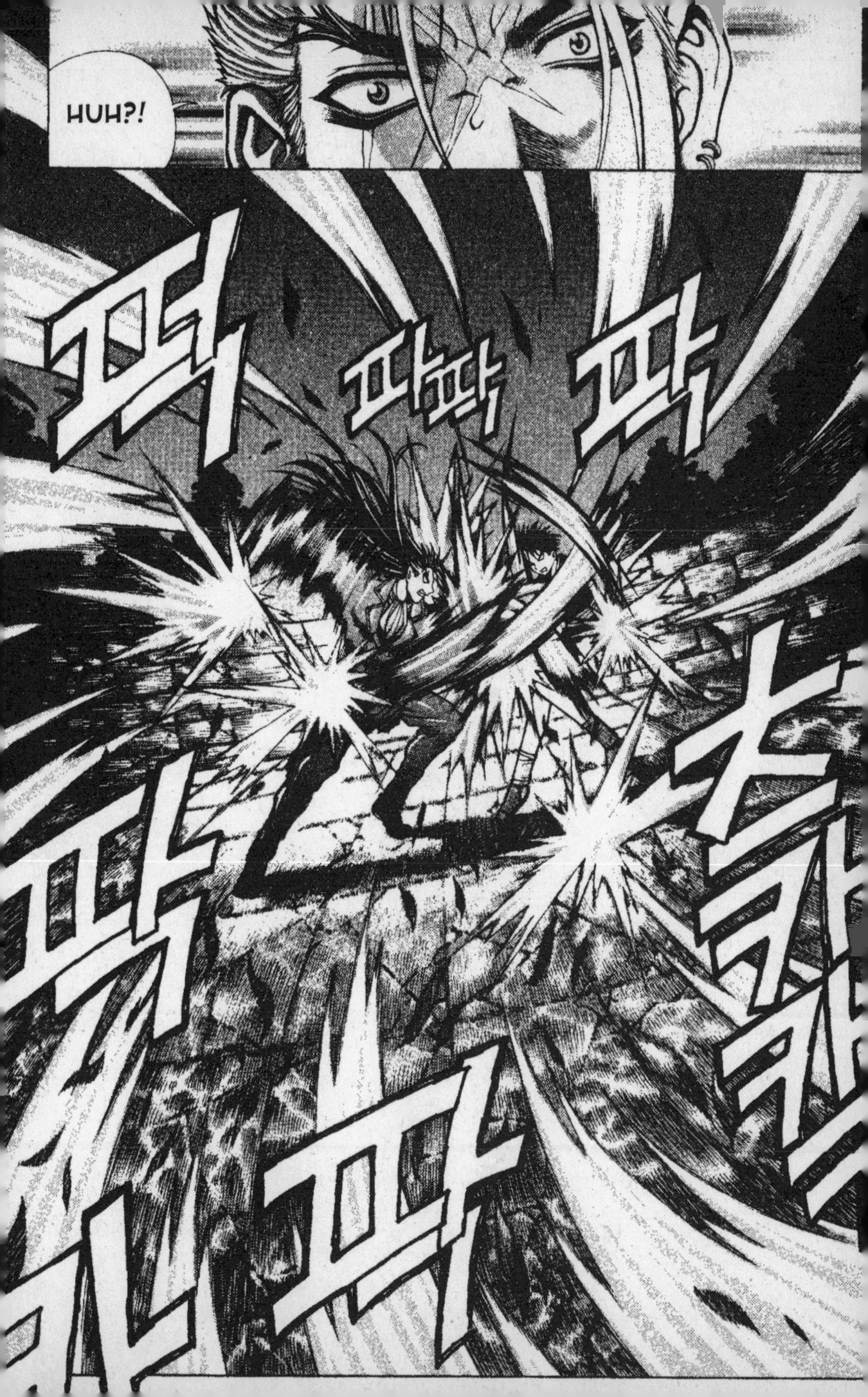
HUH?!

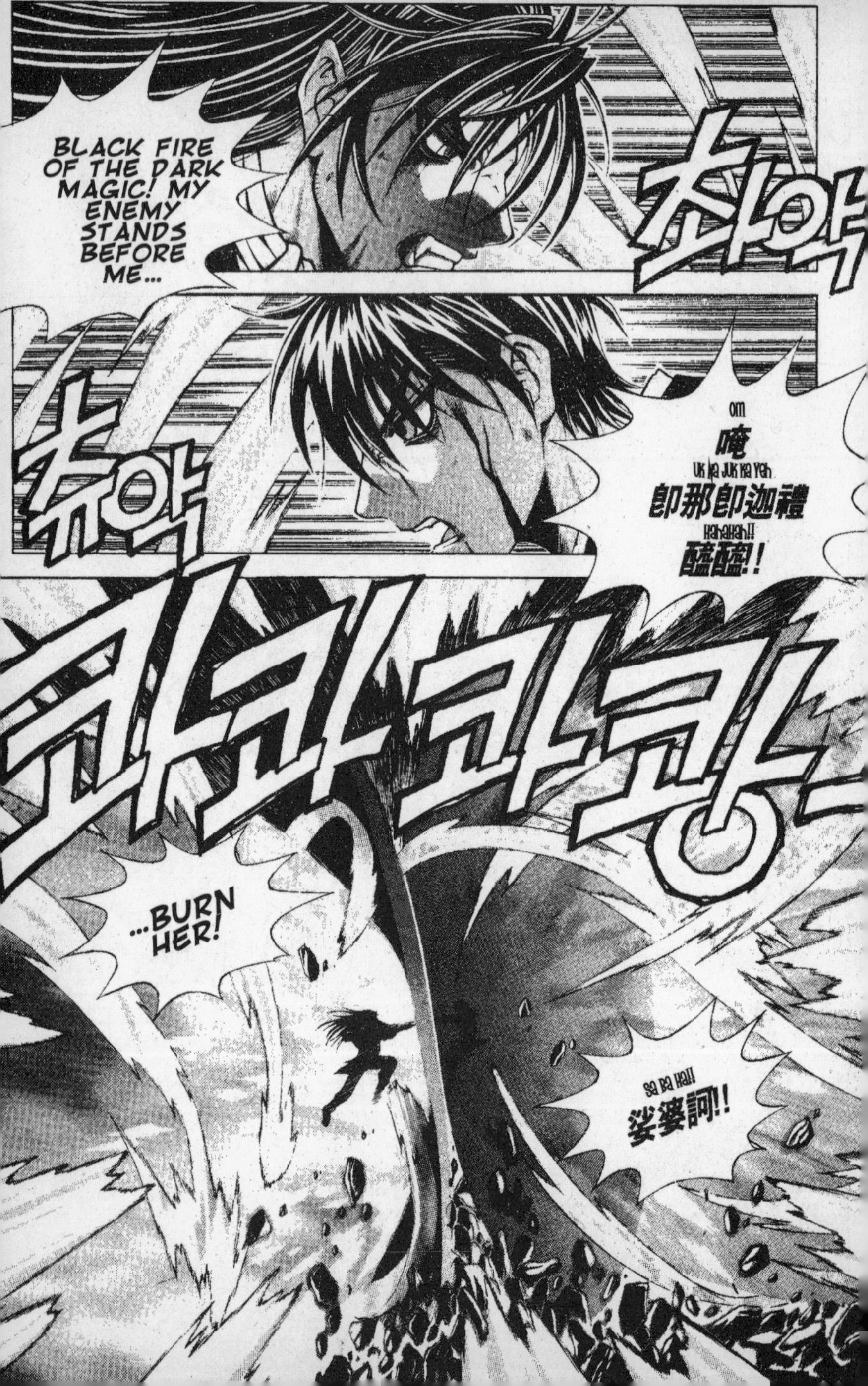
BLACK FIRE OF THE DARK MAGIC! MY ENEMY STANDS BEFORE ME...
촤아악
om
唵
UK KA JUK KA YEH
卽那卽迦禮
KAHAKAH!!
醯醯!!
...BURN HER!
SA BA HA!!
娑婆訶!!

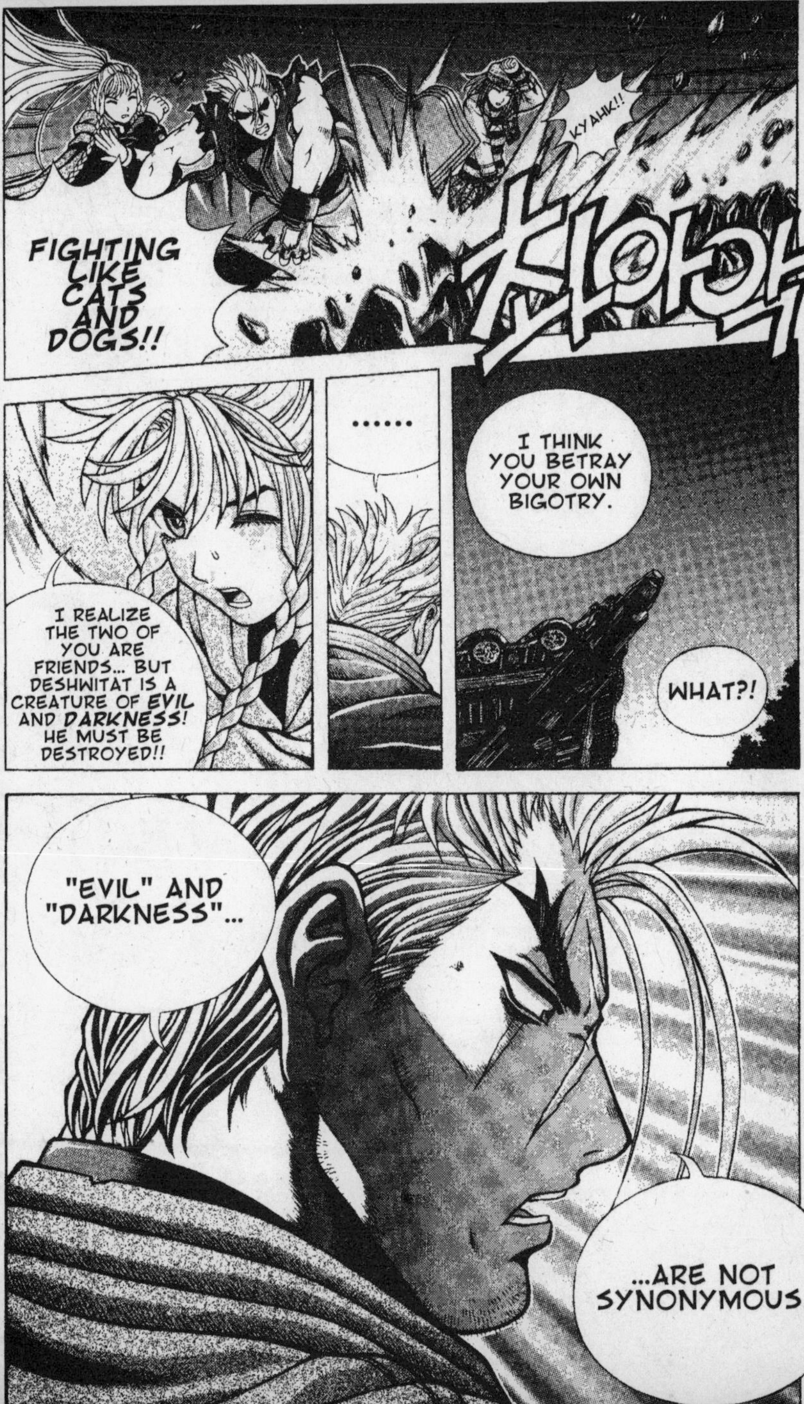

FIGHTING LIKE CATS AND DOGS!!
KYAHK!!
I REALIZE THE TWO OF YOU ARE FRIENDS... BUT DESHWITAT IS A CREATURE OF *EVIL* AND *DARKNESS*! HE MUST BE DESTROYED!!
......
I THINK YOU BETRAY YOUR OWN BIGOTRY.
WHAT?!
"EVIL" AND "DARKNESS"...
...ARE NOT SYNONYMOUS.

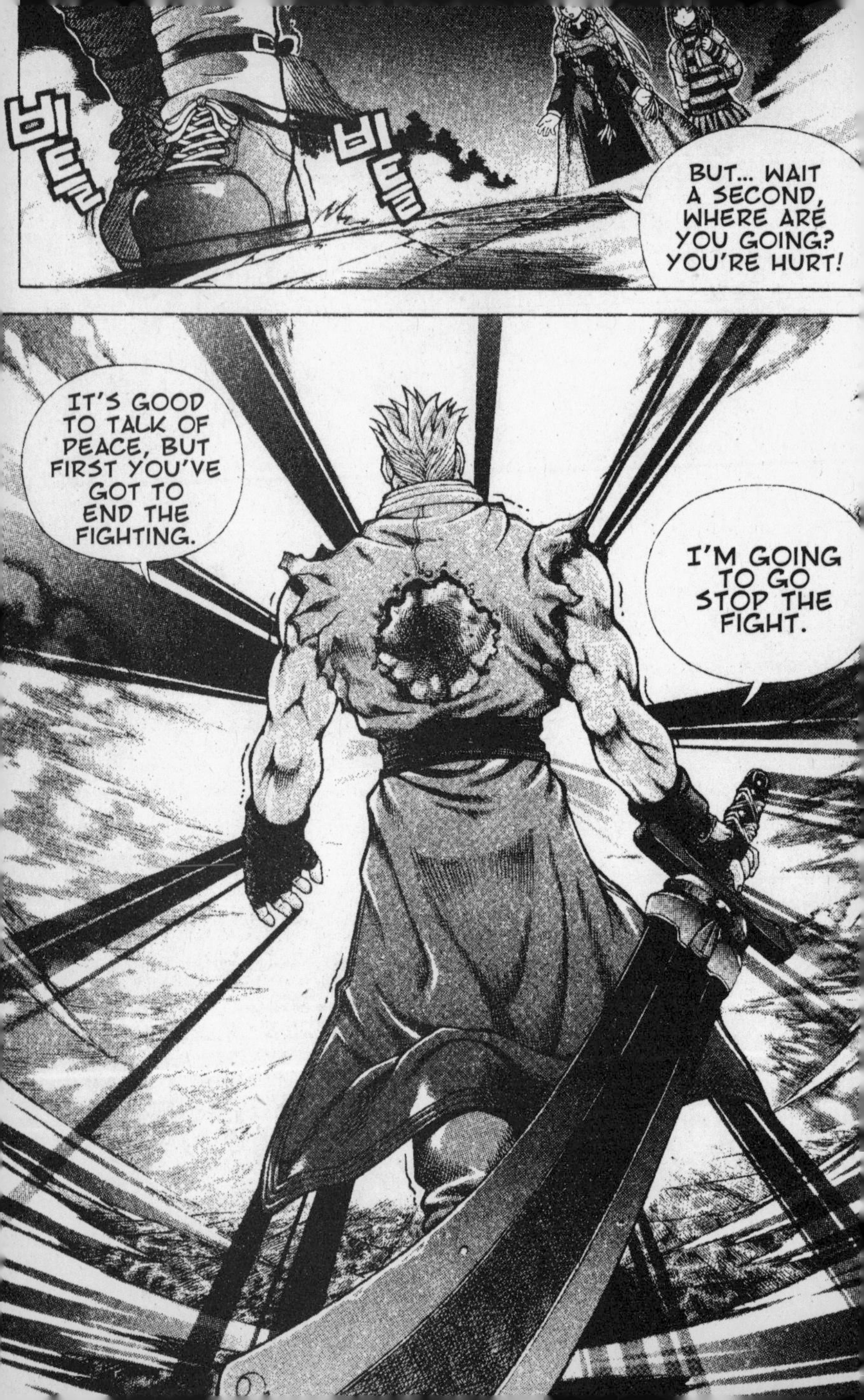
비틀
비틀
BUT... WAIT A SECOND, WHERE ARE YOU GOING? YOU'RE HURT!
IT'S GOOD TO TALK OF PEACE, BUT FIRST YOU'VE GOT TO END THE FIGHTING.
I'M GOING TO GO STOP THE FIGHT.

REBIRTH

Chapter 8: Canceled Orders

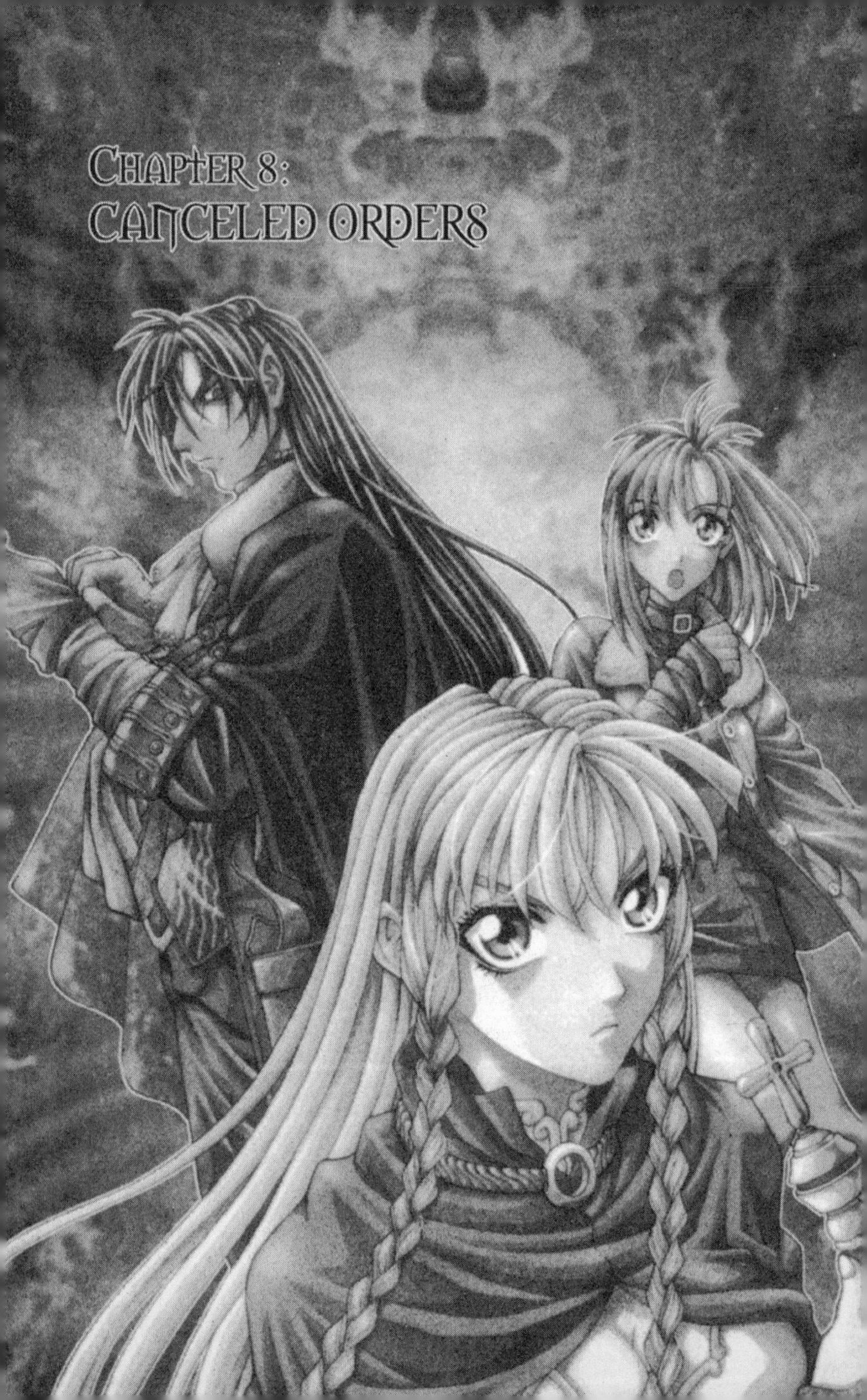

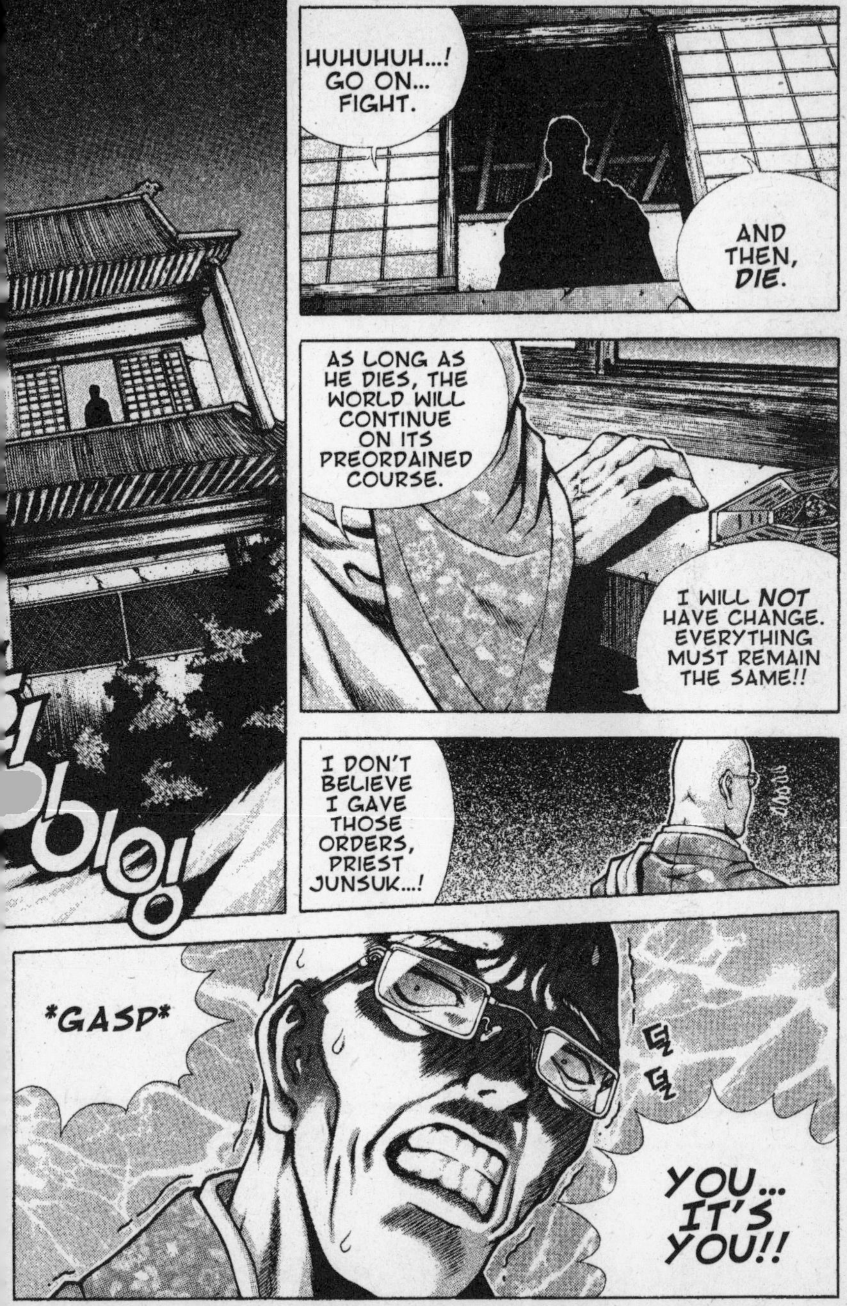
HUHUHUH...! GO ON... FIGHT.
AND THEN, DIE.
AS LONG AS HE DIES, THE WORLD WILL CONTINUE ON ITS PREORDAINED COURSE.
I WILL NOT HAVE CHANGE. EVERYTHING MUST REMAIN THE SAME!!
I DON'T BELIEVE I GAVE THOSE ORDERS, PRIEST JUNSUK...!
GASP
덜 덜
YOU... IT'S YOU!!

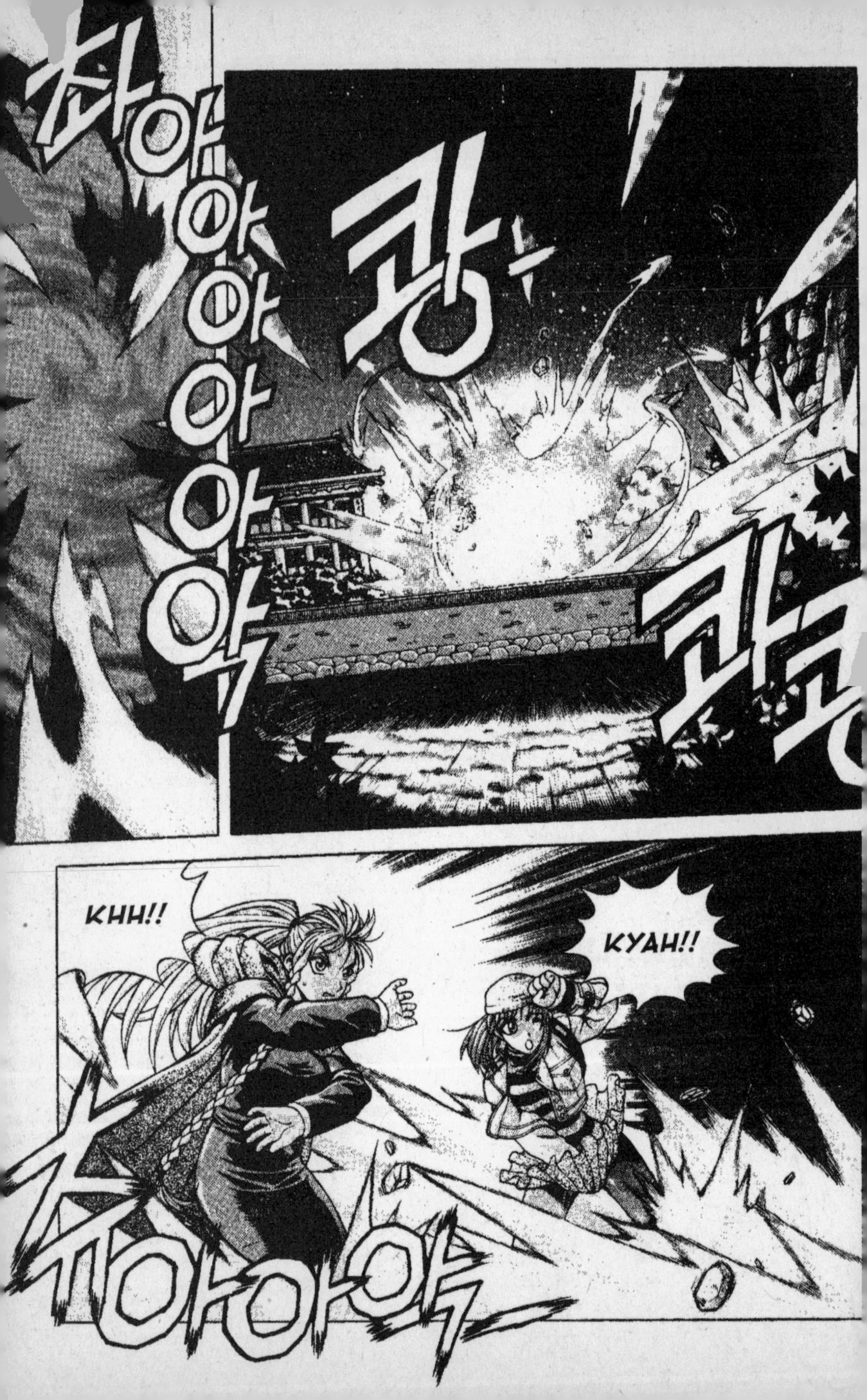
광
KHH!!
KYAH!!

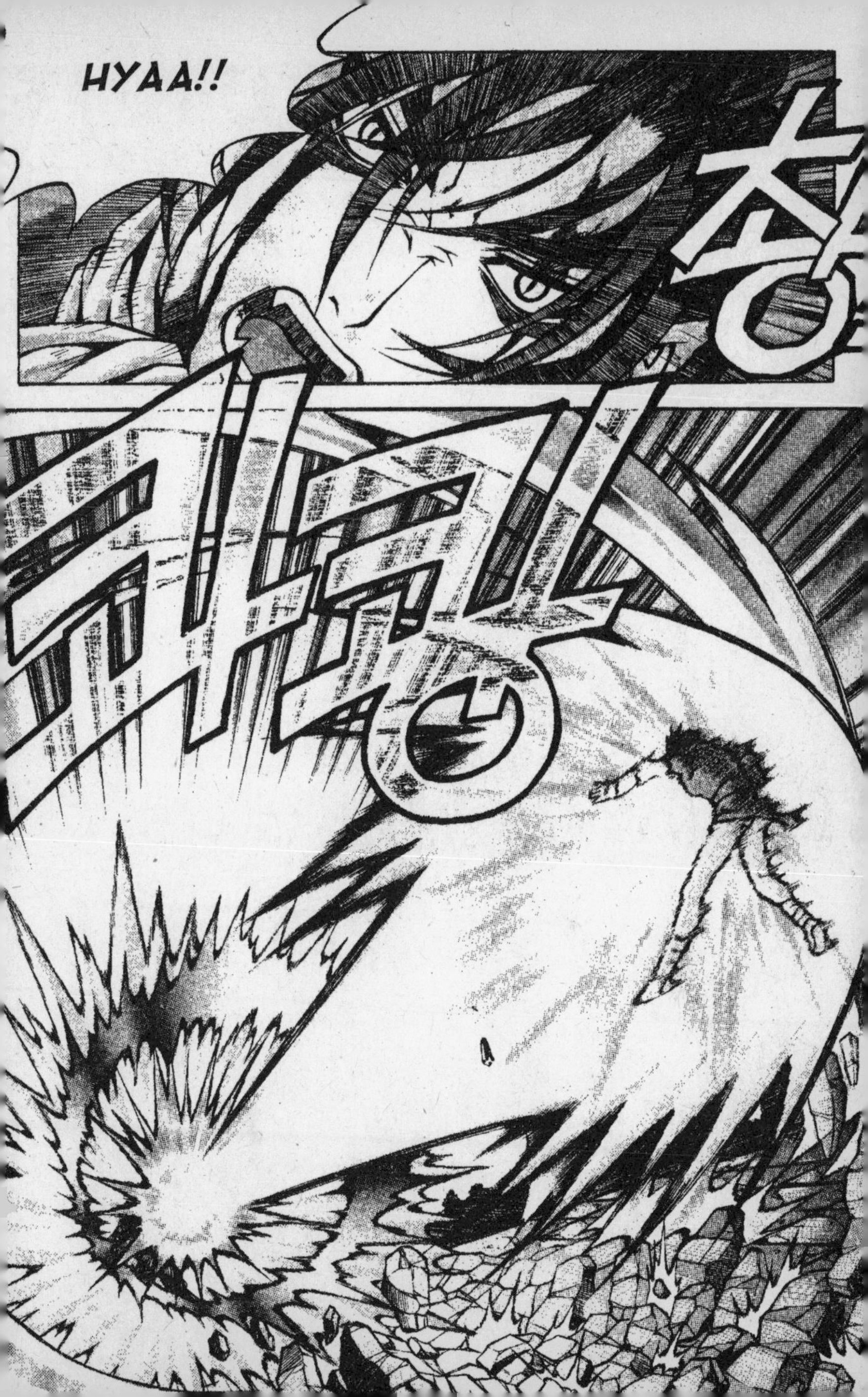
HYAA!!

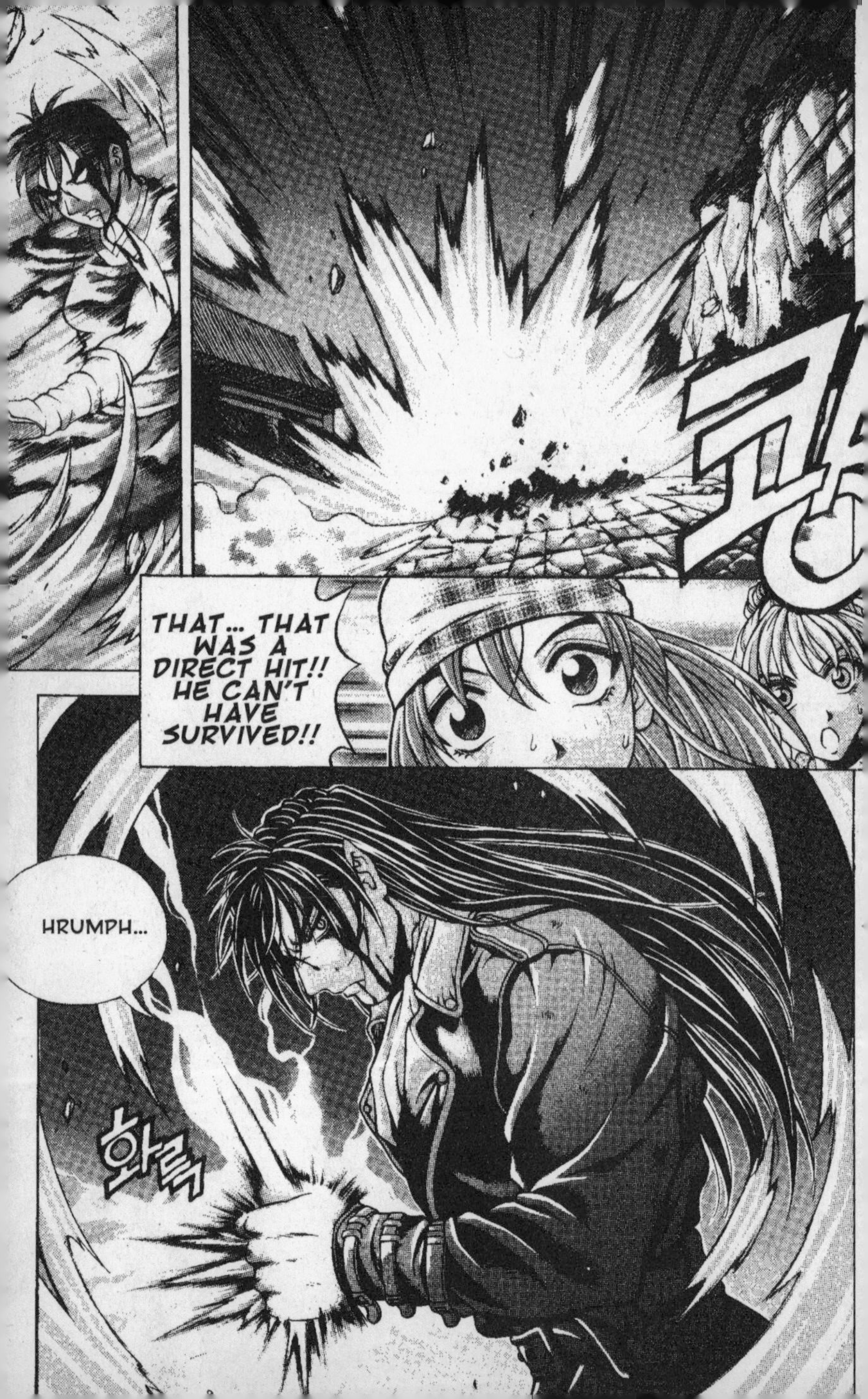
THAT... THAT WAS A DIRECT HIT!! HE CAN'T HAVE SURVIVED!!
HRUMPH...
화륵

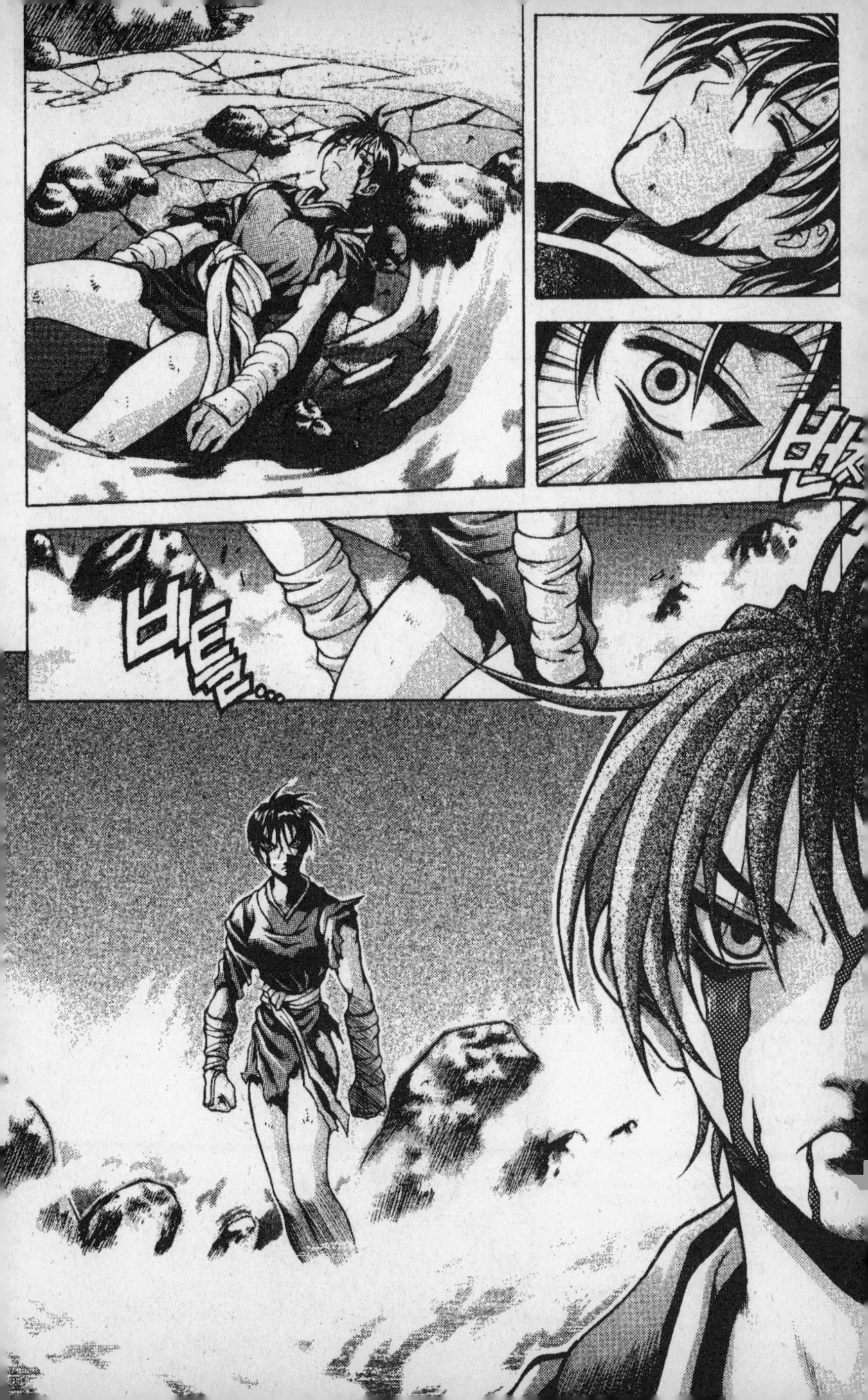
비틀...

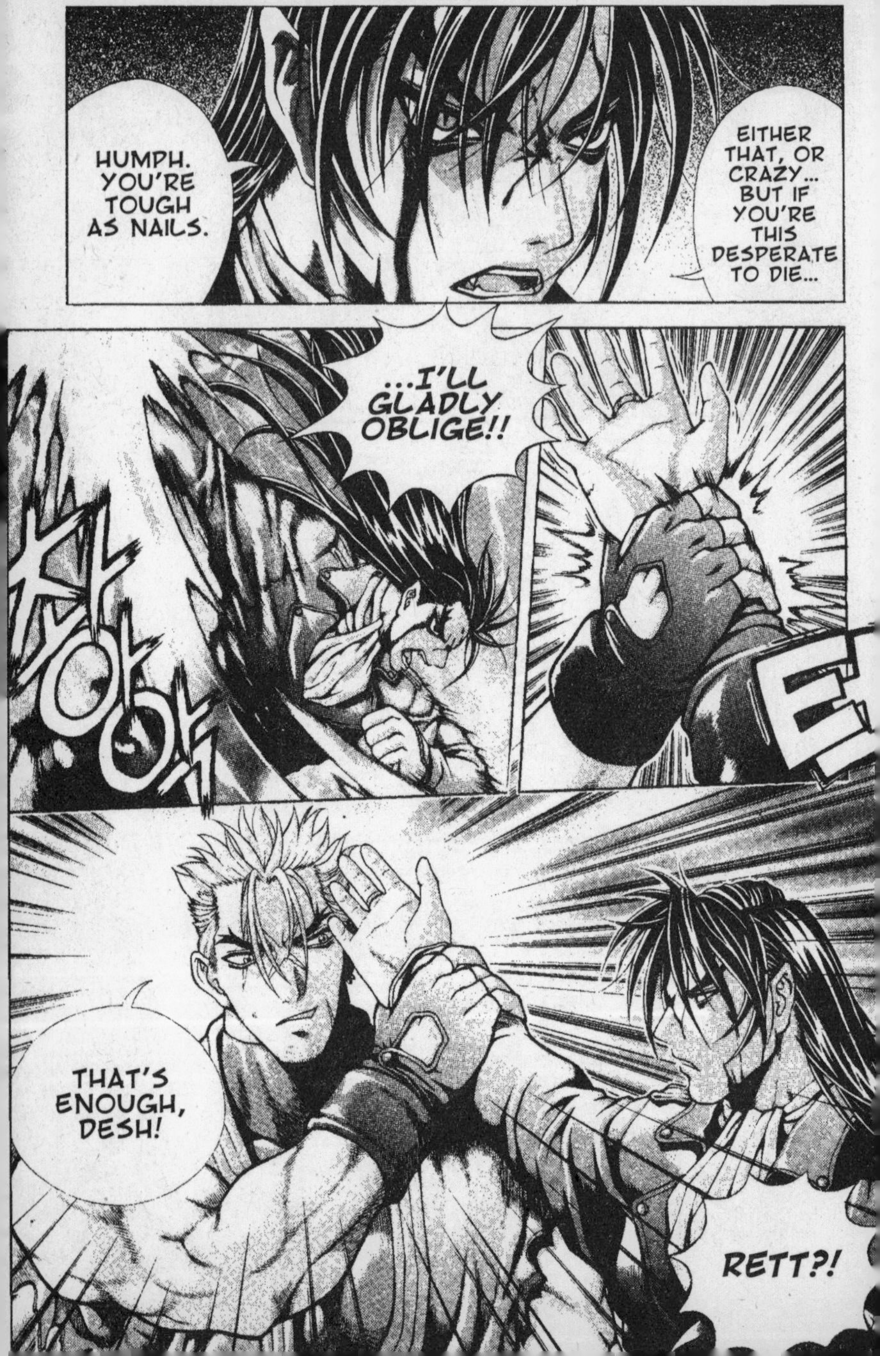

HUMPH. YOU'RE TOUGH AS NAILS.
EITHER THAT, OR CRAZY... BUT IF YOU'RE THIS DESPERATE TO DIE...
...I'LL GLADLY OBLIGE!!
THAT'S ENOUGH, DESH!
RETT?!

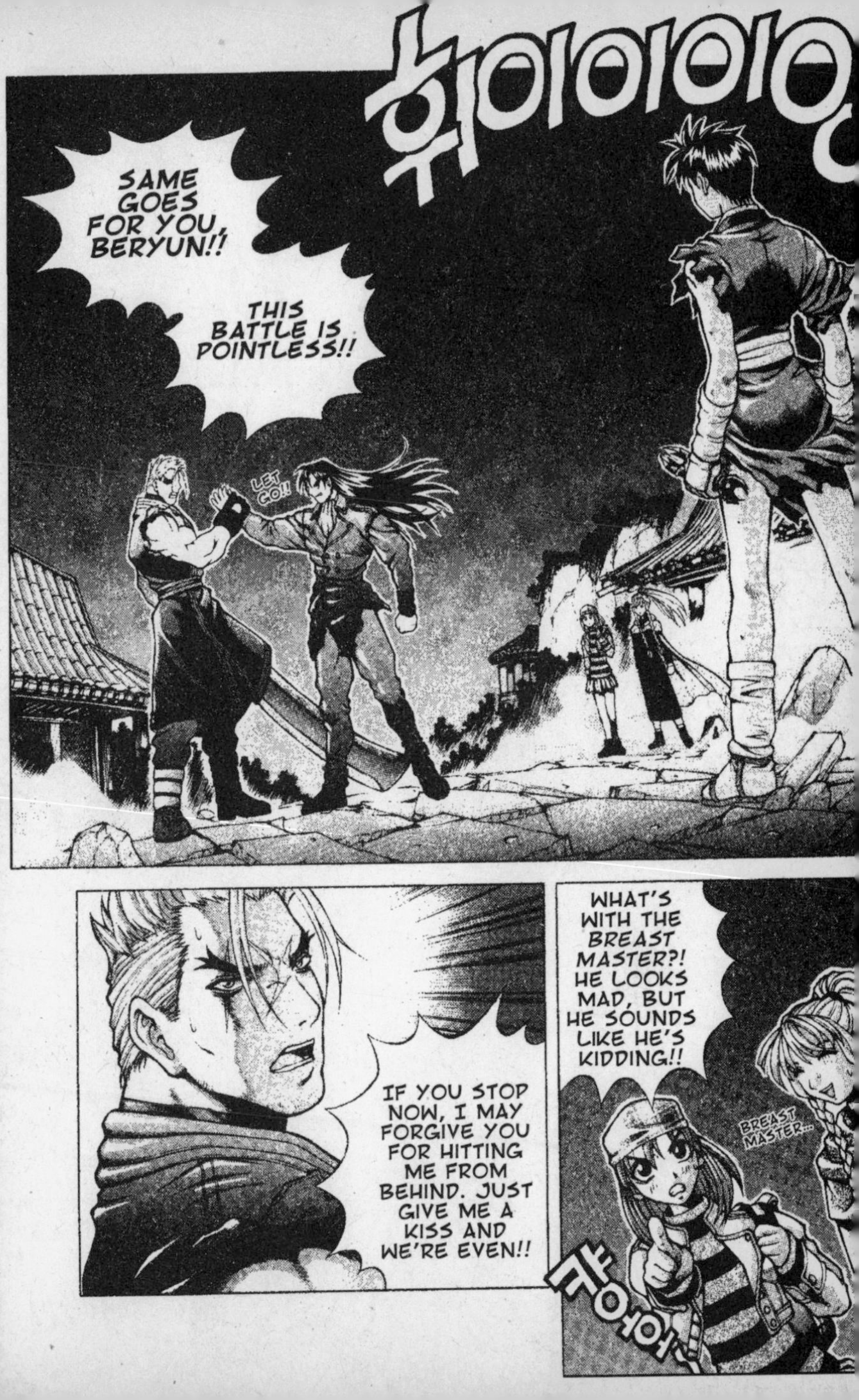
SAME GOES FOR YOU, BERYUN!!
THIS BATTLE IS POINTLESS!!
LET GO!!
IF YOU STOP NOW, I MAY FORGIVE YOU FOR HITTING ME FROM BEHIND. JUST GIVE ME A KISS AND WE'RE EVEN!!
WHAT'S WITH THE BREAST MASTER?! HE LOOKS MAD, BUT HE SOUNDS LIKE HE'S KIDDING!!
BREAST MASTER...

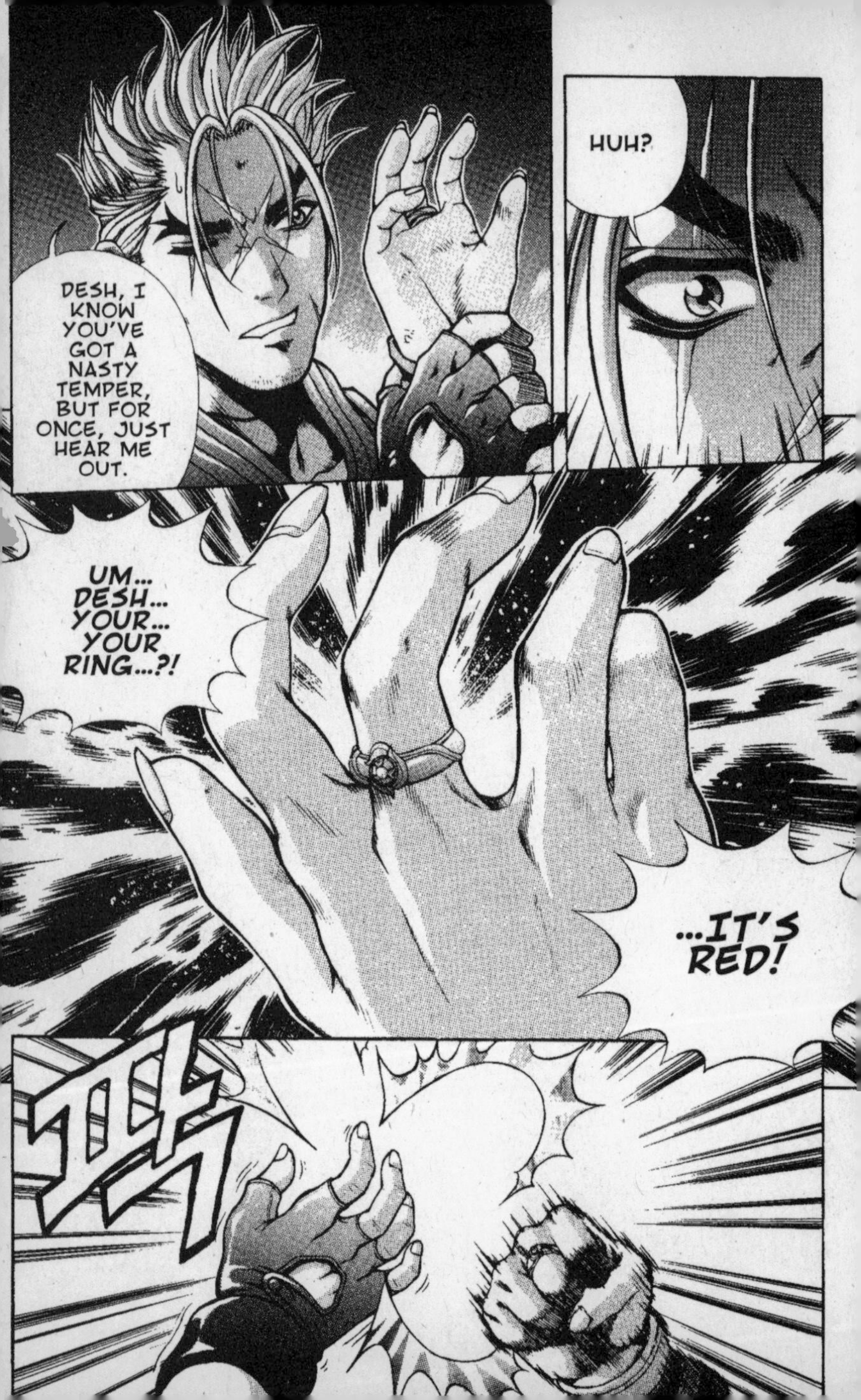
DESH, I KNOW YOU'VE GOT A NASTY TEMPER, BUT FOR ONCE, JUST HEAR ME OUT.
HUH?
UM... DESH... YOUR... YOUR RING...?!
...IT'S RED!

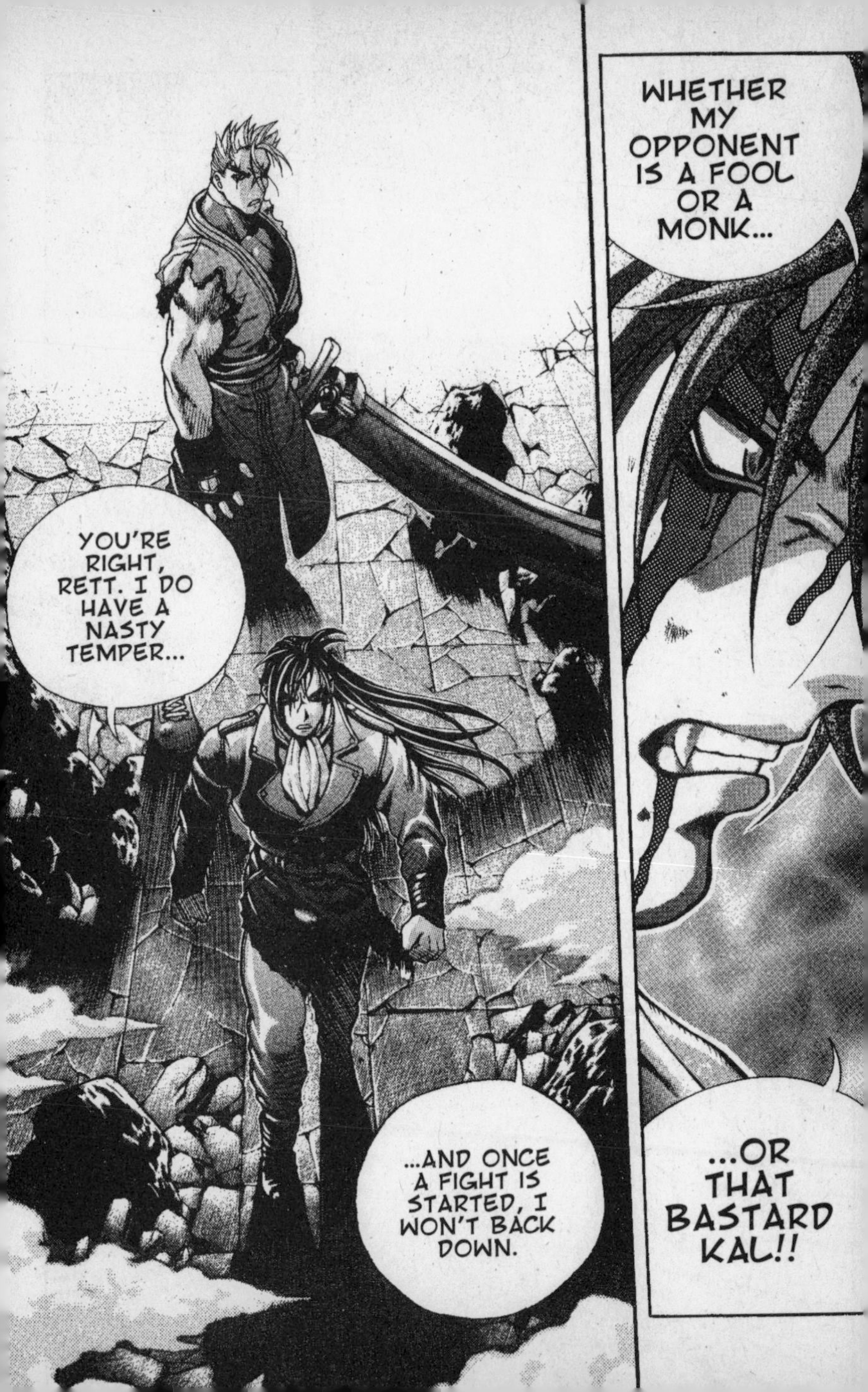
YOU'RE RIGHT, RETT. I DO HAVE A NASTY TEMPER...
...AND ONCE A FIGHT IS STARTED, I WON'T BACK DOWN.
WHETHER MY OPPONENT IS A FOOL OR A MONK...
...OR THAT BASTARD KAL!!

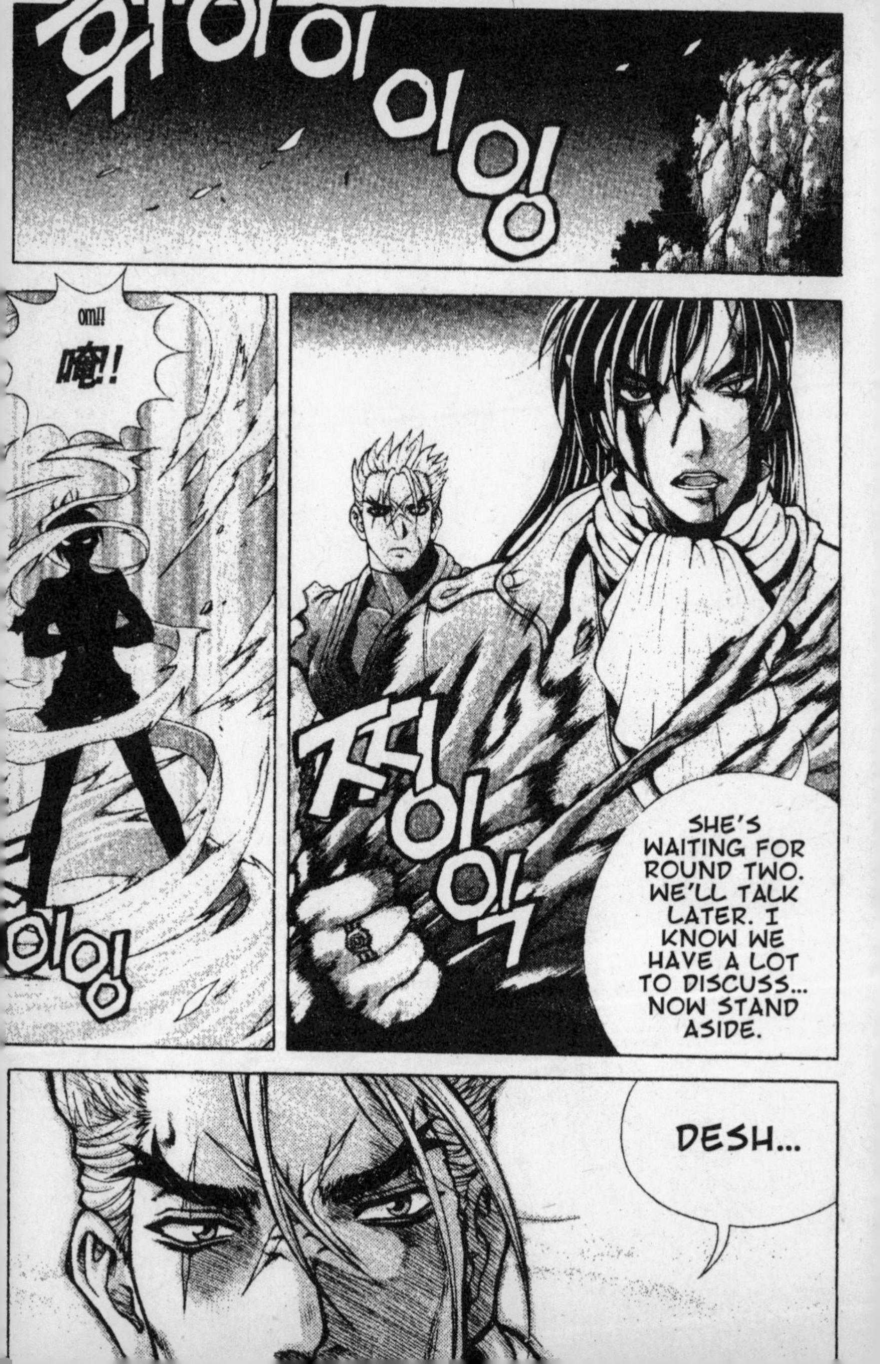
휘이이이잉!
om!!
唵!
SHE'S WAITING FOR ROUND TWO. WE'LL TALK LATER. I KNOW WE HAVE A LOT TO DISCUSS... NOW STAND ASIDE.
DESH...

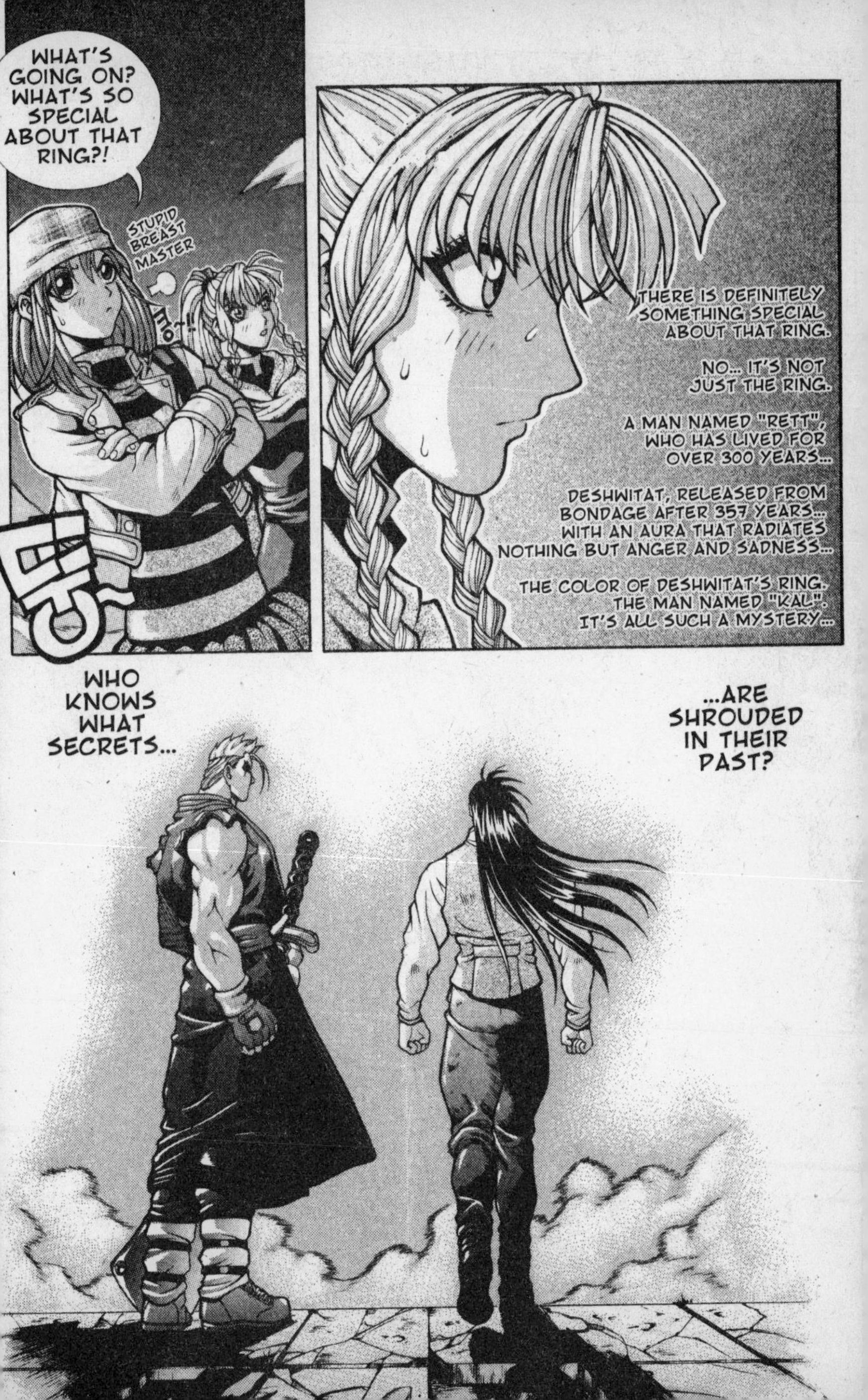
WHAT'S GOING ON? WHAT'S SO SPECIAL ABOUT THAT RING?!
STUPID BREAST MASTER
MO~!!
THERE IS DEFINITELY SOMETHING SPECIAL ABOUT THAT RING.
NO... IT'S NOT JUST THE RING.
A MAN NAMED "RETT", WHO HAS LIVED FOR OVER 300 YEARS...
DESHWITAT, RELEASED FROM BONDAGE AFTER 357 YEARS... WITH AN AURA THAT RADIATES NOTHING BUT ANGER AND SADNESS...
THE COLOR OF DESHWITAT'S RING. THE MAN NAMED "KAL". IT'S ALL SUCH A MYSTERY...
WHO KNOWS WHAT SECRETS...
...ARE SHROUDED IN THEIR PAST?

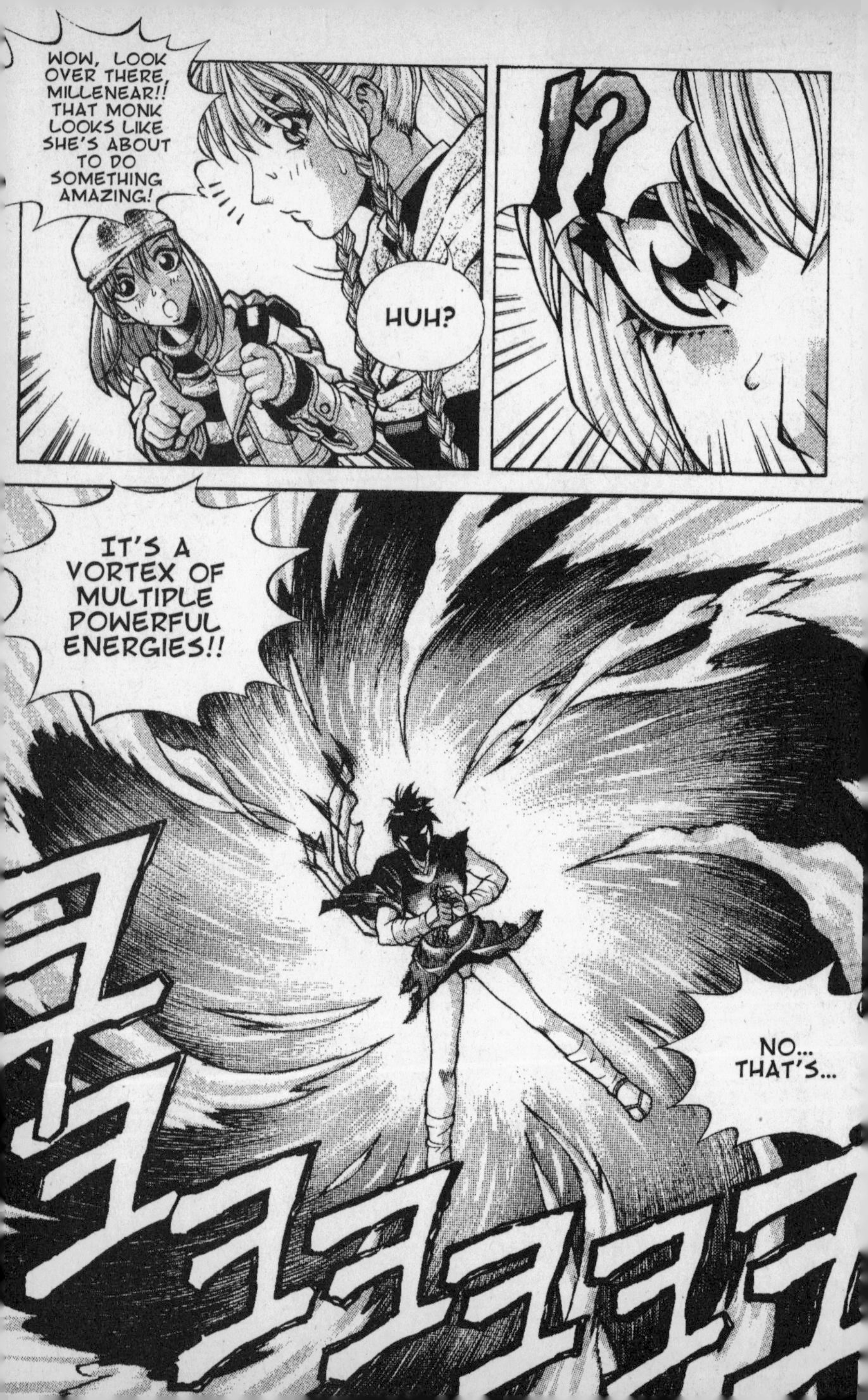
WOW, LOOK OVER THERE, MILLENEAR!! THAT MONK LOOKS LIKE SHE'S ABOUT TO DO SOMETHING AMAZING!
HUH?
!?
IT'S A VORTEX OF MULTIPLE POWERFUL ENERGIES!!
NO... THAT'S...

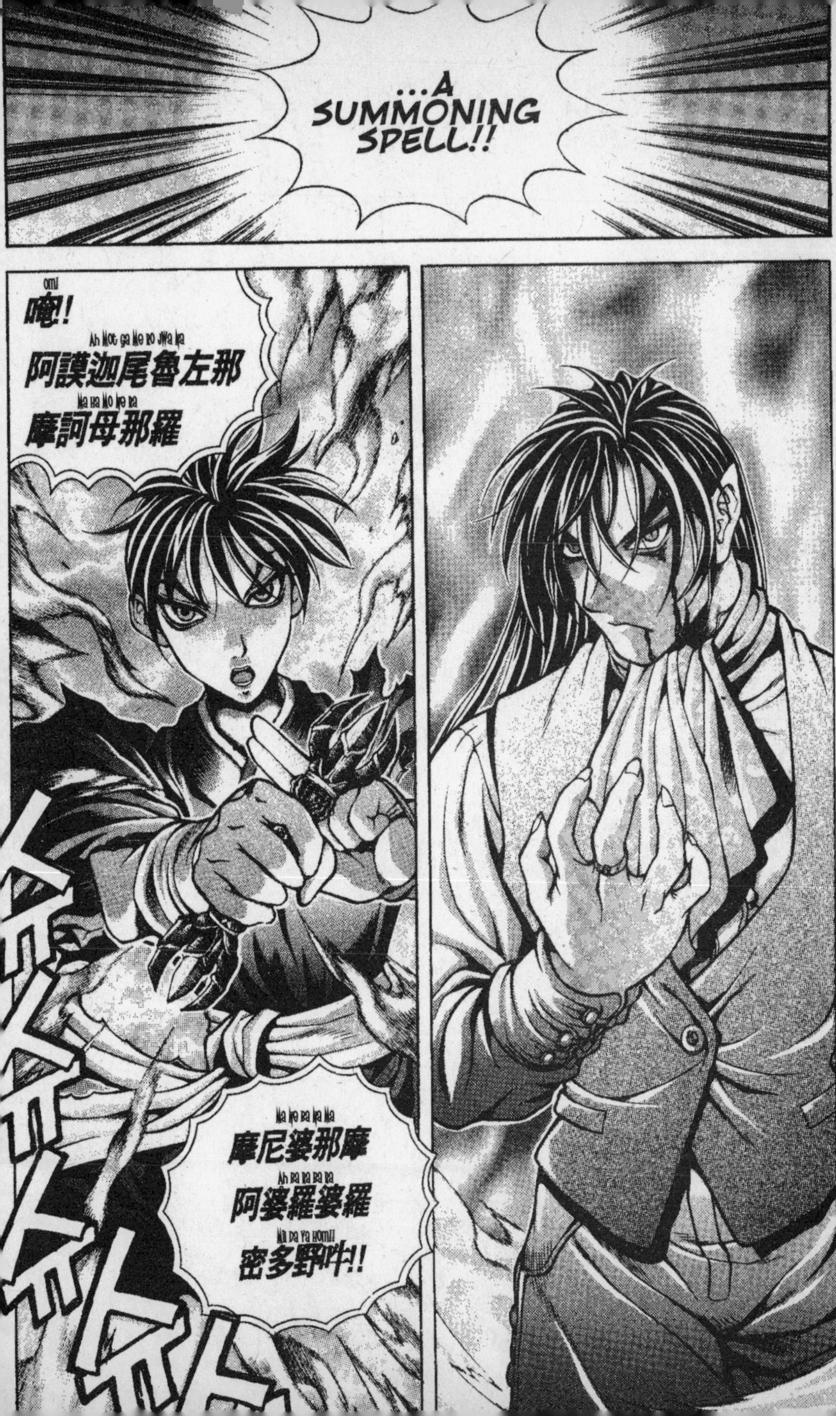
...A SUMMONING SPELL!!
OM! 唵!
Ah Mot ga Me ro jwa ka 阿謨迦尾魯左那
Ma ha Mo ke ra 摩訶母那羅
Ma Ne Ba ka Ma 摩尼婆那摩
Ah Ba ra Ba ra 阿婆羅婆羅
Mi Da Ya HOM!! 密多野吽!!

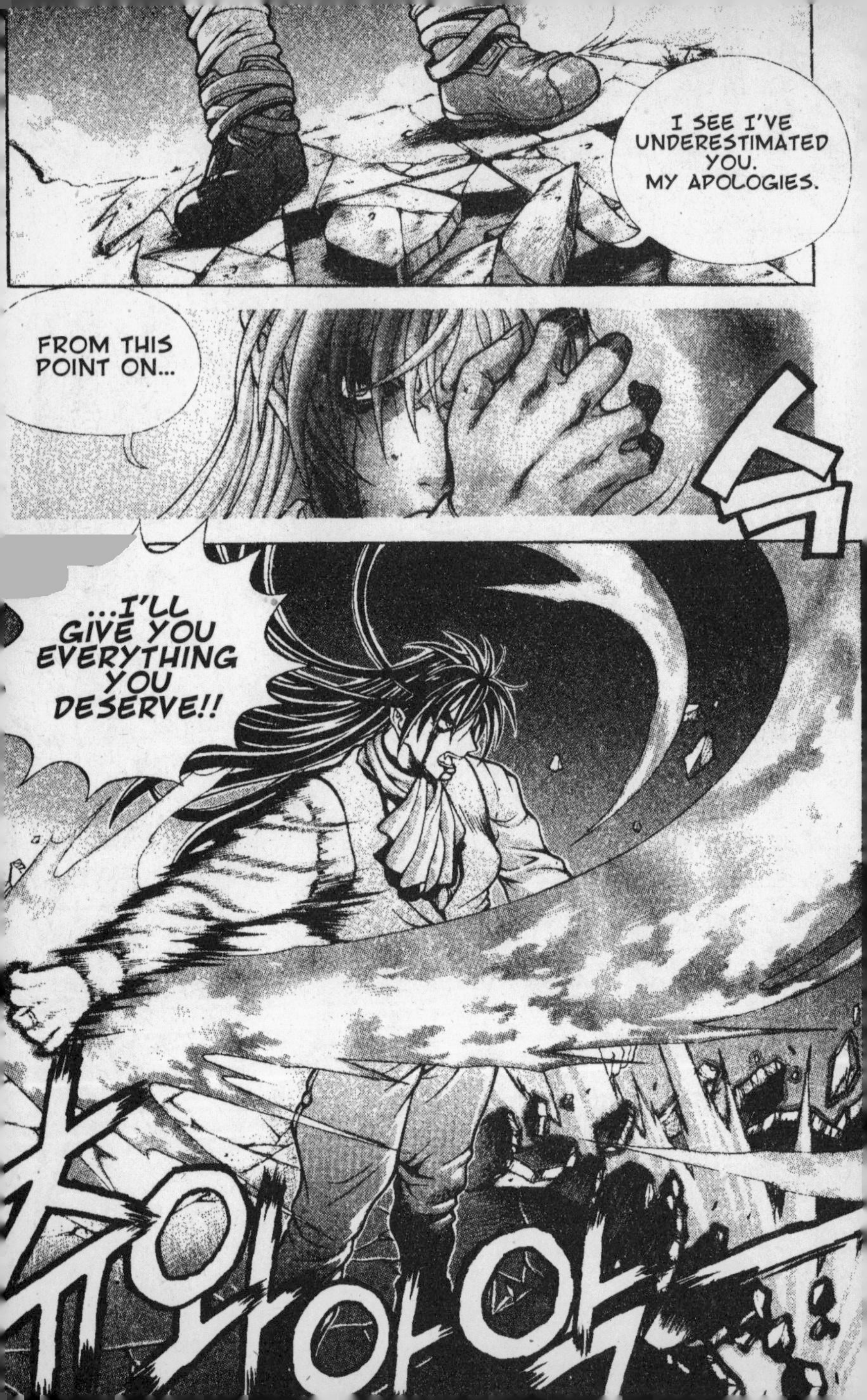
I SEE I'VE UNDERESTIMATED YOU. MY APOLOGIES.
FROM THIS POINT ON...
...I'LL GIVE YOU EVERYTHING YOU DESERVE!!

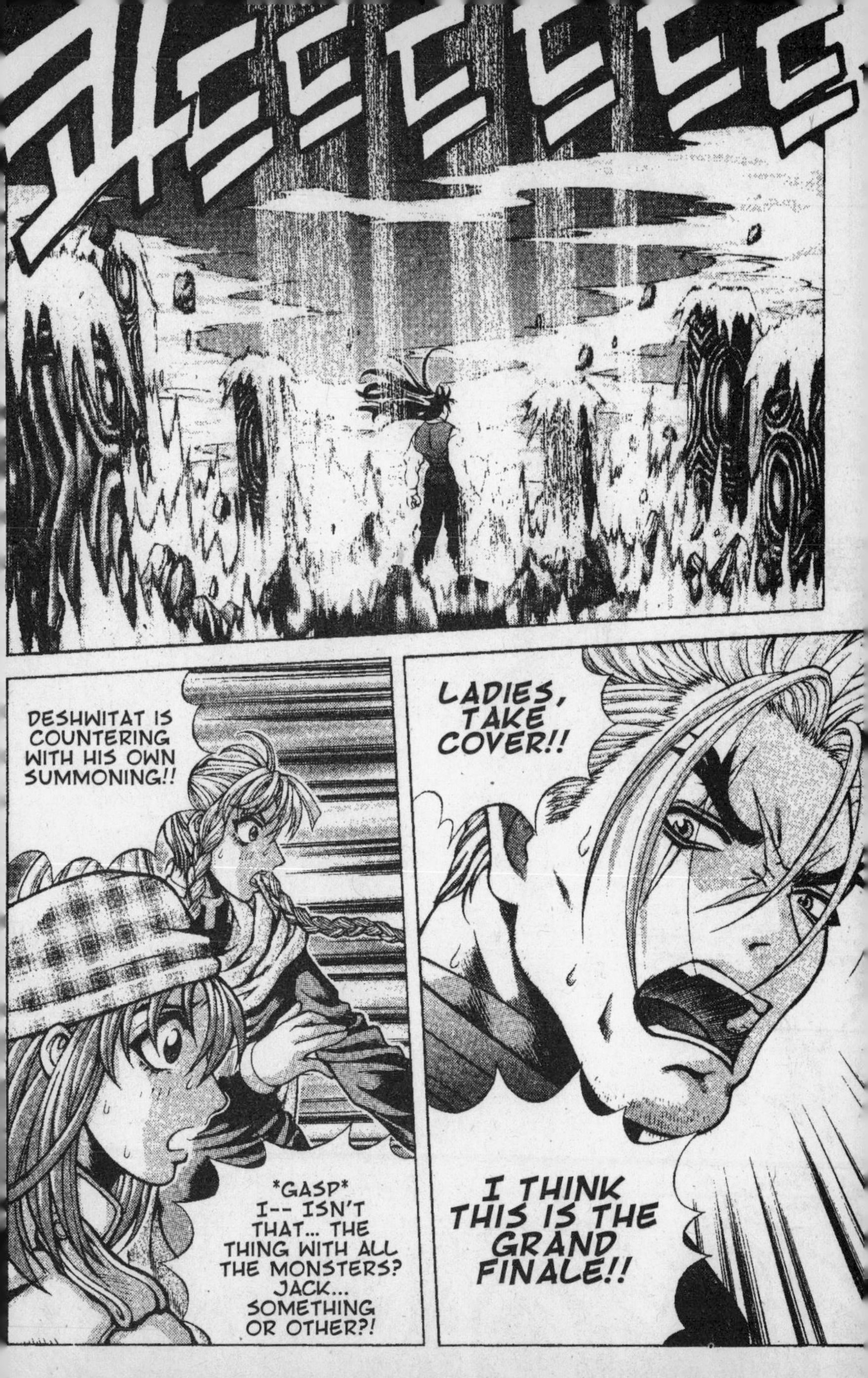

DESHWITAT IS COUNTERING WITH HIS OWN SUMMONING!!
GASP I-- ISN'T THAT... THE THING WITH ALL THE MONSTERS? JACK... SOMETHING OR OTHER?!
LADIES, TAKE COVER!!
I THINK THIS IS THE GRAND FINALE!!

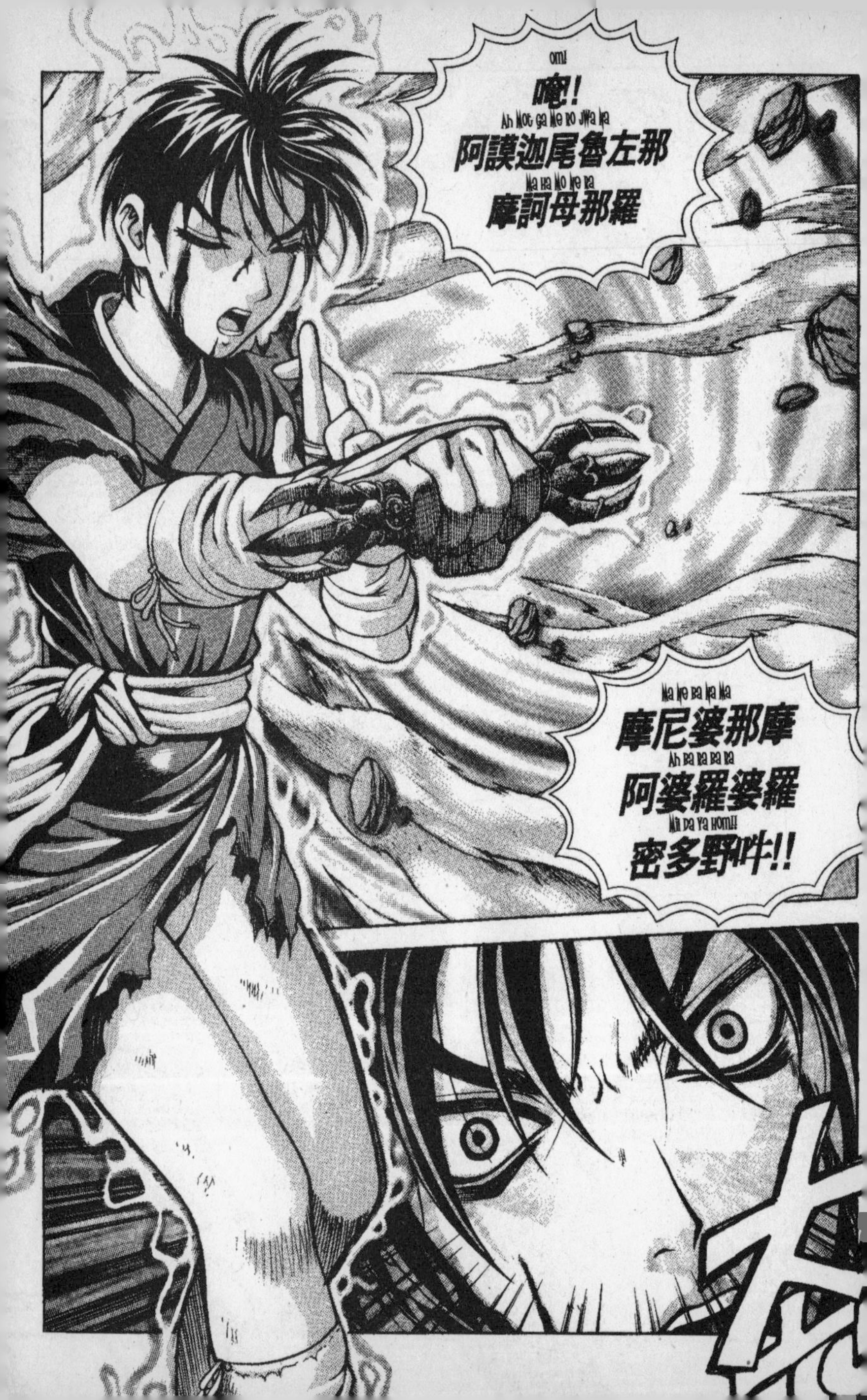
OM!
唵!
Ah Mot ga Me ro Jwa Na
阿謨迦尾魯左那
Ma Ha Mo Ne Ra
摩訶母那羅
Ma Ne Ba Na Ma
摩尼婆那摩
Ah Ba Ra Ba Ra
阿婆羅婆羅
Mii Da Ya HOM!!
密多野吽!!

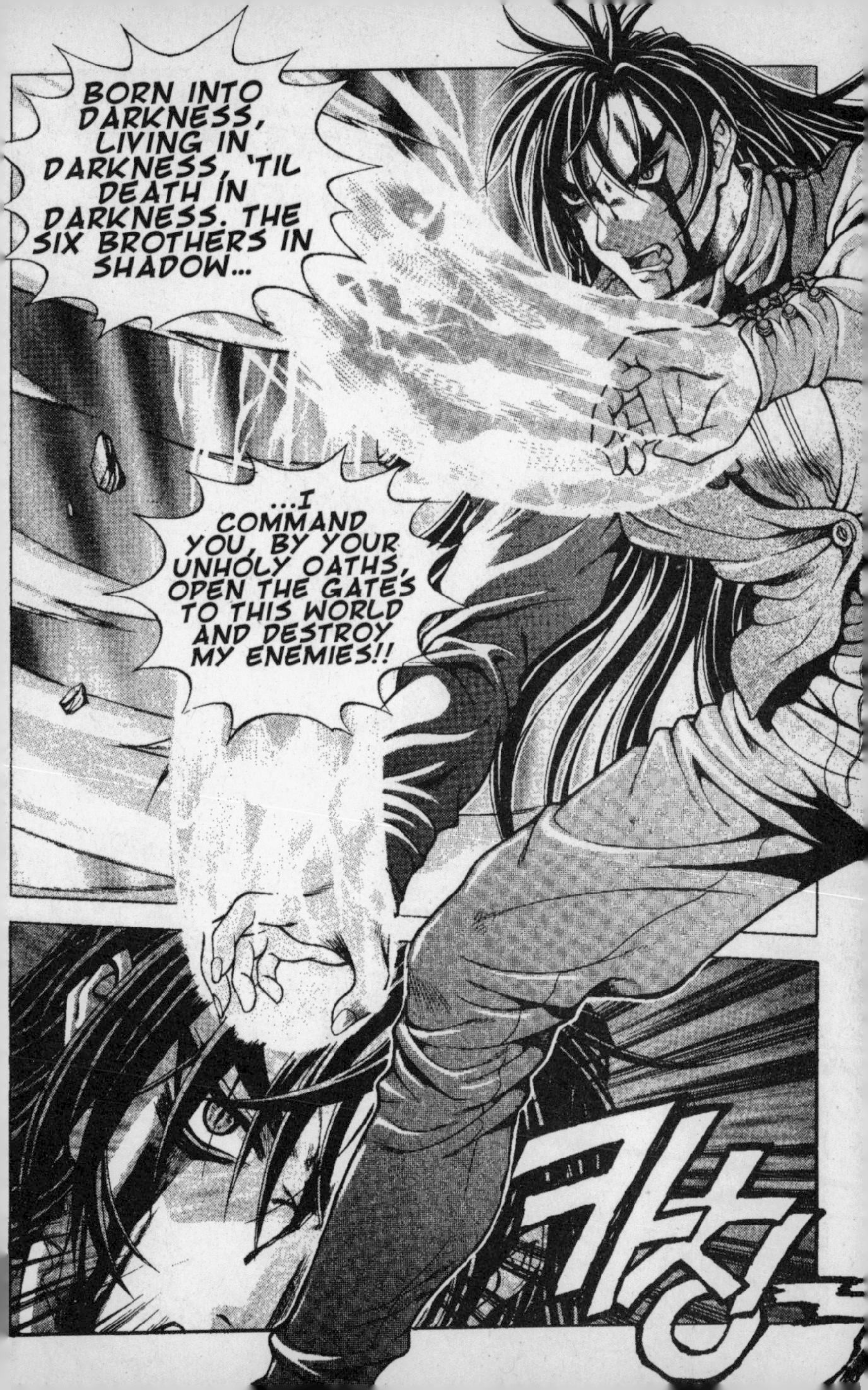
BORN INTO DARKNESS, LIVING IN DARKNESS, 'TIL DEATH IN DARKNESS. THE SIX BROTHERS IN SHADOW...
...I COMMAND YOU, BY YOUR UNHOLY OATHS, OPEN THE GATES TO THIS WORLD AND DESTROY MY ENEMIES!!

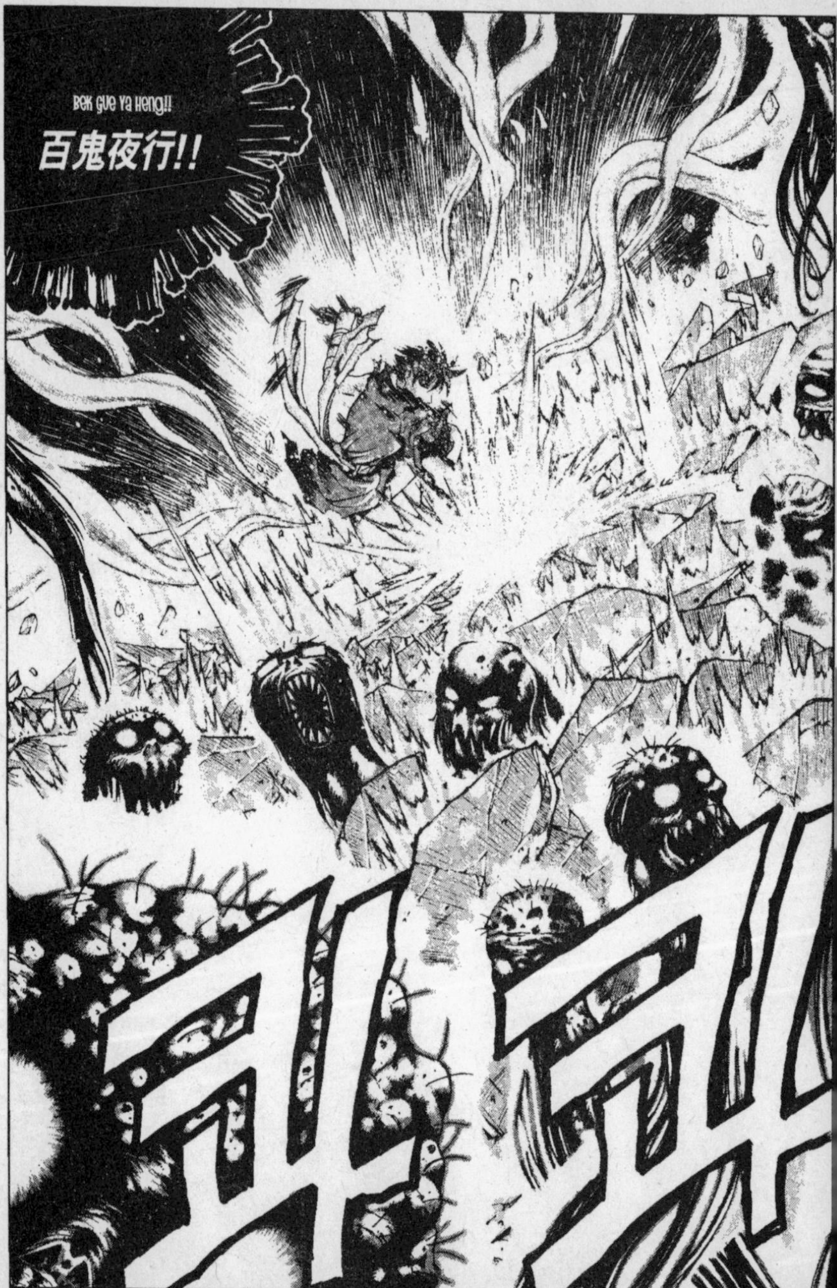

Bek Gue Ya Heng!!
百鬼夜行!!

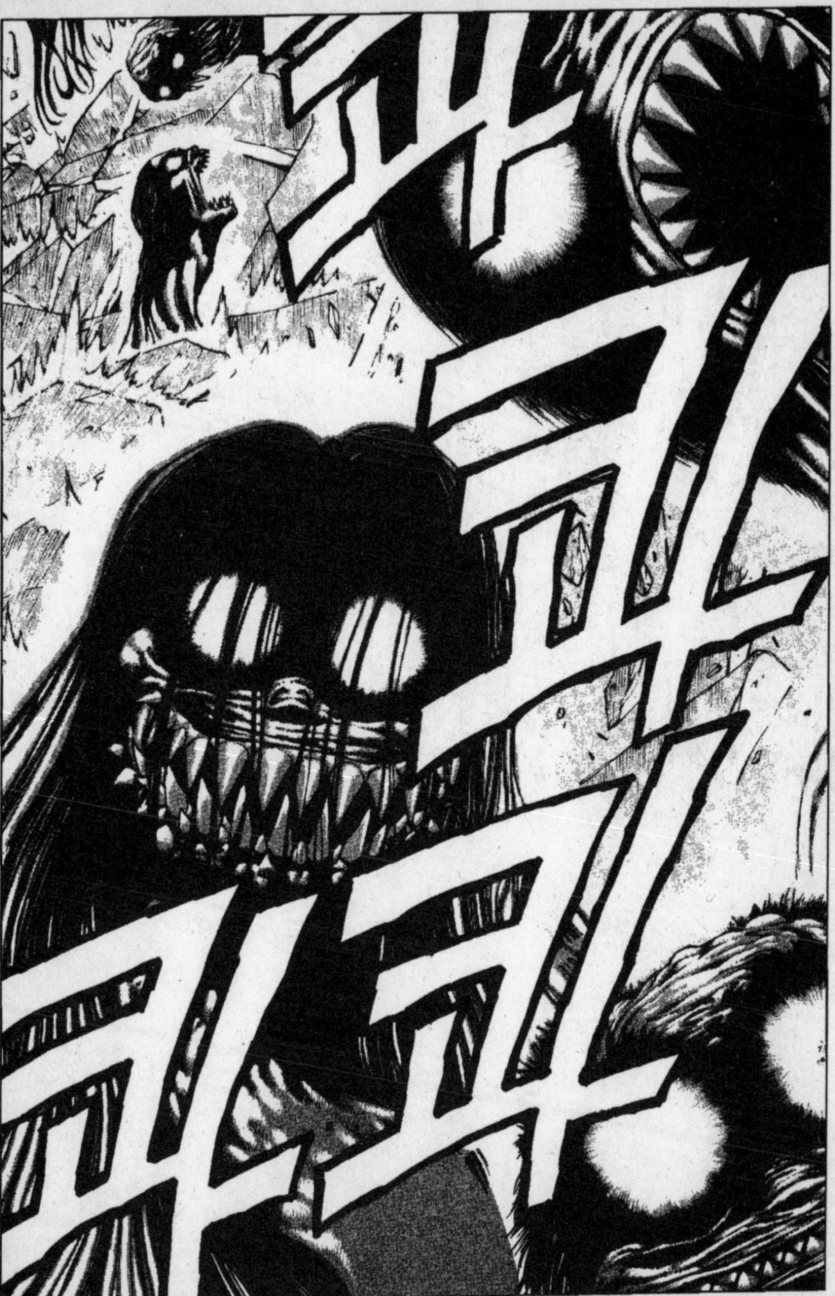

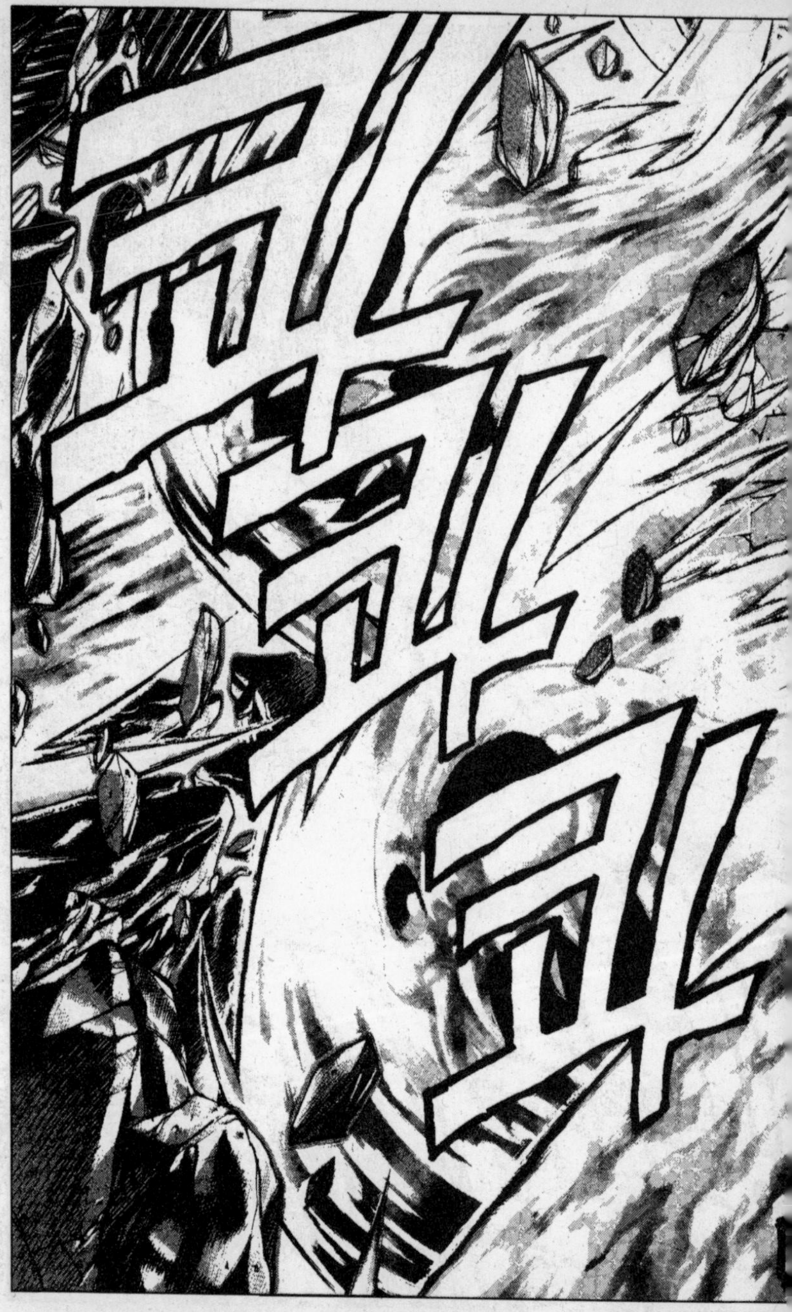

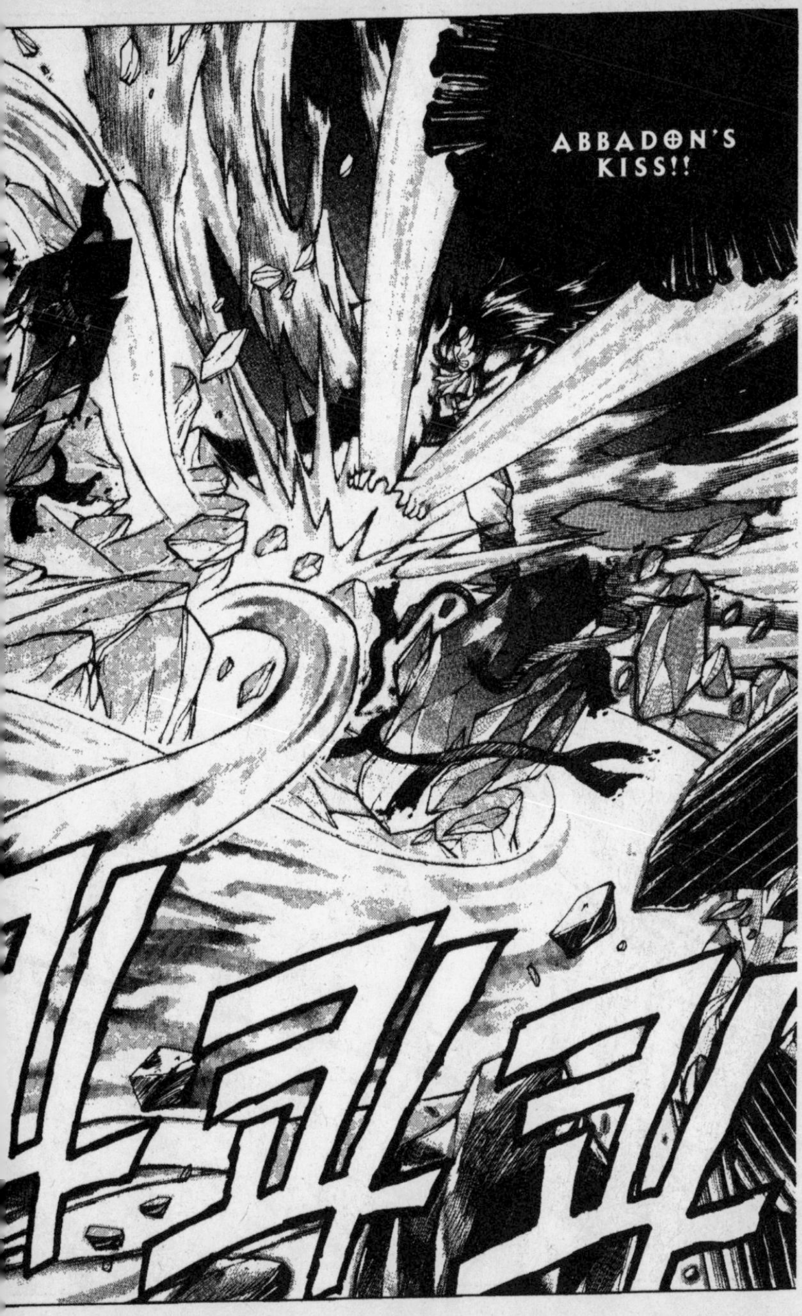
ABBADON'S KISS!!

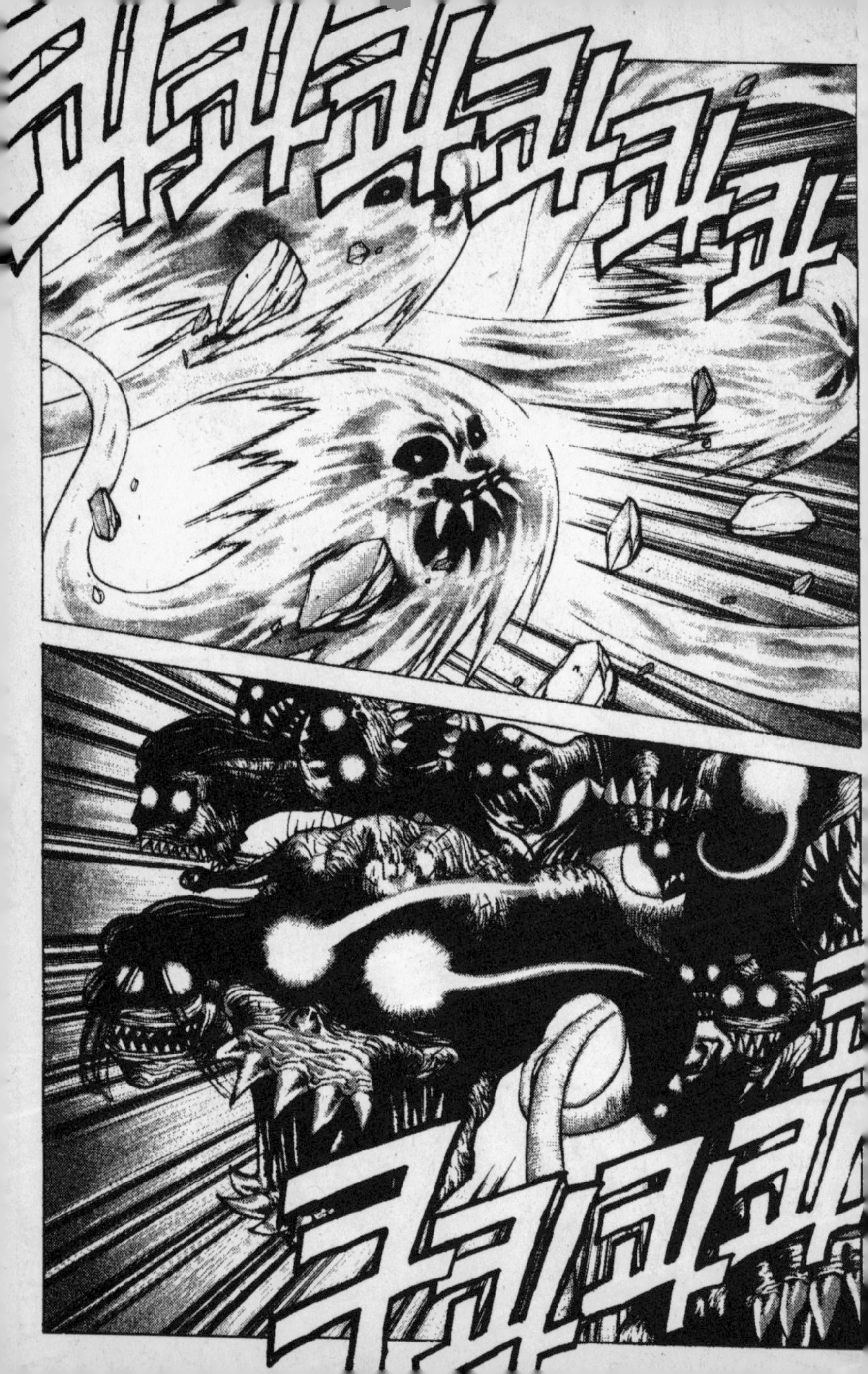

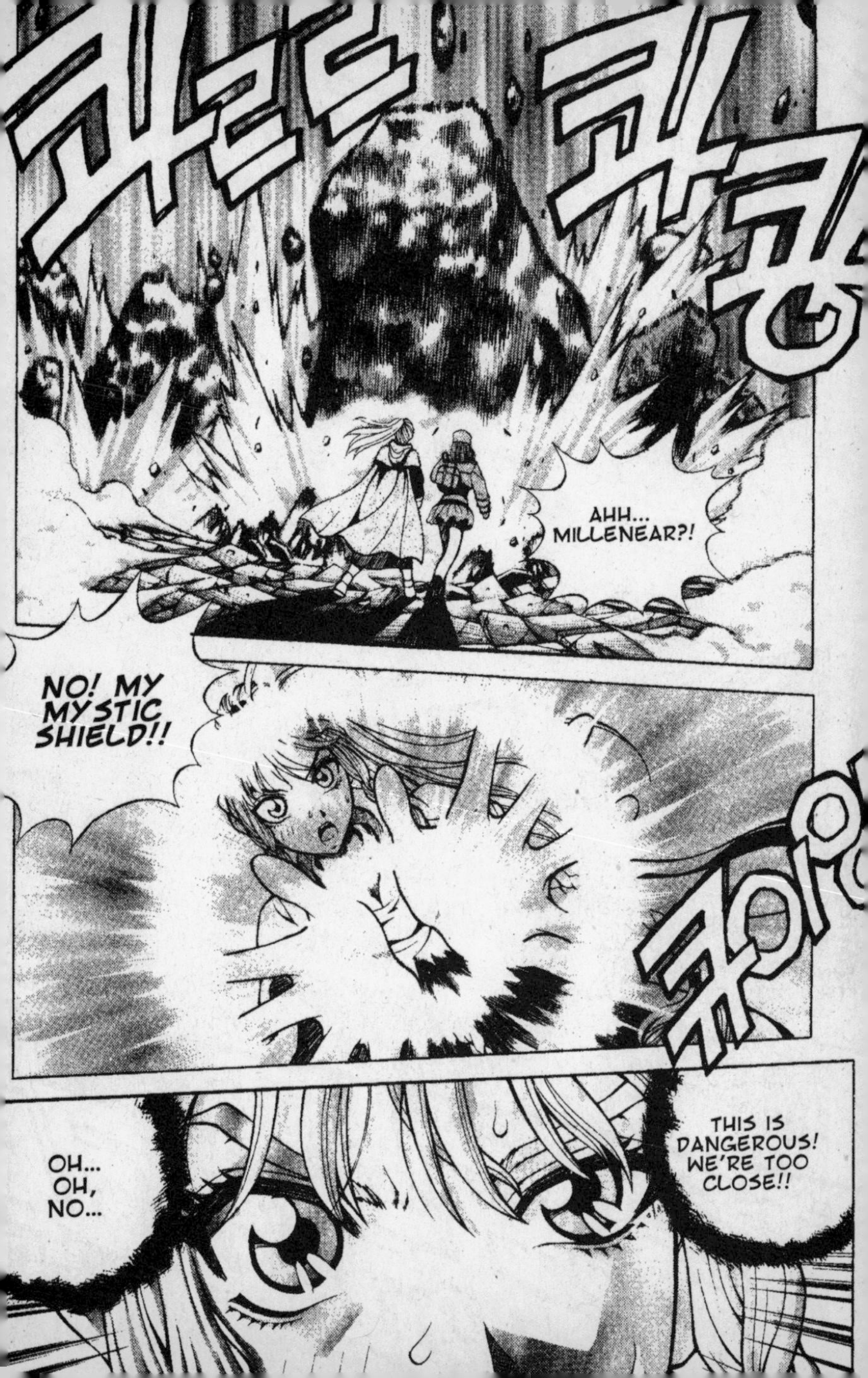
AHH... MILLENEAR?!
NO! MY MYSTIC SHIELD!!
OH... OH, NO...
THIS IS DANGEROUS! WE'RE TOO CLOSE!!

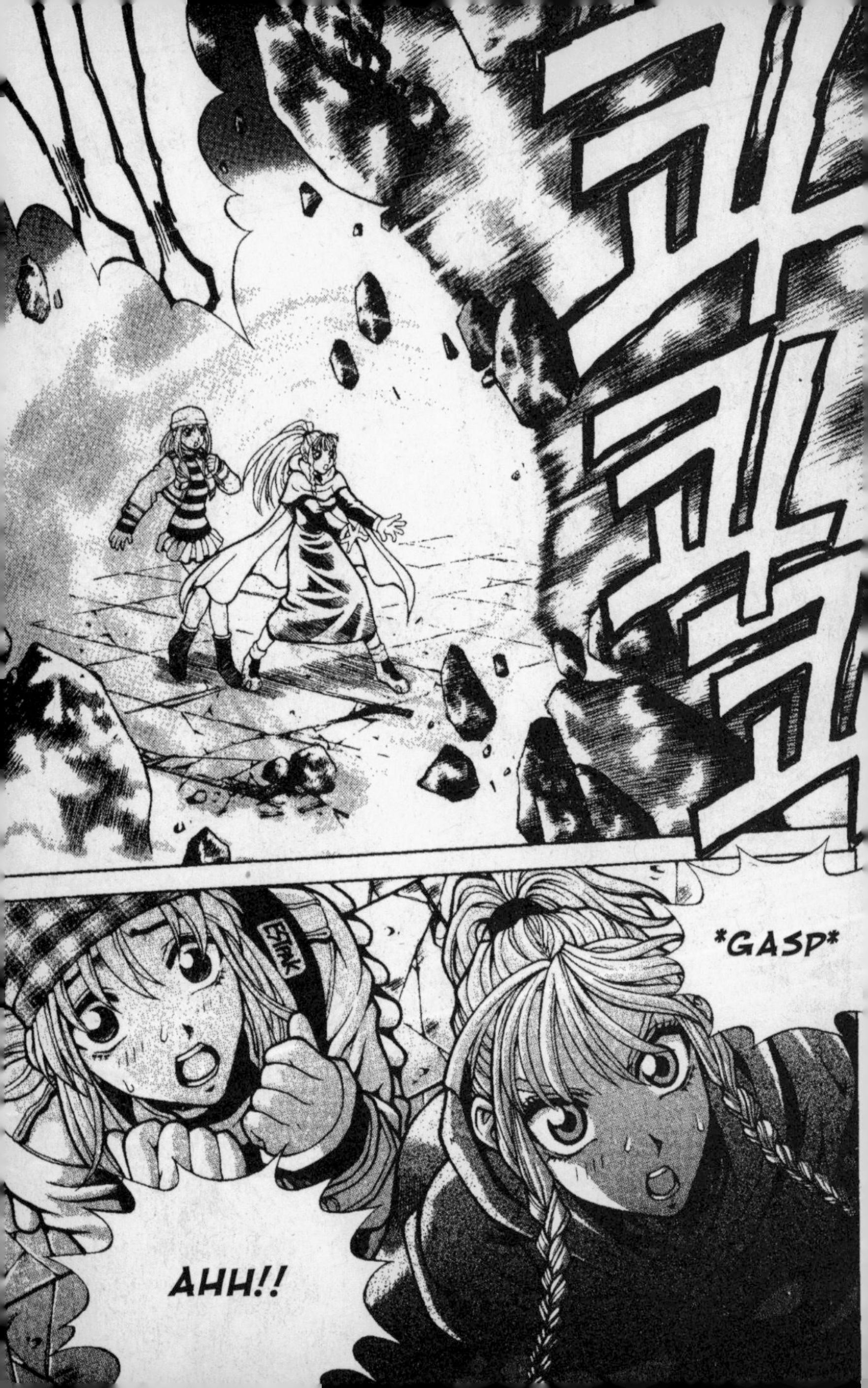
AHH!!
GASP

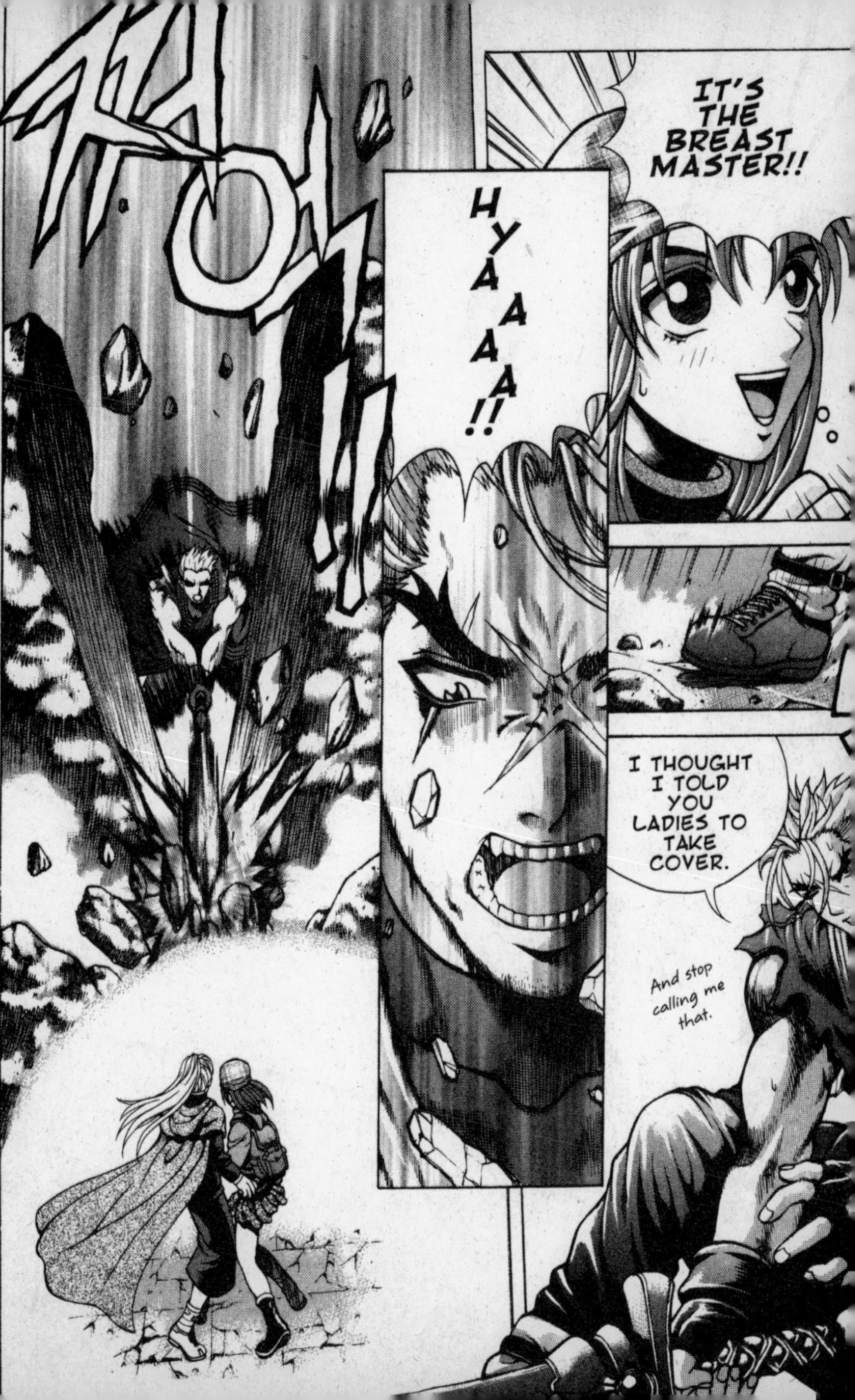
HYAAAAA!!
IT'S THE BREAST MASTER!!
I THOUGHT I TOLD YOU LADIES TO TAKE COVER.
And stop calling me that.

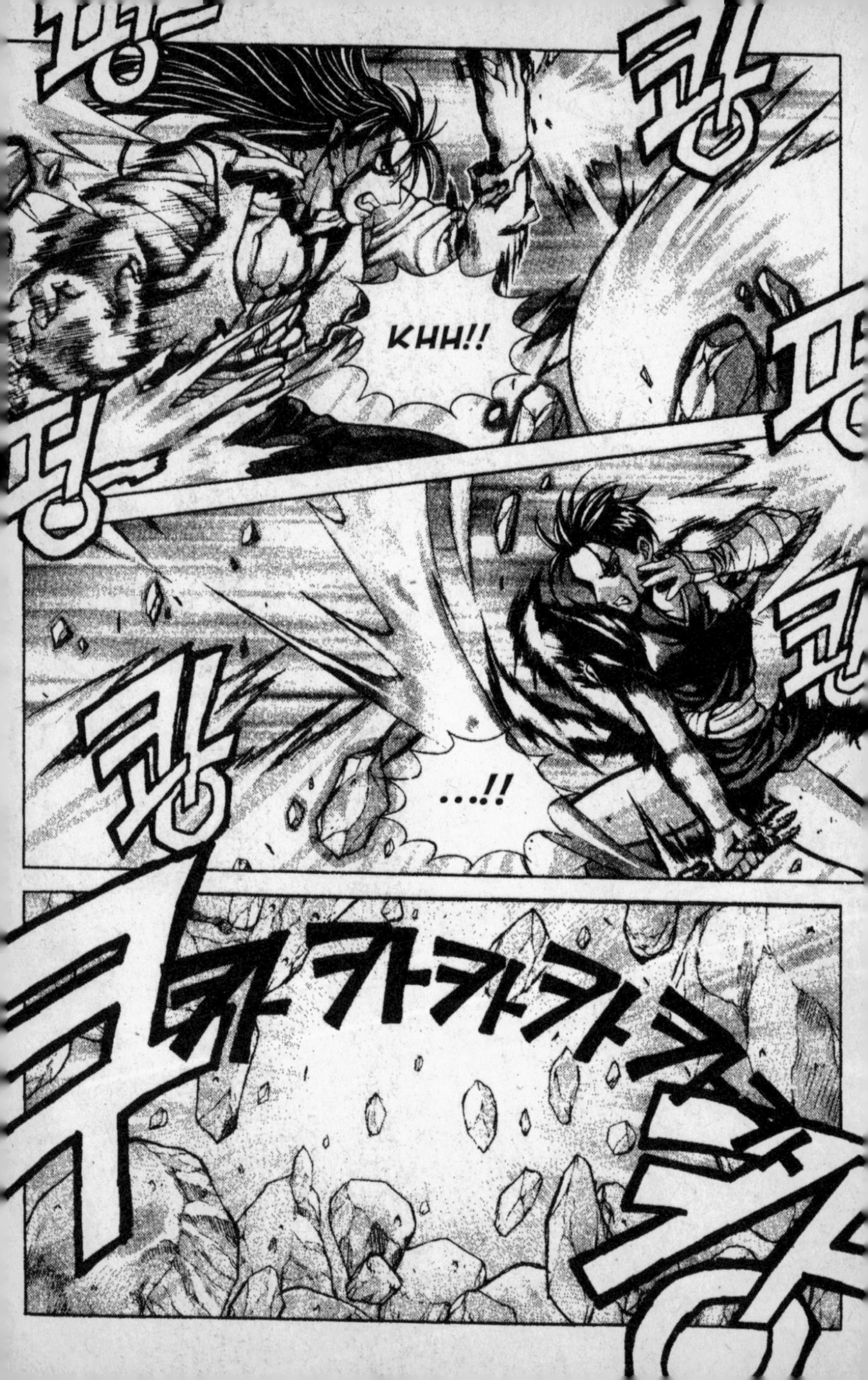
KHH!!
...!!

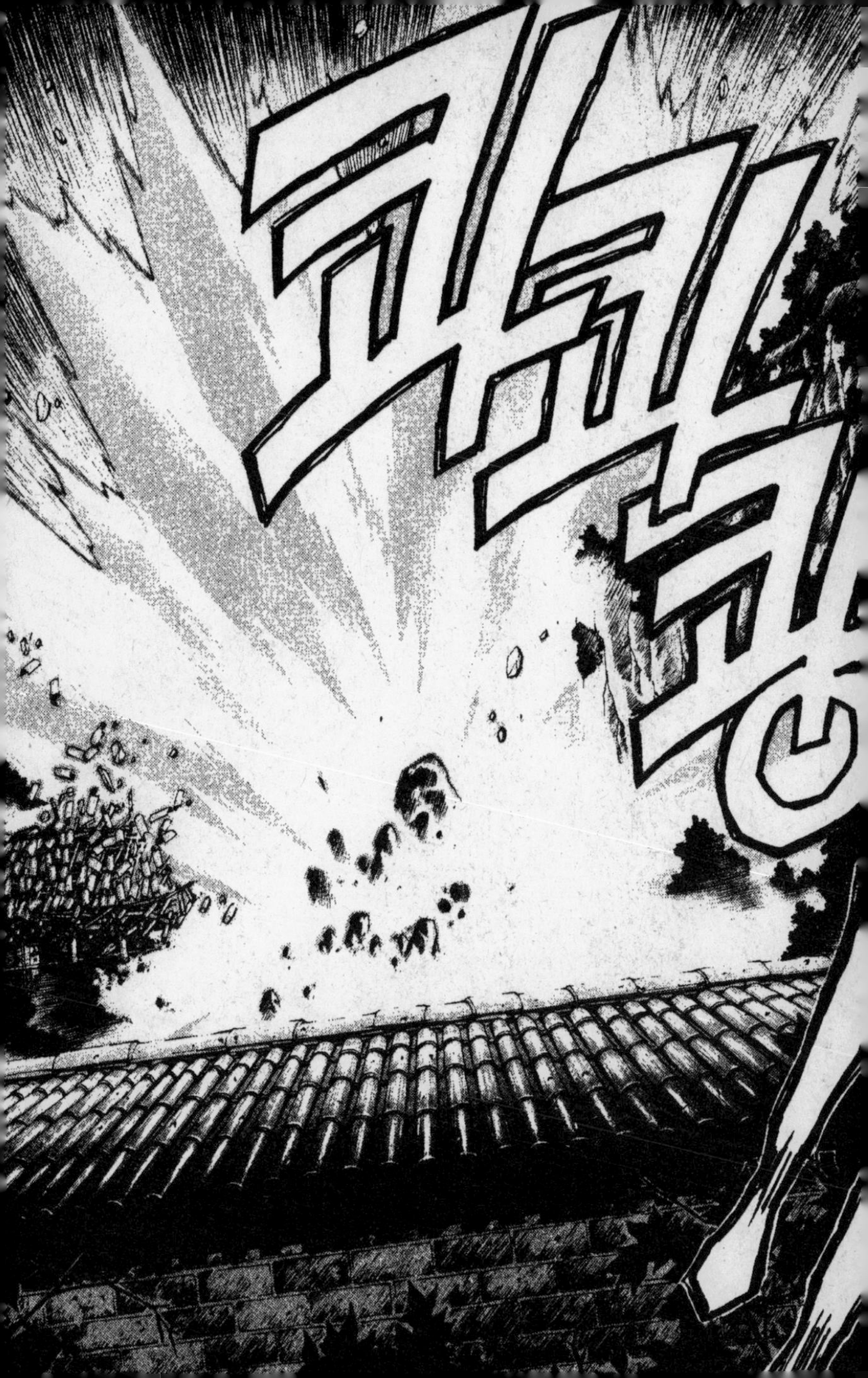

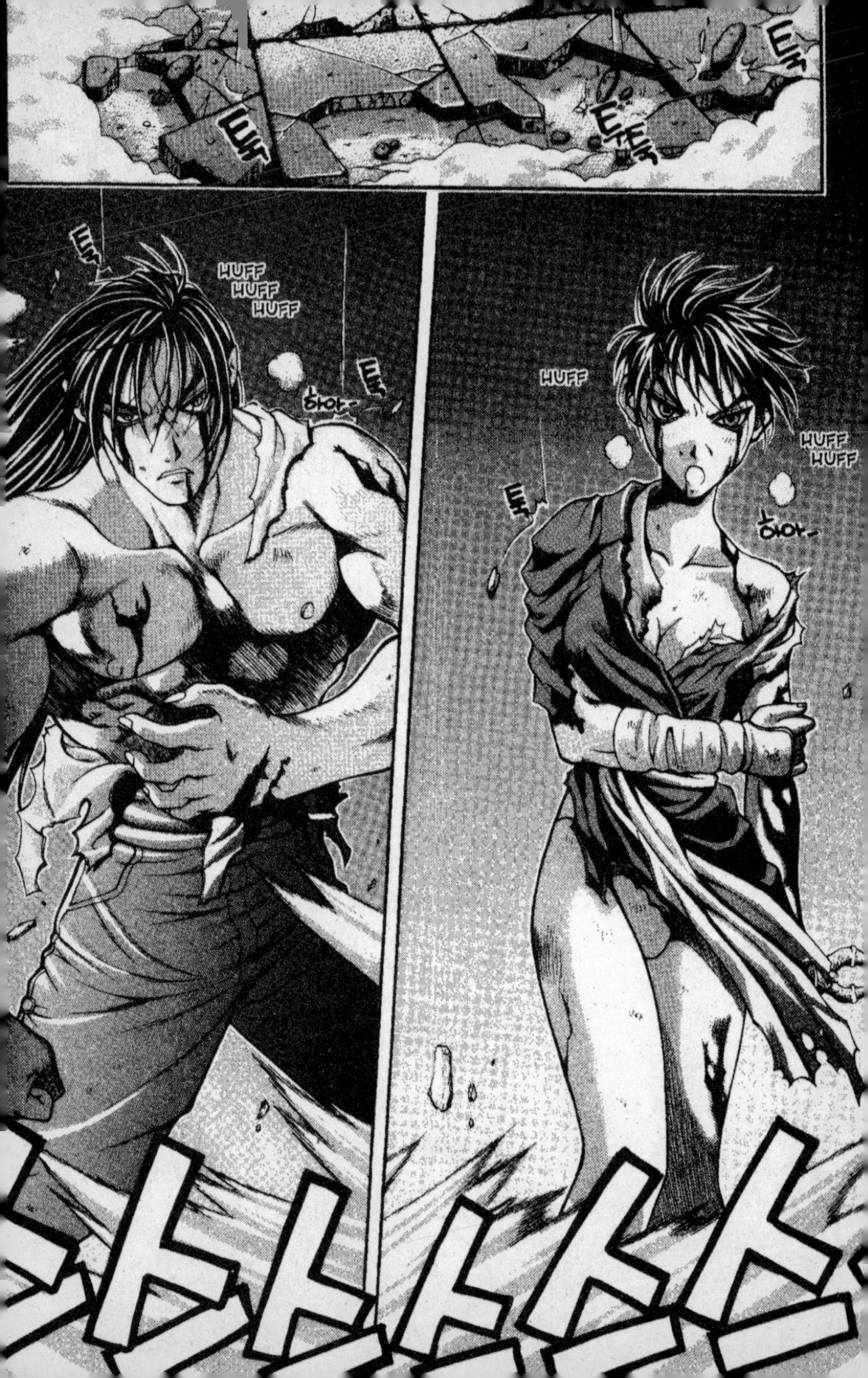
툭
투툭
툭
툭
HUFF
HUFF
HUFF
툭
하아-
HUFF
툭
HUFF
HUFF
하아-

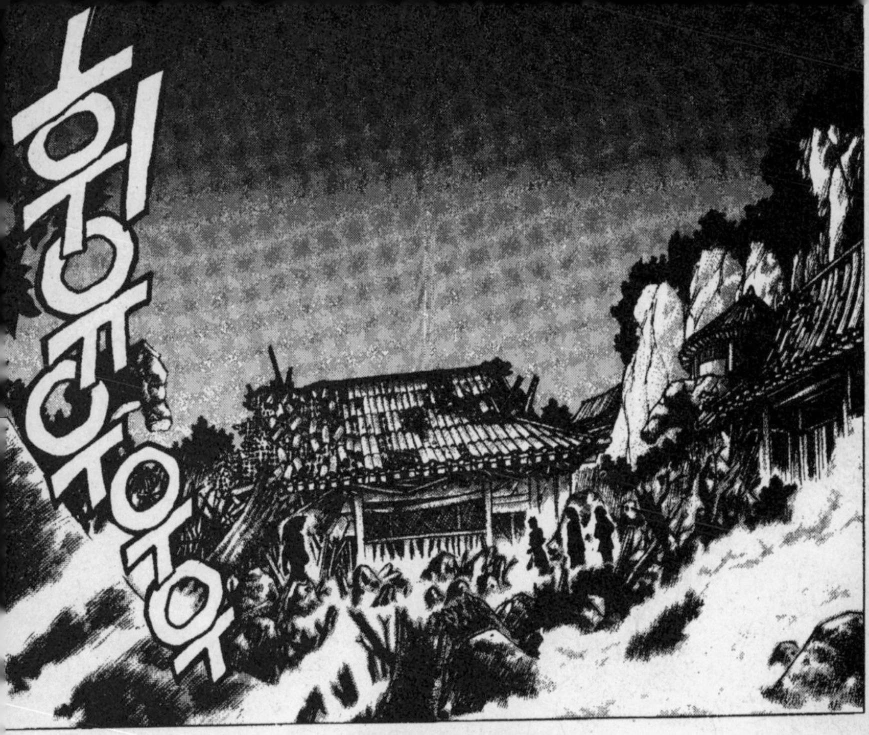

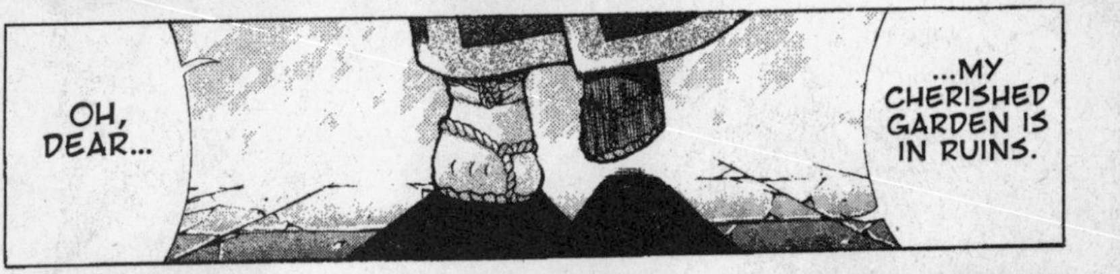
OH, DEAR...
...MY CHERISHED GARDEN IS IN RUINS.

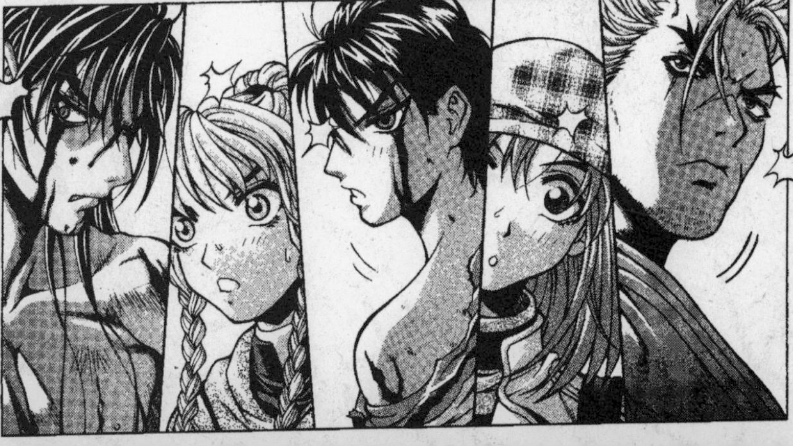

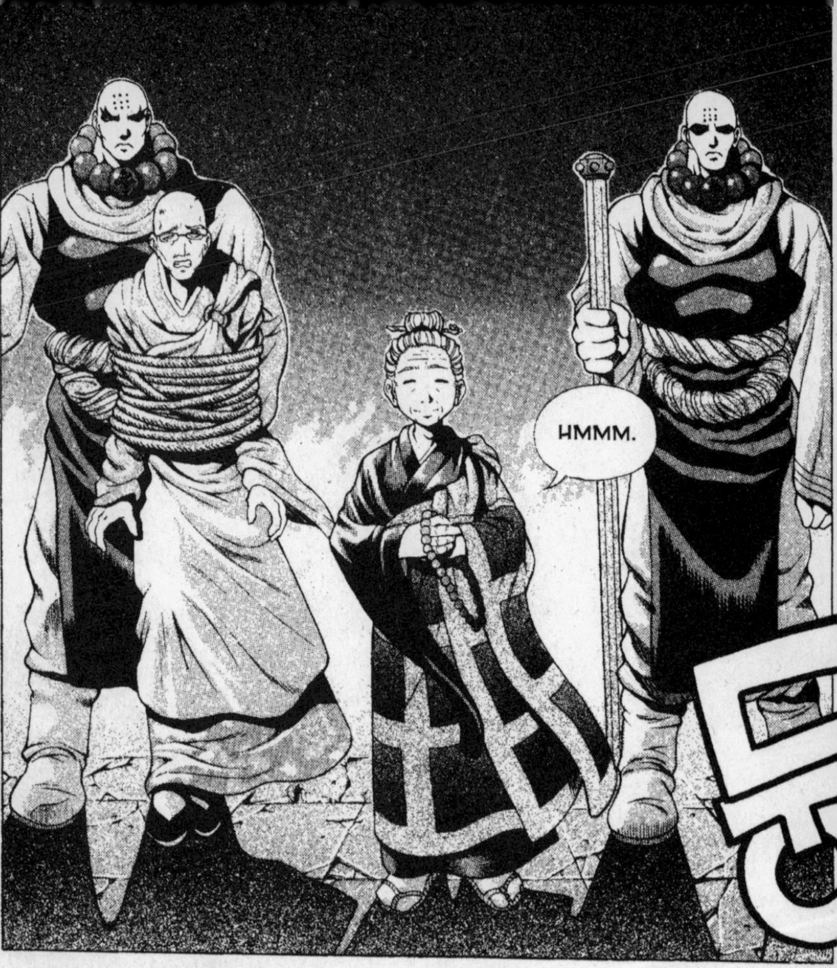
HMMM.
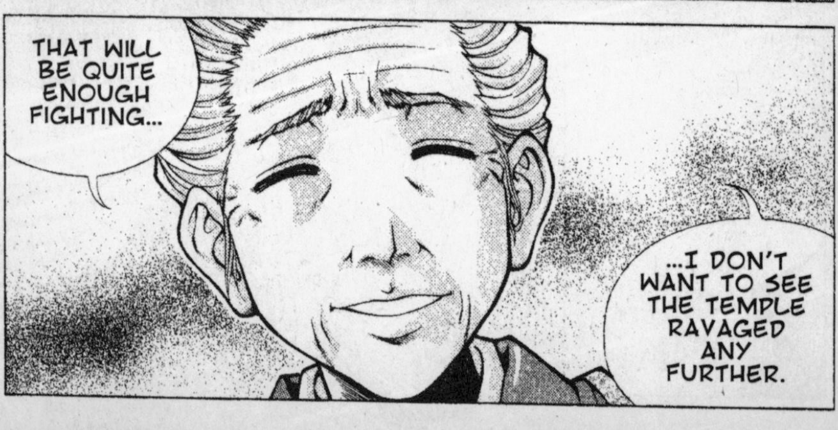
THAT WILL BE QUITE ENOUGH FIGHTING...
...I DON'T WANT TO SEE THE TEMPLE RAVAGED ANY FURTHER.

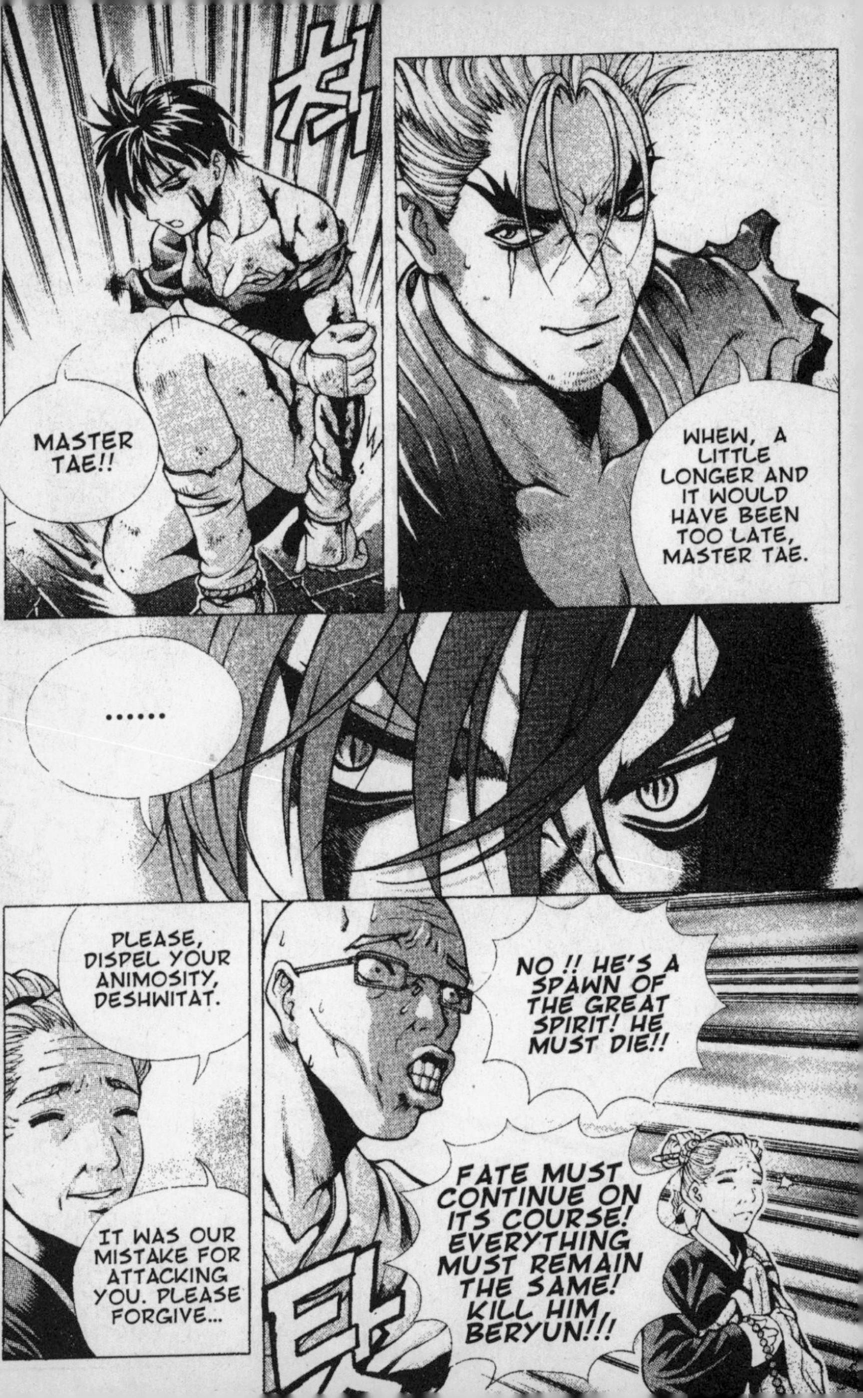
MASTER TAE!!
WHEW, A LITTLE LONGER AND IT WOULD HAVE BEEN TOO LATE, MASTER TAE.
......
PLEASE, DISPEL YOUR ANIMOSITY, DESHWITAT.
IT WAS OUR MISTAKE FOR ATTACKING YOU. PLEASE FORGIVE...
NO !! HE'S A SPAWN OF THE GREAT SPIRIT! HE MUST DIE!!
FATE MUST CONTINUE ON ITS COURSE! EVERYTHING MUST REMAIN THE SAME! KILL HIM, BERYUN!!!

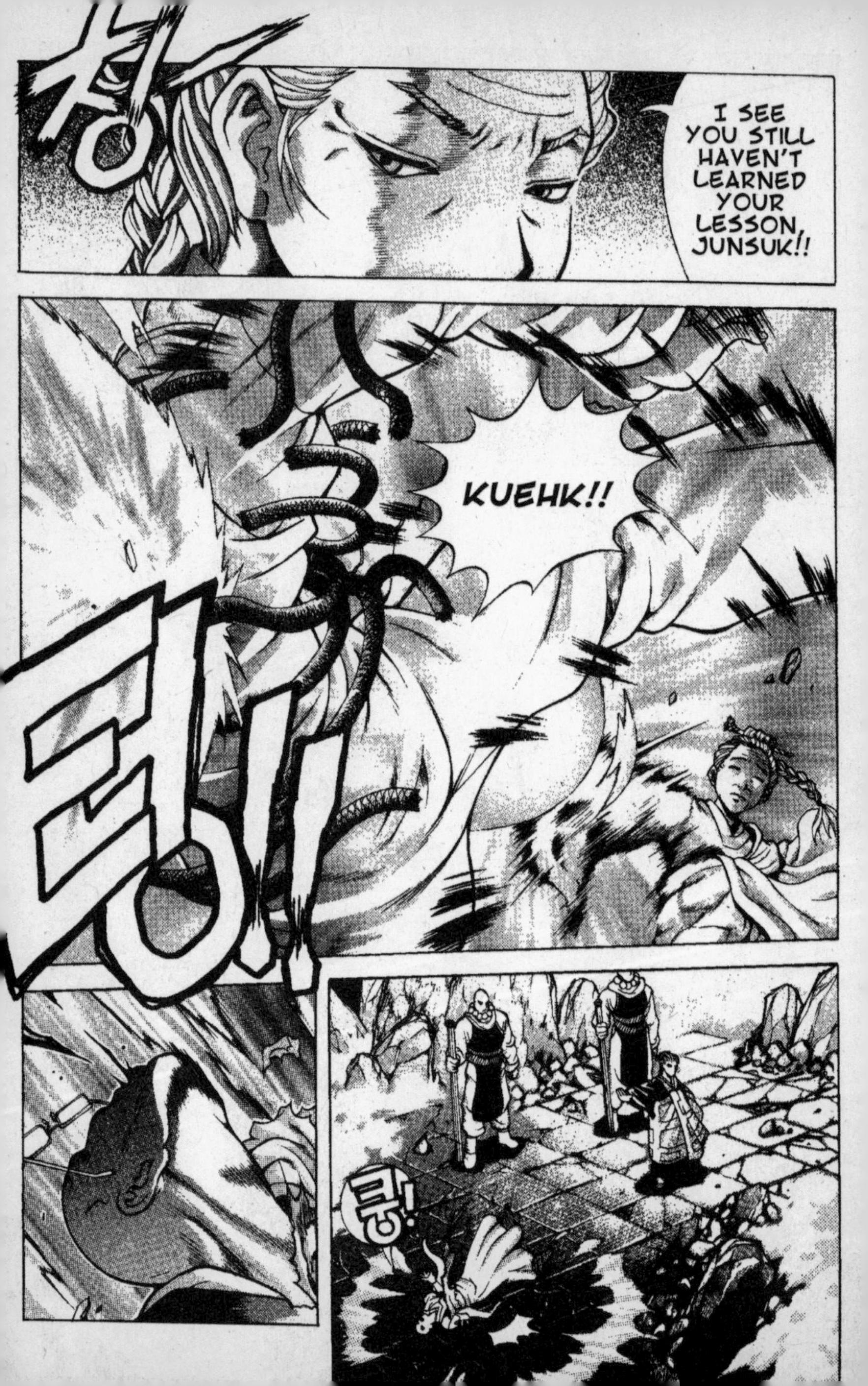
I SEE YOU STILL HAVEN'T LEARNED YOUR LESSON, JUNSUK!!
KUEHK!!
쿵!

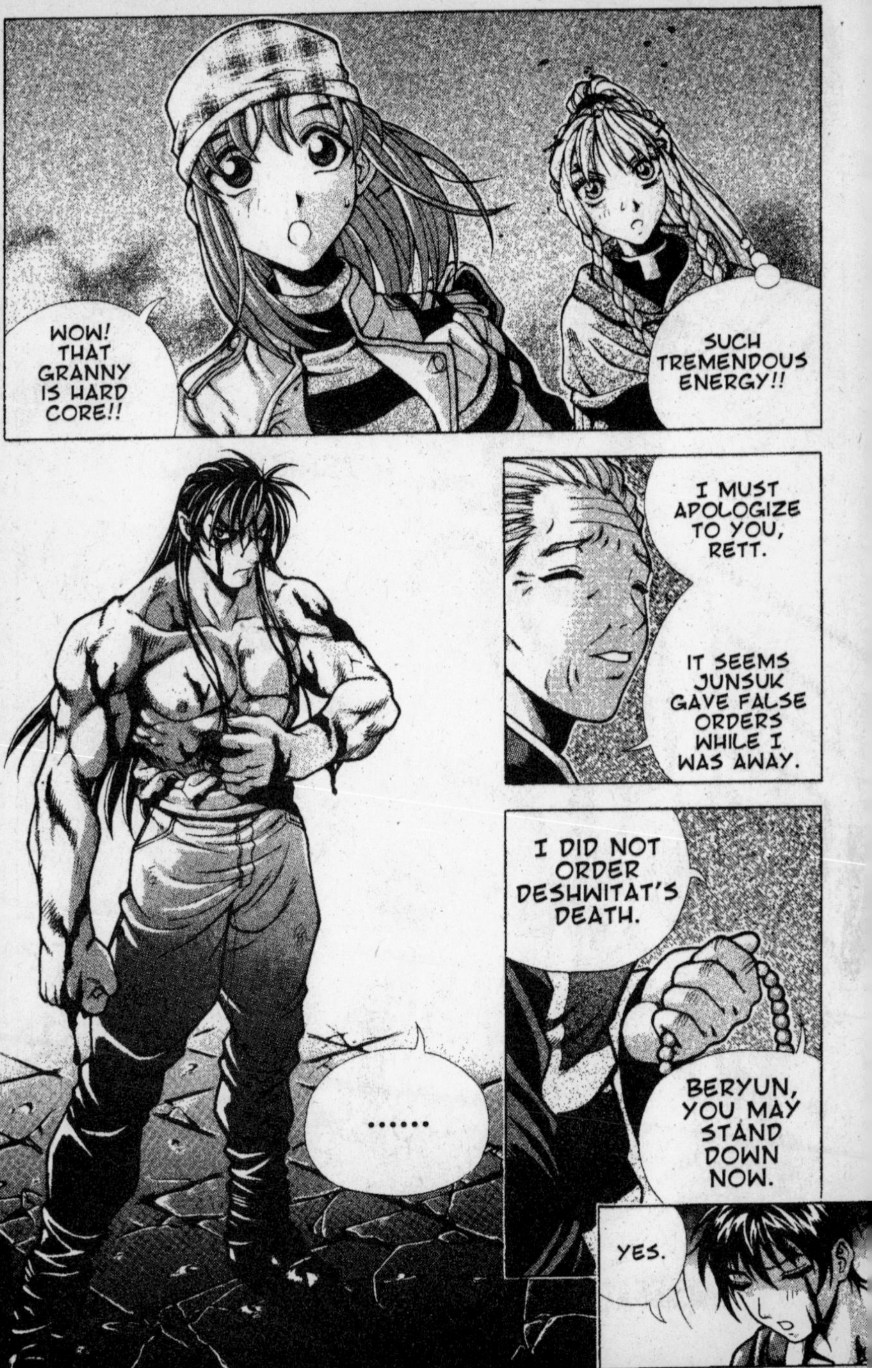
WOW! THAT GRANNY IS HARD CORE!!
SUCH TREMENDOUS ENERGY!!
I MUST APOLOGIZE TO YOU, RETT.
IT SEEMS JUNSUK GAVE FALSE ORDERS WHILE I WAS AWAY.
I DID NOT ORDER DESHWITAT'S DEATH.
......
BERYUN, YOU MAY STAND DOWN NOW.
YES.

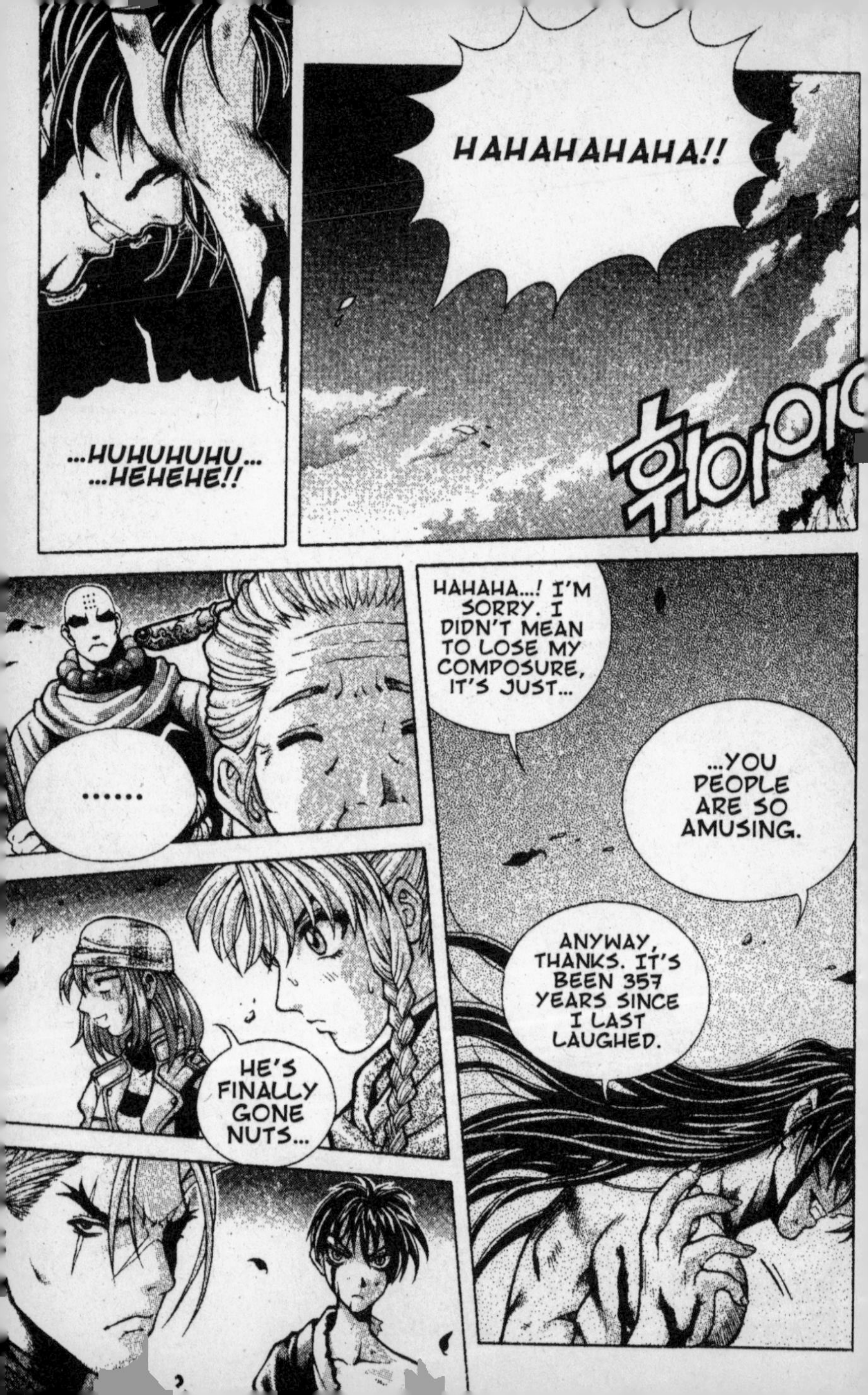
...HUHUHUHU...
...HEHEHE!!
HAHAHAHAHA!!
휘이이이
......
HAHAHA...! I'M SORRY. I DIDN'T MEAN TO LOSE MY COMPOSURE, IT'S JUST...
...YOU PEOPLE ARE SO AMUSING.
ANYWAY, THANKS. IT'S BEEN 357 YEARS SINCE I LAST LAUGHED.
HE'S FINALLY GONE NUTS...

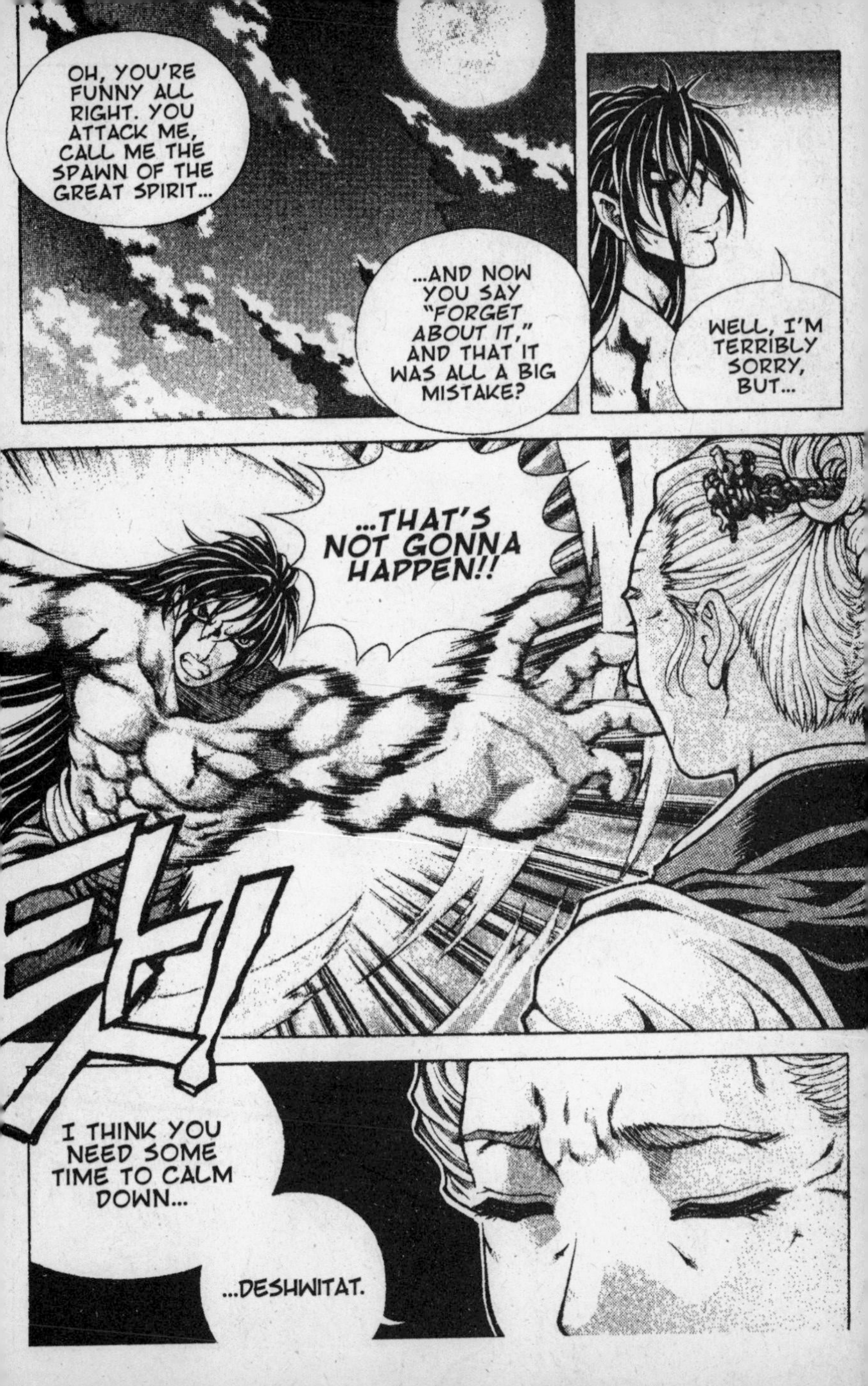
OH, YOU'RE FUNNY ALL RIGHT. YOU ATTACK ME, CALL ME THE SPAWN OF THE GREAT SPIRIT...
...AND NOW YOU SAY "FORGET ABOUT IT," AND THAT IT WAS ALL A BIG MISTAKE?
WELL, I'M TERRIBLY SORRY, BUT...
...THAT'S NOT GONNA HAPPEN!!
I THINK YOU NEED SOME TIME TO CALM DOWN...
...DESHWITAT.

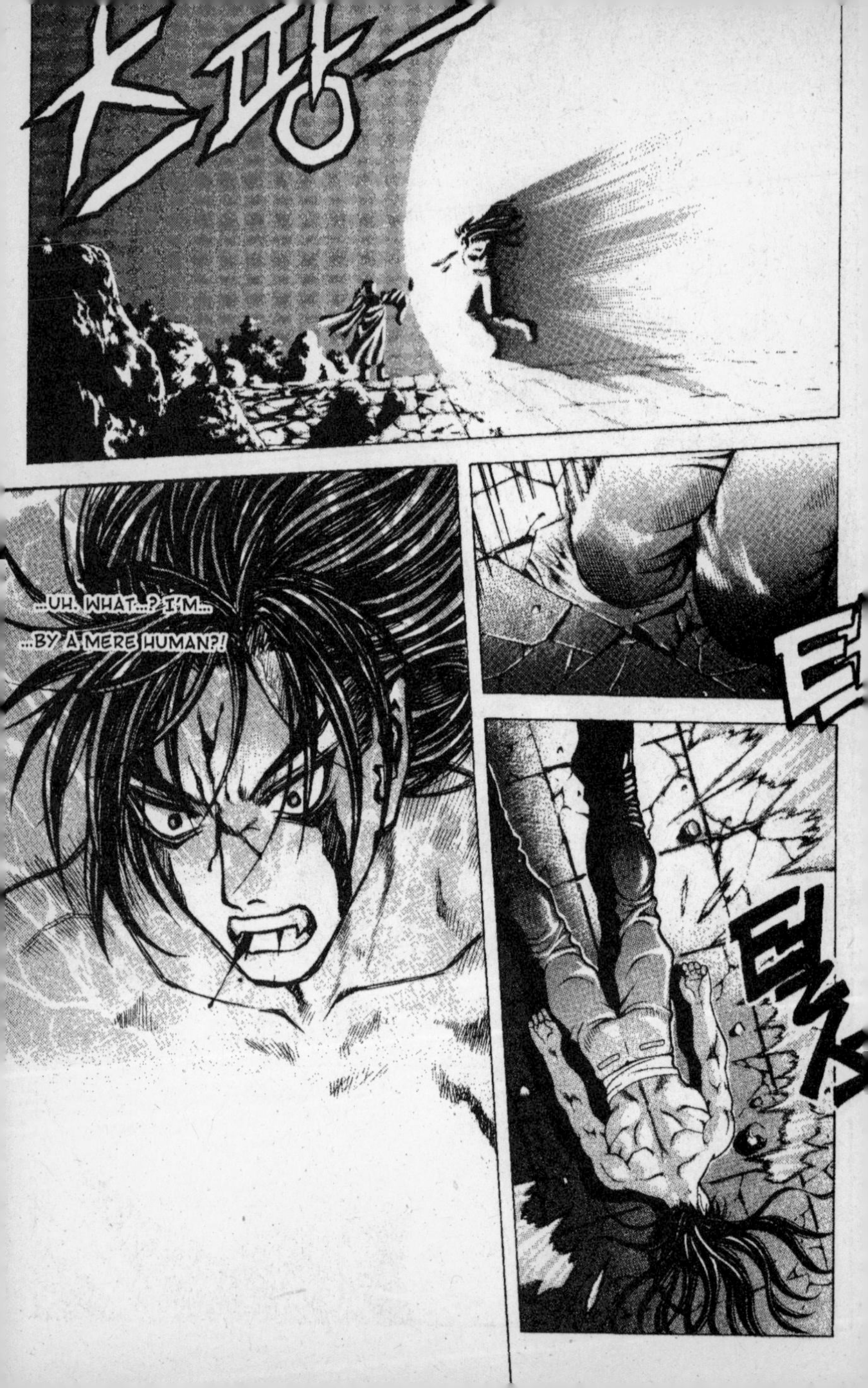
...UH, WHAT...? I'M...
...BY A MERE HUMAN?!

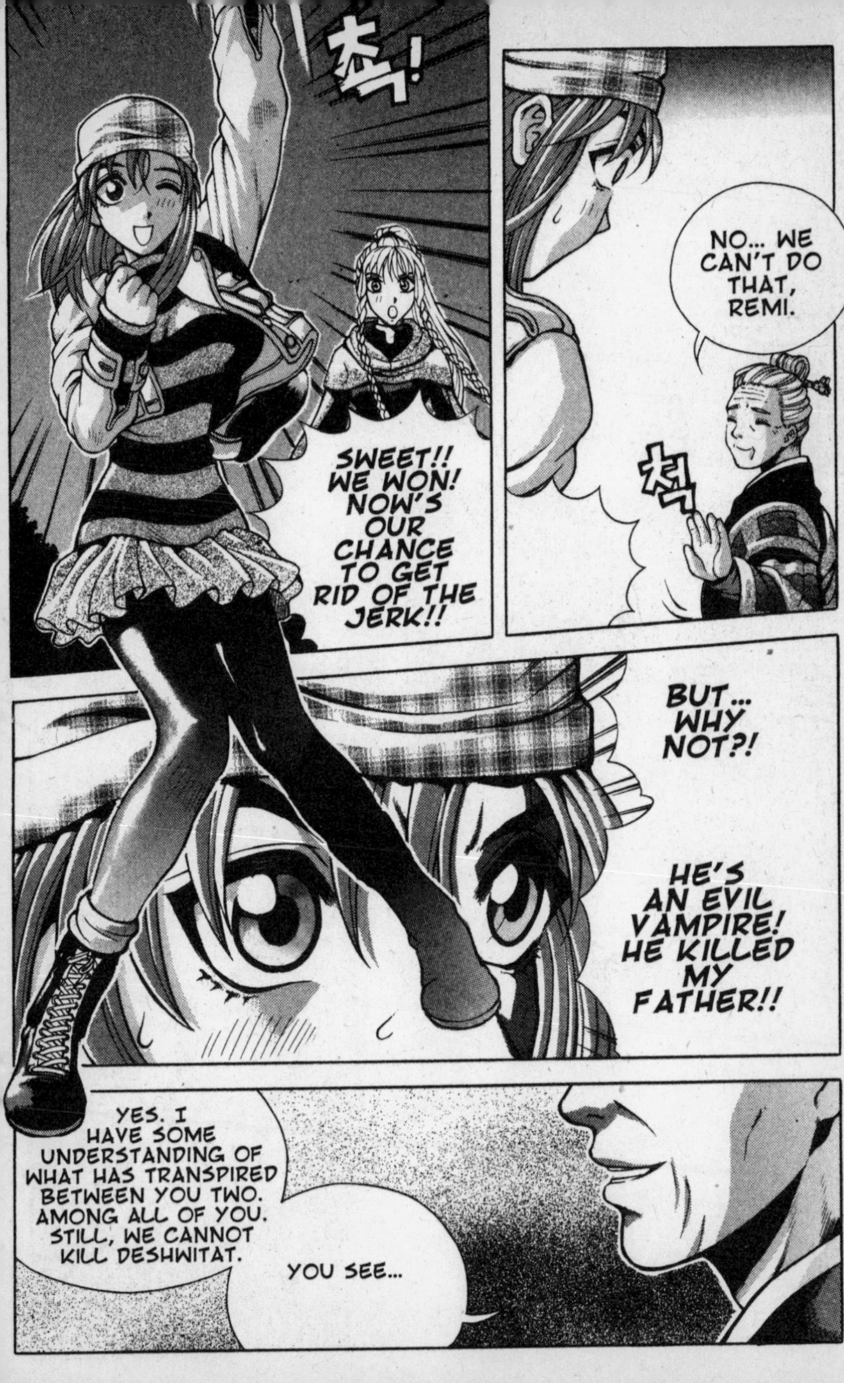

SWEET!! WE WON! NOW'S OUR CHANCE TO GET RID OF THE JERK!!
NO... WE CAN'T DO THAT, REMI.
BUT... WHY NOT?!
HE'S AN EVIL VAMPIRE! HE KILLED MY FATHER!!
YES. I HAVE SOME UNDERSTANDING OF WHAT HAS TRANSPIRED BETWEEN YOU TWO. AMONG ALL OF YOU. STILL, WE CANNOT KILL DESHWITAT.
YOU SEE...

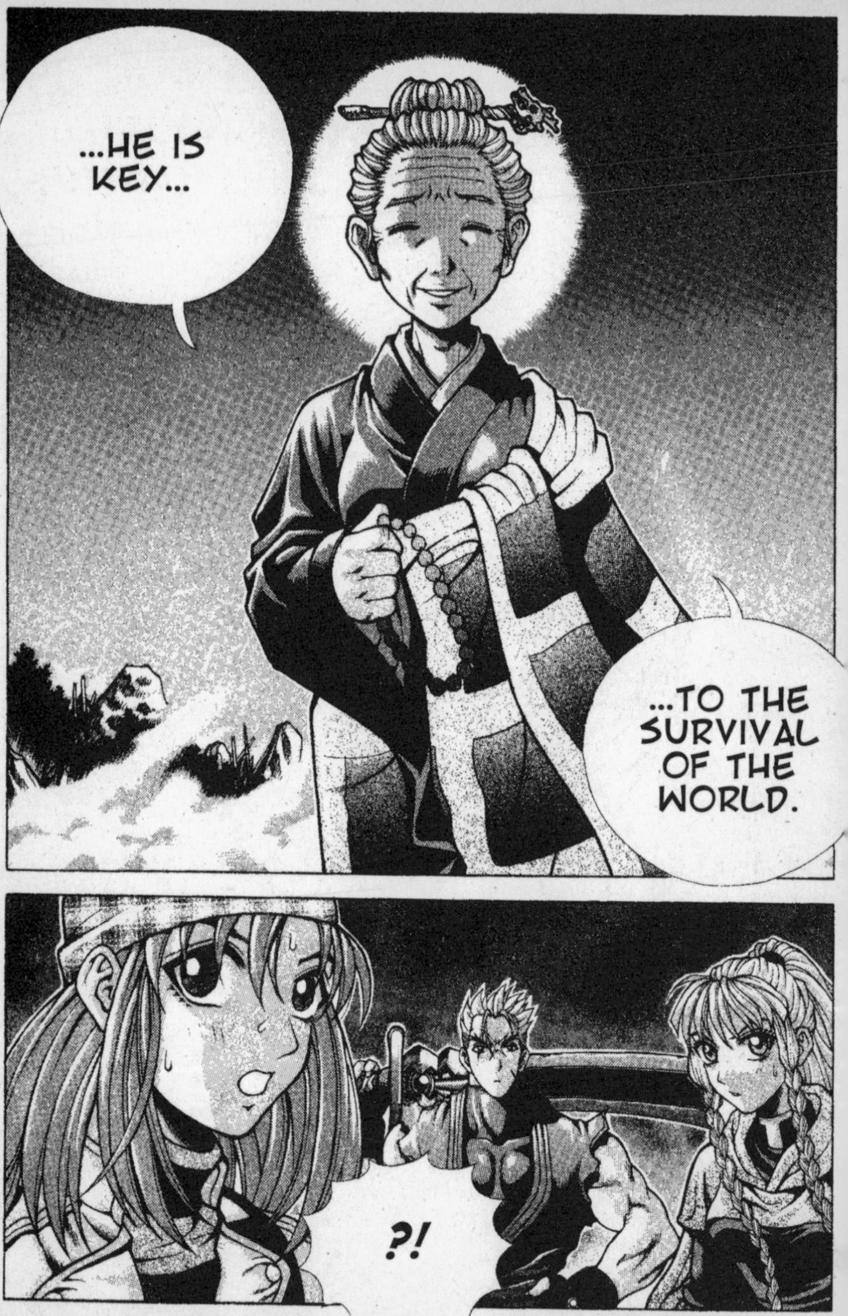
...HE IS KEY...
...TO THE SURVIVAL OF THE WORLD.
?!

CONTINUED IN
REBIRTH - VOLUME 3

From the desk of Woo:

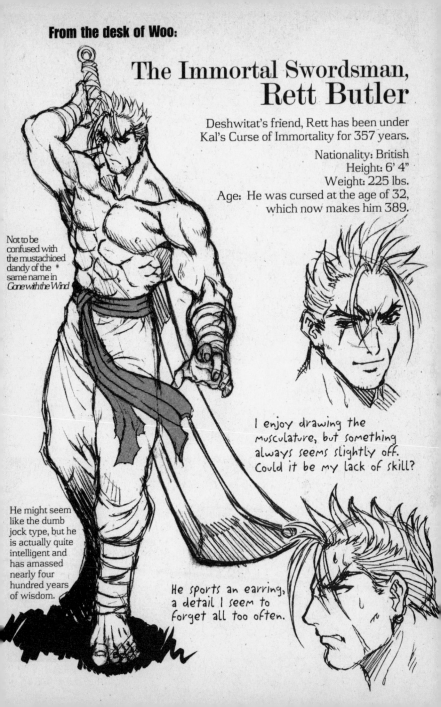

The Immortal Swordsman, Rett Butler

Deshwitat's friend, Rett has been under Kal's Curse of Immortality for 357 years.

Nationality: British
Height: 6' 4"
Weight: 225 lbs.
Age: He was cursed at the age of 32, which now makes him 389.

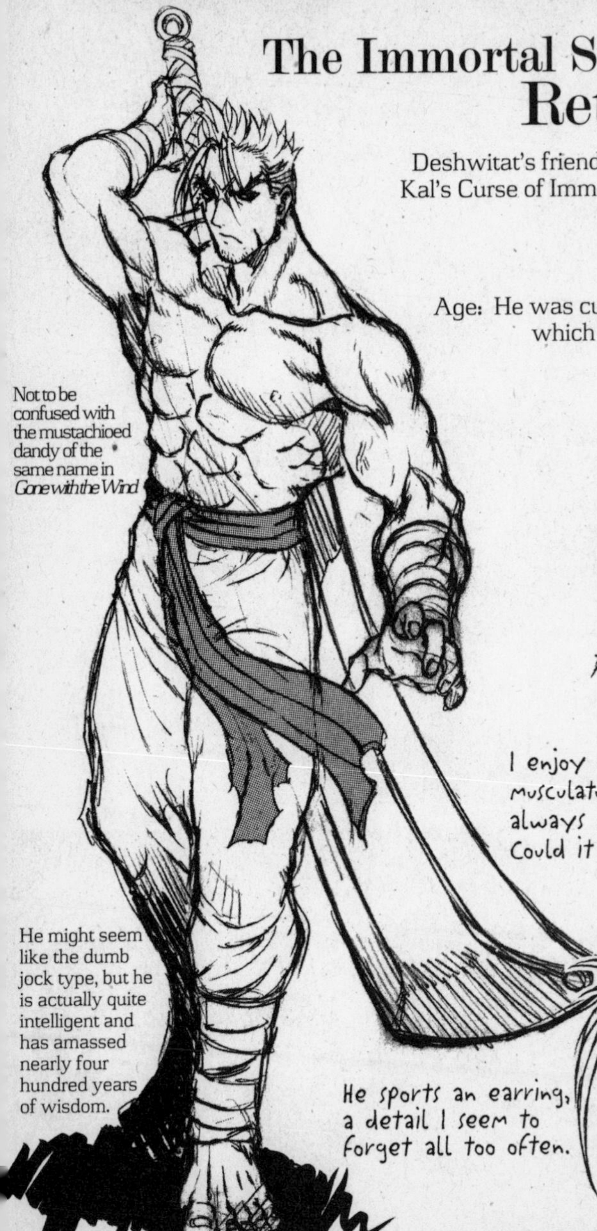

Not to be confused with the mustachioed dandy of the same name in *Gone with the Wind*

He might seem like the dumb jock type, but he is actually quite intelligent and has amassed nearly four hundred years of wisdom.

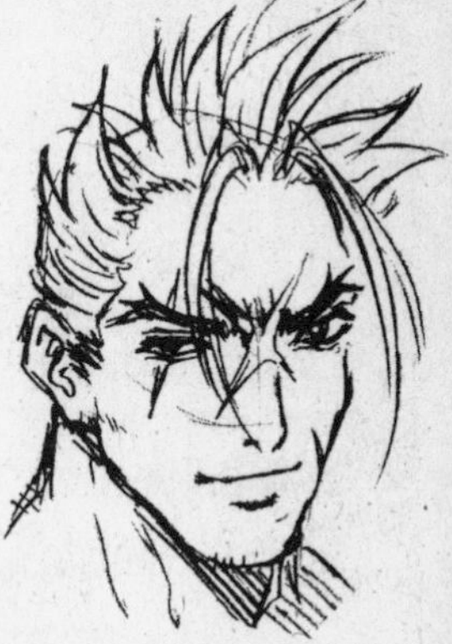

I enjoy drawing the musculature, but something always seems slightly off. Could it be my lack of skill?

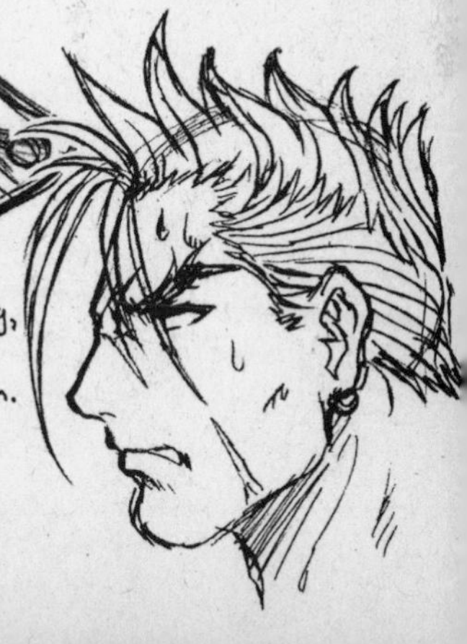

He sports an earring, a detail I seem to forget all too often.

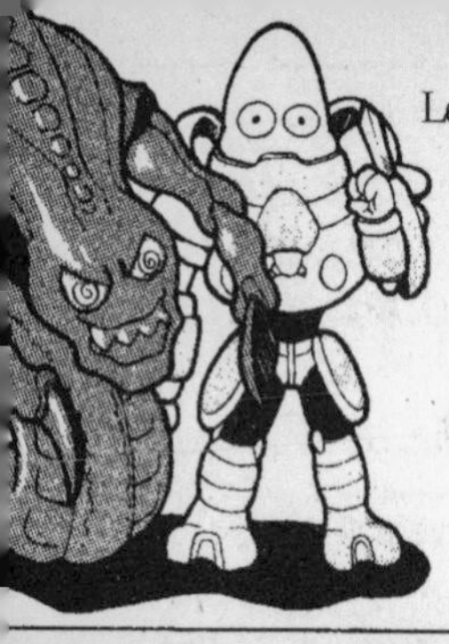

Lee Kangwoo's Game Room 1: StarCraft

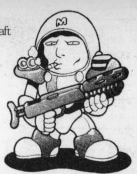

Symptoms of a "StarC" Addiction

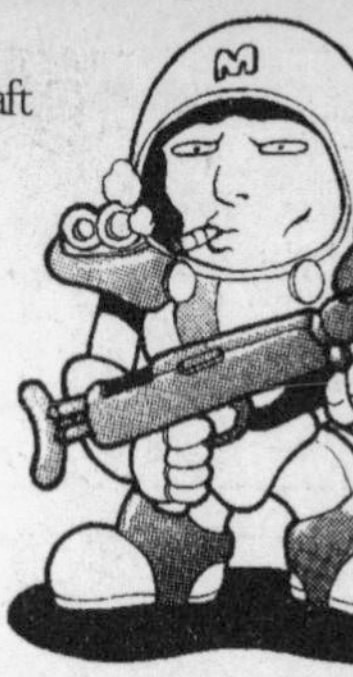

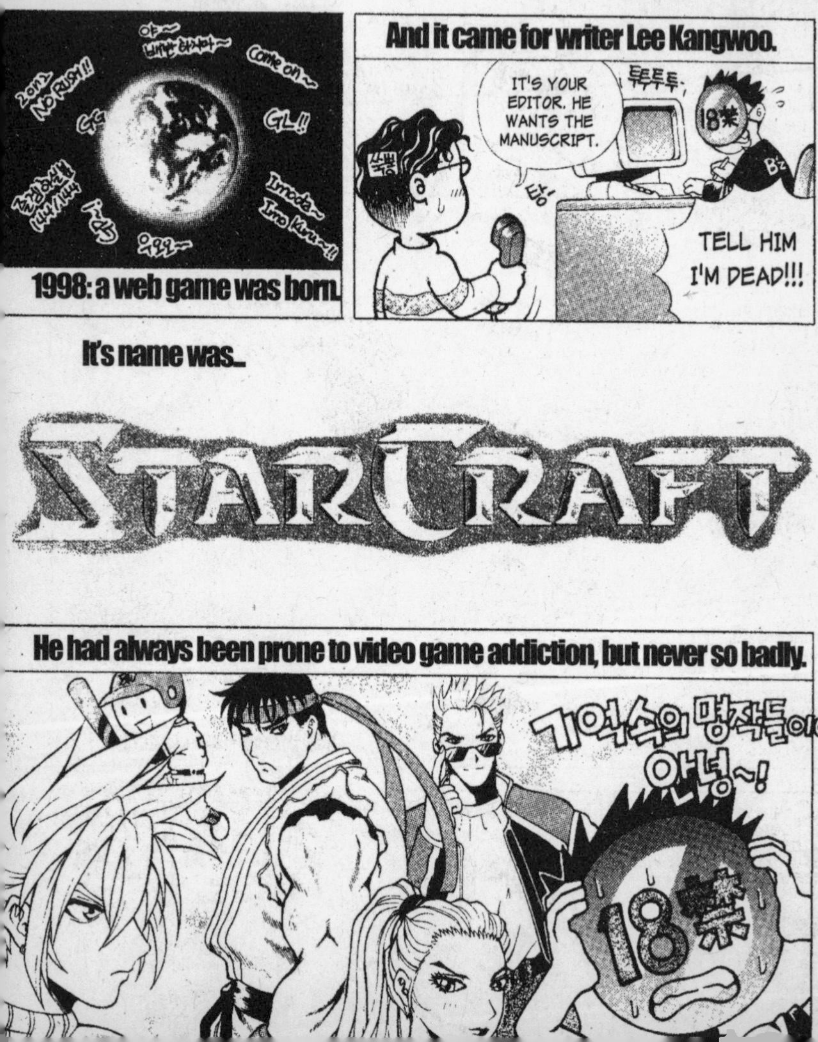

2on2 NO RUSH!!
Come on~
GG
GL!!
Imoda~ Imo Kiru~!!
1998: a web game was born.
And it came for writer Lee Kangwoo.
IT'S YOUR EDITOR. HE WANTS THE MANUSCRIPT.
탁!
TELL HIM I'M DEAD!!!
It's name was...
STARCRAFT
He had always been prone to video game addiction, but never so badly.
기억속의 명작들이여
안녕~!
18禁

WHAT I'M TRYING TO SAVE YOU FROM, READERS...

...IS THE DAMAGE CAUSED BY STARCADDICTION.

Stage 1

Starcaddiction, the Initial Phase: "SC in My Dreams." You practice battle maneuvers in your dreams. The lack of proper rest takes its toll on your health.

Testimony of my Editor, currently in Stage 1

HEY KANGWOO, I THINK I HAVE TO GIVE THIS GAME UP.

《음성변조》

I SEE IT IN MY DREAMS, I SWEAR I'M GOING CRAZY.

It is already too late for him.

Stage 2

Starcaddiction, the Middle Phase: "Hallucination." Any real object that resembles a StarCraft unit makes you recoil in horror.

For example, pickled leeks on the end of chopsticks...

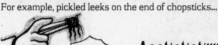

IT'S AN OVERLORD!

Overlord is a basic supply unit for the Zerg race.

《참고》
Zerg Overload ▶ = 저그 보급

AGGHGHGH!!!!

Or you might mistake a basketball for a Science Vessel.

Stage 3

Starcaddiction, the Final Phase: "Derangement." Normal life ceases to be. You are ruled by the evil hand of StarC even in the deepest reaches of your unconscious.

When there are fewer than 12 of anything, you begin to freak out.

WHAT'S WRONG WITH HIM?

NO! I NEED TWO MORE TO MAKE A TROOP.

DAMN, I DON'T HAVE MINERALS TO MAKE MORE!!!

And the color purple can send you into cardiac arrest.

DANGER !!!

THERE ARE ZERGS CLOSE TO US.

This is how I am, nowadays.

WELL, THIS WAS FUN, BUT I THINK I SHANT BE RETURNING TO LEE KANGWOO'S GAME ROOM IN THE NEXT VOLUME. I FREE MYSELF FROM THIS CURSE.

"Nuclear Launch Detected"
뉴 클리어 런치 디텍티드—

ACH!!!

Flying Lotus Blossoms, Beryun

Height: 5' 6"
Weight: 102 lbs.

One reader asked me what her measurements are. I don't know much about what's right, but someone said that 36-24-36 is ideal, so let's go with that.

This is a weapon without a verified name. It's neither Diamond Sutra nor a Taoist weapon, but I did consult a book called Mandala.

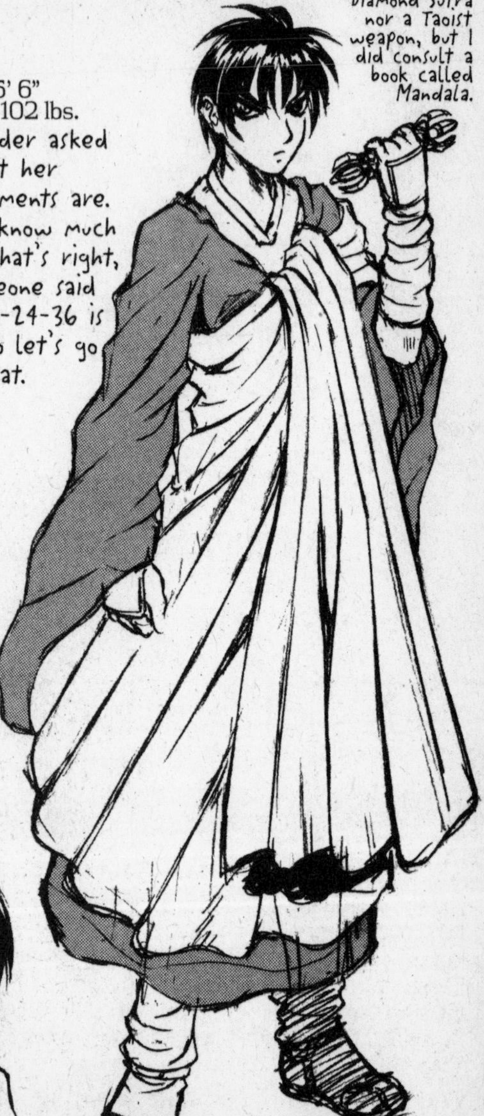

She's easy to draw because she lacks facial expressions.

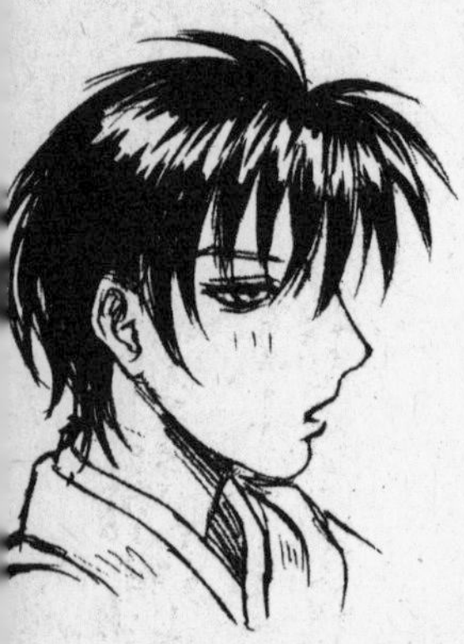

I had a female version of Deshwitat in mind, but somehow she became...

Many readers comment that she's similar to the character of Bon from Island Magic. Both of them use esoteric, existential spells.

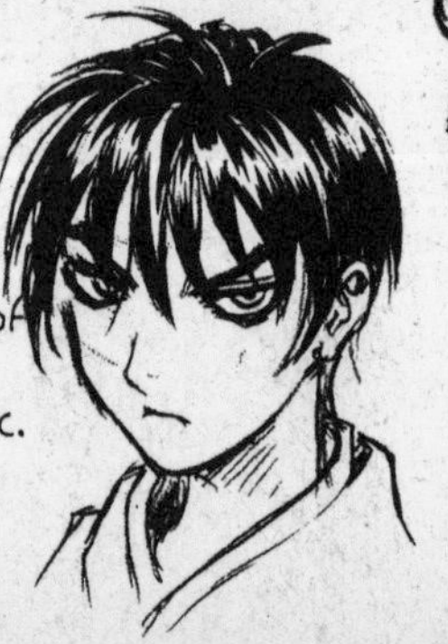

In the last volume, Deshwitat told Beryun that she is not human. I'll reveal all her secrets in the next couple of volumes.

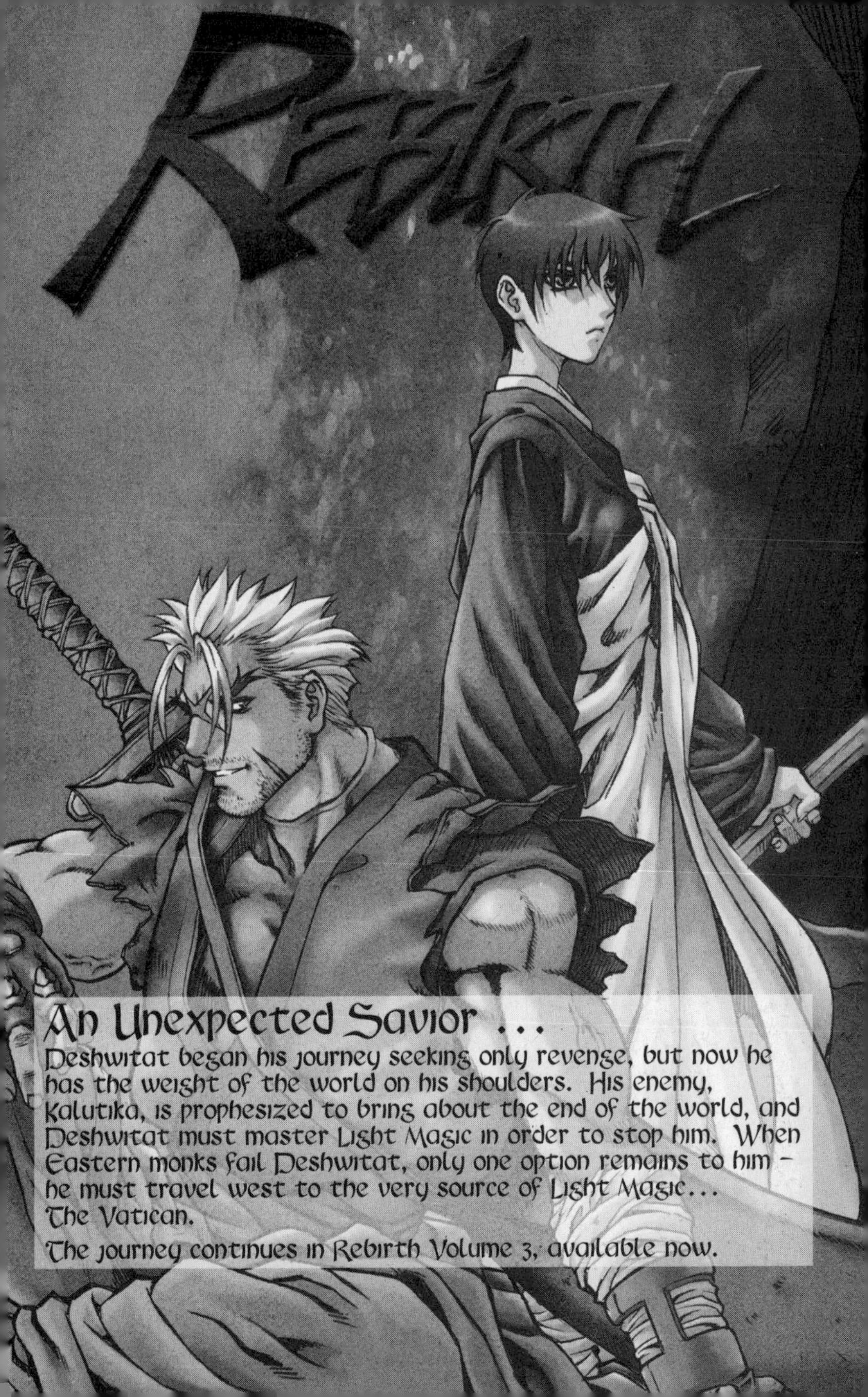
Rebirth
An Unexpected Savior ...
Deshwitat began his journey seeking only revenge, but now he has the weight of the world on his shoulders. His enemy, Kalutika, is prophesized to bring about the end of the world, and Deshwitat must master Light Magic in order to stop him. When Eastern monks fail Deshwitat, only one option remains to him - he must travel west to the very source of Light Magic... The Vatican.
The journey continues in Rebirth Volume 3, available now.

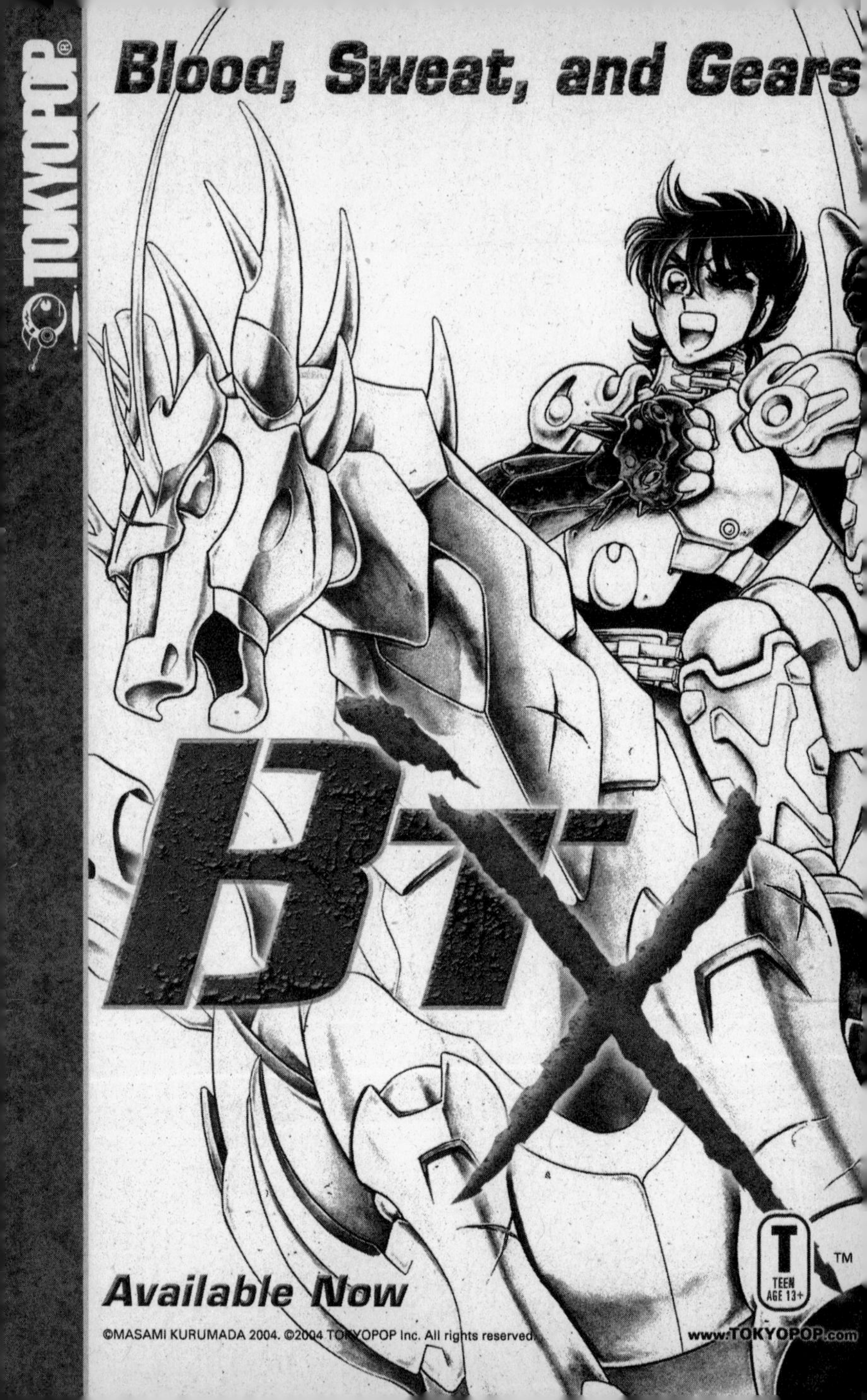
TOKYOPOP®
Blood, Sweat, and Gears
B'T X
Available Now
T TEEN AGE 13+
TM
©MASAMI KURUMADA 2004. ©2004 TOKYOPOP Inc. All rights reserved.
www.TOKYOPOP.com

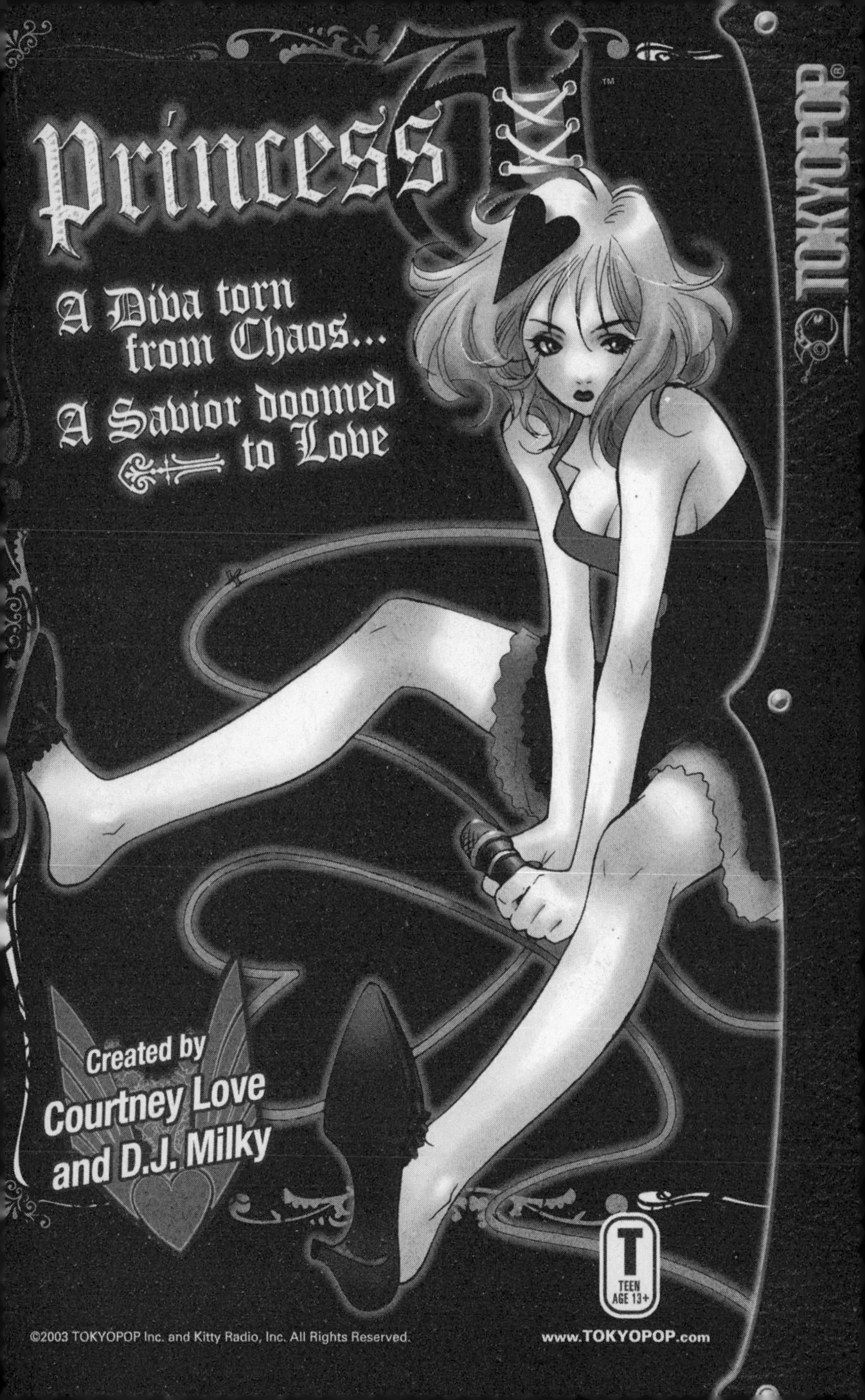
TOKYOPOP
Princess Ai™
A Diva torn from Chaos...
A Savior doomed to Love
Created by
Courtney Love
and D.J. Milky
T
TEEN
AGE 13+
©2003 TOKYOPOP Inc. and Kitty Radio, Inc. All Rights Reserved.
www.TOKYOPOP.com

DRAGON HUNTER

By HONG SEOCK SEO

SLAYING DRAGONS IS HARD...
MAKING A LIVING
FROM IT IS BRUTAL!

TEEN
AGE 13+

www.TOKYOPOP.com

SEIKAI
TRILOGY ™

The best
of mankind
locked in the
worst of wars.

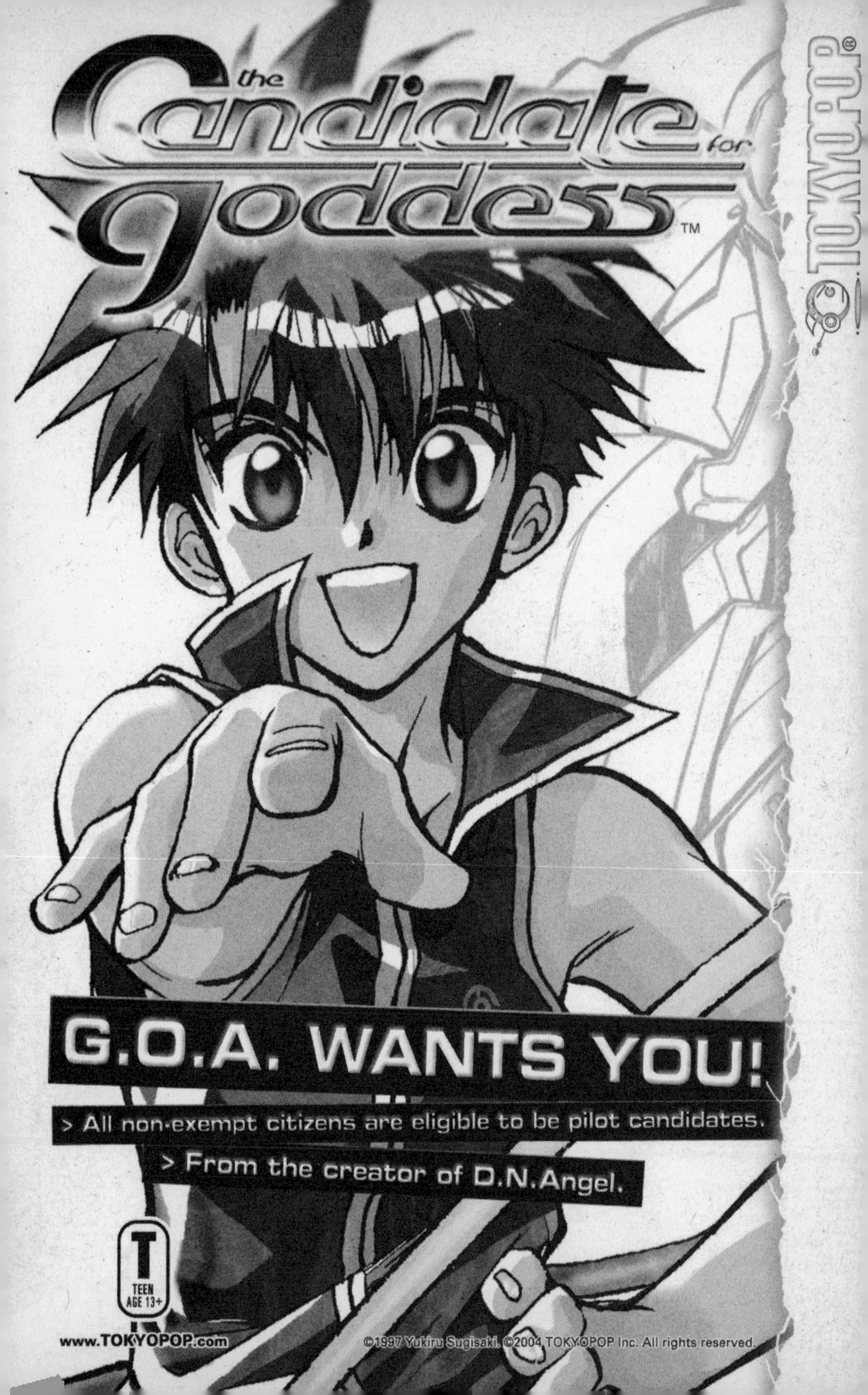
the Candidate for Goddess™
TOKYOPOP®
G.O.A. WANTS YOU!
> All non-exempt citizens are eligible to be pilot candidates.
> From the creator of D.N.Angel.
T TEEN AGE 13+
www.TOKYOPOP.com
©1997 Yukiru Sugisaki. ©2004 TOKYOPOP Inc. All rights reserved.

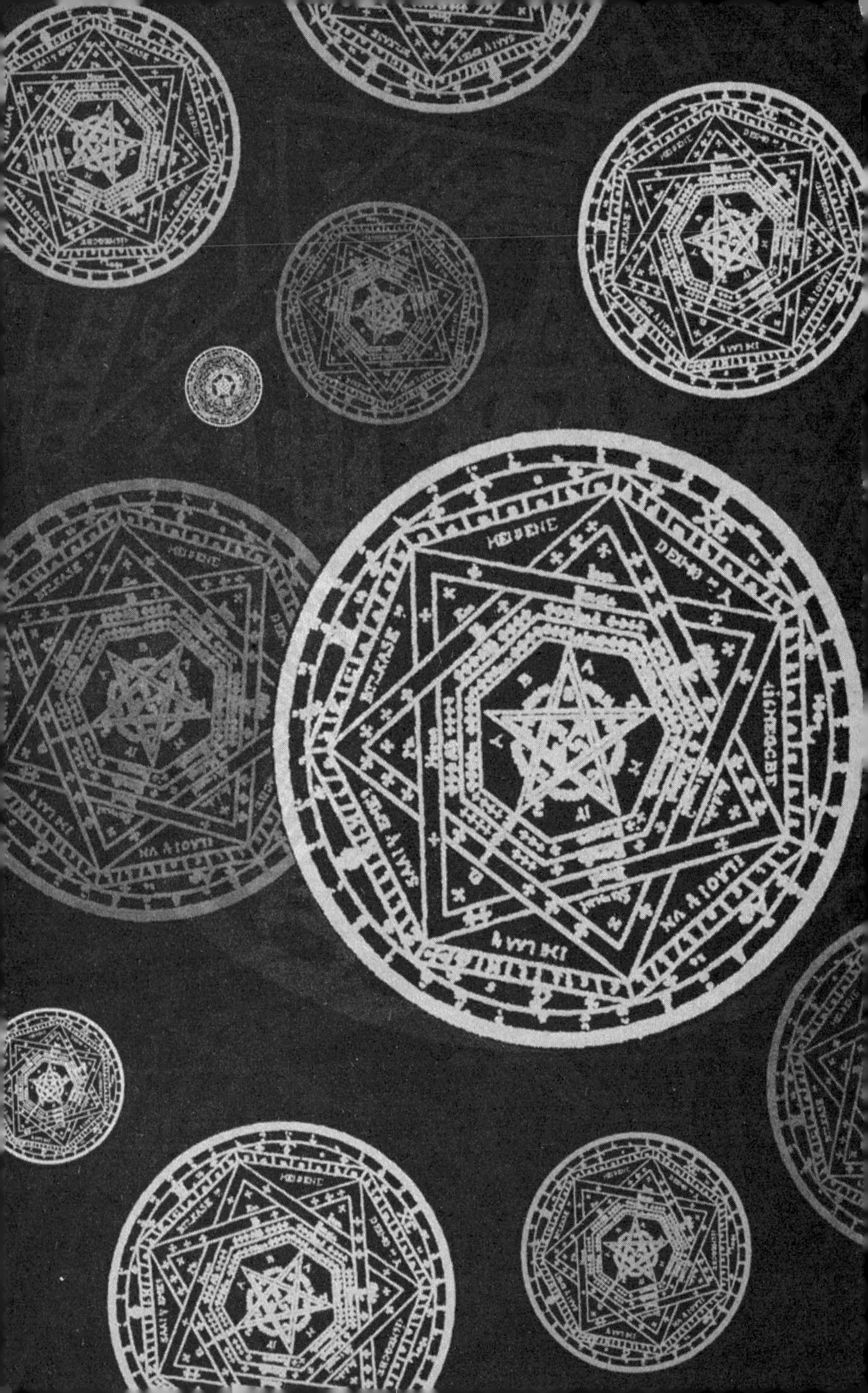